Beauty Beast

BOOKS BY MacKINLAY KANTOR

Fiction

DIVERSEY   EL GOES SOUTH   THE JAYBIRD

LONG REMEMBER   THE VOICE OF BUGLE ANN

AROUSE AND BEWARE   THE ROMANCE OF ROSY RIDGE

THE NOISE OF THEIR WINGS   HERE LIES HOLLY SPRINGS

VALEDICTORY   CUBA LIBRE   GENTLE ANNIE

HAPPY LAND   AUTHOR'S CHOICE   GLORY FOR ME

MIDNIGHT LACE   WICKED WATER   THE GOOD FAMILY

ONE WILD OAT   SIGNAL THIRTY-TWO   DON'T TOUCH ME

WARWHOOP   THE DAUGHTER OF BUGLE ANN

GOD AND MY COUNTRY   ANDERSONVILLE

THE WORK OF ST. FRANCIS

IF THE SOUTH HAD WON THE CIVIL WAR

SPIRIT LAKE   STORY TELLER

BEAUTY BEAST

Juvenile

ANGLEWORMS ON TOAST

LEE AND GRANT AT APPOMATTOX

GETTYSBURG

Personalia

BUT LOOK, THE MORN   LOBO

(With Gen. Curtis E. Le May) MISSION WITH LE MAY

Verse

TURKEY IN THE STRAW

MacKinlay Kantor

BEAUTY
BEAST

A Novel

G. P. PUTNAM'S SONS
NEW YORK

TO
*all those who have suffered because
of these things*

Beauty Beast

1

M RS. SIDNEY SHALLOP would discover the instigation of passion and doom on this day.

And while sleeping, and with those tawny eyes closed so that their haunting might not be revealed, she was still a child (actually when young she had been that misfortuned child seeming always to bring on attack against herself merely because aloofness was interpreted as challenge).

Ceaselessly mockingbirds sang out the miracles of their latest brooding, sun came lacy and spotted through five-leafed ivy. Kingly ivy was autumned ahead of its season into red and brown and rags along the upper gallery. In an interval before she rang and named her breakfast, Sidney Shallop walked to see what the weather might promise. Nicely coolish, said the day, but very bright. Lightly warm in sun, coolish in shade. All in all a llama lace shawl day. Yet fragrant.

In spite of her uncapped hair being disheveled from sleep and not yet brushed up to meet inspection, the light congratulated the woman on her restrained beauty. No painter had ever caught her properly in portraiture, although three had tried, in the United States and abroad. Scattered elements of her pale elegance could not be gathered together in a common prettiness. Sun spotted its yellow and green over her face as it came through the vine. Sun said she was a gargoyle—Away with her!— yet Sidney was not frightened into seeking reassurance from the mirror which she held clutched uselessly against her middle.

Courtesy suggested that a veritable flutter of compliments and flirtations would be necessary to melt the wax of stark white terror in which her face had long been set. Rigidity was still apparent.

A wise man might have looked into those wide eyes in the bony face, and declared that he witnessed both madness and hysteria. Yet no wise man was at the plantation, and Sidney knew only one in the nearby town whom she considered wise.

This day will mark a beginning.

Only lightest wind coming up between the pines, and then pressed back and disorganized by nearby oaks, and then finding itself in fragments approaching the gallery— Only this wind heard the words she whispered.

Ritualistically—

It's very nearly as if I recited ritual. And why should I do that? Because I'm fey?

Can I see Death come a-riding?

Can I see Love?

Twould be impossible for my hands to measure its consistency.

Age might be an abomination, but it was absolute and not to be denied. Sidney found herself well past thirty, and it had been almost two years since the horse kicked and rolled on her husband.

Though still she could shut her eyes and witness instantly.

O magic lantern. Righteously a flame burned, the glass slide went back and forth with its burden of tragedy but seeming colored and alive with sound. She could hear the horse squealings. Sometimes through perversity she held that magic lantern slide too long between flame and lens: glass cracked in the heat, the slide was spoilt. But another lay ready, hand-painted, relating the same story. Sidney's wide-set yellow-gray eyes told their tale.

I have consorted with agonies, and there may be more awaiting.

I will go to any length to protect myself against them.

Yet a perverse spirit was in her soft rounded skin-and-bones as well as in the crackling grained hair and puffy mouth. Somehow she would bring disaster on, herself.

Yea, refractory. Make a note of it.

Her plantation was called Apoxsee. *Tomorrow* in Seminole. This had been the plantation of her second husband, Pettey Jefferson Shallop. He was known commonly throughout that end of the State and over borders into adjacent States as Pettey J. Men of accomplishment would have nothing to do with him, except when they were compelled to, in essentials of business or politics. He enjoyed a kind of momentary popularity (twas always fragmentary and fleeting, twould not survive his death. What is that? No weeping?) with a few men of his own class and type. They were spoiled mothers' lambs who on gaining adult stature had become spoiled mothers' jackals or tomcats. Would never be mothers' lions, would never be anybody's lions. They drank to the affliction of their inner organs; and dissipated carelessly among all sorts and colors of women, often to the eventual affliction of their exposed organs as well. They lost or gained in slovenly fashion at euchre. They fought seldom among themselves, most had not the courage. Pettey J. had been rendered practically impotent through some sort of Venus' curse. He could not perform a sexual act in what was believed commonly to be a normal fashion. He found other raptures, pursued them avidly. He had a weapon which he used against his wife—or rather, wives, since he had three in succession. One had fallen sick and died of hemorrhage, one was believed to have done away with herself, and the third was Sidney: huzza!— she survived. His weapon and its employment were unknown among his friends, since none of his female partners had dared or wished to speak of atrocities. The weapon was a golden phallus, molded long before in Venice. It was of glass, and was large, large, and very heavy. Pettey J. Shallop wielded it with force of hand and arm. Kindly managed, the object might have been a joy to the starved and lonely. Under the manipulation of a brute—

Scorning to admit or add the sum of his own cruelties, Pettey J.

13

had sought to visit a new one upon his third wife. In a manner of speaking she had slain him.

Sometimes he came dancing and whirling on the fatal horse into her dreams even yet. Twas not her conscience that offended her, twas only remembrance and her imagination. Sometimes too he came posturing on another dappled horse, as when first she saw him. Meaty dark face, rolling brown eyes under their heavy lids, the contemptuous curl of that thick upper lip. Sidney had been attracted by what she believed to be a rare and powerful vitality, a masculinity so violent that it must be flaunted. She learned the truth on her bridal night (call it her second bridal night. Which was worse, first or second?) and walked dry and empty and sore for days.

Any deep-toned laughter which came from below stairs or from another wing of the house was a mockery. Any oath or cigar-smell or horse-whinny was common deception. Power and enticement of the male? Pah.

This was Tuesday the 29th inst., and it was on this day that an auction was to be held, whereat Sidney might buy a cook. Thus she had an appointment to drive into town and meet with Senator Ledge. Desperately, she told herself, she needed a good cook. She did not entertain, but she could command luxury. Why not command it? Goosey had gone from bad to worse. She had one child after another, and suffered from a prolapsed uterus. She could no longer remain on her feet without great pain and danger to herself. They had contrived small wheels upon a kitchen chair, and Goosey rolled about the place and along a covered passage into the house kitchen and back again. You'd hear her wheels going all the time, and it was enough to drive a body frantic, and especially if you were human, and knowing that Goosey shouldn't be cooking at all, but just lying sick abed against a possible recovery some fine day. A very fine day indeed, twould be. Still, she excelled in nothing except the native arts: could cook gator tail in a manner beyond price, could fry fish and poultry sublimely. She was capable of frying and roasting only; her soups and stews and sauces spread with grease.

14

Again Sidney assured herself that she would attend the auction and bid intently, if the proffered cook seemed able to suit and please.

It would appear that some attempt was made on the part of the legator to perform a new will, while he lay on his death bed, and I should believe that the physicians in attendance will bear out my testimony on this score. However, said legator demonstrated such uncertainty and incompetency in this behalf that it was the mutual and reluctant opinion, of physicians as well as attorney-at-law, to declare said legator of unsound mind and incapable of rendering a new instrument.

He had lain trapped, lost, all opportunity danced away from him. He lay unable to write, unable to speak, unable to carry out aspired vengeance against this woman who killed him, and with what pain. He could only track her with his eyes when she was in the room, and spew a hatred so. *Ah,* he dedicated, *his Presence would affect her future!*

He had not affected her, she felt nothing. His eyes declaimed that he would be in every parcel and ligament of the plantation, in every ounce and all fabrics of property or properties, whatever they might be, wherever.

Never once did she feel him. Had never felt him, never would.

He was dead and bricked up, munched by tiny critters; and birds sang sweeter because of it, moonlight fell softer, there were fewer thinner tears. He had been no more capable of enacting a threat after he was dead than he was of offering tolerance or lightness when alive. Sidney whispered about this to her beloved Senator Ledge, and he only grinned and said, *"Sic transit—"*

His voice trailed into space as he thought of pleasanter newer things, they both thought of them.

On an earlier day when she ate ham and salad and sipped the tea which accompanied her luncheon, Sidney had fallen to considering the oysters.

Busy above her polished cypress hair, palm fronds drew

eternally back and forth, stirring rank hot air and threatening a hundred flies which hovered.

Knowing in her mind a mellowness of imagined tides existing in the sea nearby, the woman probed deeper in reckoning.

India, she said to a barelegged dirt-dark girl who stood against the wall in the sprigged calico which all of Sidney's house servants wore. India, fetch some mint.

No mint on table, mistess?

Look, India. She spoke smoothly with no edges in her tone. And you will see none.

As mottled feet trotted out of sight toward the rear entry, Sidney sat motionless. She said to herself, quite aloud, Know you nothing but a whim of the Flesh?

As words stroked echoing into the hall away from her, the two green palm fronds flickered and nearly dropped to scrape her head, and then the old servant who held them increased the speed of his fanning. He was puzzled by growth of this habit in his mistress: the business of addressing herself to empty air, building utterance beyond understanding. Time and again she had heard him mutter, she caught mention of Our Lord, and knew that he must be praying for her. Of urgencies blazing hidden in Sidney's spirit and frame, he might only guess. Remembrance of the slave's dead master was a perplexity, but the slave accepted death as a phenomenon steady through nature. Words uttered by a widow were something else again.

To oysters.

They lived in tufts above their parent shells, long lean mounds ready to scrape paint from a boat's hull or hide from a hand. Sidney saw water receding clearly (though the shore was three miles and more buried from her in pines). Out went the tide, and great fish running with it, and pelicans marched in air above and drove down to feed.

O tide of my soul in its meager drying, she cried whispering, and the old man by the luncheon table bending close to try to hear her. O tide take me loose with you and lose me in the Gulf. Let me drown rather than— Rather than—

Back came India with mint dripping.

Did you wash it, India? There are bugs this season, there are tiny bugs any season.

Yessum, mistess, I never wash it, Goosey wash it.

Mrs. Shallop rolled a treasure of mint tightly between pale narrow hands, and juice came dark as the leaves were pressed. Into her green glass the mass drifted, and tea spread over it in a wave. Sidney's father had brought that notion of mint tea in returning from a Northern African port before Sidney was born. His name was Philip Sidney Veck and he said that his son should be named Sidney. The child appeared as a female but still the name was applied.

Now in widowhood she was suspended joyless, reckoned wealthy. In truth she was so sensuous that sensuality claimed her private illusions. Not one other breathing human had ever dreamed the truth about her, least of all the latest vicious husband.

Over her head the fronds capered. Basil, she told the servant, that will be enough.

No more, for flies' sake, mistess?

I'll sound the bell if I need you. Go get your dinner. India, you go as well.

India stalked away. Basil ambled behind her, linen pantaloons too short for him, his blue figured calico shirt clean and billowy, silver head bent in tight little curls, neck like live-oak bark.

Now I am rid of them. I can talk.

Words she wished to utter began to assort themselves in her brain but found no access to her lips.

Take the oysters once more. They were resplendent, honeyed with juice, fattening again at this time of year. A bit of milk might flow as each was opened, and faint color still pinked on their inner shells: it might have something to do with spawning, Sidney supposed.

In recollection she rebuilt an evening many months before, in that same house. (They lived briefly in Savannah after the wedding, then went abroad for two years.) On that night she watched her spouse eating oysters. The servant had fetched them on a silver tray.

The woman said stiffly, Thank you, I'll have none.

Pettey J. looked at her. Pray try them. I sent boys to the Gulf at half-low tide. They're my favorite.

Thank you, she told her husband, but I've never been able to abide raw shellfish.

Do try them.

Please. Thank you. No.

You've never tried these. The most tasty dish in the region.

She shook her head, attempting to form a smile as she did so. She played with the pearls about her neck, and then remembered that they had been bound in packets of living shellfish to begin with. Her hand fell.

Silas, called Shallop to a cadaverous butler, you leave us now.

After Silas had slouched from the room, Pettey J. stared at Sidney for a time and then asked, One bite?

No. She shuddered.

If you're ailing they're good for what ails you.

She sat without moving.

One oyster, my dear.

No, she said indistinctly, contributing a long sad N-sound to the word.

He arose and took one of the shining wet open things between his fingers. They're good for debility, he insisted. They put strength into the weak. Sap in a man's tree trunk. Or a woman's.

He came near, holding thick dark fingers spread wide. The oyster tilted and some of its juice spun in a string to the table linen. Put fire in your breeches, he cried coarsely. Somehow he rid himself of the shell and held only the cool pulp.

He was behind her and around her, one hand paining cheeks and chin and jaws, compelling her lips apart and trying to make the hard-clamped teeth widen. He forced his thumb between her teeth, and then with his left hand sought to feed the oyster to her.

Now, she cried throughout her being, my teeth have become

weapons. I will use them. With such ferocious power as she could own, she bit long and well. She felt her incisors go through, go through, and hot salt blood was tasted. All the way to his bone she bit, and even rubbed her fangs grating on the agonized bone before she relaxed her jaws and let him loose.

Slut, slut, you damn slut, he kept pouring words in the frightening quiet. It would have been easier had he screamed.

I'll die!—he did scream, a few weeks later when he lay broken by his horse. I'll die, and there's no one else, so you must have it. He murmured on, but made no sense by the time his family lawyer and a physician, and then a second physician, had been summoned. They thought him witless, whereas Sidney believed him robbed only of any power of communication.

You'll have Apoxsee but I shall be here always. I will live in shadow and stick, along ditches, in candlesticks, in nigger shacks, everywhere.

This was the import of message in his unearthly eyes.

In all ditches, and in chips round a chopping block, and in scrub, and among the testers. In skeeter drapes and ewers and andirons, I shall dwell to watch you.

Sidney thought of yelling in reply (twas but a thought, the doctors were there, and Senator Ledge) , Shall I be able to hear you mouthing at your sport with Jiggy and Yellow Martha? As I listened to you panting in so many nights? Pity you couldn't have taken them down in the pines somewhere, and not into your chamber to let me listen.

I wanted you to listen.

Yea, dear husband. And then you'd come creeping with that glass thing in your hand!

But after he was safely dead she never saw him or felt him lurking.

Sidney drove near the Gulf in her light carriage. Over the coachman's protest she prevailed, and insisted that he turn the horses along wheel-tracks which curved far between humps of mangrove. Should have a cart, cried Nineveh. That old two-wheeler or such, cause we mire down for certain. Nineveh's was a scrolled ebon face which might seldom change expression because of excessive loose folds of flesh. Only when he roared in wide laughter or when you looked closely into his deep-pitted eyes did an alteration occur.

Mire they did, in a bayou where high water from a tropical storm had softened the rooty world. Nineveh feared that his straining team would damage the carriage. He calmed the horses, standing at their heads and being kind to their noses with great hands, while he sent his grandson to bring a few field negroes who were cutting wood in Neighbor Bonaparte Wilkey's pineland. Lucky they were to have the tiny grandson in his tow shirt; but the child had pleaded with imploring gaze for leave to sit upon the box with Nineveh, and Sidney was sensitive to children of whatever color, and sought to make them glad.

Off Coony trotted. Sidney removed her shoes. Ordering Nineveh to keep his glance turned aside, she lifted her skirts and loosened her tight pink garters of puckered silk, and thus removed her stockings. Barefooted she stepped down into the muck and went wading toward the sea with her gown and underskirts lifted. Fiddlers inched away on every side among mangrove roots—mulberry and purplish crabs they were, each lugging his wide claw so out of proportion to his tininess: they seemed to be bearing violins, thus their name of fiddler crabs. The largest had a body not much bigger than a silver quarter-dollar, but so vast was their number that a light rustle and click rose from sand where they made their dens.

Free of the shrubbery Sidney walked amid sedgy grasses. Here was a path which fishermen had made, and she traversed it until there was no more grass around her and the sand glared like flour. Waves edged up, green and blue were the dyes, surely they would stain her limbs with pigment if she immersed them. Into the Gulf she strolled, and chuckled at the water's laving, and her skirts began to float and then grow soggy and fall heavily around the movement of her legs.

She stopped. Oysters sprouted just beyond. There was one short depth where the little white rays sped to hiding, and then

20

the shoal turned water to a ginger hue, and gray-brown shells stood like twisting tusks on higher regions of the bar. There was distinct horror in this reminder, but still Sidney lingered to stare. Because in intimate recesses of her soul she was vulnerable to the great moving song and sermon of salt water, the holy sun blazing, gulls yelping above a horde of jackfish, wielding their pure wings like sickles unrestrained and full of light power.

He too was a portion of Nature's force? Pettey J.?

Aye. But he was malignant.

She spoke both question and answer to herself, not yet in a voice to be heard, but conversational in intent thought because of her ruling solitude.

Was there anything of God in him?

No more than in any breathing sprite or monster. Yet— God in all, God in gulls, God in the crabs, God in weevils as well as in furious salty tints of this storied water.

Merely he must have wanted to possess you because of your comparative youth and daintiness? When balked he lowered himself into the brute?

Born a brute.

Remember how he ate the oysters? He did not chew them. He swallowed them entire, the gleaming mass gone down his throat and into his body in a single lump; and he rolled his eyes with each swallowing.

How simple it would have been had you nerved yourself to minor distaste, and nibbled delicately, and said, Mr. Shallop, I fear I cannot share your enthusiasm, but sometime I shall try again! Then you might not have slain your husband.

For slay him you did, indirectly it is true, yet well you know it. The bitten finger mortified, pain was constant, and Pettey J. would take himself off to town to consult a surgeon. He was bound to ride instead of drive and thus renew his lie of masculinity and vigor.

That hard-mouthed Watson horse, with wide satin chest, Arab ears, bulk and height, his mean eyes, long jaws hating the bit and worrying it. Twitch of rein, the spurting oaths the hands heard as they looked up from their hoeing, hurt oh hurt

21

of the mortified finger, struggle in the road, the whipping and more oaths which became a single shout, the dancing and rearing amid palmetto scrub as still the whip fell flailing, slippery tangle, lunge and falling, the kicking and spasm and the roll, the roll, the beetle-shape in its white linen suit mashed like a roach on a doorstep.

You recognize all this, though he told aloud that it was a hound which bit him? No one else is aware of the peculiar truth, but you are aware. Do you feel as a murderer might feel?

Nay.

Say it in antique accent, and it will have the import of Scriptures. Say to yourself not No, but Nay. I hold no guilt. Only I hold a sense of relief, and wonder at the ways of blood and bitten fingers and horseflesh.

Ah, flakes of shell seem created of tin, and now the loose discarded shells stare up to mock me as I go near them, and oh my heel was cut a bit by one sharp wicked shell. Yet on I go. The impulse flows with current of this sea's recession.

Sidney put down her hands and strove to lift one mass of the crusted living things. Those clusters bloomed like tin cabbages, slick and dry where sun had cooked them into grayness, edges waiting like fluted razors to cut her skin. Cut again. This thumb, that side of her hand, and how red the color runs into the light wet green tenderness.

She gave up, she could not budge the thing. But a savage excitement was possessing her as she journeyed back to shore with wet garments trailing. It was as when, a child, she had indulged in trivial wickedness behind closed doors, pulling up her dolly's pretty gown to see that the dolly's private portion was not made in the complex fashion of her own. Any little girl might have done that, Sidney now supposed; doubtless many had. Yet her black nurse peeped in and caught her, and lectured severely between shakes and more shakes. Ah, naughtiness, naughtiness, yet what a flutter of the pulse. Now she felt it again.

Nineveh had sent Coony to find his mistress. Cutely the little figure beckoned and waved. He came grinning leisurely, kicking stony feet through the sand, chewing on his fingers. Mistress, his voice trilled like a frightened instrument of reeds, Nineveh telt me look for you.

Has he got the carriage loose, Coony?

Yessum. He wait way up there where he got turn roun.

I'll hold the horses, Nineveh, she said when she was again at the carriage. Give me the reins. There. Do you go to the Gulf and fetch some oysters. I tried, but cut myself slightly.

Ain't got nothing put em in.

Just one cluster will do. You can put them on the floor of the box. I've decided to return to the plantation. It's too blistery today for driving, even with my sunshade.

In ten minutes he came grumbling back, wet-footed, but bearing cautiously the oyster clump like a trophy. When they reached the house and she had alighted, Sidney sent Goosey the cook to clean the oysters, and ordered that she serve them then and there, and not wait for the dinner hour. Goosey was to arrange them on a silver platter, with pepper and lemon accompanying.

Didn't know you relish em oysters, mistess.

That will do, Goosey.

Soon they were brought to the little tea-table where Sidney sat in the library, with flies humming ceaselessly, with her dead husband's dead father accusing in his naval uniform, and her dead husband's dead grandmother wearing the cut attributed to British dragoons. Sidney sent all servants away, and then examined the tray minutely. It was identical—the same tray which had held Pettey J.'s oysters in an earlier season—the same nick and bending of a scroll around the edge where some careless person had battered it.

Sidney felt breath pushing rapidly in her throat and chest, but eat the thing she should and must. In that moment she recognized that she had never put a bit of oyster into her mouth before. It was not that she could not abide them: she feared the rawness, the clammy texture, she had always feared without tasting.

She took up a small fork and watched the creature slide loose

23

from the shell where Goosey had cut it cleanly. She neglected pepper and spray of lemon. Only this thing as it had grown within waters, this pure crudity with its own animal flavor.

Also she saw the minute wounds upon her hands where she had dabbed them with camphor, and she thought of Pettey J.'s mortal wounds that she gave him. She closed her eyes, feeling her temples ring like drums, and immediately her gesture had obeyed her agonized will, and the thing was in her mouth. In utter stupefaction she found it good. It was as if through the more than three decades of her restricted life she had awaited this ointment, thus fluency and savor. Sidney opened her eyes and shook the tears loose, and quietly employed her pocket handkerchief as she chewed. There had been nine good oysters in the clump, and all were served to her. She ate seven, then knew that she could eat no more. But the very next day she sent a hand to the Gulf with a bucket.

When she rose like a ghost by night (as so often) and went walking rooms and galleries, she recognized that a truth had been driven like a stark nail into her being while she slept. Some unseen Jael crept and had a sly way with her.

The piercing nail was a sharp wrought-iron fact.

You consumed oysters because it was essential.

In eating them, gloating and ravening at their taste, you were demonstrating final rebellion.

You broke yourself loose from any last strings of power which his remembrance may have had over you.

You did it to be free.

And she was free at last. His specter had never plagued her, yet there'd always endured the feeling that he might persist or threaten in some odd way.

Now Pettey J. Shallop was a Nothing. She was even freed from hatred of his remembered image.

She felt rinsed and cool.

She returned to her bed and lay for a long time before she slept again, looking out through thin moonlight, or looking in across the floor where his spook might have come to trance her and yet never did.

She was powerful and wise.

Once there had been a mighty obsession in her life, a strange and rather horrid love, a Possession as by demons or a demon. It had ended abruptly in the homely familiar words, Gone to Texas.

Now that she was rich and might dominate and might persist in spite of any discouragement, it was well within her power to engage an emissary, send someone to Texas, to hound the man down, spy him.

What? And then pounce on him and cry, Ah-ha, I've found ye out? I've run ye down?

Frankly those words could have been uttered by her first husband. His paltry vengeful brain might have sought to employ them—and to employ that spy or emissary and all the rest. She thought in scorn, A fit deed for one like Calvin to perform! Tis not for me to do.

Again she slept, again she rose, the moon had moved, it was lowering, its light lay richer and thicker and yellower than when on high. She thought of going into water, into her private pool. No, late night was too chilly for that, she'd not be comfortable, and she wanted only comfort and new-won peace.

Nonsense, she wanted much more than that! She wished to be up and doing, to race like a girl, to skip spritely and even chattering.

Twas ridiculous!—she'd never been able to chatter at small talk. She could not squeal and squeak with other women, had seldom squealed and squeaked when a girl.

She turned in bed and looked toward her east gallery doors again, and saw traces of color. She was gratified by the dawn, she'd needed it. She thought, How I welcome them: trivia of hunger and the munching that follows, trivia of breakfast, the day to claim me.

What's ado on this day? Ah yes, I must to town. I exchanged notes with Senator Ledge. He told me of the auction wherein he will offer five servants. There's a cook among them.

In this way and in this mood, with feline grace and power supple throughout her being, she approached the ultimate disaster.

2

S HE SAID to Nineveh, There will be two baskets today. Linnet is fetching the basket of pistols.

Linnet was her lady's maid.

But I am in need of new targets. Everything at the tree is broken. Do you, Nineveh, get a large willow basket from Fairy or Goosey, and fill it with bottles from the cellar.

She added, Then set them on the opposite seat. And fetch some bits of leaves or grass or moss to stuff between. I can't abide their chinking and clinking.

When Sidney referred to the cellar it was not to a wine cellar, but to a storm cellar. A great many bottles had been emptied each week in that house, and originally they passed into the hands of slaves who desired bottles for various uses: to contain hair oil, home-made medicines, sundry poisons and potions. They were toys for children as well. But bottles accumulated in monstrous force. After Pettey J.'s death, Sidney discovered with wry amusement that an old storm cellar had been the repository. A barn door had been placed over the excavation, and there was a cat-hole cut in that door, and through the cat-hole bottles were dropped by servants.

Nineveh lugged a mound of them piled amid the withes: brown, green, blue, colorless. They were of all sorts and sizes. Following his mistress's direction, he packed them cautiously, he stuffed pine straw so that the bottles might not play a tune or crack. Linnet brought out a smaller basket containing Sidney's matched pistols and ammunition, and placed it on the seat. Linnet was pale ginger in color, and exactly the size and shape of her mistress. She could wear Sidney's gowns, and did (amid loudly voiced criticism and jealousy of other servants) whenever Sidney was gone away from Apoxsee for any length of time and felt disinclined, for one reason or another, to take her maid along. But Linnet was clever enough to earn easy treatment and even coddling through unfailing demonstration of a polite innocence and a willingness—nay, a passion—to serve.

Pleasant drive, mistess, said the shy voice.

Thank you, Linnet.

You home for you lunch, mistess?

Twill be late. Why do you ask?

Cause— Bashfully. —Cause if you ain need me I walk across Divide Field to Mr. Bonaparte Wilkey's place an see my Aunt Eve. I hear tell she laying poorly.

Sidney said chidingly, Your Aunt Eve! Poorly again! Tis her own fault, Linnet. But do you go.

Well, said Linnet in concession, she do eat like a horse.

She is notorious, poor soul. Where are the Hostetter's?

Hostetter's Stomach Bitters in masta's old chamber, I bleeve. In the washstand draw.

Take them to your Aunt Eve. And pick her some geraniums from the gallery.

Yes, mistess. Pleasant drive.

Before they left the circle, Sidney saw a place she loved, and told her driver to stop the carriage. She sat worshipping and doting. This beauty below the hill she had created for herself, and she called it Lake Tannin. That was because live-oak leaves went thick into the water and brewed it dark. The very clay beneath the surface was dyed by leaves' strength. A small creek, one of several on the plantation, had meandered adjacent to the wide house-yard; it bounded both flower garden and vegetable gardens at the foot of a slope. Sidney thought that it would be wise to dam the creek and thus create a pond for bathing; and she mentioned this project, but got nowhere with Pettey J. He scorned the idea solely because she'd suggested it.

Bathe in your chamber, Mrs.

Empowered by the act of death, she had dammed and managed.

Cypress logs made the dam. They would last as long as she had need of the lake or need of anything. Sidney ordered all stumps and underbrush to be grubbed out; her lake should offer no danger or entanglement. The peaceful pool filled a shallow saucer between slopes. There was one little peninsula which ran out into Lake Tannin, and on it grew an oak reddened with lichens, the oak found its ornate twin on the smooth surface. O joy. Sidney had flowering bushes renewed and relocated along the margin; some were stolen from the garden itself. But still not enough concealment to suit her. She desired utter privacy. Accordingly a fence was contrived of slim green willows, smooth bark against smooth bark. Perhaps a clever rat could have gotten through but nothing bigger. As for snakes, they were a consistent danger at any time in any season. You had to live with snakes and know the ones to fear, just as with human beings. Some snakes had even been found in the house, coiled cozy in laundry or on beds. But no use in dealing with gators as well.

After consideration Sidney had iron posts installed. They ruled the creek bed, perhaps six inches apart, both immediately below the dam and upstream above the pond. Only the tiniest gator might ever glide between the posts, and a tiny gator was considered to be a pet. Sticks and logs wedged themselves within the iron but those could be removed. Sidney swam nude as she wanted to swim, guarded by willow fencing. By night she could mingle wet and loosely with stars.

Very well. Drive on, Nineveh. Wheels rolled again, hoofs ladled up the dust.

The Big Gate was nearly two miles from the Big House. Shortly before they reached it Nineveh turned his team to the right and drove into a pretty winding sluice through a hammock. The way was creased and trampled. Sidney Shallop went there every day except under the most trying conditions of weather. Often she rode by herself or walked when she was in the mood. Here lay her target range. She did not choose to shoot near the plantation house. Black children gathered, stood around, they applauded, chattered, even their whispering was a trial. Furthermore she held always the fear that some of them might creep into bushes at the target area, stupid and unheeding. She did not often fire wildly; still a heavy spring might take the hammer away from her finger when cocking.

Here grew a lounging thick-trunked oak with lateral branches running out and far. Sidney deplored seeing these wide-spread generous things snapped off in storms. When first she came to Apoxsee she had gone about with a wagonload of field hands, showing them which limbs must be propped. (Her husband berated her savagely for this: twasn't ladylike.) Thus sodden props were set in place beneath these wide limbs as well, already channeled by insects but strong enough to serve. The upper portion of the trunk on the northern area was crimped with lichens but there were few lichens left farther down. That area stood pocked and torn by Sidney's pistol bullets. She had put hundreds of rounds into the tree. She speculated with lazy amusement at times, considering a future. Suppose that oak were logged off, suppose saws bit into the lead?—and what a wonderment might ensue? Various little shelves and pegs had been arranged to hold targets. Earth at the foot of the tree, grass and moss were all ashine, spangled fragments lay in a jeweled carpet. Elements were endeavoring to turn whiter fragments into that frail lilac which is the heritage of elder glass.

Nineveh's feet were a worry. He went slopping about the place most of the time without shoes, and only cackled with glee at her concern.

Mistess, I tell you, I could bust you a bottle with my bare foot and ne'er feel it.

Well, you shan't try.

Now she asked, Nineveh, are you wearing shoes?

He was hurt. I always wears shoes when I drives you to town.

Then set me up some targets.

He decked the tree. Some bottles were placed upright in a row upon a shelf, some presented only their bottoms in a smaller array.

Sidney owned two cases of matched duelling pistols. One had belonged to her late husband (not that Shallop could hit the broad side of a cow barn at ten paces). This bore the graven initials RAJ, and again and again the woman speculated on who the original RAJ might have been. These were of comparatively ancient construction, smooth-bore, huge as to caliber. They had been converted, however, from flintlocks to percussion. The other pair of pistols was smaller and rifled. She had also her own private weapon carried in a reticule or in any other bag kept handy.

Nineveh tied the team against a rustic horse-rail put up at the opposite side of the glade. Horses knew what was coming, they busied their eyes, their ears were back and sharp. Nineveh admonished them.

You keep quiet, now. She going shoot. You know she going shoot. Ain't going damage you, and you be quiet.

But the horses considered that explosions might indeed damage them—although they were not obsessed, were not about to panic and rip the rail and run. Nineveh kissed Betty on her gray muzzle and Bill promptly put his head over to be kissed. Nineveh peered out from behind the team. You going shoot now, mistess?

I'm just capping up.

Mrs. Shallop always kept her pistols loaded but not capped. Except for the .28 caliber revolving pistol in her bag.

She would fire the heavy weapons first.

She took a big pistol and stood at a distance of ten paces from the target tree. The position was marked by two white stones which Sidney herself had set into the ground. She put her toe on the smooth roundness so that always she might be standing in the same place, firing in the same direction. The first shot banged out and smoke was dense. She waved smoke away with hand and arm and narrowed her eyes to see. The target bottle stood stolidly intact, and Sidney murmured a soft curse. A flinch, she had flinched again. Should she never be able to discipline herself? Why anticipate a loud report? She took up the other pistol, and drew the hammer against its taut spring,

33

and felt it bite and hold. She aimed. These were large weapons, and weighty. Her hand was shaking, she steeled hand and arm. Now squeeze lightly, steadily, and do not anticipate, do not warn yourself that there will come a snap and burst and flare.

The snap-boom came, surprising its author, but the bottle was a splash of fragments against the tree trunk.

Nineveh called, You want me to clean?

I fear that there's not time today. I'll fire only these few rounds.

She opened the other case, and this bore hinges and lock of gold plate. She had bought it in Savannah, and the gunsmith assured her that these were excellent pistols of British make but he knew nothing about their history. They were more satisfactory, more to her size as to weight and as to comfort of the butts, and as to curve of the triggers. Sidney selected two of the small targets with only bottoms exposed, and broke them both in deliberate shots.

You shoot you little pistol today, mistess?

No, Nineveh. I'm three-quarters perfect at the moment, and I'll leave well enough alone.

She added, Do you, however, bring the basket of bottles, and fetch away these that are left on the tree. Hide them yonder in the myrtles. Otherwise children may come round and break them for sport.

She sat on a log while he was performing the chore, and swabbed out all four pistols but did not clean them otherwise. This was a lazy joy which she would undertake at home; she would oil the weapons to perfection, then wipe them free of oil, so that the felt wherein they reposed might not be stained. Yes, they would be nearly free of oil, yet they would be charged: powder would be stuffed into them, bullets stuffed against the powder, the weapons at readiness except for spark-giving life-giving caps, and those would be handy too. And the .28 revolving pistol stowed in her reticule. No man might dare torture her again.

Senator Fenton Ledge was both attorney and banker. In one capacity or the other all of Mrs. Shallop's business affairs were in his hands. Or rather, hand. He had but one. Senator Ledge had run away to sea at the age of fourteen, and was on the *Chesapeake* when it was captured, and when Lawrence fell. Ledge lost his right arm in that engagement. He had been some years in the State Senate and was now years out of it, but the designation of Senator was still applied. He was an affable bald-headed man. His nose, which should have grown in sensitive shape with a narrow high bridge, had been bashed lopsidedly against his face when he was young (handiwork of a mate appropriately designated as Mr. Meany. Mr. Meany was guilty of other similar misdeeds, and, on a voyage home from the Mediterranean, was carved into a wad of red embroidery by some eagerly-intentioned members of the crew. Mr. Meany had to be bound up in a sack and weighted and slid from a plank. Cheers rose from the rear ranks of an assembled ship's company—cheers which the captain pretended not to hear. Senator Ledge related the incident often, with zest). Ledge's invariable attitude of easy cordiality did not belie the firm but affectionate soul within. Ledge had admired Mrs. Shallop from the first day he set eyes on her, and they played at a game. The pretense that he was her uncle and she a somewhat spoilt and frivolous niece. The angular constantly-complaining Mrs. Ledge did not think highly of Sidney Shallop, and accented the first syllable of that family name whenever she drawled it.

Mrs. *Shallop*.

There were criticism and implied sneer in her tone. No one missed the effect.

Always a young man could be found reading law with Senator Ledge (several such had gone on to give good accounts of themselves—a fine reflection on their mentor). This one was Mr. Heyward, a frightened-looking youth with silver-rimmed spectacles and a mop of tousled taffy hair. He limped in to announce Mrs. Shallop's arrival, and the senator came out, took her hands, intoned a welcome, led her to sit in a carpet-covered rocking chair and to be guarded by blank-faced busts of Cicero and Caesar.

You are early, my dear Sidney. The others have not yet

arrived, and it must be a fair auction if a small one. Pray rest, and give me the benefit of your smile.

My deepest apology, sir. Somehow we made better time on the road than I had anticipated. Even then I was telling Nineveh to hold the team.

I'd thought you might come a-horseback in your handsome green habit.

He was teasing her in recalling one of the occasions when she had whirled into town at a speed which scandalized all observing ladies, and had herself thrown in Oglethorpe Street (unhurt) to the town's terror.

Actually I yearned to do it, sir. But, should I acquire a cook today—which I think unlikely—she'd need to be transported to Apoxsee.

Behind a piled and confused table Senator Ledge leaned comfortably in his leather chair and sat with fingers of his stout left hand playing with a Masonic pin with which he kept his empty right sleeve fastened against his jacket.

Why do you think it unlikely that you will acquire a cook, child? Many wrinkles deepened on his smooth-shaven face as he smiled.

So few of them are up to snuff.

Ah, but you haven't heard about Beauty Beast.

Sir?

No wonder that you're amazed. But that's the black woman's name, and she's remarkably trained. Ledge took his fingers away from their play with the pin, and let them seek amid papers.

Sidney said, I thought it remarkable when my sister owned a scullery-maid named Idgit. But Beauty Beast—

And long ago, Ledge told her, our neighbor Mr. Hebb actually had a coachman named Jehu.

Ledge found the paper which he sought. Here's the list. There are five girls to go, in all. Melissa, forty-two, laundress; Caro, thirty-six, nurse; Johnny May, seventeen, housemaid; Ellen, eighteen, kitchen-maid; and Beauty Beast, twenty-eight, cook. I take it that they're choice. Mr. Justice Bracket, rest his restless soul, wouldn't have countenanced any others. He was always seeking perfection in every department of life; which, I may say, led to his unpopularity in certain quarters.

They both chuckled, and then Fenton Ledge went on brightly, But take this girl Beauty Beast. She must be a wizard. He read from the paper: *Beauty Beast is highly skilled in the culinary arts, and performs skilfully with the French cuisine as well as with our own traditional dishes, having accompanied Judge Bracket to France during his stay there. Is also highly literate, musically inclined, and has proven a great comfort.* What say you to that, hey?

I fear she may be uppity. And I couldn't abide her if she were.

We'll soon see for ourselves. The servants are over at Mrs. Dowson's place. You know—Judge Bracket's granddaughter? Her husband came here two years ago and bought the cedarwood factory. And also he ships smoked mullet. They've house servants many and to spare, and don't need these.

The last time I made bold to attend church, said Sidney, Mrs. Dowson cut me.

The more fool she.

Young Mr. Heyward put his head in at the door to announce the arrival of Messrs. Cuzzen, Rosenbach and Merrill.

That's the *tout ensemble,* so we may as well go along.

Ledge rose, came round the table, and extended his hand to Sidney, drawing her from the chair. They went out to where three men stood with hats held against their chests. Sidney bowed to each of the others but not to Mr. Cuzzen, a man with protruding eyeballs and slabs of iron-gray hair.

When Shallop was still living, LeRoi Cuzzen had often been a guest at Apoxsee. He annoyed Mrs. Shallop particularly by leering after her personal maid, whom he was bound to observe from time to time, and openly offering to buy her. There came one of those evenings occurring all too frequently, with men much the worse for wine. The others were all drunk or still playing at cards, or attempting to, and Cuzzen staggered into Sidney's room to embrace Sidney and, as he chose to minimize the occurrence, to *steal a kiss.* Sidney sliced his nostrils and upper lip with fingernails, and stamped a hard leather heel upon his boot. That boot, with its fellow, had been made for Mr. Cuzzen in New Orleans, and its material was of leather scraped thin and gentle as velvet. The boot held in its forward portion Mr. Cuzzen's toes, studded with sensitive corns. She left him hobbling and cursing, tears squeezing from his plump eyes and dripping to mingle with the blood and water which came from his mouth.

God damn you, lady. You're a hell-cat.

Yes, said Sidney.

Child, I'll hand you into your carriage, and the rest of us shall stroll. It's the former Boddling mansion. You know? Across from the church, on Yeehaw Street?

Sidney had Nineveh drive around two extra squares, that she might not anticipate the gentlemen's arrival. Air was lazy with dust, smoking in sunny places; oleanders built a pink-and-white luxury above every wall and in all shade. The carriage turned into Yeehaw Street just as Senator Ledge and the others filed through the yard gate. The senator waved them on toward the gallery, and then returned to the driveway to hand Sidney down. A tiny black girl, barefoot but wearing a fresh gown with blue dots, came waltzing across the gallery and down the steps in welcome.

Mistah Senator Ledge, sah. Mistess say she *otherwise occupied,* and beg to be excused.

Sidney thought, I should be in no wise surprised at this.

Where are the colored, Little Mag?

They out on back gallery.

Then, Little Mag, fetch them here. One at a time.

Ledge guided Sidney to a chair in the shade: the one farthest from Mr. Cuzzen. Ledge knew the story. He had no use whatsoever for the Cuzzens of this world; but on the other hand he was dutiful in an effort to settle the Bracket estate on the best possible terms for his client. Cuzzen, with an ailing child at home, had asked the senator to look out for a competent nurse.

One by one negresses were brought forth by the guiding

Little Mag. Cuzzen seemed to be the only person in the market for a nurse. He asked Caro a few questions. Yes, she had attended white folks with lung fever, several times.

Both the plump Rosenbach and the gaunt Merrill displayed interest in Melissa, the laundress, and she was kept standing longer before them. In each case Fenton Ledge read from his paper the brief description of the servant.

The two maids were fetched, the housemaid first, and were appraised and questioned.

I wish that I had brought along my Mrs., said Rosenbach. She'd know better about those girls than I. But she refuses to leave the house on a hot day like this. Absolutely! I declare, we spoil our servants. But the house people have grown so lax that I must either have them whipped, or sell them. I prefer to do the latter.

Selecting niggers, said Merrill grimly, is a man's business. Don't let anyone convince you otherwise.

Now for the most expensive item on the list, Senator Ledge told them. That'll be the cook. Fetch her, Little Mag.

The child rolled her eyes at him. Sah? she asked, not seeming to understand. Sah?

I said *fetch her,* Little Mag. The cook. Fetch Beauty Beast.

Yessah.

She danced away, but still looking back over her shoulder. When she returned, ushering the cook, they could understand why she had behaved in such fashion.

Beauty Beast was a man.

He stood graceful, there was splendor about him. His skin was not deeply toned, twas amber. Jet hair, wavy, with not a kink in it, was pomaded tightly against a sculptured head. There lived a gentle elegance in this creature which, to the undiscerning, might have seemed as a kind of studied insolence. But he was not insolent, he was courtly in politeness. He bowed in turn to each of the white people on the gallery, and his deepest bow was directed to Senator Ledge as if by protocol.

Sidney Shallop had closed her eyes. There was riot within a locked-up portion of her heart and spirit, and seemingly the riot

39

began to extend until it occupied the entire nearer world. Voices shouted, yet there were whispers as well. She directed herself: Don't swoon. You dare not swoon here, with these men. Even the senator. Twould be an admission too horrible, and someone might guess.

Then she thought again, No, no, they could never guess.

It was a thing too unruly, too vast, too mysteriously demanding. She managed to open her eyes and look upon Beauty Beast again. Her lips shaped a word. Very nearly she spoke the word aloud. The word was *Joel*.

Melissa, forty-two, laundress, had been first on the list; in turn she was the first to reappear and to be bid upon. Ledge, in protection of his client's interest, specified that bids begin at twelve hundred dollars. Rosenbach offered objection. He said that there was little use in considering Melissa's skills or state of health: her age must be taken into consideration. Forty-two was forty-two, and perhaps twenty years of activity were left before her, perhaps but ten. Senator Ledge acquiesced, lowering the stipulation to one thousand dollars. Rosenbach placed his bid for this amount, but Merrill went up to twelve hundred immediately, and Melissa was sold.

Rosenbach also vied with Cuzzen in an exchange of bids over Caro the nurse.

She is but thirty-six years of age, Fenton Ledge reminded them. Six years younger than Melissa, and of course much more highly skilled. In deference to my client's wishes, I shall consider no bid below the figure of fourteen hundred.

Bid, said LeRoi Cuzzen. Obviously he believed that Caro was the answer to his child's need of the moment. Rosenbach bid fourteen-twenty-five, Cuzzen fifteen-twenty-five, Rosenbach fifteen-fifty, Cuzzen sixteen-fifty. What want you with a nurse, Mr. Rosenbach? he demanded, emphasizing the German-Jewish quality of the name. Are you planning to speculate with this property? Rosenbach shrugged, and bid no more on Caro.

Mr. Merrill craved the gentlemen's indulgence, and asked Senator Ledge if he might not scratch his signature a few times, and proceed home without delay. This is what I came for, he declared. A laundress particularly.

As always, methodically correct to a fault, Senator Ledge had had Mr. Heyward draw up papers the day before, and only the name and date and price need be inserted in each case. Merrill went round-shouldered into the garden and found two of Mrs. Dowson's boys: one was spading manure into an empty flower-bed, and the other squatted against the wall, watching him, talking and tittering. Merrill sent the watcher-titterer to Ogle-thorpe Street for his French chaise, and gave him five cents in currency when the boy came driving back. Melissa and her bundle of possessions were loaded into the two-wheeled chaise, but not before tears had been shed. Sidney Shallop observed that Beauty Beast shook hands with the departing Melissa, he embraced her with respect and affection. But Sidney retained the notion that Beauty Beast held no relationship to this negress beyond the fact that both of them had been owned by Judge Bracket, and for a long period of time. Here was tenderness engendered by proximity—ah, solely by proximity. Caro and the two housemaids sobbed and clung to Melissa, while Mr. Merrill stood waiting, seeming annoyed but still sympathetic.

I hope to see you soon, little Johnny May was sobbing. See you *soon*.

Melissa's reply was muted, doubtless she was reassuring the girl. She walked to the chaise holding her head high, bowing in thanks to the new master for his sufferance, before she got into the vehicle beside him. The horse trotted away with them through sun and shade and dust and golden patches of midday street.

There had been a misplacement of papers during the con-firmation of Mr. Merrill's purchase. Ellen, the kitchen-maid, came next for sale. Messrs. Rosenbach and Cuzzen bid steadily against each other, Mr. Rosenbach going up by his usual twenty-five-dollar units, and Cuzzen advancing by units of fifty dollars. He was bound and determined to have Ellen, and Sidney remembered how the man's swollen eyes had gone over the girl when she stood before them.

Yet *you* thought of *Joel*.

When Cuzzen's head was turned to one side, she looked at the flare of his nostril and saw a tiny scar. It was the one she had inflicted. She felt satisfaction, and thought, I should like to scar him again, but he's too frightened, he'll never offer the opportunity.

These were only a kitchen-maid and a housemaid to be considered, but they were young and seemed vigorous. They were handsome, both of them—one in cushiony manner, the other in slender fashion.

Mr. Rosenbach was deploring prices. Why, I can remember— And not so long ago— Eight or nine hundred was an adequate, a more-than-fair price for any maid. You could buy field hands in their prime for a thousand or eleven hundred!

Senator Ledge said, You might as well talk about the days before our time, when they could be had off the boat for a few pounds sterling. Times change and prices change.

True, sir. But you demanded that these bids start at eleven hundred dollars and—

Judge-Bracket-bred, or Judge-Bracket-trained niggers, said the senator loftily, are something a bit out of the ordinary. Unique, shall we say?

Somewhere short of thirteen hundred, where Ellen was concerned, Mr. Rosenbach began counting his five-dollar gold pieces if not his pennies. He would now raise Mr. Cuzzen's bid by only five dollars on each occasion, and Senator Ledge stirred restlessly in his chair and looked vexed with himself. He could have imposed a unit system of twenty-five dollars or whatever, and had not done so. LeRoi Cuzzen finally bought Ellen for fourteen hundred and thirty-five dollars. Johnny May went to Mr. Rosenbach for considerably less.

For a time Sidney Shallop had battled to observe, to take note; and then she capitulated and let herself be ruled and occupied by a single concentrated awareness. The thought was as a liquid pumped into her body by queer means (but never through the vaginal opening) and then it occupied her within trunk and skull and extremities: the thought congealed to a solid core, extending every which direction, a mass to push her organs and notions—even her dreams—aside. The thought was, *Never reveal. Never let be known.*

From girlhood Sidney had been subject to shabby treatment or to outright and outraging brutalities which she had never courted and which she did not deserve. (Sidney was extraordinary as to emotion and imaginings, but not as to intellect: for all her sum of human experience she did not yet recognize that there is no functioning Justiciary to measure out benefactions or penalties. She felt that she had hurts stored up unused, like seeds saved in a granary. The bags lay hoarded, applied to her credit.)

Let us say that one needs a certain amount of cruelty visited upon one's self, in order to keep her name on the rolls of normal bruised humanity?

I need no more.

I have a granary full.

Still there would be equity in suffering her awful motive to be explored and the findings disseminated. Twould be just, yet she'd not tolerate it. She'd give no one the chance to probe.

If the man whom I trust and admire most in the world— If Senator Fenton Ledge himself knelt and asked me, and said that it'd make all the difference, and it'd keep him from death, I—I—

If that knowledge were the last panacea, I could not give, could not award, could not tell.

The business of buying a second Joel. This will be?

The first was there, yet I could not have him for my own.

The second Joel.

Sold? To the lady yonder?

Before the fifth slave was offered, Senator Ledge spoke in routine fashion, as he had done with each of the others. E'er the bidding begins, should anyone wish to examine the property again?

I should, said LeRoi Cuzzen.

The men looked at Mrs. Shallop keenly, since she had come

43

to the auction and yet had bid on no one of the other four; so her need must be for a cook. She did nothing but to incline her head slightly, as in acceptance.

Little Mag owned an assortment of wilted japonica blooms which had fallen in the garden, and she was arranging these on the edge of the gallery. But now the senator interrupted her play, and told her to fetch Beauty Beast. She went dancing to the task, going side-wise, jigging along on big-toed feet. Soon the white people heard her barefoot dance repeated, with a heavier tread coming behind. And the tan man reappeared, walking stably but not heavy-footed.

Oh, grace, Sidney thought. Grace and balance as he goes.

There's no mention of illness in the description, said Saul Rosenbach. Let's ask the boy himself. Beauty Beast, have you ever been sickly?

Only when a child, sir.

This was the first time he had spoken to any of them, and Sidney's eyes crushed shut once more when she heard his voice. But only momentarily. She forced her eyes open.

Had the fever? Hey?

No, sir. Not the bad fever.

Cholera? Rosenbach went on naming complaints, including the pox.

Senator Ledge spoke with natural gentility. It's customary to strip the field hands, I know. We all want to know what a man can bring to his task. But house servants—

I must say that he looks like a very healthy article, said Rosenbach.

Cuzzen leaned forward, puffy hands plastered against his knees, eyes bulging.

So you've been across the water with your master. You have lived in France?

Yes, sir.

Please to say master.

Yes, master.

Whereabouts did you dwell with the judge?

In Paris principally. If you knew Judge Bracket, master, you

44

knew that he enjoyed travel. We went to Brittany, and also were in the Champagne country and in the Haute Savoy. Also long in the Lot valley and the Dordogne. We drove about by coach, and for a time my master took a house in Aix-en-Provence.

Ah. Then your cookery is of the Provençal type?

Not entirely, master. I have many recipes, and can also prepare dishes of the Breton and Parisian persuasions.

Sidney spoke, the men jumped to hear her. Your coat, Beauty Beast, she said. Your jacket.

The young negro looked down at the garment, which was of rough tow-cloth with wooden buttons. *Madame?*

Was it given you by the judge?

Yes, madam. He said that he found it in an old chest. He wore it when he was young.

But—the color?

Beauty Beast lifted one arm, smiled at the tint of his own sleeve, let his arm fall easily. I did dye it myself, madam.

She could not have described the hue, except to say that it was somewhere in the range of palest lavender or wild mint blossoms.

Did you employ boughten dyes or natural dyes?

Natural, madam. He hesitated, and then smiled as he explained: We had an old nigger woman on the place, who was said to be part Cherokee. She taught me a great deal about dyeing.

What did you employ?

Indigo, madam. But it was scorched first, and then mixed with a broth of sugar berries.

Sugar berries?

They grow in the swamps, madam. Left alone, they give red, but with the indigo, and in the thinnest of broths—

Cuzzen broke in, chuckling self-consciously (as to label his jeer). Is dyeing important in a cook's lore?

Senator Ledge said, It might be, to a lady.

Seems to me, said Cuzzen, that would be a task for a laundress.

45

Senator Ledge was aware of implied criticism of Sidney, yet he could not quite identify it. He asked, Are there to be any more questions? Any further examination of the property at hand?

No one spoke, and he signalled to Beauty Beast that he might return to the rear gallery. The servant went unescorted; but Sidney saw his strong amber hand come down and touch the tight witch-knots on Little Mag's head as he passed the child. Yes, yes, there was much kindness in him.

But she had known, all the time.

O Almighty *God.*

Senator Ledge declared that no bids for less than eighteen hundred and fifty dollars would be considered.

Incidentally the stipulation is not mine. It comes from the estate.

Mr. Cuzzen leaned back in his carpeted rocker and wrapped his lips inward in a smile peculiar to himself. Then he let the lips roll out for speech. Two thousand dollars, he bid without equivocation.

Rosenbach cried, Now hold, sir, hold! What—?

Senator Ledge ruled, The bid is legal and allowable, if a trifle premature in the scale.

Cuzzen said pompously, There is no need for amenities which are not prescribed, in the course of business conduct. I am willing to pay two thousand dollars for the property.

Sidney Shallop said, Two thousand five hundred.

All turned to look at her. Mr. Rosenbach wrenched up from his chair and half spoke, but only half. Sidney was under the impression that he was muttering an indignant curse, and certainly he was not a man given to swearing, and especially in the presence of a lady. He settled back forlornly. The bidding was gone beyond his financial ability to participate.

It remained finally for Cuzzen to put the opinion into words. In the meantime he had been fairly gulping for breath. That is preposterous, he said with rage.

Sidney turned and smiled at the senator. May I request, sir, that you quote—or perhaps reëstablish is a better word—the comment which was just made about the bid offered by this person himself?

Certainly it is legal. Ledge was nodding at Cuzzen. And certainly good to hear, to the ears of this referee, who was hopeful of securing a bargain for his clients.

Bargain!

From our point of view.

LeRoi Cuzzen's face had turned to wet rust and he fanned himself with a white silk handkerchief. He moved to the steps, down into the garden, walked to and fro for minutes, seeming oblivious of the others. When he breathed back to the gallery, Sidney offered him only the corner of her glance. There were Macartney roses hedging thickly along the path, so critically she kept regarding the roses as if suspicious of their diet and reckoning to change it.

My own good cooks, Cuzzen exclaimed. Mother and daughter. Both went down when the fever appeared last May. In one package, Mr. Rosenbach! The loss of a small fortune, which I'm sure you will appreciate.

Cuzzen was momentarily pleased with himself at condemning, by implication, Rosenbach's Jewishness. (He belonged to that portion of mankind who believe or pretend to believe that Jewishness is synonymous with cupidity.) He grew expansive and went on to say that with cooler weather ahead, and seasonal increase of commercial activity in the region, his social obligations would be numerous.

I have more need for a boy like this than might any lady dwelling by herself in, shall we say, voluntary seclusion.

Ledge looked sharply at Mrs. Shallop, but she appeared aloof. The senator asked, Are we to assume, sir, that you are hoping that the lady may desist from any further bidding, merely because of your urgent need for such a servant?

I am explaining why I choose to utter a preposterous bid of twenty-six hundred dollars for this property.

Mr. Rosenbach exclaimed, the vocal syllables came out, no one knew whether they were German, Yiddish, Hebrew. Sena-

47

tor Ledge's forehead was scrolled as he looked down to examine the Masonic gaud which sustained his empty sleeve. As if he found lint or foreign material there, he went exploring the pin with fingernails of his left hand.

He said, A bid of two thousand, six hundred dollars, for the property Beauty Beast, is now entertained.

Sidney heard her own voice off yonder. She considered it thin but was glad of the sound. (Why is my voice remote? Like distant ringing. Silver? Sometimes people have said—)

Away off, voice speaking, clear metal, jingling to mention money. Three thousand dollars.

Mr. Cuzzen's face was no longer solidly dark-colored, it became painted in miscellaneous patches. Sidney counseled herself in an instant of human sympathy and not in detestation. That man is not long for this world. I pity him. Could I compose a sympathetic note to his relatives? But I have no saintliness.

Cuzzen's eyes were marbles pushed out of his head by the goiter inside. I can go over to New Orleans! Or Mobile. I can go and buy two excellent cooks for that price, possibly three. May I state that I have no higher bid to offer? I cannot contend against madness. I had crying need for a cook, and especially one skilled in the French cuisine. But if Mrs. Shallop purchases this boy— and it would seem that she has bought him—there is assuredly no one whom he might serve except herself.

Sidney made up a melodrama in which she played the starring role. She was often doing this, had done so ever since she was a child. Often she felt ashamed in contemplating her own silliness, yet twas an amusing retreat. In imagining she heard Senator Ledge saying pompously, Mr. Cuzzen, it would seem that your final remark requires some elucidation, sir.

Senator, please— Sidney continued her fiction. Allow me. She left her chair and walked to Cuzzen. Despite any original intention to stand firm, he retreated and very nearly fell backward down the gallery steps. Mr. Cuzzen, should you like to repeat your attempt to steal a kiss? I'll be delighted to oblige in kind.

Sidney held chamois-skin gloves in her left hand, and swung

them full force across Cuzzen's mouth. You are a coward, sir. Have you friends? There must be someone who can act for you. Might you be able to resolve your statement into a matter for discussion with pistols? I shall be rewarded in meeting you at any time and any place designated by those who may represent us.

She saw the field where they met, twas Mr. Wilkey's pastureland. Grass grew long. Cuzzen was quaking, and she chided herself, Of what extensive bullying are you capable? Why murder as in a lark? Distance was paced off, they stood apart, signal was given. Cuzzen jerked up his pistol and fired askew, the bullet keened off a nearby stone and went singing. Sidney called to her seconds (vague people), Might you request that Mr. Cuzzen lift his foot and turn it sidewise? Coolly Sidney shot the heel off Cuzzen's boot. There came plaudits from the watching crowd. (Earlier there had been only principals and seconds, and a driver or two, and the doctor; now there were hundreds.) She shot the heel from Cuzzen's boot to show how easily she could have killed the man had she chosen to do so.

Absurdity and charm of her private pantomime were over and done in a flash. A catbird spurted its miaow, an old negress *yah-yah-yah*ed somewhere in the tall house, squirrels flicked in a sabal palm. Then Sidney was speaking to the spritely black child (observe her skin: black, so black, and yet as if seen through wood-smoke). Little Mag, do you tell Beauty Beast to make ready to go in the carriage.

~3~

S HE HAD picked a flower, caught a fish, been rewarded by
her schoolmistress. She had achieved, acquired. The posy
prinked in vase or bottle where she might behold it; trout
toasted on the fire ; the teacher saluted her. You have spelt well,
Miss Sidney. Move to the next bench.

Senator Ledge appeared self-consciously inscrutable as he put
her into the carriage.

At times you are given to extravagance—

I fear.

Then when shall I be invited to dine at Apoxsee and taste the
fruits?

Sidney, nerved and ready to protract a conflict in some direction, said (her voice rang, did not lilt or tinkle), Whenever
Mrs. Ledge shall see fit to honor us by accompanying you.

You know she won't, he said mournfully. Somehow he reminded her of the boy he must have been before he went to
sea.

He gripped her hand with muscular fingers and pressed it
twice in characteristic gesture. She'd often thought that this was
the Grip. It was their lodge, they belonged to it. You gave the
Grip, you signed with your fingers and were recognized.

She was carried off, carried off, dust drifted loose and somehow had a lenient smell in the sun. Dust was always the color of
spice, one spice or another, but this dust tasted of spice.

Can that be ascribed to blossoms nearby? Or the very taste of shade itself?

Of course shade.

Shade and sun. Sun's always had a taste. But I can't remember the flavor of shade, and am savoring it only now.

And is that because something strangely dark—? I mean, darker than—? I mean, there is shade and shadow, new, coming into my life?

Dragged into your life. You doin' the draggin'.

She held her sunshade (how odd: I've been estimating sun and *shade*) low against her, and appreciated its ruffles—pink, and a kind of cloistered blue.

The day came on warmer, she said. Much warmer than first believed. I loosen my shawl.

Sidney tilted the gay fragile umbrella and thus saw Nineveh and Beauty Beast together on the box. Nineveh round-shouldered, elbows proper, strong hands a-holding, relaxed in the conventional crouch of the coachman which still had solidity and a bearing about it. Beauty Beast tall beside him, storied delicate-dyed jacket gleaming, its color a wonder.

His color a wonder.

Ah, not only color. Stature and body, the eternal Joel quality of him.

Captive fish, plucked flower, hard-won honor in the class. Also there was a moth, many years before. She'd wanted it for hours on two successive nights. It attended her secret illegal candle, there was a glass chimney round the candle, the moth rippled close and tried to walk there, hurt its furry feet. It rose into dull golden-lit air as if wailing for a moment, and then it might have cried, No, no, the tradition is too strong! I am a moth, and here is flame. I must tilt once more.

The creature brandished wings of gilt splotched with purple, but you had the feeling that the purple was applied by God with a loose and urgent brush. He did not care, He slapped paint heedlessly, and perhaps one such moth was not exactly like the next. As with changing leaves in a cool climate—never two the same.

54

She coveted the fairy because of its hugeness and mystic qualities. Wider of wing than her stolen peach was thick (fat peach soft beneath the corner of her pillow, half-eaten now, and making soaked stains on a tea-towel in which she'd bundled it). Sidney kept in bed with her also a novel. She'd been told that she should not read it, so of course was bound to explore each phrase. Had it been work set for her by Miss Pam, the schoolmistress, twould have been a dreary task; but here was only titillation. One of the two heroines was pronouncedly *giddy* and the other (whisper) had been accused of being *fast*.

Sidney read into wan hours of the night. The moth returned and went away again—a bit scorched perhaps. Then reappearance: the lure, bold candle sustaining its wide bright tongue within glass. How she longed to hold the moth and feel its satin hair gently delicate on its body, close against her fingertips. Nor would she squeeze, nor would she press and sweep too closely and rapidly with her hand in making capture.

Ah, try again—

Then she had the moth, loose and live, body squirming, wings trying to blur. She prisoned it between her fingers, and promptly felt a sense of loss replaced by capitulation.

She had no one to whom she might display this prize. She dared not wake her parents. Her sister was recently married and gone.

The attraction of the novel was as nothing now: an essence cheapened, one not to be wanted. It was proved vulgar merely by comparison with this flapping protesting prisoner. Yet take care—

You have it, your hand has the innocent, to let it live or to slay. And necessarily a wise management of your fingers—nerves and muscles or whatever contrivances control your fingers. The choice is yours. The superintendence thereof.

How may one enjoy that which he may not exhibit? Enjoy it in secret?

But he who relishes a glory in pure secrecy must be a miser.

(Eternal picture of a wasted old wretch wallowing amid rich coins and flinging them about.)

55

The acquisition is not good unless we may share. Or at least display before the world.

A hurtful thing to learn when young, so very young, and able barely to read a purloined novel.

Her little soft fingers began to loosen, fell apart. Moth rose high. It dove through torn mosquito net, came back, whirled past the candle in its chimney, flapped off, came back.

I'll cheat, she thought. Tis your only salvation.

She puffed, and there was then nothing but blankness and smell of the wick. And yes, insignificant glow for part of another minute, with tallow frying as the wick smoked and dried. But she felt the moth pass her cheek a time or two before she settled back upon her pillows a-wondering. And then indulging in tears, she knew not why.

She'd bought an organism on this fair day, invested in a new human. The first time in her life that she'd ever made such purchase.

What to say? Heigh-ho, I went me to market and bought a new slave?

Heigh-ho, to market we go.

A pig—

A pig going to market to buy something?

Or is it you yourself going to market with a basket to buy a pig?

Markets and baskets and pigs. Inseparable in childish ritual and belief.

Do you say, I bought that there boy for a wild price?

Or should you coo (as women are expected to coo among themselves) and say, Darling Jean or Darling Prue, you have no idea what it means to be a widow, and to require a cook. Then you needs must go and bid against the menfolk. An unladylike experience, I'll be bound.

I saw the look.

Indeed *tis* a concern of mine. Field hands, the outside servants, are immediate responsibility of the overseer. But a mistress looks after house servants.

I could not well have Mr. Irons frittering with Linnet or the maids, trying to get work out of them; and no doubt cozening them into bed, if he could do it without his Lora witnessing.

I saw the look that Linnet gave—

How did Beauty Beast look upon her? This I did not see. This must be imagined.

A. He paid no need. She's but a juiceless thing.

B. He himself is yellow in tone but black within, as are they all. But he—

C. Come, come, he's like a youth. Linnet owns the well-turnings of thigh and breast, slimness of ankle, its sudden taper into the calf. All this is like my own. We could be sisters—*Hey!* —were the tints not so dissimilar, together with the shape of our faces. Linnet has nigger nose, nigger lips. But he'd find it natural to look upon her with favor.

D. No, he's too wise. Slave or no, there's much of the human sophisticate about him. So he'd not bother with this namby-pamby wench. Twould be no appeal to his intellect or his erudition.

As in parenthesis, I note that I should have called all the black people together, let them assemble in the yard, be sure that all were there, and addressed them thus:

This day I have bought a cook. This day there is another slave to join you. This day is not the first day I have dealt in flesh, for previously I have sold but never bought. I sold Jiggy and Yellow Martha because my husband was wont to disport himself with them, and I could hear. Surely his first decay was not achieved when they were sold off and gone sniveling—the one to Mobile, and other up-country somewhere. And Mr. Irons shook his head and said that I'd let them go for a song. But I was bound to rid myself.

So now, good black people and bad black people alike, be notified of the power which I feel and have discovered. It is the power of means. I have means, have ownership.

I know not where my path goes, but let nothing stand in it. Let *no one* stand there.

You, Linnet, give especial heed.

Churned and affected as she was, Sidney Shallop yet walked calm, she walked in control and said, India, bring this. Basil, do so. Goosey, you do thus.

At once Goosey was to be moved to the cabin of her family at the quarters. The cook's cabin, where of necessity she had dwelt adjoining the kitchen, in back of the Big House—this would now be Beauty Beast's own. Goosey's elder children helped their mother in the moving. They gathered up her hair oil, combs, her gowns and aprons and kerchiefs, grinning shyly as they did so. They would be content to have their mother with them. It would not have done for the entire family to be there nigh the cooking. Too mad a mess, with little ones nibbling underfoot, and all the squawks and confusion which attended. So they should dwell together, along with the rotund husband and father, Caesar Augustus, known commonly as C.A. Goosey, diligent for all her illness, and conscientious to a fault— She was ordered to lie abed as she needed. The young folks to assist would be ordered up if Beauty Beast desired them. Or he might select his own helpers among the other blacks. Twould be his choice.

He owned several pieces of baggage. A well-stuffed carpet-bag; a long extension case of stiff hide and rivets, bound neatly with straps, and still marked with cryptic chalk and crayon symbols put there in European places; and a satchel containing favorite kitchen knives, spoons, and scales.

Such a cumbersome package which you have strapped upon your case, Beauty Beast.

My music, mistress.

Do you indeed play an instrument?

When there is opportunity, mistress.

I prefer that you call me madam, as you did over yonder.

Yes, madam. When much younger I learned the harpsichord, which was my owner's especial pleasure. But my **great** love, if madam will pardon me for expressing it, is the pianoforte.

Why, we have one.

Do you play, madam?

Poorly, and thus rarely. The piano, a Broadwood, was the property of my late husband's—first wife.

Yes, madam. He dropped back with bags in his hands to yield to her direction.

It was in this hour of his arrival at Apoxsee that Beauty Beast told his mistress how his peculiar name had come about. His mother's name was Beauty, and when she presented her scrolled Simian infant to the world, the women with her laughed and said, He a little beast. Later they referred to him as Beauty's Beast. In common slurring of their careless speech, negro children adjacent (as he grew older) called him Beauty Beast instead of Beauty's Beast. For some reason this tickled the fancy of Judge Bracket who owned him. The name was put down, so, upon plantation rolls, even in days when the child was reckoned as only half-a-hand.

Judge Bracket, he said without rancor, promised me my freedom.

A manumission. But why did it never occur?

Beauty Beast shook his head slowly. Madam, I'm reluctant to criticize the dead. And most of all to criticize Judge Bracket, for many reasons. But he was in some ways a selfish man, much more selfish than people believed.

Sidney spoke gently. I think I understand. When it came to the deed itself, he could not quite manage. Because he was afraid that he would lose you. You would go away.

He bowed, said no more.

Sidney would not rest until she had made him familiar not only with the abode, but with equipment, whatever conveniences were contained therein, whatever eccentricities existed. She knew that many a chatelaine would have turned him over to the retiring cook and to other house servants, and let them have their darkey riot together. You'd hear shrieking chatter, high vibrant shapeless laughter out the kitchen. They'd agitate within their colored world, being a part of each other to begin with; and you, white mistress in distance, a part of nothing they owned, even though you owned them in turn.

59

Sidney Shallop loved her kitchen, even the cook's quarters adjacent. So she went along the covered passage, signing Beauty Beast to follow, and thinking how winning was the whitewash on squared logs inside (even though flaking and peeling here and there, needing a fresh coat). But shadows and light made it bluish. Somewhere there was a bucket of water a-sitting, bucket of something. Little light danced in bubbles on its surface and ordered a reflection on the whitewashed ceiling rafters and shakes. Misshapen pennies of elegance stole across the ceiling.

Beauty Beast exclaimed, It's pretty.

What say, Beauty Beast?

I spoke out of turn. *Je regrette, madame.*

The mistress wanted to tell him that he must speak out of turn whenever he felt the impulse. She did not know how to say this. She desired to reach across, communicate with him, make him understand.

She said, In the old days twas all done on a spit, or over open fire.

Yes, madam. We came across such places abroad.

But my late mother-in-law had this iron stove erected, you see, bricked in. And here is a small charcoal grill, when it is necessary to get up a hasty snack.

He identified it, spoke the French word for the thing— *potager*— and Sidney listened in courtesy.

For all her aches Goosey had paid a visible duty to cleanliness. Everything was crisp and white, and wooden cutting-blocks scrubbed. Everything on the surface was serene. It was only when you dug and delved that you found odd saucers, lumps of meat wadded up and forgotten in careless crockery; candle-stubs abed with chicken bones; palm roaches so dry they might have been scarabs.

Sidney told Beauty Beast limply, You are to turn the place inside out. Initially it appears clean enough but—

He turned from investigation of a cupboard, and smiled. There was that which (it frightened her suddenly: could there be treachery in the smile?) diverted and beguiled when he grinned.

I understand, madam. I have just discovered a ham butt well past its prime.

They heard the rolling of Goosey's wheels as she approached, and two of her children blathering along with her.

Goosey is returning and can now tell you where things are kept. But manage your own dispositions in the future. Also be sure that you inquire as to whether she has made the bed freshly. I'll go to rest now, but shall come back later to see how you are doing. By the bye, Basil is at station in the dining room with India as serving girl. I should prefer to keep these, but you may make your own selection for the scullery. If the young folks are told off to other tasks already, I'll see that it be arranged. For a kitchen boy, I suggest the coachman's grandson, Coony. He is bright and able, though still very young.

She went up to her room in a tremble of excitement (dare it be termed anticipation?) and wondered how long it had been since she lay in a tremble of excitement. There had been such meager recompense in her life, so little warm investment by her to be rewarded. Her only treasure was that hoard of cruelties—bags put away in the vault, the meal-chest never empty of miseries.

Stay. There was the glory (by means of oysters) when she had rid herself of any subservience to, and even active execration of, Pettey J. No need to concern herself with that longer. Rinsed-and-cool-and-emancipated—well she remembered that night. But it was long since such emotion overwhelmed her.

There was another form of emotion in which she dealt privately some nights (twas necessary to do). Yet she looked back and reviewed each occasion with furtive shame, as a little girl might do.

Late that evening she sang the hours of this day, the piping melodies and undertone of percussion with which they were stuffed. Sang them over to herself. Disorder and savagery were therein contained. But so were there disorder and even tragedy as well as savagery, in the better symphonies.

Morning, shooting, driving— The few remarks exchanged

with Senator Ledge— Sitting and hearing the talk and seeing the slaves, seeing Beauty Beast, seeing a version of Joel.

Bidding and the buying—

This latter was nothing of her choice. She'd had no decision to make. Sidney became poised as an actress and this was a part she had learned for a play—her lines and her stage directions. Go perform them. Do. Speak the lines, walk the stage.

Buy the man.

There is some portion of ancient madrigal here.

This music has been thumbed by others and long ago. As, in picking up a book of child's tales, one finds the dried crumb of apple pressed between pages. Someone has been here before. A child read, and ate while he read. Conceivably in the case of the music, those who sang had the grease of Christmas goose still on their fingers. Still they held the music. Sang.

There existed Brown Bertha, and my parents had her with us for a while when I was very small; and Sister still with us, not yet married. And how Brown Bertha taught us to sing. She'd been nurse to children of a government official, she told, and went with them to England.

She had been freed.

>My father bought me an acre of land.
>Ivy; sing ivory.
>My father bought me an acre of land,
>And a wreath of green holly and ivory,
>And ivory.

So Tuesday the 29th was devised on a scale with clefs, with measures, quarter-notes, quarter-notes. Now follow both music and words, and chant again.

>Ivy! sing ivory—

One song was as they drove the two miles from the gate to a wandering turn before the Big House. In this course they lived with live oaks and scrub and cabbage palms; and they appreciated ditches regulated by Mr. Irons, who surely was an engineer in heart. Whenever no immediate necessity of field work was claiming, Mr. Irons might superintend parcels of black people to work on the roads. He had even extended these activities beyond the actual borders of Apoxsee, and had rebuilt and drained properly some of the contiguous tracks. This was an influence of value among the neighbors; and the next-door neighbor, Mr. Wilkey, even loaned dozens of his own people at various times to Mr. Irons to be so employed.

In any event the drive was gladness, and Sidney felt pride of possession go through her fiercely as her sensuous recognition went out to touch, to fondle.

Here. This wax myrtle is getting plump, a silvery joy.

Now these three, at the next turn: vast amiable oaks, all dead together, and looking as if they had died in the same hour; and oh their excellent burden of moss. And when I was very young I believed that moss stifled such trees, they were strangled in its bearded beauty. But now I am wise in matters of tillandsia: The stuff is not parasitic.

(Some humans are parasitic, aha, aha. Living off the sap of others. *Mirror, mirror on the wall*—)

Look, ah look, wild grape changing to yellow and pink along the limbs. Look, ah look, air-plants glowing red when we go toward the west and see color contained.

Behold!—we have here more wax myrtle, and palmetto scrub showing so very green beneath it, as if the scrub were a shredded salad and ready to eat.

Then— I declare— Impossible to tell whether the long moss is more beautiful with sun lying fat upon it, sun at our backs. Or when we go round another curve—now, *now!*—and see white sun coming through, penetrating the beards with intent.

Behold again. Arching shadow here as in a cathedral's transept, and crows streaming across by the dozen, talking discordant as they come.

So well may it be seen that I wish for him to love the place as I love it at last, being disassociated from Pettey J., no lingering tumor of hatred still in growth. Because the place is in itself a beauty, and beauty can taste of beauty.

And beauty can beget beauty?

63

That moment was before I knew the genesis of his name.

But he has kindliness and whatever is the masculine equivalent of daintiness. They show in eyes and voice, in the way he manages his extremities. Thus I desire him to love the place, as I'm sure Nineveh loves it, and many another of the blacks.

Come, come, Mrs. You've acquired a new servant and have toted him home. You've fetched no bridegroom.

I wish—

He must love Apoxsee. He *must.*

4

M RS. SHALLOP knew little of an owner's career, had not been long an owner. She knew of a slave's career. She had been a slave, sold to a man named Calvin Tensley when she was sixteen.

Bill of sale was arranged in the form of a matrimonial certificate. Price paid was in the form of cancellation of one mortgage and three notes which Mr. Tensley held against Mr. Veck, Sidney's father. The Vecks lived still in the same bustling Carolina seaport where their daughters had been born.

The first girl was nine years older than Sidney and had been parcelled off in much the same sort of sale in her own time. But Sister Emma found herself consigned to a husband who was a pleasant-tempered lout (except when in his cups. Then he drank himself into an insensibility so profound that it was easy enough for wife and children to stay out of his way).

Calvin Tensley's commercial pretense was that of being an artisan—a cabinet-builder and coffin-maker. By reputation he still possessed the two broad pennies which had lain upon the eyelids of his first corpse. Actually he was in the Trade, the Black Trade, and had been for years. He seldom had possessed enough money for a solitary venture, but was customarily a sub-partner or co-owner. He looked out at the world through the mask of respectability which was his woodworker's domain, with a separate entrance into a closed office at the rear, and pungent shavings rolled in mats, and fresh sawdust smelling like fresh bread. He'd suffered some reverses: they'd lost one cargo and the ship in a storm; had another cargo pirated in the Bight of Benin; suffered further vicissitudes at the hands of captains whose cupidity was as great as Tensley's own.

To him were attributed (principally because of his appearance) a Maine conscience and Maine attitude. He had been born in Portland and came to the South at an early age after being apprenticed to a ship's carpenter. Some few of the men along the waterfront still called him Chips.

He was a bleached reed of a man with a net of muscles over the hard skeleton of him. He was blotched with freckles and wore a meager growth of sandy-colored hair on his scalp, on cheeks and chin, on other portions: all the same color, with the same wiry curl to it. He looked as if he might secrete no moisture within, yet had enough and to spare of the sexual fluids which went spattering into his young wife's body, night after night. Sidney thought in considering them that they must be more acrid than the juice of other males.

There had been nothing in her religious or ethical training to provoke profound thought. But under harsh treatment her brain went stretching beyond its original elasticity as she wondered, sought, doubted, feared.

In immediate awareness during the forty teen-age months which preceded her marriage, she supposed that the world witnessed agonies which were not necessarily, with will and purpose, made into agonies by men and women. But they were wickedness inherent in Nature: thus if you explored too far you'd see that they could have been ruled and decreed by God. And thus in turn, exploring too deeply once more, you would become that reeking specter, the avowed atheist.

Sidney dared pursue no further. She tried to accept her own current tragedy with meekness, attempted to consign herself into God's hands for the future, preached to herself that those were capable and physicianlike hands. For a long time she witnessed no demonstration of His mercy.

Calvin Tensley had a small house into which he dragged

Sidney almost in the same hour in which she became entitled to his name. There were a black couple whom he owned—the one was supposed to keep stable and yard, the other to cook and do chamber work. But both were already cowed into incompetence. They feared Tensley, having heard stories about his affiliations in the Trade, and believing that he might ship them off to Brazil any time he took a notion (actually he had threatened to do this) .

Rats came in from wharfsides and infested every area. They scooted openly at night, and even in daylight hours when tempted by food. They squeaked under the floor, you could hear them. Neither Caleb nor Tessie might get rid of them. You'd hear them (rats, not the servants who slept in a cottage at the rear) chewing through partitions, bound to penetrate the kitchen storeroom; and champing even against tin which was nailed in pathetic hope of blocking their passage. The sound of their merciless little jaws grinding away, and ghastly bird-song squeaks they squeezed out, were not the worst horror of Sidney's nights. The worst horror was her husband.

When first he marched her to the bridal cottage she had been appalled at notion of sharing a room with a man, and had prayed to be permitted to keep a chamber behind the parlor downstairs for her own. This continued as a domestic habit, but her tenancy there brought no escape. There were two cubicles above stairs, and in the larger of these Calvin slept. The other was reserved as a storage space and often had rats fighting there. Sidney's room lay directly below her husband's. She would disrobe, slide into bed, lie tense and waiting. Eventually, all too often, there sounded a pounding on her ceiling overhead (a pounding on his floor in the upper room) . Calvin did it with a chair—a warped chair, cheap, of cottonwood or some such stuff. It stood beside his bed, and he would lift the chair and pound with that.

Frequently she pretended not to hear, pretended to be asleep, although she knew that in the mere refuge of silence she was being guilty of a falsehood, and she had been instructed that falsehoods were deplorable in the sight of Heaven. But should

69

she not nerve herself and respond to his poundings, then he'd steal downstairs and open the narrow door that closed off the stairwell.

Wife.

Yes, Mr. Tensley—

Come upstairs.

In earliest phases of matrimony she cried, Oh, not tonight! Please, husband, not tonight! I'm too tired. I have a sore tooth. I have—

She improvised many excuses, all of which he met with the assertion that it was her bounden duty to come to him. Infrequently he would approach her bed, jerk back the covers, tumble down, embrace her body with grunts and straining arms. But usually he made her ascend the stairs. He was a tall man, if skinny, and complained that her bed was too short, his feet hit the footboard. Then, in his upstairs couch, the same tough clinch would ensue—straining, pounding, the kneading of her tender shoulders beneath his carpenter's hands till her hide bore perpetual marks.

There was gasping against her face, condemnation and challenge which he uttered. One of his favorite snarls was, You won't bleat! I'll make you bleat! Then he would keep on striving, crushing his hard mouth with the dry hairs rimming it, crushing it on her tenderer lips, and the smell of him and his hair enfolded them both. Twas a parched mouth he had, a leather mouth.

In her lunar periods (however inconvenient and painful they were at that early age, and in the disorganized emotional and physically repulsive manner in which she was introduced to copulation) she found a degree of escape from her husband. She did everything possible to protract each period: took concoctions which she had heard might turn the trick; went out into the fields and dug herbs which were rumored to have such effect; she washed and boiled roots, drank the tea. A cleverer and less scrupulous girl might have forced her spouse to believe that she was perpetually, eternally incapacitated. But Sidney feared to speak a lie even though she might live one in silence.

Shyly at first, then with bolder intent, she urged him to seek the favors of a woman who lived on the edge of town, in a chaste brick house surrounded by pines. The woman's name was Louella Tripwood and her notoriety was wide. Yet her bony figure held a charm in the eyes of men. She could not get enough of men, twas said.

Everything concerning Louella Tripwood was told in whispers. The whispers were tense, charged with mystery which the whisperers might not understand. It mattered not to Louella that public opinion refused her the right to set foot in the very edifice where her father once presided as pastor. She had become heiress to several business properties when she inherited her mother's estate. So the local dressmaker attended her because she was afraid not to—even though she did not approve of Louella, scorned her, spoke of her as a Jezebel, was credited with having done so to Louella's face. She said as much when she went a-sewing in other people's houses. But she gave her skills to the task; and so Miss Tripwood walked abroad stylishly gowned—always trimly be-ribboned, be-bonneted, be-shawled.

To Sidney's suggestions, first inferred, then in desperation stated, Tensley turned a deaf ear. Lolly Tripwood doesn't tempt me a mite. You do. By gum, I'll show you. Show you right now!

Exhaustion would take him out of bed at last, and send him thudding away up the stair. Or, if she were in his room, exhaustion would cause him to roll from her body and begin snoring. Then she could creep to her sad retreat below, bruised and sore, hating the day of her birth, hating worse the hour of her marriage.

A weaker person, or one less starkly reared, might have drowned herself. Twould be so easy to do, wharves were handy, and the river beyond. Also there was a mill with gushing race on the slope above them, and sometimes the girl thought of letting herself be drawn under that wheel. But lip service to an ordained God and ordained Scriptures which her parents practiced, and with which they had suffused her, would not permit Sidney to make such disappearance.

When she counted the days until her next period she was not fearing pregnancy. She sought only the temporary redemption which those days might offer. Early it had been apparent either that she was barren or else Calvin could not beget. Instinctively Sidney sensed that the latter was true, but people did not talk about such lacks in the male. Her relatives muttered that Sidney must be at fault.

One August day when she had been almost six years married to Tensley, a ship came up the river and was tied for refitting. Rumors ran concerning this craft, and there was a smell: you could sense it even when you walked on the far side of the waterfront, could sense it when wind blew across the harbor. Ordinarily vessels employed in the Trade were cleaned out elsewhere before being brought into port, but in this case weather had interfered. The vessel was at hand, impregnated, oozing stench.

Two officials called on Calvin Tensley as part owner (his partners were conveniently out of town) and informed him that the vessel must be moved from its anchorage to a more distant spot. That was attended to, but it necessitated Mr. Tensley's presence aboard. In all he spent most of two days there. Hearsay had it that he attempted to resist forcibly a tour of inspection which some officers wished to make.

A week or two later he became paler than usual during a supper hour, and complained of various pains. That night he came down with raging sweats, raging chills which alternated. His wits were addled, he moaned in that chamber above.

Sidney tried ministering to him. Once he was so cold that the jerking of his body seemed to shake the room. In desperation his wife brought more quilts, more. Still he suffered, but profanely refused to consider the summoning of a doctor. Sidney gathered up the very rag rugs from the floor and put them about him on the bed, wound him in an immense cocoon. Ultimately sweat poured.

By morning he was enfeebled, and faded freckles stood out above the pallor of his face. Still he ruled in self-opinion as a man who held himself to be immune.

72

These perils can affect other people. I am too important. Hence armored.

Calvin nourished sublime hatreds at which he'd worked actively (in the manner of one who is aware that most people despise him, and therefore wishes to pay Humanity back in acid coin). Beyond all others he held loathing for a doctor named Dickerson, with whom once he had appeared to be on fairly good terms and who accepted him as a patient to be treated for minor ailments or injuries. But Dr. Dickerson had been present at an exhumation soon after Calvin Tensley was wedded to Sidney Veck. A certain family planned to remove to Virginia, and did not wish to be so far parted from the remains of a little daughter who had died. Dr. Dickerson happened to mention that the coffin fell apart during the process of disinterment. Calvin Tensley regarded this statement as blasphemy against his skill as an artisan. He said that Dickerson was a liar, and that no coffin of *his* ever fell apart after only eleven years in the ground. Had he lived in another stratum of society he would have challenged Dickerson, but his class indulged in fisticuffs only. This he sought to do, the first time he encountered his enemy in public. The doctor was an old military man who had been in brawls aplenty in his own time. Promptly he wrestled Tensley into a humiliating position, and was seen to kick his posterior before departing.

From that time forth Tensley frothed literally at the mouth at mere mention of the doctor's name. In this morning, conscious again, he demanded that Sidney fetch a Bible. He made her swear on this Bible that she would never call Dr. Dickerson to his bedside.

She managed to have the oath amended to, I swear on these Holy Scriptures that I shall not summon Dr. Dickerson so long as you forbid me to do so.

Soon Calvin fell unconscious once more. The room smelled like a privy-box, the bed was oozing. Calvin had lost control of his faculty for retention. Vile liquids spewed from him, and his wife and the slave Tessie could not cope. Sidney screamed at her rotting spouse, Do you still forbid me? In God's name, *do* you?

He could neither hear nor reply. She sent Caleb hustling. The old negro trailed Dr. Dickerson on his rounds until he found him assisting at a birth. Nor was the doctor hypocritical when it came to application of his Hippocratic pledge. *Whatsoever house I enter, there will I go for the benefit of the sick.* He did come in another hour or two, and stood beside Sidney in the horrid atmosphere of the low-ceiled bedroom. Said he'd never seen the like.

It must be an affliction of the direst nature! Worse than enteric fever or any other febrile disease I've witnessed. Observe: there are curds of pitch showing both in the process of regurgitation and in evacuation of the bowels. He is losing blood internally. Some peculiar form of worm must have gotten into his innards!

Dickerson sought to give the sufferer a febrifuge, but Calvin heaved loose whatever portions of the dose had descended from his throat. They tried to wash his lower bowel by means of tubing, but the water could not penetrate far. The doctor shook his head, prescribed damp cloths, left powders to be administered if the patient recovered the ability to assimilate them. Calvin Tensley died the second day following. The doctor said that his heart could not stand the strain, but doubted that a recovery would have been achieved were his heart ever so strong.

There existed no close friends, no one intimate with Sidney except her mother and sister. But a few women did come from the neighborhood or from the church to snivel and fret. A wraith named the Reverend Mr. Belton Lasher presided over the obsequies, since Calvin Tensley had offered up a few reluctant dollars in membership of his congregation. A well-waxed coffin was set up on chairs in the narrow parlor, and Sidney could look through the door and see. Yes. One of those chairs was the same which had stood beside his upstairs bed, the one with which he used to pound at night on the chamber floor. Somebody had brought it down.

Voices continued, handkerchiefs were wettened, the air was laden with scents of lavender and smelling salts, with underneath the creeping taint of death. *Mind, tis hot weather.* The widow sat with face mainly expressionless, although now and again the corners of her lips twisted as if she fought to conceal a smile. Some of the numbskull mourners thought that this might betoken hysteria, and they waited eagerly for the young widow to break and writhe in a conventional paroxysm of grief. Sidney was not smiling at the death of Calvin Tensley, especially in so agonizing a departure. Hers was not essentially a cruel heart. But she found mild glee in facing the fact that these neighbors and few relatives and fellow disciples were so undiscerning as to think that the only wretchedness which might ensue between her husband and herself was related to his passing. They must think that all partings were a sorrow, sweet or bitter. They must think that all marriages were made in Heaven, and perhaps even believed that a man was worthy merely because he was a teetotaler (Calvin had been one). They thought of a wedding ring as being a symbol of human peace and security, and not a weapon worse than a tomahawk. They believed that extravagant cruelties were practiced only by wild Indians, or done somewhere else beyond the seas, or perpetrated by wicked jailers and drunken sots. They could not recognize the depravity which had overwhelmed Sidney, did not even know that such devilment existed.

Acting through no parental advice, but fumbling purely by instinct, Sidney consulted one Lawyer Ashford, and put all her affairs—claims, responsibilities, and whatever inheritance she was to possess—into his hands. She had admired Ashford from a distance when he sat in church, grave and infirm, looking like the sketches of Henry Clay. He was a man who attracted trust merely because of his serenity.

He listened with sympathy to Sidney when she stated her situation and placed in his keeping the papers she had come across. Also there lived a quarrelsome man named Sohnfester, a lawyer as well, but one with whom the late Tensley had had dealings. He appeared at the small house adjacent to cabinet shop and office, only a day or two later, and presented some forms which he wished Sidney to inscribe. She suggested that he

75

take them to Mr. Ashford. He was reluctant to do so, and yelled coarsely at her stubbornness. Nevertheless he was compelled to visit Ashford in due course, and the old man rather delighted in playing at St. George, with Sohnfester as the dragon, and Sidney an unchronicled princess to be rescued. Mr. Ashford succumbed to a lung complaint a few months later. Sidney wept at his rites as she had not wept at her husband's.

Tensley owned only a portion of the wealth ascribed to him by local gossip; also much of this was dissipated through the connivance of Sohnfester and surviving partners. Still in due course Sidney was established as a widow woman modestly well off. She sold the negro couple and the rat-ridden house near the wharves, and went to live in a country cottage which Calvin had picked up through a foreclosure. Cash accruing from his estate was put out at interest in solid fashion, and there were two business properties in the town itself which brought in rents. But Sidney's father's dreams of exciting financial gambles and gambols to be exercised with the late Mr. Tensley's means were not to see fruition.

The home Sidney chose for herself was two miles out on a quiet track called the Blackwater Road. The yard ran down to a brook lined on the opposite bank with willows. There was an open patch of firm sward at the edge of Sidney's lawn bordering the stream, and there she might angle for catfish whenever the mood struck her.

She went back into all sorts of childish reversions at this time. Hawked off to the ugly New Englander when she was barely past her puberty, she'd had no chance for the little pranks and gaieties ornamental in most girlhoods. She found them now secretly with rare delight, telling no one, exhibiting herself to no one. There was a swing hanging from the limb of a gum tree behind the house, a child's swing strung there only eighteen months previously when a young family occupied the abode. Often Sidney sat on the board, twisting herself in strands, slowly untwisting as ropes pulled against their constriction; not whirling as she had been bound to do when small, but enjoying the thrill of imprisonment and then the turning release. She recognized symbolism accruing to an adult who had been in her desperate condition, yet found also the tiny rapture which a tiny person would find.

They had an open winter that year, spring showed itself in February, there were bees and a droning in thin fragrant sunlight. Sidney took note of tubs spaced over her front yard: these should hold petunias and nasturtiums. She found an old free negress who lived half a mile up the road and was eager to earn a few shillings. Aunt Sedalia came to her a day or two each week to wash and iron, chores Sidney detested. Nor did she enjoy most cooking. But preparation of pastries was her common pleasure—joy in the making, not ludicrous addiction to the consumption thereof. She liked to bake cookies, sweet cakes of every description, and give them to children who drifted past. Clusters of white children, ragged caravans of black children who idled there: she offered the cakes and watched the shine of their eyes, heard their chatter, saw them dance as they munched. I should like to be a child along with you, she thought. Should prefer to start my youth afresh. And then imagined that she was doing so.

At other times she considered herself as a mouse or a lonely bird nesting (with eggs? Ah, no) in some remote thicket. But a mouse or a partridge would be in danger of being victimized, done away with, and Sidney felt that she was in refuge for the first time in her life. She called the cottage Willowhurst to herself but could not make bold to divide this notion with either her parents or her sister Emma. She might have told Mr. Ashford, but now he was dead.

She burned many a candle in its chimney that spring, hoping that a moth might come. None ever did.

When she bathed her body she saw that the marks which her husband had put there were at last eradicated. Like an infant grown quickly ecstatic at thought of a treat, she hunched her naked shoulders in spasm, hugging and loving herself. If ever she should countenance another husband in her life, he would be at a polar extremity from Tensley. But she could not see this new husband yet in illusion nor did she wish to. The desert area of her young years was bedewed and in a manner irrigated for the first time. Absence of pain, absence of ugly encounter, absence of bitterness and jibing—these awarenesses became as waters flowing together in easy enrichment. Flowers began to bloom here and there, as did the miniature plants which she bargained from Aunt Sedalia and planted herself, on her knees, with trowel and watering-pot. She planted them in old tubs before the cottage, and painted the tubs green because that was a vernal tint.

What'll I essay this morning? Gingerbread? Thimble cookies?

Suppose that I were to make ginger biscuits? Shouldn't the children relish those, with butter and sugar spread?

She baked the biscuits, baked them thin so that their crust would crunch when younguns ate them, gave them to the little things. (Darkies always accepted shyly, as if convinced that such trophies were not for them no matter how many times she tried to prove it.) She saw the biscuits disappear, learned to laugh within herself in greedy joy of sharing. Brightly she said to the children, No, there are no more. You've eaten the whole lot.

Also there fell the fierce and haunting experience of her first venture into the world of books. Previously books had never lived for her, never occupied her being. There were some school books, the Testaments New and Old; and stories wherein infants stalked like characters in a miracle play and might have been labeled accordingly Pride, Treachery, Benevolence, Honor. There were newspapers and the few magazines which came her way; and some Walter Scott; and other novels trivial by any standard of judgment. These and little else.

Then, here in her fancied Willowhurst, she found two small volumes, chocolate-colored and bright with gilt and crimson on the spines. These were discovered on a high shelf unexplored during the earlier months of her abiding. They could not be seen by one standing on the floor, were he ever so tall; and Sidney found the books only when she went aloft on a ladder to replace the rusty cover of a stovepipe hole which annoyed her.

She whiffed dust from the volumes and found that they were

almost mint-fresh, and had been published in London—a new edition, by claim—in 1834. *The Sketch-Book of Geoffrey Crayon, Esq*. She was impressed by the dedication to Scott, felt herself momentarily if vaguely in the hands of friends. But only when she had reached Page 41, and saw the name of Rip Van Winkle, did she recognize that already she held at least a speaking acquaintance with the author.

During the rest of the day, on throughout evening hours and into the night, she kept reading. She fetched the largest lamp she owned to the bedside (thought briefly of a moth's appearance, but oh no, twas far too early in the season) and fell asleep only when confronted by "The Mutability of Literature." Her reading had been of the slow and savoring kind. Almost she found that she could look at herself from a critical perch, and find that this was good for her— It was— (Once she started up in blind shock at this knowledge.) *It was the way books should be read*. And well enough that many of the words had been so difficult or even incomprehensible, and she'd had to go back so many times to try to learn what actually was meant by *pragmatical* or *factious*. Next day she would buy a good dictionary.

There was a public stage which operated on the pike a quarter-mile to the north. She went swaying in to town in the old vehicle, next day. Mr. Caddy, the bookseller, dozed undisturbed behind his counter much of the time. (There were of course customers who came in for licorice drops or patent medicines such as Aromatic Schiedam Schnapps. Sidney had once bought a bottle of this brew, on advice of the minister's wife, but it made her throw up.) The bookseller was glad to be disturbed on this occasion. He sold to Mrs. Tensley not only the dictionary she coveted but also Shelley's *Essays, Letters from Abroad, Translations and Fragments;* Mungo Park's *Travels in the Interior Districts of Africa;* more Irving in the shape of a battered and scorched two-volume edition of *Bracebridge Hall* — Recollect, asked Mr. Caddy, when Mrs. Captain Sidwell's place burnt down? He sold her *The Iliad of Homer,* the 1820 volume of Keats, a set of Shakespeare; he sold her Thomas Jefferson and Lamb and Montaigne. Sidney sent Mr. Caddy's boy for a liveryman, and she drove to her cottage with books tumbling down upon her feet—forgetting utterly that she'd had no midday meal, and charming her spirit in this unexpected kinship with Elia. *For what satisfaction hath a man, that he shall "lie down with kings and emperors in death," who in his life-time never greatly coveted the society of such bed-fellows?— or, forsooth, that, "so shall the fairest face appear?"—why, to comfort me, must Alice W——n be a goblin?*

The driver said on his return, That widow-lady, she funny one. She just a-reading little book all the way, and she laugh so.

Indeed she laughed so, she wept so, she marveled. She meditated, How can it be explained? I feel the necessity of explaining to myself, yet is that essential? Perhaps. Then let us say that I am now awarded the gift of speech, whereas before I was mute; I am now given the courtesy to listen, whereas before I was deaf. My hands wait naked and sensitive for the world, whereas before they were mittened thickly and could touch nothing.

She read on into spring and summer, and looked at all around her, and felt that objects had size and color and dimension for the first time. She wounded her eyes, reading.

Sidney laughed aloud, alone in night, and only the mad or the wholly redeemed could do that.

Ho, what would Louella Tripwood think of me—solitary, without a man to my name, and no desire for one? Ho!

For nearly a year, whenever she thought of the mortifying Calvin, clearly a scent came to her nostrils: smell of those critical juices expelled from his body during his illness, the foulness of the bed. It'd come sharp and dark and her gorge would rise. She'd run to fling open a door and stand in the doorway and breathe deeply. Later the suggestion dulled, stench grew thinner, eventually twas non-existent.

Rarely her parents came to spend a night, and more rarely did Sidney engage a chaise and travel to the house whence, nearly seven years before, she had gone forth to be a slave. On one occasion her mother asked her why she had not had a stone cut for Calvin. Her mother said that people were talking about her failure to do so. Twas the proper thing, the dead must have stones. Sidney went to confer with the community's gravestone cutter, another free negro named Jamie Bliss. Jamie Bliss had a regular stock of symbols which he carved: lamb for a child, sprig of flowers for a woman; often a hand for a man, with one finger pointing upward to indicate the direction in which the departed spirit had flown. Jamie Bliss was taught the mason's trade while still in slavery, but had evolved his own gravestone vocation during later years of freedom. He'd accumulated a fund of memorial doggerel which he tried to sell to customers. (He was fond of telling how his late mistress had declared that she would make him free, once he'd learned to read and write. So he did, toiling through the fourth and part of the fifth decade of his life in order to win the promised boon.)

For Calvin Tensley's stone Jamie wished to indite the familiar, *Take heed, O stranger passing by.* Sidney believed that such adjuration was too unlike her departed husband, and said so. Jamie Bliss came up with a somewhat shorter verse stolen from one source or another, and perhaps mildly amended. *Weep not for my dear husband, his noble spirit fled. He sweetly sleeps with Jesus among the silent dead.*

Jesus? She wondered. Well, there was the belief that all would be forgiven—

She said tartly, Jamie Bliss, we shall bid for a few changes. It must be as follows. She wrote it down, or rather printed it upon paper so that no error should be made. *Weep not for my dead husband. His spirit now is fled. He sleeps at last with Jesus among the silent dead.*

That was the way it came out in the end, except that Jamie Bliss misspelt two words—*husbend* and *silunt*—because, as noted, his literacy was of late and difficult acquisition. Well, said Sidney, so is my own.

Once the stone was set in place she never stood beside the grave again.

She did permit herself the luxury of commiseration at odd times in considering what she knew of Calvin and the life he had lived before she was mixed with him. Certainly she had never been able to pity while enduring the tortures which he bestowed. But now (recognized familiarly as dead) she could see him in completion, and he was not merely a spotted monster. He'd spoken seldom of his earliest life, yet piece by piece she learned. She could recognize the starved stiff-necked orphan taken into the household of a too-frugal carpenter when he was five or so. She saw the boy whose feet were clammy with frost because of holes in his boots, and who had to start his rigorous morning chores long before dawn if he wished to attend the schoolhouse; and who was whipped severely on Monday if seen to doze during the long sermon of Sunday. Such scolding and privation might nurture eventual tolerance and affection in a being with a larger soul; but she realized that the souls of people like Calvin were dried like prunes on the very vine of their youth.

Sidney understood him better in those months when the worms were yet working in him, but her compassion was only the accrual of a native sweetness (also it was demanded of her by the dictates of Christianity). She felt no personal glow, no response to the defunct man, no wish to warm his memory. He'd come a-pillaging against her soul and body far too fiercely for that.

Solitude and books became a healing poultice, so did insignificant plays and charities in which she indulged. There were bouquets on her table and dresser, sun on new nasturtiums. Sidney grew to concede that she might be able to tolerate affection for a man—even feel a desire, a keenness for encounter with some certain male.

Then suddenly stars fell from their appointed places and thunder burst in her ears. She recognized that she was yearning for the person of her blood nephew, Joel Airhart.

~ 5 ~

S IDNEY RETURNED to the kitchen long before dusk and found Beauty Beast in peaceful occupation, trimming a flitch of bacon. This was for the house servants' supper, and already he had yams roasting for them.

Pray do not devote too much attention to my own supper. There's no opportunity in this short time for special preparation. We have chicken—

The cold chicken appears to be of good quality, madam.

Goosey can fry fowl very well. That will do for me, with perhaps some small vegetable accompanying.

She looked through the doorway beyond and observed that the cook was neatly conditioned in his room. Clothing lay spread on the crazy-quilted bed in order that creases of packing might disappear. On the dresser Sidney saw a small picture in a frame, and suffered curiosity.

Your room was properly prepared?

Yes, madam.

I could not but see that you have— Is that a daguerreotype?

No, madam, a miniature.

Hesitating only a moment, Beauty Beast wiped his hands on the towel fastened at his belt.

(I must have aprons stitched for him at once.)

He stepped into the bedroom, necessarily bending his head to avoid the low lintel.

(That also should be arranged: the doorway made higher. No need for it to be so low.)

He returned with the portrait in his hand, holding it gently by the frame so as not to mar the surface.

Who? she asked.

Judge Bracket, madam. It was a miniature done during the first year we went to France. He left it for me when he died.

She studied the painted face. She had never seen a representation of the judge before, but had heard much about him, especially from Fenton Ledge; and she was eager to understand why Bracket was held in such esteem. She divined an impetuous nature, obstreperous in youth but disciplined by experience and resenting it somewhat. A magnificent skull, with thick curls of a much younger man painted by time to resemble lead—bright lead, hot and fresh-moulded. Beetling brows, straight fierce Indian eyes: a man of passion who could have been patterned either into commander or murderer or both. His presence in a room would have been felt almost before he entered, either for good or ill, but it would have been felt, and remembered afterward.

I never saw the judge, Sidney said. He left this neighborhood before I was married to Mr. Shallop. But I've heard much.

The easy politeness. Yes, madam.

There had been some suggested sharing between them as she studied the miniature; yet she could not determine how it came about. Her voice hardened slightly in saying, Then the simplest of suppers for me, Beauty Beast. Tomorrow I shall be more demanding.

Her evening meal was served an hour later. Twas Goosey's hen, she knew. Nevertheless there seemed a subtle distinction. And here were some bits of green—wild cresses?—for garnish over the pale and dark scraps. Goosey had been forever removing the skin along with stiff dried batter, when serving her product cold; and here shone a rim of delectable yellow, bordering each bit, and Sidney loved skin. Here also a dish of braised celery. And a lettuce salad with the *soupçon* of garlic which whispered, Hillsides in Provence. Remember?

86

Goosey's left-over biscuits had been split, dampened with butter, toasted brown. Preserves, the coffee.

Why am I in such concern, reckoning one viand against another, twittering about this business? Food for the poor is vital, and so also the food of armies, the bread of entire populations. Food for the rich is a trivial caper. My lonely meals are trivial in the extreme. I inaugurate a public demonstration in pampering myself. And then—

What am I about? Attempting to excuse myself *to* myself? Going bail for the belief that a mere braising, in some Continental fashion, affects the opinion of Providence? When there is so much of agony and destitution in the world at large? I should ask our Reverend Mr. Fortunatus Stephens about this matter. Should inquire for his interpretation—not in Scriptural terms, but in those of morality and ethics.

Or, she thought in postcript, am I endeavoring to justify a three-thousand-dollar expenditure?

She awoke from a bad dream, dreamed again, dreamed better. She stood with a choir singing more madrigals, and the remembered Brown Bertha directing them while holding a wooden spoon as baton.

Sidney saw the color of morning, hid away from it, and then slept in peace. She rose at last to meet her day, feeling hardy and hungry.

She rang for Linnet. Soon, wearing robe and slippers, she skipped on her way to Lake Tannin. She shuddered at the first smash of cold water, but swam the length of the pond twice. She rubbed herself with coarse toweling, laughed while she rubbed. She ran to the Big House in haste and starvation.

She'd ordered omelet and coffee. They came. Fantastic coffee touched with the taste of chicory, and how long since she'd savored that? Hot milk with it, pure *café au lait* to build a gourmet's content. And oh the little rolls and oh the omelet itself. Mushrooms! Had he invented them, concocted them from nothingness in the kitchen? By what miracle did these obtain?

Sidney could not wait to discover. She summoned Linnet,

and presently Beauty Beast appeared as she sat with her tray on the upper gallery with her hair bound in a pale green scarf and with a green wrapper flowing.

Good morning, madam.

Good morning, Beauty Beast.

You sent for me, madam?

She said, *L'omelette aux champignons,* and he began to smile.

Madam, I was walking at dawn—

You walk in the dawn?

Indeed yes, madam. Tis a weakness of mine.

I love those hours myself, she said, and they both waited understandingly for a moment.

Then he explained, I recognized these as belonging to the genus *Agaricus* and knew them to be flavorable. So, although madam did not specify an omelet of mushrooms—

Delectable. Where did you find them?

Near that pretty pond.

Ah yes, it comes to me now. I'd seen something which I took to be toadstools—

Under those pines?

She nodded. I trust that there will be more.

Beauty Beast did not hold high hopes. The ground is very dry, it is of note that I was able to find even these. Will there be anything else, madam?

Well, for luncheon— If there were more of the mushrooms—

Only two left, madam. And I haven't yet explored the smoke-house. *Pardon, madame.* Is there such a thing as a *pigeonnier* on the premises?

No one keeps them in these parts, but there should be plenty of squabs above the pole stable. Do you have Coony fetch you some.

He's a bright child, madam. He helps willingly.

Beauty Beast seemed about to inquire if he might be dismissed. Hastily she saw him lift his head, and observed the muscles of his neck tightening under clean amber skin. Do I have my mistress's permission to introduce an unpleasant topic?

What could that be?

Tis merely— Madam, I dislike— And so newly in the household— I dislike to complain of another servant. But—

Who? she demanded sharply.

He told her that it was Adam the gardener. He'd gone out in his early walk and found the big black man at work among vegetable patches.

I asked him about herbs, madam. If there were any savories of that nature in growth. I could find almost nothing dried in the kitchen. A few little envelopes, but mostly too old to be of any use.

Sidney said, I'm well aware of that. Goosey never understood herbs.

So he had asked Adam about such things, and was rudely denied any right to do so. Adam said that he didn't want to be bothered by any yellow— Any—

Beauty Beast choked himself into silence. Sidney knew on the instant what she would say to Adam, but still there was the matter of herbs.

Whilst you were telling me this, I was thinking. Our neighbor, Mr. Bonaparte Wilkey, owns a cook who is reputed to be skilful in that line. Linnet, many of whose relatives belong to the Wilkeys, declared that the cook—her name is Dolly—has herbs growing in pots. So do you go to Mr. Wilkey's. I shall write a note which you are to deliver, requesting his kindness in this matter. Linnet will show you the path across Divide Field. I do not mean, she added hastily, that she need accompany you. But I'll bid her take you out and point the way. Beg for some slips to plant, if possible.

And any fresh dried herbs would be welcome indeed!—he finished warmly for her. Madam, will a pass be required?

They're not used commonly in these parts. You mean a walking paper?

Yes, madam.

The Wilkey place borders ours, hence you need not walk by the public road. There's no regular patrol hereabouts.

Immediately she regretted that she had said this to a new

89

slave. Citizens of the neighborhood varied in opinion as to the efficacy of a patrol system or the pure necessity for one. There were always those old grannies (Sidney typified them thus: men or women) who lived in terror of a slave insurrection. They envisioned jungle menace pervading all darknesses, heard mysterious padding feet outside their windows, shuddered at considering witch-doctors and spells.

There might be some justification for their fright. But why dwell in frenzy if indeed there *were* no reason?

And some folks felt, on the other hand, that the mere presence of patrollers would cause a distrust among the slave population which did not exist to begin with. Exploring black males (at least half the younger ones) roved at night on romantic adventures and misadventures. Everybody knew that. Sometimes there were ructions: these were a wild people, hence often predatory in their amours.

She bade Beauty Beast wait a bit, and had Linnet fetch a tray with writing materials. *Respected Neighbor,* she addressed herself to Mr. Bonaparte Wilkey, *May I request a courtesy, one of those many unfailingly awarded through your generosity? The bearer is my new cook, Beauty Beast, who desires to confer with your Dolly regarding the culture of herbs, of which she may be able to award him seedlings or some small quantity of the dried article. Pray do not allow her to beggar you or rob your cuisine of distinction! I trust that Mrs. Wilkey's health remains serene, and that Daughter Nell is recovered from her throat affection. With gratitude, and please believe me to be Your Admiring Friend.*

Take with you a basket, she told Beauty Beast and sent him off.

Now for Adam. She did not have the head gardener ordered to report until she'd gone below stairs. Though somehow there'd seemed nothing impolite in the situation when Beauty Beast came to the gallery while she was still breakfasting.

Surely I would have had Basil come to me under the same conditions. He often has.

Or—

Or Nineveh, she thought weakly. But Nineveh is a very old man: he has three sets of grandchildren, different generations.

At any rate Sidney was gowned and coifed and cleaning her pistols when Adam came. She'd let the weapons go overnight, and that was not treating them with respect. Twould be clean again, fire again that day. Clean again. She was not averse to having her people discover her absorbed in this occupation. Fantastic tales about her marksmanship went far and wide. These stories she sought to nurse, and even let them expand in future tellings. Dwelling as she did, lone white woman in a large colony of blacks— Many of them were capable of savagery, some had demonstrated it. Mr. Irons was the only white man on the place, but the blacks knew that he slept with a black and fathered her children. Such relationship was not uncommon among overseers, but frowned upon still. The minister who preceded the young Mr. Stephens as local presbyter had mentioned the matter of Irons to Sidney in critical fashion. In effect she told him to mind his own business.

Ant-ridden floors shook under Adam's bulk. He wore a face beaten out of metal. Sledge strokes had been used instead of moulding when his skull was shaped, when his jaw was jutted. Then he'd been polished to a fare-you-well, and his nostrils were caverns going into a monstrous hill. (An Englishwoman who once visited Apoxsee marvelled at his weight. Twenty-two stone!—she kept declaring. Twenty-two stone or more.)

Withal he talked gently, pleadingly to seeds and shrubs when he put them into the earth. Sidney had overheard him making such magic with his deep voice, and she wondered in the hearing.

There was this about it: liquor must be kept from Adam. When the rest of the people received their tot—say, in the Christmas season or at some other generous holiday—Adam was allowed none. He lurched off and sulked at this, and even then danger persisted. The previous Christmas it seemed that he arranged with some of the hands for them to divide their ration with him, or (nigger gossip had it) he bargained with some to take their entire portion. He rampaged around, vicious and irresponsible. He struck a boy named Binny so wickedly in the eye that later a doctor had to remove the eye itself. Adam was bound by the drivers, once he'd become groggy and less dangerous, and lugged to the calaboose in town. Sidney ordered that he be whipped, and he was whipped. But he had been beaten before and no permanent benefit seemed to accrue. His sullenness was traditional even when he'd touched no drink more exhilarating than spring water.

He stood glaring before her.

Adam, what's this I hear?

Dunno, mistess.

The new cook went to you to ask after herbs and vegetables—

Yellow-skin, said Adam. I hates yellow-skin.

Tis nothing to you what color skin he bears.

Adam said that he was too busy, he had no time to waste in fooling with the new cook.

What if I should tell you that I sent him to you? What if Mr. Irons sent him?

Still ain't got time. Got my cabbages—

What are you doing with the cabbages?

Ridging, mistess, ridging. I got too much to do, and them other boys ain't no good.

They're young, and you must teach them. Adam, I know that you are a capable gardener but also I'm sick of your being such a crosspatch. It is necessary for us to know what sort of herbs we have available, if any.

Don't grow no herbs, ain't got time. I got my pea beds to fix with the manure. Got my early Dutch turnips to sow.

That will be no excuse for your failure to observe my wishes. If you've misbehaved, I shall remember it when it comes time for Christmas gifts.

He mumbled incoherently but did appear a trifle more contrite.

Now then, she said briskly, I'll say nothing to Mr. Irons if you promise to behave properly when you're asked to help again. What shall be done is this: Beauty Beast'll come to you and we'll have a census of vegetables.

Who Beauty Beast?

He is the new cook, the one to whom you were unpleasant this morning, and we'll have no more of that. I shall give him a tablet and pencil and he will write down—

He write? asked Adam in wonderment.

Yes, indeed. He belonged to Judge Bracket and has many skills. Pay strict heed: you are to take him among the patches and let him see what is available and what isn't. What's still below-ground waiting to be dug, what's been put down—if anything's been put down yet—

Ain't scarcely nothing put down, he grumbled. Too early.

In any event he can see what you've got. If he desires to make a herb garden of his own, you are to help. And let him have whatever soil or—manure—

She got the distasteful word out. Or any sort of fertilizer the soil needs.

Then in a sharp tone, Do you understand?

Mumble, nod.

You may go.

The Wilkeys received Beauty Beast hospitably, Dolly was liberal. After he lugged his huge willow withe basket home to Apoxsee, he sent India to find Sidney Shallop.

Beauty Beast he say maybe mistess be good enough come see what he get from Yaupon.

Yaupon was the name of the Wilkey plantation.

When Sidney came he was all smiles. Just see—they'd given him several fresh heads of artichoke. And please to observe, madam. Endive! so beautifully blanched. He'd seen no endive since returning to the States. And this pot of chives! And— here—several choice heads of fine fresh celery. Then there were all the slips ready to put into pots, though perhaps this was not the best season in every case. But here were tarragon and thyme and chervil and cress. And—ah, he'd almost forgotten— Beneath this newspaper: a pot of sorrel. And then—but see—shallots. And in these papers: savory, marjoram, bay leaves, mustard seed, marigold flowers. And seeds of borage and dried fennel and dill, caraway seeds, coriander.

This envelope of rosemary.

Here a quantity of sage. Dolly insisted she had much more than she would ever use.

He said simply. People are open-handed hereabouts.

He said, It made me glad, madam, that I might bring you so many things. In several cases, now, we shall soon have our own.

Later Sidney heard him singing as he worked. She stopped to listen. A *chanson*. Her French was limited, but she recognized the ditty, and swiftly remembered some children clambering over an old Roman bridge, chanting as they climbed.

He sings like that, and he is a slave.

When I was a slave I did not sing.

There are slaves and slaves, masters and masters, mistresses and mistresses. Surely I am a better mistress than was Calvin Tensley a master.

Pettey J. was no master of mine. I was not sold, except in the sense of the word of being tricked. To Pettey J. Shallop I herded myself of my free will, and to my damnation.

Yea, refractory. Make a note of that.

But never did I fetch such fortune as Beauty Beast. Ha— I know the price paid for *me*. God knows I heard it often enough. *One mortgage: nine hundred dollars. First note: one hundred. Second note: eighty-seven-fifty. Third note: forty-six dollars.* A total of eleven hundred and thirty-three dollars and fifty cents, paid for the small bride yonder.

Yonder indeed. All those years yonder.

Beauty Beast declared that it made him glad to bring me so many things. Does it gladden him as well to recognize that I now own him? Oh, is he truly happy that—since he's black and must be owned—that he is owned by *me?*

Truly? Truly?

She pondered later on the simple delight certain people could generate merely in the fact of their existence, fact of their arrival.

Is it because so honestly they appreciate, and are gay in the possession of, small things? A few seeds, few slips, tiny pots of vegetable shoots?

Tis not merely that these were given him freely. He'd be quite as pleased had he found them in the shop of some *fruitier* on a village street (though not if he'd had to lay out too much of his mistress's money in dealing with the shopkeeper).

Apoxsee is more merry, and all over nothing except his arrival. The servant girls linger watching him as if tranced, and then they giggle together. He possesses what some of the elder writers used to term a livelihead. The thing which says, This hour yields joy, and I am wrapped in it, and you are here as well. So let us identify it and hold jollity in concert.

One may not do that to prove a meek subservience or manufactured politeness; the quality cannot be assumed. It springs vivid from the heart, and sometimes children feel such enchantment easily and exhibit it. But sometimes children are sad, as mostly I was sad when small, even unknowing of what was to follow. So some folks cannot find it until they are older; and sadly enough many children who laugh lightly when they are young have lost all their laughter by the time those first lines are pickling their faces. They've lost the ease and luxury.

Some never have it, early or late. But they are dullards, not to be considered.

Sidney was able to sit with Mr. Irons and have him trot out his fortnightly accounts, when frequently she fled from him. She'd been able to discuss, plan, deal. She felt alive as she had not felt alive by day for a long time. (In some nights, mind, she was charged with exuberance.)

She thought she pranced in fresh youth and came from a hearty strain. She ran lightly up the steps when going above. Said to Linnet, Very well, fetch the pistols. I'm going alone today. I had Nineveh put that sober Rodney horse into the chaise, and he's the only one I wish to drive. He will stand alone and decently when I fire. Nineveh has to baby the team, but Rodney cares naught how much gunpowder is burnt. He is usually munching green leaves!

She chirruped to the old horse on the way, and he obliged her by getting up a gait, going at his jovial lumbering trot for a

95

time, and then looking around as to say, I did that well enough. But don't ask me again immediate.

At the target range she shot to perfection.

One thing which she had not observed to Linnet was that there were other uses for Nineveh on this day. Sidney sent him into town on an errand. The man sought there could not come to Apoxsee on Thursday; but on Friday morning Mrs. Shallop was happy to discover Mr. G. Washington Heyward in the back parlor, engaged in the task to which he'd been summoned.

He was the father of that young man reading law in Senator Ledge's office, an elder but identical image. Perpetually strained of countenance (as if alarming news had just been told him) he owned similar silver-rimmed spectacles and a mop of tousled whitish hair which must have been taffy-colored as his son's when he was younger. Fortunately he did not possess the club-foot which compelled his son to limp, but there must be numerous other pains and worries besetting him. He was known throughout the region as Mr. G. Wash Heyward, or simply as Mr. G. Wash. This man was of an old family, but fortunes had dissolved, and through most of his years it was incumbent on Heyward to give voice lessons to young ladies or conduct singing schools among the less elite. He offered instruction in the art of the water color as well, and occasionally did oil portraits, starkly primitive, whenever he could secure commissions. The voice of Mr. G. Wash was girlishly fluttering, and you would not think that he had fathered six children, but he had.

He was the only man thereabouts who might tune a piano.

Most unfortunate, he said to Sidney Shallop, but I recall telling you some time ago that we might expect trouble here.

It's been neglected sadly, I must admit.

He'd opened the piano, and corrosion stood exposed, and one could see wreckage of moths on felt. What a shame! This instrument always held a superb tone! But our weather is brutal to the pianoforte, no matter what care is taken. And, if one doesn't *take care*—

96

Can it be cobbled together?

But see. The listing cloth is in poor condition, and in some areas should be replaced. And *but see* these resistance bars!

Can it be *played?*

Tis a question of whether the strings will yield to increased tension. After all, this is a Broadwood, and deserves better attention than I can possibly command. Yes, I can attend to the felt—yes, some of it. And then, I was driving my old Will horse, and he seemed to go lame in the final mile. It's a two-day task, Mrs. Shallop. Two days *at least.*

You can return tomorrow?

Well, if Will horse hasn't fallen *completely* lame, I can—

Might Apoxsee afford you hospitality for the night?

No, no! There are materials I'll need to fetch.

Do you by all means leave your Will horse here overnight, Mr. Heyward. Nineveh can carry you back to town this evening, and call for you tomorrow morning. My stable boys will make your horse comfortable, if the poor thing needs to be gentled for a day or so. Then— Perhaps the piano would be in condition for playing by tomorrow evening? Perhaps?

G. Wash rolled his eyes behind spotted spectacles, said that he would pray.

Repetitive complaint of the strings rang and tingled. Such sounds were excruciating to Sidney, but she nerved herself to bear them. During those two days she spent little time below stairs, but roved the plantation or clung to her chamber on the second story. There was of necessity a session with Mr. Irons which included also a brief meeting with the plantation drivers. These people, the white man and the two blacks (conferring with Sidney on the downstairs front gallery), seemed puzzled at anguished thrumming which issued from the back parlor, but did not make bold to comment.

Only in her bedroom might Sidney win relief from lingering tautness of the strings' outrage. Hour after hour, existence had become a whine which ended with snarl or groan. For once she delighted in the fact that the house was of such odd construction. Like most Big Houses in the area, it was individualistic, peculiar in design. Senator Ledge remarked that obviously the place was not delineated by Thomas Jefferson. No more was his own mansion!

The Apoxsee house was constructed principally of cypress. As usual there was no closet in any room, nor any cellar underneath. The thing rose on piling and mortared boulders with high space beneath for air to go through. Inequality of the ground made a seven-step stair necessary for the front gallery spanning the first floor, but at the rear one stepped upon level flags. There the air-ducts were dug out and lined with stone. Water rushed down and under the house along rock-built stream beds in heavy flood when rains came. Two galleries, upper and lower, at the front; one gallery only, upper, at the rear. There were four large rooms above and four below. Two enormous brick chimneys rose at each end of the house, to accommodate fireplaces in every room. Conventional dog-trots ran from front to rear of both stories, but on the second floor there was an additional hallway bisecting the structure from north to south as well. Thus each upstairs room was an island. In hottest weather the proprietors of Apoxsee had been envied by neighbors because of the excellent circulation: chamber doors which could be kept open in every case on three sides, and windows opened on the fourth. It was told that Pettey J.'s grandparents, who had built the place in their old age, kept a retinue of slaves hanging up damp linen sheets over the open doorways during stifling nights. These servants would doze on the gallery stairs (both stairways, north and south, were exposed to the weather; but at least sheltered by gallery roofs) while master and mistress slept in a contentment established by constant renewal of cool water on the sheets.

Every wall was doubled, its contained space stuffed firmly with cotton, which made for warmth in winter and also kept household clatter and yapping of black folk to a minimum. Now Sidney appreciated the ruling acoustic condition which made the old piano's torture less audible.

She took her midday meal in seclusion, both on Friday and Saturday. She was reluctant to hurt his feelings, but G. Wash

Heyward did not represent the ideal table companion. He gestured expansively, and his observations were confined to emphatic remarks of disapproval or rapture about the obvious. Cardinals trilled divinely, sin was wicked, pain hurt *terribly*, water was wet, wasn't it a *tragedy* that President Pierce's little boy had to die in that railway accident. He was a man trying eternally to please—sweating, striving, panting, pushing to please—and thus of course pleasing no one.

Instead Sidney kept company with Voltaire. She read this master as she had read Montaigne years before: constantly she felt the compulsion to stop reading, close her eyes, relish the truth for a moment, and then reread the portion aloud to herself. Sidney trusted that this might make her mind more retentive but the prodigy of conception and artifice slipped from her. She lost cadence of the words, eventually even the sense of them was gone, she felt impoverished. Why might we not retain that tart brilliance to which we were treated? *Such is the wretched stupidity of mankind that they revere those who have done evil brilliantly.* Condemnation like this was a joy soon taken away by the impact of new material confronting.

Do you, Linnet, tell Beauty Beast to come directly.

He was ordered up to discuss the menu for the next Saturday evening, a week hence. Sidney had dared to invite five guests— her first guests following the advent of Beauty Beast. Once discussion of *Petits Soufflés de Poisson* was ended, however, she observed a persistent smile affecting the corners of Beauty Beast's mouth. Some people might call it a smirk? Sidney thought of the previous Tuesday when she feared she'd observed a suggestion of treachery.

I could not help but mark, madam, that the piano was being tuned. But—

He hesitated for a moment. Then— Madam said that she played but rarely.

Which does not mean that I wish to continue living without music.

She watched the driveway and a posse of midget slaves running there. Please to deliver a message to Mr. Heyward, who is

99

at work on the piano. Say that I request him to send me word when he feels that he has done all he can do. Then we shall have it tried. You are to try it, she said.

Beauty Beast's eyes turned down, the lids came over them. Yes, madam.

Perhaps you should fetch some music?

Madam, I can play many things by ear.

As you choose.

Accordingly she went down when the message came, a little after four o'clock, and found Mr. Heyward clasping his hands. He exclaimed that he had performed a miracle—at least so *he* thought—and trusted that Mrs. Shallop would agree with him. Ah, the excellent tone was there.

A Broadwood can *never* be deprived of it! But at best, as I said before, my tuning will be unstable. Such instruments are *pestered* by humidity.

Pray leave the thing open, Mr. Heyward, in case some further adjustments be required.

Oh, I've already done my level best. He ran a scale.

Sidney sent for Beauty Beast. There was only the pause in which the cook might remove his voluminous apron, then he came to the parlor. On this day he was wearing for the first time one of the sprigged calico shirts—the household livery of miniature blue blossoms.

Joel again.

Mr. Heyward, this is our Apoxsee cook, who has musical aptitude. Do you, Beauty Beast, sit down to the instrument. And— And try, she finished lamely.

Beauty Beast drew out the bench. He sat down, touched the keys, there were a few ripples as he tested the pressure. He flew unencumbered into the Mendelssohn *Spring Song,* played a few bars, looked up beaming.

Splendid, madam.

So say we all! crowed Heyward. So say we all, boy! You possess a *beautiful* touch. Who taught you to play the pianoforte? Do play *more.*

If mistress wishes me to comply—

Sidney realized that she was clenching fists within the folds of skirting around her hips. Do, Beauty Beast. Do.

He gave more serious consideration to the keyboard. I'm without my music for this, sir and madam. It is written down somewhere but became misplaced, possibly in an album of other music.

Beauty Beast let his racing fingers go into their dance upon the keys. The complex lilting which he sought was beyond ordinary accomplishment (when last had he opportunity to touch a piano?) but obvious errors came from a clumsiness easily forgivable; even he forgave himself and grinned to do it. For the rest, peasants might have been weaving intricacies about a maypole, and surely pipes tooted in a village beyond, lambs were prankish. Sidney breathed rapidly in listening. An almost supernatural familiarity was inherent in this quaint rapture, but it seemed leaping out of a century gone by.

Mr. G. Wash Heyward waltzed about, whispering ecstatically, Lovely, lovely! Imagine—a slave, a cook!

Dark faces shone at two doorways. What befell here? Beauty Beast, taken into the back parlor and placed at the piano which no one played— Mistress tried painstakingly at times, but the instrument had been so out of tune, and— And she preferred the people's voices. Often she urged them to sing for her.

Yah, yah. Beauty Beast, and the white gentleman, and our mistess. Beauty Beast, he just a-*play*ing.

Yah!

If madam will excuse me, I must see to my stew.

She asked in weakness, Was that baroque?

Telemann. Actually a portion of his Sonata in F Minor. The *allegro*. I think that originally it was scored for the bassoon or oboe or flute. But I did make a piano transcription, solely for Judge Bracket's amusement. Excuse me, madam, sir. I must to the kitchen.

He went lithely. Heyward was gasping still, gaping after the yellow man. This is fantastic, Mrs. Shallop. Fan*tas*tic! His familiarity with— With *Telemann*. And transcribing a sonata for a pianoforte solo— I must confess, the word has been around town about the *exaggerated* price which you paid—

He giggled coyly. I can see now, dear Mrs. Shallop, that you knew *exactly* what you were about.

Mr. Heyward, if you'll be so good as to close the piano then I shall have Nineveh prepare to drive you to town.

Thank you, oh thank you, Mrs. Shallop, but I've talked to your stable boys. Will, who must have strained himself *somehow*, is not *too* lame. I must drive him home where he can be—

He kept gushing about the sonata transcription.

Sidney brought out a purse and paid Mr. G. Wash for his labors. She hastened to the upper gallery, tears coming.

Glory! To have, to own, to command, here in her own tight corner of the world, own tight corner of a day or hour, to command when she chose.

To have, to have—

Later she would inquire, Are you a devotee of Mendelssohn, Beauty Beast? And he would say diffidently that he was.

I've always been, she'd tell him, since first I began to listen to music. Tis odd: I arrived in Leipzig the morning after he died. Word had got about, and people were speaking of it, standing in groups, talking of the death of Mendelssohn.

Beauty Beast would say, after reflection, Twould have been better for both of us, madam, could we have arrived in Hamburg—not Leipzig—the day after Mendelssohn was *born*. Then we might have followed him throughout his life. And listened.

6

TELEMANN strains echoed with Sidney for many hours. That night she pondered keenly and memorably upon her nephew, Joel Airhart. The introduction of Beauty Beast into her life had revived certain recollections, let them go loose and soaring.

So he'd been wearing one of the new shirts which Trudge the seamstress sewed for him on Sidney Shallop's orders. No one else in the area kept house servants swathed in identical fabric. Sidney picked up the idea abroad, when first she saw livery, and she thought her notion quaint and favorable.

It would not have been possible to have held primitive passion for Nephew Joel when he was an infant but she did retain memories of him. Still, nothing in his appearance or miniature personality seemed important at the time, when he looked to be a chick and she was in maidenhood. Sidney felt for him and for his younger sister Mame (there had been two children in between, both lost to diphtheritis) only that natural tenderness which any aunt might experience.

The pattern of Beauty Beast's shirting affected her: an infinite array of tiny blue flowers and leaves, seeming to hold adjacent fruits, and rigged as on a vine. She'd sampled the material in the days when Pettey J. still lived, and a man came offering factory goods. Certain coarser cloths were always bought by the bale, as essential for clothing of the field hands. But lighter and more expensive goods was often gifted out in small quantities at Christmas time. *Joel again.* Sidney was struck by remembrance immediately (but this had not been true when other servants were so costumed: only when this tall metallic man wore the pattern).

The goods resembled a dress which Joel owned when a baby. Joel was addicted to the garment, believed that he could not prosper without it. Since the colors were pale and the background whitish, the gown suffered severely in its dressing of a boy baby. He was bound to hustle and jump, go under stoops, dig in sand and dust, work up mud puddings with bare toes. The little dress was doomed within an hour or so; but if his mother stripped it from him he'd want it back. Emma kept a wicker hamper in which soiled clothing was piled. Should one scrap of telltale hem be showing, Joel would demand that he be garbed in that same gown once more. He'd drag his wrecked adornment from the basket, wailing in fury.

Should be but one answer to this, said Emma. That's to make all his gowns alike. But there's no more of this goods to be had.

Years later, Pettey J. only snorted when Sidney broached the idea. He cared not what the servants put on themselves, or how they were accoutered, just so it was of no unseemly expense or nuisance to him. Gradually therefore, as clothing wore out, Sidney spread her uniform about the place. The pretty calico was as close to pattern of the recollected Joel-baby-gown as she could come. Females wore aprons or dresses of this material, the men wore shirts. Lady visitors at Apoxsee clucked approvingly over the idea, but there were very few lady visitors.

Tis my queer way, I suppose, of keeping It alive. Yet why should I wish to keep It alive? I'll never see Joel again.

Silly thing, you, It was never alive. It only *sought* to be alive.

Can a woman be overwhelmed by that *which lives not?* Yes, yes, for I was overwhelmed. Am still.

You whispered *Joel* when first you set eyes on Beauty Beast, and counseled yourself at the time, No one must know. Ah, you might have had wit enough to change the livery before he was adorned with it!

That would have been yielding to a fear.

Fear of what?

Fear of admitting to the ownership of an entity before which, before whom, I stand enthralled.

When first Sidney saw Beauty Beast come walking with buoyant zeal, flesh of her nature lay scorched again. Possibly there had never been applied the ointment, bandages, the tincture of Time?

Pulsation within the ears night and day.

Joel Airhart reappeared at the beginning of Sidney's second year in the Willowhurst house. He'd been living in Charleston since he was twelve, apprenticed to a German artisan. Now he was taller than most cornstalks. Mr. August Grempel had died, and Joel Airhart's prenticehood was at an end.

Sidney chided herself in reflection, When children are long out of sight they remain static, they stand as last-glimpsed, motionless on the pattern of the years. You fancy their ringlets are the same, if indeed they were ringlets; for you the tilt of their mouths is congealed; their thin voices persist in echoing memory, caught like ferny frost on the windowpane. Growth and the world have had their way with them, but of this you hold no evidence. Time may have done something to you, but Time has done nothing to the image of the child, because you have not witnessed its workings.

When Joel was small there had been that little-old-man quality about him which some young sprouts own. He preferred society of his elders, and if his elders happened to be in dotage so much the better. He liked to visit with the white-haired Bentleys in the next cottage. He'd go in politeness to call on superannuated Grandma Ives, or Captain Eames of the fragile voice and shaking purple hands: a relic who'd fought against Governor Tryon at Alamance Creek when he was a boy, and loved to tell about it, even though it was difficult for most people to understand what Captain Eames said. But Joel would sit solemnly on a battered chair made from a rum keg (his aunt had seen him sitting so) with thin bare legs a-dangling, while

Captain Eames mumbled on and chewed his gums between thoughts.

Joel's mother Emma said of her son, He's an orderly little trick, if queer.

When he'd grown a trifle taller, and his quavering friends dropped away, the boy was given to extensive solitudes. In a pastime like picking berries it was told that he always picked by himself, not with other children. It seemed that they respected him but demonstrated no great fondness. No one was close. Much of the time his black eyes seemed perceiving distances unshared, unexamined by his mates.

Now back he came in 1845, treading once-familiar planks and porches as if he were a giant stranger who moved there for the first time.

Sidney would look at him and then look away quickly, catching her breath. When she'd known her early erotic dreams long before (and suffered chagrin and guilt which all young people suffer because they know not that their supposed vice is a universal phenomenon) she'd envisioned a creature like this Joel, except of course unclad and rollicking through the woods. He was black-satin-haired but there was something like a sword in his glance. And despite the smoothness she perceived a hidden shaggy quality. Might he not blow a primitive flute for her, as she'd witnessed sylvans scooting and fifing away in illustrated legend? He'd extended over two feet in stature since last she set eyes on him. His father shook the weak worm-eaten verandah of their house when he stepped upon it, but Joel would pass as if he put down no weight. He spoke with the resonance of a man, yet was only in his seventeenth year.

I feel prideful about Joely, said Emma.

His father spoke with honest appreciation. He'll be a mainstay.

John Airhart was ailing nowadays. His innards were disturbed, he'd drunk too much too steadily, and had been supine and corpulent. The fact that his original capital was mainly squandered in a variety of ventures did not soothe him now in reflection. He was still pleasant-humored in spite of the dissipation which puffed his face. But often there rang a fretful note in John's voice. Tone and charm of the bell were gone when it became cracked. The last ambition is a hurtful thing to lose, thought Sidney. Even when often ambition has been impractical, even lurid—perhaps a scoundrel's notion.

She looked out through the window and saw Joel with his long powerful arms and broad palms coolly swatting into the stable those same lumbering oxen from which he had shrunk four years before.

His aunt thought aloud. He should go to the Academy.

Airhart said, Don't know precisely how we'd manage to get his fees together, Sister Sidney.

I could manage that, if indeed you'd permit.

Don't know precisely how I'd pay you back, and John got up and left the room.

Sidney spent that night with the Airharts, sharing the room of her niece Mamie. Recognition that the lean human package, that bundle of excellence and incitements which was named Joel, lay a few yards distant, though separated by a wall— This did not engender somnolence. Long she lay awake and staring. There began growing within her a potency heartened and intensified by the mere knowledge that this youth existed.

Indeed he must go to the Academy.

I possess the means, plenty and to spare.

And college beyond that— Even a Northern university?

So she drifted in planning, with innocent little Mame slumbering beside her. Eventually came a prowling sort of dream in which she herself followed Joel—no matter where he went, to what university.

Through the window next morning she'd seen him again. In the yard lay an old bench with shingled roof put up overhead so that one might work at that bench in shade, or be preserved from moderate rains, when weather was warm. A vise at the end of the bench had gone out of repair through neglect, and Joel was making it right.

Sidney ran out and perched gaily on the bench as a girl might do, and asked, Joel, do you mind if I talk with you a while?

109

Sheen of his hide, unstudied elegance in the use of his arms. Faunish ways and tricks aforementioned, the mystery attending the varmint— Good varmint (not hateful one to be destroyed) which went knowingly along the underbrush at night, four-footed and cocky and chuckling about it.

She wanted to stroke him, her fingers quivered to get at his hair, she willed them into motionless submission. Was there not, somewhere extant, a black deer or black antelope? Sidney knew she'd heard of such animals, and sought to envision one. Twould be his symbol and companion.

Joel, your father and I— We were discussing how it should be with you.

Be with me?

I mean for the immediate turn of events.

Well, Aunt Sid, it's just this: Mr. Grempel had a stroke and died, and his folks decided to sell out his gunsmithing business.

You should have let me know. I might have bought the business for you.

He laughed. Aunt Sid, I reckon I'm too young as yet to be a sole proprietor. But truly I'm fascinated by firearms. And trying to learn a little something about them.

Tell me.

He spoke of many facts he'd acquired, or mysteries which he would like to penetrate. He mentioned weapons she'd never heard of, made allusions foreign to her ears. The bulk of his words went fragmentary and irretrievable above and beyond her hearing.

She could not look at him and think, How might I have missed the essential quality of yourself, Joel, when you were young? Yet miss it I did, never saw it.

Perhaps twas not there?

No, no, that couldn't be true. It *must* have been there, but I did not see.

Now I see, now feel.

Feel? Gad, *yes.*

Like water that's so icy that you cry out when you lave in it. Yet you are drawn to repeat, to keep splashing.

Like biting a strange berry, instantly sweet, instantly tart, or sweet and tart by turns, you know not how to describe it. You are impelled to eat another quickly.

He said that he was stimulated by the mere thought of guns and their handling and manufacture, and the thriving belief that sometime he might be able to better the weapons *themselves*. Be able to invent improvements.

Polish came back into his eyes as he talked, and it was not like blued or browned steel, it was silver.

Jewelry. Private gems in his eyes.

Joel said, Eli Whitney didn't only invent the cotton gin. He grew disgusted at difficulties he faced in trying to collect monies due him for the gin, and he went into manufacturing guns. Yes, ma'am, right off he got a contract from the National government for ten thousand muskets.

Joel said, What they call the old Queen's Arm was really the first Brown Bess. British used the Brown Bess for at least a hundred years. Mr. Grempel had a specimen with a forty-six inch barrel. This one had a wooden ramrod, but the French used to make ramrods out of whalebone too.

Sidney said, her voice unnaturally husky, You've learned so much.

Just little bits I picked up.

Tell me more about— Gunsmithing.

Well. You've got to have rotation to get accuracy. That's the reason a rifle outshoots a smooth-bore and always will.

I see.

Joel said a hundred things but all to her alone. His family used to babble about how the cat had got Joely's tongue, but the cat hadn't, not when Aunt Sidney was about. Joel said a thousand things.

He said, Mr. Grempel got a beautiful color on barrels. He'd rust them with salt water, then rub off the rust with a scratch brush. Then you got to make a just-right solution of bluestone and hot water, and wash them in that. Looked kind of purple and softly shiny, like ripe plums.

Mr. Grempel thought the coming thing in pistols would be the revolving pistol idea. Like that man Colt invented. Could be for carbines too, and maybe larger caliber weapons.

Indians just ruin rifles and muskets! Man came by the shop who'd lived among the Indians, and he said he'd seen them put a trade rifle in a pond when it got fouled, and leave it there two-three days to soak.

Good way to start a curly maple stock is to char it slightly in between the curls, and then you rub off the soft wood with real fine clean sand. That lets the curls of maple sort of stand out, see? Just beautiful. Then you take some linseed oil, with alkanet root— You take some soot, too, and—

They didn't change the 1831 Springfield much from the 1821 Springfield except they put a fence on the pan. And they left off the brown finish—I don't know why. Neither did Mr. Grempel.

I got an old blunderbuss of my own. Show it to you when my box of things gets freighted home. It's got an anchor sign on it, and that means it was manufactured for the Navy long ago.

Mr. Grempel believed that the best flints are English ones. They call them Brandons. They're kind of black.

One notion I've got, Aunt Sid. Time's bound to come when ball and charge and cap will be *self-contained*. I mean, in a single catteridge. Lot of people tried, and still trying, but none of them's done too well yet. Just a question of figuring out the right metal, or maybe alloys and so forth, for the catteridge. I lie awake, of nights, thinking on it.

There was that about the Veck blood which would not tolerate idleness among those persons within whose bodies it was veined. They must be up and doing, successful or no.

Sidney considered her father Philip Sidney Veck and his schemes. They ranged from patent well-drilling machineries to erecting a mock of the ruins of Pompeii, for edification of young and old and the enrichment of his own wallet. In her mind she likened him to a mariner who might flounder curiously, boring holes in the hull of his own ship to see what would happen.

Like his father-in-law, John Airhart had delved into numerous businesses, and wasted substance in highly speculative activities. But a few of these were experiments which might have come to successful fruition in the hands of one less indolent, and less disposed to fritter time and money, to pamper a handsome body, let a brain grow fat. John was not so much harebrained as lazy. He'd yielded to a natural weakness for losing interest in an activity almost as soon as it was commenced. The high enthusiasm of initiate and initiator was his, but did not flicker long enough to sustain him.

His son Joel demonstrated the zest of the Vecks. In that week he went scouring through town and surrounding villages, but failed to find employment as a gunsmith. He would have been willing to renew an apprenticeship in order to do so, though he'd begun to consider himself something of a journeyman. His father, who was a Freemason, smiled and said, I'd no longer typify you as an Entered Apprentice. By now you must have become a Fellowcraft.

Joel was aware sharply that the household purse lay scrawny; there was very little real property unencumbered. For that reason (as well as compelled by the energetic stew which worked within him) he had to be employed, and immediately.

The best that he could manage was to engage himself as clerk to Chat Hendry, a ship chandler. Promptly he made himself invaluable to the owner. Why not?—he was always at his tasks. Part of his wage was in found—an enviable condition of affairs, since the chandler's wife set an excellent table, and Joel's room had two windows and overlooked the wharves (not a rat in it or behind the wainscoting) .

Aunt Sid, what brings you here?

Just thought I'd drop past, Joel. I had a little trading to do in town, so I came in on the stage, and— It's only a step down here from Rice Street to your warehouse.

Mind that bale, Aunt Sid—got tar on it. Please to come over here: I'll clear a space for you to set down.

Can't stay but a minute.

Well, set down anyway. Oh, here's Mr. Hendry. Mr. Hendry,

may I make you acquainted with my Aunt Sidney, the Widow Tensley?

Greetings, ma'am. Glad to see you looking so well.

Good morning, Mr. Hendry. Yes, Joel, I'm already acquainted with your employer. He occasionally—did business—with my late husband.

Mrs. Tensley, I declare you look younger by the minute! No, I ain't just a-flattering. You do. By golly, you do! Joel, I got to hustle down to the dock; but you go ahead and check the rest of this order on the manifest, piece by piece, just the way you were a-doing. And you take good care of this pretty little aunt of yourn, you hear?

Haven't seen you in nigh onto a mouth, she told Joel when Mr. Hendry was gone.

I knew it had been quite a while.

Thought maybe you'd come out to my little cottage on a Sunday, and take some dinner or something. I looked about for you at Divine worship, but you never seemed to be there—

Oh, I went, first Sunday I was to home, before I took this job of work. But I declare, Aunt Sid— Don't like to be critical of the clergy, but I can't abide that Reverend Mr. Belton Lasher. He's just too whiny and angelic.

Well, she said haltingly, I do not seek the congregation as—as often as I should.

(In honesty she might have admitted that she had not been inside the church for months previous to Joel's homecoming, and went now only in the hope of encountering him.)

I'd thought too, Joel, that you might come by sometimes of an evening. We could talk and you could tell me more about— Oh, it was so interesting.

What was interesting?

All those historical facts relating to the firearms.

Joel said ruefully, I'd a lot ruther be reaming a barrel right now, or maybe building a new lock, rather than what I *am* doing. But I don't want to be a beggar, and I can't be a chooser, cause there's no other choice open to me.

Joel, I was speaking with your mother and father. They say

114

that in so short a time Mr. Chat Hendry has grown to depend upon you.

You talk about evenings, Aunt Sid: that's the reason I haven't had any evenings. Too much work to be done here. Maybe a whole shipment comes in late in the day, or maybe an outgoing shipment has to be packed up before dawn. No time for skylarking.

She spoke primly. I said nothing about skylarking.

He appeared meek in the belief that he had offended her. Sidney took her departure, and Joel blurted out something about seeing her soon.

Hence she was not overwhelmed with surprise, only fluttered and delighted, when early the next Sunday morning Joel appeared at Willowhurst. He'd walked the Blackwater Road, twas no distance to one with his stride. A bright whistling announcement brought her to the door to watch him wipe his shoes in thick grass at the gate.

Just let me get this dust off, Aunt Sid, and I'll volunteer to escort you to church.

To think of those feeble implorings and mannered reading of the Scriptural passages, and dismal chants and the smells—Twould be like holding another funeral service for Calvin Tensley.

No.

Let us be heathens, she said softly when he was come up to the porch. Let us not attend worship. Let us run away.

Once more those miraculous splinters of metal, little knifeflashes were shafting in his eyes. Run away? Where?

Right here at Willowhurst.

Where on earth is Willowhurst, Aunt Sid?

This is Willowhurst. I—I've never told anyone else. Joel, have you taken breakfast?

I et a bite. Haven't you had yours? I'll set by and watch you, and maybe drink some— Coffee? he asked on an inquiring note.

Certainly there's coffee. But mayn't I fry you a slice of ham?

Now that you mention it—

And I baked oatmeal cookies yesterday.

He quoted with gaiety. The way to a man's heart— Immediately there swelled warmth within her, but twas coziness and comfort, not a warmth which addled and upset. Rather a feeling of pleasantry, a pleasance.

She asked after his parents and Mamie. He said briefly, I saw them a-Thursday. And then they talked no more about the family.

Ah, Sidney had a surprise, something to offer Joel, something she'd found unexpectedly. No, no, she'd not produce it *now*. It must wait till later, it was a *surprise*. They giggled with the breakfast. Sidney had not eaten earlier, she was hungry, she joined willingly in the fervent appetite of the young.

Rarefied blue day. Autumn smoked its nostalgic bonfires among landward distances, imaginary files of Indians went treading in moccasins through woodland below the horizon. A dog belonging to old Sedalia (the free negress who dwelt up the road) came a-begging as he did often. He smelled ham and kept scratching at the back door. He was named Maury, with hang-dog eyes and ears. Joel offered a scrap of bone which Sidney cut loose from the ham, and remarked on the hound's lugubrious appearance. Sidney cried that perpetually Maury looked as if he'd just been found guilty of forgery.

Joel had a trick of throwing back his head and flinging his mouth wide open when he laughed. Sidney loved to see him do that.

Ah, mightn't she leave cups and plates and cutlery for the darkey woman to wash next day? Joel shook his head. Said that he couldn't abide a cluttered kitchen. Hoped that, if ever he married, his wife wouldn't keep one.

(Alarm, hidden alarm. Joel *married*. Married to whom? To— to what young woman? Married and— Gone from her? Forever gone?)

He rolled up his shirt sleeves—he'd taken off his jacket long before—and began to ladle hot water from the reservoir of the little iron cook-stove. Sidney would have none of this; she sighed, got out soap and dishcloths; and Joel ended by drying dishes and polishing them brightly with Sidney's best tea-towels. He detected two table knives with black wooden handles in which the blades were jiggling. Joel said that soon they'd be coming loose altogether, though Sidney shrugged—they'd been that way for months. Joel set to work to repair them. So he did repair, working with improvised tools on the porch bench. The knives were solid when he'd finished. His Aunt Sidney couldn't imagine what he'd done to them, but gave thanks and praise.

She put away the dishpan and hung towels and wet cloths on a line to dry. She stood in dreaming open air with the tall youth beside her. She saw his hand go up to brush back a lock of oiled hair; she wished that he would not use so much oil, yet that was the thing: most young men did employ it, so nowadays one had to put out antimacassar doilies on the chairs.

He was the first young male who'd ever stood within the precincts of Willowhurst since she lived in the place.

Joel, she thought, I must not put my hands in your hair.

Joel, she thought, I shall die if I am not permitted to put my hands in your hair.

Whose hair, Wanton Widow? Your *nephew's?*

Aye.

Custom and relationship will not permit.

Condemn custom and relationship!

Infidel, take care you commit not the Unforgivable Sin of damning the Scriptures themselves.

Why, why, why— I would not pretend to damn the Scriptures. Would much prefer to cling to them, quote them. Hear me now.

Stolen waters are sweet, and bread eaten in secret is pleasant.

Sidney and Joel hovered above the rear steps, looking down at creek and willows, contemplating hazy secrets of the day, thinking again of Indians. After a time they were on the steps side by side, giggling at their own fables. Or foibles, said Sidney. She told Joel that perhaps hostile Tuscaroras crept up behind the woodpile; he'd best hasten for a gun.

Joel closed his eyes tightly as he laughed. He asked, Maybe Yemassees? Seems like I've heard tell of them.

I'm not sure that I know which ones were around here in the old days. Cherokees? Do you know?

No, Aunt Sid, not for certain.

Everyone should read more history. American history. I know almost naught of it.

I just got those little portions that I picked up in learning about guns.

If you went to the Academy, you'd have an opportunity to read more.

First place, don't want to go to the Academy.

You just say that.

Second place, can't afford it.

I told your father that I'd be—

You did indeed, Aunt Sid. *He* told *me*.

This unexpected remark of Joel's put her promptly in a state. Sidney drew back, switched away, shook out her skirts, frowned off from him, did all the female tricks. Behind her his low steady voice went on explaining.

Father told me of your suggestion, and I'm glad he did. For I'll have none of it, any more than he wants to. I guess Father is poorly because— Well, he used to have a lot more of the world's goods, but somehow he's lost out.

Immediately Sidney forgave him for his rejection. Joel, your father feels guilty, poor soul, because of failures.

Reckon that's true. But, you see— Me, myself— I'd feel guilty if I took *favors*.

Any aunt should be privileged to help her nephew if she wishes to do so.

In another moment he muttered, Sometimes you just don't seem like an aunt.

There came skip and pounding within her breast. Twas difficult to breathe, difficult to sit; twould have been still more difficult to rise; twas difficult even *living*.

Something to invoke, some discipline, some management of self?

Maybe they should read—

Oho, that was it. They'd have a Scripture reading. Be close

118

(touching?) together and read a Chapter or two, and be informed again that lust was abomination. They should approve a recipe for wickedness and let it frighten them into submission.

For without the law sin was dead.

In tenderness she asked (it was a whisper because she was a woman, no woman could have done other than whisper, she asked the question which any woman would have asked, oh any woman, every woman, any time, every time) —

You say I don't seem like an aunt. What *do* I seem like, to you?

Ah— Could be that— I don't know. Not an aunt. Some other lady. I mean— Girl.

He added cheerily, You crack little jokes and such. That's not a very auntlike way of doing, is it? I never heard tell of any other aunts a-jollying so. You know. About that hound, and how he looked like a forger. Then— The Indians—

We're nigh to the same generation, Joel. Though I must seem sadly old to you. Still we're only seven years apart.

Let's get back to this Academy business, Aunt Sid.

He had no wish to be a lawyer or a doctor, no ambition to go into the military. Assuredly he didn't embody the makings of a clergyman—Heaven forbid that. He eyed no eventual goal such as being the Honorable Mr. Joel Airhart bound for the Legislature, or some such dignitary. No, *sir*. No, *ma'am*. No, Aunt Sid. When very young he'd thought that he might wish to tussle in irregular encounters as Captain Eames had done. At nine or ten his desire was for piracy, and later he wished to be an explorer like Davy Crockett. And through all his years since hearing of the Alamo, Joel had wished to invent some sort of gun which would slay quantities of Mexicans, one after the other.

At home there was a family shotgun, and his father had a pepperbox revolver; but John Airhart said Joel must not put his hand upon these weapons until he'd grown into elder responsibility. Joel was impelled therefore to invention. Whilst other boys were capering at their high jinks in holidays on Wednesday and Saturday afternoons, Joel was off to a round of the artisans' shops, places where there were lathes and forges, hammering going on. In most locations he found an over-supply of midget darkies to run errands.

Or rather you might say, said Joel, winking at Sidney, to *walk* errands. And that tardily.

But at last he'd rather tickled the fancy of the Henderson brothers, friends of his father. They fitted steam pipes, repaired ships' boilers, rebuilt stationary engines. Joel offered to run errands at one cent per errand, and he earned fourteen cents during his first two afternoons of employment, even more in the next week. Assembling materials through purchase and donation, Joel built his first weapon. He'd thought of a multiple-barreled affair, but wisely concluded that he'd stick to a single-barreled muzzle-loader in this beginning. He shaped butt and stock out of walnut which had been cast aside as spoilt (in Calvin Tensley's shop, of all places). His smooth-bore barrel was a bit of lead pipe given him by Mr. Saul Henderson. Joel smashed one end of the pipe shut to form a breech. He then drilled out a vent hole to accept a hollow nipple for mounting percussion caps. Naturally the plunger, or hammer and trigger, gave him the most trouble of all. He ruined many horseshoe nails a-trying.

Joel's pistol, when finished, did not blow up in his face. It worked too well for peace of mind. He killed, the very first time he fired it. He'd had no wish to do so, meant damage to no living creature unless to future Mexicans. He put in powder charge and essential wadding, but what should he use for a bullet or shot? His last cents had gone for powder and a few fearfully expensive percussion caps. He returned to the Henderson's, asked permission to sweep the floor, and gathered up in this way some iron filings and pellets of shaved metal along with them. This might serve for a charge, he thought, and rammed it home. Then he hastened all palpitating to affix the cap and shoot his pistol.

There was a sea-gull sitting on a wharfside post.

God knows why I did it, said Joel in confession.

Cap was exploded, charge was fired, the spray of death went

forth. Gull sailed up and out with a squawk, tumbled to the pier planks, flapped wildly for a moment, and then lay still. A trickle of blood oozed out of its open beak, and one dead eye was cocked dolefully at Joel.

He swore then and there that he would never slay wantonly again. Perhaps he would never even hunt for birds or other game. He might not even *fish* again. He pushed the dead gull off the dock and watched it drift and saw living gulls circle above the thing as it sank or was tossed up again, heard harsh screeching.

Joel said now, See, Aunt Sid. It's not that I crave guns and like to be with them and have them and work with them because they *kill*. Not that. It's because they *shoot*.

He told her that he went home, gravely cleaned his weapon, hid it, was long saddened.

John Airhart said when Joel was twelve and at a time when he himself paraded in a mood of ambition and expansion, My son, I must sail down to Charleston this week on business. Should you like to bear me company, and see the big city? Scarcely did Joel sleep for the three intervening nights. He decided that there might be hard characters in Charleston (it seemed that he'd heard there were) and twould be wise to take along his home-made pistol for protection. He was permitted a carpet-bag of his own for the voyage, and spent hours at packing. The pistol, its existence still unknown to his father, was hidden amid a nest of clean stockings, wrapped in an extra nightshirt.

He said, Aunt Sidney, it's droll. When I was packing those clothes, I recollect now that I thought of a dress I wore when just a little fellow. It had kind of flowers on it. Twas my favorite.

I know, she said, I know.

Charleston brought the great change in his life. Silently he followed his father up a stairway and cooled his heels for an hour in the outer office of an attorney named Grempel with whom John Airhart needs must consult. When they came out, the youthful Mr. Grempel (anxious to demonstrate that he was a full-fledged adult who knew how to deal with youths) clicked his tongue at Joel and snapped his finger on Joel's skull. He said, Mr. Airhart, sir, you should take this fine young sprout into my father's shop—it's but two doors below the corner. He'd relish seeing the firearms in Father's collection. Many of them were fetched from the Old Country long ago.

Thus ensued the first encounter with a round-shouldered *Thüringer* whose fingers were broken, scarred, knotted, yet still strong as pincers. This gnome displayed a Swedish matchlock, a Spanish wheel lock, a Dutch snaphance. They were in perfect condition. *Ja,* they could be fired today! He showed pistols, and Joel confessed bashfully that he had constructed one.

What's this, young man? his father demanded. I never heard the beat.

You make *ein pistole?* cried old Mr. Grempel.

Joel volunteered to run and fetch it, twas only a stone's throw to the inn where they'd settled. He was allowed to do this, and scooted with excitement through crowded streets, dodging carts which the negroes were pushing, and hearing cries and conversation in dialects unfamiliar to his ears. He seized his pistol, fetched it back to Mr. Grempel. The gunsmith was amused vastly by Joel's workmanship but lauded him in principle. John Airhart, anticipating favorable news from Mr. Grempel, Jr., spent that evening and most of the next day and the following evening in the taproom of their hotel. News came at last from the lawyer, expressly unfavorable and hope-shattering. The original investor in Airhart's current project had withdrawn his entire support through a very small loophole. Result was that John spent the following two or three days inert in his own room.

In contrast to this sad spectacle, an extremely contented Joel occupied himself during the interim at Mr. August Grempel's shop. After being permitted to sit observing but silently undisturbing for some hours, he was given little jobs to do: he turned the grindstone, worked a treadle, fetched water, pounded chemicals in a mortar, and actually delivered a valuable carbine aboard a vessel which would sail soon to South American wildernesses.

Let him stay with me, August Grempel begged when John Airhart was sober again. There is much that I can teach.

Don't know how I'd explain to his mother. She'd want him to have more schooling.

Next day John Airhart carried Joel on a homeward voyage to the boy's regret. Joel agreed to finish out his school term; still he bade his parents examine facts. He was an average reader, a third-best speller, but he led his class in ciphering. He was the only lad in Master Graniter's school who held any algebraic skill. And he'd read both books on geometry which the schoolmaster owned, nor had any other lad done this.

Joel was a month away from his thirteenth birthday when he sailed once more for Charleston, sailing alone, leaving a weeping mother and little sister and a grim-faced father on the shore. He was to be gone a year; actually he stayed nearly four.

No Academy for me, Aunt Sid, were I ever so fat of purse.

With temerity. You might change your mind.

Shan't.

Sidney knew that he was telling truth and had a gift of prophecy as well. Softly she spoke again, but with such obvious sincerity that her conviction reached across to tempt and alarm the boy.

Then if there's to be no Academy and college beyond that, you must have your gun shop.

I don't see how, he said almost angrily.

I'll buy it for you, Joel. Please understand that I long to do this. Buy tools. And— Guns. Whatever you need. Reamers and— Alkanet root—

If I had my ruthers, Aunt Sid, I'd ruther buy my own. Thank you just the same.

You're my sister's child. I'll set you up.

Wouldn't feel twas truly mine.

Couldn't it be both of ours? As— Partners?

It's all right to support children. Folks are supposed to do that. But I'm a child no longer: I'll be seventeen in November.

I've known people to marry when they were seventeen. Boys, I mean. Girls younger. For instance: Mother. And you.

She asked shakily, Do you have anyone picked out, Joel? Some girl you plan to marry?

Why, I don't know any girls. Here *or* in Charleston.

He looked down at her. When the gay stars splintered in his eyes again, she felt that he was giving back to her, in intimate appeal, the plangency of her own voice.

Don't know any girls, he repeated. Except you.

Sidney had never glimpsed love (she'd participated only in a travesty of physical performance), had never felt its motion across her life. Her embracement until this time was solely of an immaculate model. She'd supposed that true love must be pure and wide-spread, probably white in color like a bolt of linen unwound. You could wrap yourself in it. Or widely made of marble, a solid but worshipful substance as in shield or escutcheon. You hung it on the wall to admire and to bow down before.

Pure love was to her notion congealed and permanently established. A pillar, column in a colonnade, perhaps twas an entire temple. No one might speak ill of it, twas past belittling.

Or could it be a chalky liquid measured out by ministers at a Lord's supper?

If a fabric, then it must be soaked, scrubbed, rinsed, dried, sprinkled, neatly ironed. Would have no odor except the simple suggestion of beeswax under pressure of a clean Holy iron.

Think again. Love had to do with lilies, roses, babies. If it smelled at all it smelled of mother's milk, because the process of love eventually put a baby into the mother, and later milk into the mother's breasts.

Love flew with doves. Its cherubs were fat-cheeked and had dimples in their knees, and thighs like pillows, and were always writhing around with garlands, if little suckling-pig-like bodies could be said to writhe. A Madonna beamed upon love, upon all flowers, all true lovers (two lovers always went to the altar and knelt to be prayed over). Love spoke with an archaic voice as did Quakers. It said Thee and Thou. Love sang, *I sent thee late a rosy wreath, not so much honouring thee as giving it a hope that there it could not withered be.* Love sang, *So let us rest, sweet love, in hope of this, and cease till then our tymely joyes to sing.*

Besides the doves there were the dicky-birds, besides the harp there was the lute, besides the primrose the buttercup. Despite its alleged presence in royal chambers, love was mainly bucolic and had again to do with milk (dairymaids? Harvesters and gleaners?). There existed naughty love in French prints: people peeking in boudoirs, or men sliding their hands beneath girls' petticoats or into the bosoms of their gowns (ordinarily this was done in gardens). But that was not true love, that was false love. It was dalliance, not to be dignified as honest affection.

True love—*actual* love—had rather to do with the woodcuts of maidens who sat pensive, holding their sewing, perhaps listening to canaries while waiting for their lovers to appear.

True love was apt to be more substantial in humble cottages than in great houses.

True lovers were always forthright about their attachment: that is, the men were. The women were supposed to flutter, lower their eyelids, hasten in their breathing. But still lovers always went *stealing softly.*

Aunts were supposed to love their nephews, and nephews their aunts; but that was the filial type of love, having to do also with grandparents and grandchildren. By every injunction an aunt dared not entertain the feeling which she entertained for Joel.

Had he given indication of knowing, or did she only imagine?

You mean, she asked herself with point, that you wonder whether you'll manage to seduce him?

If you confess, and say Yes—

Let the Furies who guard all true loves—their appurtenances, their caravans and constituents, their paraphernalia and symbolism—come down upon you. Lambs, doves, cherubs, all, all. Let lilies drown you in their pools, rosebuds scratch you with their briers. Yea, you'll witness God and Jesus and the entire sum of Supporting Angels stalking toward you, admonishing as They come, and promising the stoning or the burning (well-justified) which you shall receive.

How dare you cry, Now I, for the first time in my life, have a love? I love him, I love him! Tis true love! There's no mockery about it!

Bear up boldly then, Wanton Widow, and stop God and Jesus and Their minions of Church and Law in Their tracks.

In imagination she drew a deep breath, stood motionless but not tense. Said with strength, I shall hold firmly before Them. I swear it.

Even as she took the oath unto herself she felt that she could be uttering falsehood. Something might occur to give the lie to any such affirmation. She'd cowered before, she could cower again. Thus be reduced once more to enfeeblement.

Illusive fiddle playing its baleful Buy-a-Broom remembrance and parody.

When I was a weakling
So puny was I.

What riot will ensue when this prodigy is gone from me? What argument of a thousand voices fencing round or far away? This is my first love, and I have come to it all unwarned. Why was I not informed by voice or book (if thus apprised I never heard) that love might be a charmful damage?

No one told me. No one.

But had they told, I would never have accepted it as gospel.

Love was neither bud nor jewel, love was a *mélange,* hotch-potch, potpourri, rag-bag, a pretty mess. In one hour it smelt as righteous as cinnamon buns in an oven, an hour later it was gone scurvy.

Term it dust-devil posturing across trampled plantation yards or summer streets which led down to the river docks. Such infant whirlwinds came to bite up feathers, corn-shucks, dry powder of clay, and spin them giddy, and then drift into nothingness, letting the residue fall from their clutch.

In thinking of dust-devils you mentioned the possibility of devils' existence.

Have you come now to the belief that The Devil has sponsored a considerable portion of all the true love ever witnessed?

There are poets other than Jonson, and love has been not always A Rosy Wreath Not Smelling of Itself But Thee.

Far gone in the past, Brown Bertha sang a bearded lay.

> What care I for my house and lands?
> What care I for my baby-oh?
> What care I for my ain wedded laird?
> I'm off with the raggle-taggle gypsy-oh.

Surprise, surprise, oh ne'er-to-be-forgotten surprise, elegant and valued surprise.

O face ashine. (Folks tell of faces glowing. His is a strong brown lantern.) Dear Lord, I give thanks. Privileged I was to light the wick at this moment, and see the brightening.

Aunt Sid, what— What *is* it?

You should be able to tell me.

But— They're so hard to come by.

Then I'm glad I was able to come by it for you, Joel.

He stood tranced, the cloth which had wrapped the gift in one hand, the cannon-barrel itself in his other hand.

They call these the old Queen Anne screw-barrel weapons, but there's many a one still in use. Aunt Sid, where on earth did you find it?

Once it belonged to a man you followed after when you were small. Twas Captain Eames'.

He never showed it, I never knew he had it.

Sidney explained that she had thought to find some sort of treasure which Joel might fancy. It occurred to her that such a man as the captain might have willed an antiquity or two to his descendants.

So I stopped by Mrs. Graniter's place—

Her husband used to be my schoolmaster—

And Captain Eames was her grandsire.

He was with the Swamp Fox, in Revolutionary times. Must

have captured this from the British! Look at these proof marks, Aunt Sid: they're of English type. And but see the silver plating—All embossed— They speak of this as a mask butt—

They speak of this as love and sometimes it too must wear a mask: the world would blow bullets through its bewildered face did it not do so. They speak of a vigorous young customer a-calling on his aunt (how favorable an act!) and her a-fixing breakfast and further Sunday fare (black Sedalia fetched down a pot of stewed oxtails last evening, we'll warm it now, and I'll bake biscuits, twill be enough). They speak to an aunt; say, How nice your nevvy came. Most would wish to be off gallivanting!— And how they'd blink if they were to ask, What did you in the afternoon?—and you gave back the actuality and said, We read a Chapter.

Awake, O north wind; and come, thou south; blow upon my garden, that the spices thereof may flow out. Let my beloved come into his garden, and eat his pleasant fruits...

They speak of this as love, but name it hurly-burly.

You saw him away on the road to town before the sun was down, gay in carrying his gifted pistol, and turning to wave and call thanks once more.

Come again, Joel.

Will try, Aunt Sid.

Next Sunday if you can?

The momentary silence. Then— I'll do my best.

And you in confidence anticipating the return; yet certain too that there would come a farther journeying, deeper cleavage in a future time.

Gone to Texas.

That would come.

Nine years afterward, in the Apoxsee house of which you never dreamt during that momentary Reign of Joel, you beat your fists upon your bed at night because you lay a-thinking.

The music tore you, moderate as it was.

Shall Beauty Beast play more?

Yes, yes. Let him practice. *Make* him practice. He shall play.

While you lie sweating in the agony of renewed memorial.

7

B EAUTY BEAST.
  Madame?

I did not hear the piano all morning.

Je regrette—

You're spending entirely too much time at your cookery.

Madame. There were those mullet, fresh caught. Flash had lugged in that great basketful, besides whatever amount the other niggers might have stolen, either at the shore or after they fetched them home to Apoxsee. It was urgent that a fire be started in the yard furnace immediately, if the fish were to be smoked before they spoilt.

You offer one excuse after another.

Madame, I—

Now I must to the infirmary, and do a little dosing. See whether Mosey's sprain is mending, see whether Vant's fever is down—

The wenches said they'd heard from the nurse that she was still feverish this morning. Very.

Sidney said, Then I fear that I must sweat her again. Poor thing, she's frailer all the while. And Dr. Crampton can't be expected before tomorrow at the soonest, or perhaps not until Friday. And, Beauty Beast—

Comment, madame?

I—want—to—hear—that—piano.

(He looks out at me with impish attitude, as to say, I know I've been naughty but it's in my nature. Yea, yea, mistress, I know that I myself told you that hours and hours of daily practice are required of anyone with pretense toward capability. But I'm a critter of color, mistress. Pray recall that we are born to antics and caprices. Assuredly I did concentrate upon that Schumann yesterday, I did, I did!)

Work well with your Mozart. You cried that you were in difficulty—

He smiled lugubriously and said, Constantly, madam.

Beauty Beast, I shall look forward to this evening.

Sidney wished to add, As I always do, but dared not speak the words because their implication progressed far beyond the mere admiring of an art.

She said only, I require that you practice incessantly. As for the cuisine, you are to omit fancy falderols and flib-flabs, unless we have guests. Just so I don't starve.

Did I starve you, madam, I'd pray to be fettered and whipped.

Beauty Beast had memory of his mother being carried to the plantation hospital by other slaves, and his bawling along behind. Distressing remembrance and, he believed, the very first. He could not recollect when his mother died but it must have been soon afterward. There was pictured a moment when he visited her while she lay sick abed. He recalled her pretty tan face, face the color of dried oak leaves; and thought it right that she should be named Beauty; but she lay soaked with perspiration which wettened the sheet. The little boy crouched awed and crying. She managed to lean out to touch his head and run fingers across his brow, then some woman guided him away. The infirmary was not an evil place, he'd heard no wails except his own. The kind negro woman there, perhaps a nurse— She gave him three ripe persimmons.

Judge Bracket towered strong and fierce above his black people. He was rated as a kind master nevertheless. The darkies on his plantation, named Shearwater, ate the best and slept the best of any hands thereabouts, and were compelled to be cleanly. He even had one driver, Wat, whom he called his sanitary engineer. Wat was made to inspect the quarters with terrifying frequency, recommending for punishment those culprits who were careless and did not live up to the law.

Elder women explained to Beauty Beast later on: they said his mother died of inflammation of the bowels. The attack came on a-sudden.

His first well-fleshed recollection concerning Judge Bracket was recited in detail. Beauty Beast was out with the shirt-tail brigade as they were called—all the worthless yapping white-eyed midgets who were almost ready to be taught their first chores, but not quite. They ran about in single garments made like sacks, with heads coming out at the top and holes for arms to go through. Many of them, especially the boys, loved to take off these shirts when they went tussling down hedgerows or to the brooksides or along cattle and horse ponds (from which they were forbidden, and got cuffed soundly if caught there). It was an endearing thing to remove the shirts and scamper naked, although frowned upon by plantation code.

Sidney told him, I know, I've seen them at it here.

(She did not add that she'd observed the tiny nudes hopping around, catching at their rudimental organs and holding them for girls to see, and then poking fingers at the girls who ran screeching. Something they must have learned from debased elders? Oho. Could be they'd managed it through instinct and plot, all by themselves.)

Beauty Beast was gone with the children, and then a horn blew and someone ran, and a driver came to seek him. He was a bullying driver named Rudley, though not permitted to be as harsh with the people as he would have liked to be. Rudley was not supposed to administer stripes, but did so behind the overseer's back, behind the backs of other drivers.

By that I mean not to administer stripes until the case had been *tried*. As you know, madam.

I aim to keep it so. One can't always.

Rudley took him between fingers at the scruff of his neck in a kind of pinching grab, and how that hurt. He said in a deep voice, Nig, you put you shirt on.

133

Beauty Beast put it on, and then ran to the Big House, as ordered. Massah want you on the gallery.

The master sat with two friends, they had some bottles and glasses. It was late in the day, and they were refreshing themselves with wine. Perhaps noggins of rum or grog? Beauty Beast didn't know. He did remember a basket of pecans, and how the men were cracking them. Judge Bracket crooked his finger, and said, You're my boy who dances. Dance for the gentlemen.

Beauty Beast obliged. He had a chant to which he swayed and stamped. I know not whether I'd learned it from others, or made it up myself, he said. But it was the one I used, and it seemed that I had done this many times before.

Danced for the pleasure of Judge Bracket and his friends?

I know that there were other times. But this— Tis the first that I can see in my mind.

Later, he said, the gentlemen must have gone away. But he knew that it was the same day, same occasion, because the pecans were still there. Judge Bracket grinned at him, and let him sit at the edge of the gallery, and let him have pecans of his own to crack.

Judge Bracket went to sleep in his chair, stayed there long.

I must have slept on the boards of the gallery, for I wakened and still remember the moon. Twas like a slice of wild orange. We had a tree at Shearwater but the fruit was bitter.

Beauty Beast thought it not too long after this event when he was marked as half-a-hand, and sent to assist an old man named Jeems with the poultry. They were mostly speckled hens, with a few gaudy torn roosters ruffling about. And he hated the odor of the chicken-house above all. Hated hens, hated the roosters. He thought that he should never like to touch them dead or alive; but sometimes twas necessary to drag out the dead ones. They'd die of battling each other, or perhaps just die. He remembered with horror how the living poultry would pick the brains and bodies, the entrails of those who lay dead.

Unless we got to them first. I'd always been taught to be disgusted by the idea of cannibals.

Who taught you?

134

Judge Bracket, madam. Twas one of his joys to chaff, to ridicule. He warned me: some of my ancestors had been cannibals as well. And I must keep them in mind as a bad example, and must learn to stay as far from the condition of being a cannibal as ever I could.

He said seriously, It made a great impression.

I have a thought.

Madam?

She searched meticulously for the exact phraseology. I have a notion that at times the judge was most amusing to himself, yet ruthless to those within his grasp. Perhaps something like that wicked Marquis de Sade?

Oh, no, madam. It was seldom that he'd allow anyone to be whipped, even the hardest lot. He sought to govern by force of character and by example. He sought to have his overseers, his drivers do the same. Of course only a few were capable. Twas a small empire which dissolved when Judge Bracket was gone away.

He'd bait you, Beauty Beast. You tell of it.

Madam, please believe. I do not say these things with the purpose of building criticism against the judge's memory. I've told you only because you are my mistress and you asked.

Abjectly. Please forgive.

He whispered, she could scarcely hear his whisper. Can a slave forgive? Has a slave the right?

You have the right.

He turned away, shaking his head.

Do you play, Beauty Beast. One more. I'm weary. Do play another melody. We'll speak no more of Judge Bracket.

His hands trailed out some Schubert for a time. Then Sidney had risen, and Beauty Beast stood quickly to make his bow. He carried a candle for her to the gallery stair, where wind whipped the flame.

If *madame* will wait, I'll fetch a shielded candle.

Unnecessary. The stars are bright, and even if this flame blows out I can make my way.

He bowed again, she went aloft. She heard him retreating

135

easily along the gallery. She knew that they would talk of Judge Bracket again, were bound to do so. The tale was there, it must be told.

Aha, aha, ooh, ooh, oooooh
Tickle dead. She *dead.*
Ahhhhh—
Lord, Lord, she *gone!*

Dr. Crampton had come to make his rounds of adjacent plantations, had been at the Wilkeys' just before, then was come on to Apoxsee. He stood in the infirmary (as Sidney described it) or sick barracks (Mr. Irons used this term, and so did most of the people) prescribing for the only three blacks who needed prescription. He was shaking out some powder when screams arose from timber at the creekside below the quarters. This area was beyond a horse-pasture, well below Lake Tannin: willows grew thick, and sometimes a bayou formed. Children had been playing there, and on a sudden they hustled shrieking across the field. They wailed that Tickle was still, so very still. They'd found her amid dead water-logged willows and she would not move. They thought she'd been witched or maybe snake-bit. They yelled to high Heaven, gyrating in circles. Came one of the man-grown blacks a-running and he had Tickle in his arms. They toted her to the infirmary but no use. Out on the step Dr. Crampton dumped water from her lungs, and pressed and pulled, he sought to breathe life into the tiny corpse, women chafed her cold wrists. Naught to do. She'd been in the bayou too long.

I tell her never *go.*

The distracted young mother wrenched at restraining arms. Tickle was stretched flat and covered with a crazy quilt.

I say, You never go by that old water. I say, I biff you if you do.

Most of the hands were off with field gangs, but flowing from their quarters came the senile, the far *enceinte,* the infant-tender. They ringed with piteous lament and posturing.

Oh Lord, oh mistess, oh Lord Lord, she gone, she gone.
She *drown.*

136

Oooooh-hooooo-hooooo.

Sidney thanked Providence that Dr. Crampton had been in attendance at Apoxsee. Recognizing his presence, momentarily she felt relieved of ghastly responsibilities which otherwise she would have needed to accept. The Doctor was there, and even he could do nothing. (Once The Doctor was gone, guilt came back upon her.)

The mother, one Sarah, jerked in convulsions. The father, one Coot, stood mutely behind her, holding his mouth open. Spume dripped from his lips, tears seeming even oilier ran from his eyes, his very silence was rending.

At night Sidney asked Beauty Beast, Where was I at fault?

Twas not your doing, madam.

We could have built a better fence? A high fence to keep them out? Should I have such a fence made at once? As in a fortification? Sharp stakes mounted and pointing down, so that children cannot clamber there?

Still there are the horse-ponds. And cattle must drink. A small child could die in any of those pools.

I do not know, she said. This night— Whether I can bear music—

(And after her uneaten dinner.) Do you choose, *madame?*

The grief of simple folk, she said. Primitive people. An agony to witness.

But people who are more complex— Is not their grief even worse?

This lean young yellow man, he sat as nurse or comforter. His hands went down upon the keys and he played a dirge for Tickle who was drowned. Sidney Shallop had never known that a dirge could be so winning. And Beauty Beast was saying soft words with priestly grace, they were poetry barely whispered. Poor little child. Poor little black girl. Run and play in sun and water. So cruelly gone. But escape so much. So very much escape. Preacher maybe call you little lamb. But you always small black girl, run and play, running in sun. People see you running, hear you laugh. In bright clean water always. Sun bright on pretty water. Poor little slave.

Music skipped into silence as it were the dead child skipping from the room. Then distinctly Sidney heard Beauty Beast say, Authority and majesty of death itself.

Here were minor chords firm and terminal, but bell-like in their acceptance of a rule laid down and now enforced. She'd heard them often, thought they were done by Chopin, was limited in her musical recalling, could not be sure. Kept saying throughout this enforcement— Kept saying within herself, God. God Almighty. Thy will be done.

She thought that Beauty Beast had spoken (not as slave to madam or *madame*) and told her, Please cease to build for yourself a grief you do not truly own. You cannot feel all grief within the world. The spoil of it is vast and stands in stacks. You cannot touch it all.

She came nearer to him. He looked up, made as if to rise, candles above the piano were welcoming them both. Sidney motioned Beauty Beast back upon the bench.

The music. What you've just been playing—

Chopin, *madame*.

From— The preludes? I heard Liszt— Or Thalberg—

Madame, my feeble efforts should not be mentioned in the same breath with such performers.

She cried, Don't say things like that. Hear?

Je regrette—

Which of the preludes?

They're all of Opus Twenty-eight. The first one I played— light thing, nigh onto laughing—was the E-Flat Major. Followed by the C Minor, *madame*.

She told him abruptly, Never before have I been addressed as madam or *madame* by any other servant, except those abroad. If you had a fancy— Had you your own choice, could call me anything you wished to, how would you address me?

Presently Beauty Beast said, Had I my own right— Something which no one might tolerate in a slave. Had I lief, I'd call you Misty.

Misty? Why so?

It seems like you. He thought, and then said, A suggestion of mystery. The two are much the same.

It's as if I dwell in fog? In mist?

If *madame* will pardon me—

There's to be no madam-ing or *madame*-ing any longer. I shall be Misty. As you have chosen.

What will the other— The servants—?

They'll pay little heed.

But—white folks—?

It has the sound of a pleasant diminutive. A friendly way for one to say mistress or mistess. As a—

She was about to say *pet name,* shied hastily away from that. I find it tolerable, Beauty Beast.

He could not manage to address her as Misty immediately. He sought to avoid the madam or *madame,* was mannerly until disturbed. Only when Sidney spoke in a way which brought them closer together did he use the Misty as she'd suggested, as she'd drawn it out of him.

Even then it was in almost apologetic fashion, as if underneath he were praying, May I?

Aye, you may.

She was fated to share emotion, to speak of Judge Bracket again, to ask that Beauty Beast tell more. He told.

I did appreciate the act of guarding the poultry against predators. I remember those nights, lying in wait with old Jeems, to rout polecats, raccoons, other critters. I enjoyed that. It was as if we fought in war.

Judge Bracket had accustomed himself to lecturing me extensively. The judge enlarged on valuable disciplines attendant to my employment, but I begged to be put at something else. And went into pout when a transfer was denied; and got a hiding from the master himself. He used to admonish me constantly when at Shearwater, though often he was gone to Washington during that period. He demanded excellent performance of everyone, in everything. Of course no one might attain, to his reckoning, a perfection. Twas impossible. When he himself failed at perfection in a given task, his display of temper was appalling. Then he'd try to choke it back. He'd grieve because he had given way in unseemly fashion. He— It was difficult to be with him, madam.

Misty. (As in a separate telling.)

Misty. He said that my work with Jeems amid those chickens I despised— Twas not so much despising: almost I was in fear of them— Judge Bracket declared that it would firm my character. I must have been nine when he ordered me from the hens. He had me scrubbed, made the old nurse cut off my hair so I'd be harboring no mites or other insects unwanted. I was dressed in new clothes, and I jigged merrily, feeling that I cut a fine figure. Truly my labors were just beginning. The judge had decided to train me as his personal boy. His valet was old and sickly and ready for the rocking-chair. So when Judge Bracket next sailed for Washington, he took me with him instead. And now he had become Mr. Justice Bracket, although his own people—and neighbors and other familiars—referred to him consistently as Judge Bracket, and still do. I couldn't have been more than ten, for Andrew Jackson was still in the White House.

The President was to our house a time or two which I can remember. He sat with Judge Bracket in the library and they drank. When I was in the room on one errand or another, I heard them talking of British and Seminoles. They were laughing when they made reminiscence about the British, but when they spoke of the Indians they did not laugh at all. I remembered ospreys and eagles we had at Shearwater. Sometimes they used to carry off small animals. I had a cat by which I set great store but one day she was snatched away by an eagle. It did not help my spirit to be told that I too might be captured in similar fashion, did I not be on my guard and run quickly when one of the big birds hovered. Therefore I was very much afraid of President Jackson and trembled when he appeared. He looked like an eagle.

There was so much, so very much to learn. Too very much to learn. Sometimes when I went late to my sleep, drearily late to my sleep, it seemed that there were mountains piled ahead of me—each mountain a mass, a knot of knowledge which in some fashion I must ravel away. There was the mountain of sewing at first: the judge demanded that I learn the needle, and well.

There would be times when stitches would be needed in the wardrobe, and no seamstress about. He said that I must learn to be dexterous with my fingers in all ways. He had important plans for me. So he did. But, *madame*—

Misty. (In fog? Mist?)

Twas the mystery and fear of those plans which kept me sleepless many times. I did not know, yet I suspected.

The harpsichord.

Gold. It stood dominating one of the parlors, however small its size. A frightening implement. Judge Bracket loved the plucking sound and had moderate skill himself. He could play a few bright things which he learned with effort. But those were committed to memory: he was not adept at reading a score. Notes and musical symbols baffled him, it took him too long to interpret them.

In the house was an ancient clavichord as well. But this instrument lay in a state of disrepair, always pulled apart by men who could do little for it. I was introduced to the clavichord but briefly. Twas the harpsichord which shadowed across my life. And then, almost overnight, I became hospitable to the shattering flashing tones which had aggravated me earlier. But it was in the same week when Judge Bracket announced, Come, Beauty Beast, I've news for your ears. You're to go to Monsieur Menies tomorrow and begin with the pianoforte.

Actually of course I was incapable of valeting Judge Bracket properly. Too green, too inept by youth and lack of experience. Also the small size of my hands was a problem in my work as valet, as well as in my attempts at the keyboard. But I did grow apace: hands grew out of my sleeves, wrists grew long, they were disproportionate to my size as a boy. You've observed how we niggers grow: a growth here, a growth there, and our hands and feet forever flopping.

The judge bought a Jamaican. His name was Arnold, and he had been recommended as a property by some diplomat who was retiring. So he bought Arnold to valet him, instead of putting up any longer with my fumbling attempts. Judge Bracket preferred to keep me at books and music.

There was little love between Arnold and me. He was always

bent on slapping me or belting me. He was a sneak, still to be scorned after these years. Frequently I'd see him steal a small amount of money—a few coins only—from Judge Bracket's purse, when there was opportunity. He did not rob enough to make the judge suspicious: only those few coins. He became conscious that I had spied on him, and he muttered about murdering me. He chased me around the house when no one else was at hand, but I was too fast and agile. However, when he realized that the master seemed to regard me with high favor and had put me to elegant purposes, then Arnold changed his tune. He fawned over me and after me. Which I abhorred as well.

Forever a burden. The sharp pains ground into me, as if I labored along carrying weight, carrying some sort of box strapped to my back. Box or boxes; perhaps trunks of anguish, larger and heavier than I could support, and their corners thrust into my flesh as I tottered. Often I grew dispirited, wondered whether I shouldn't do away with myself. But that wickedness was forbidden by laws of the Church. When Judge Bracket read Scriptures aloud to us assembled servants there was never any doubt about where he stood. He stood on the side of the Lord, and admitted it. Except of course in the matter of the Sixth Commandment.

The Sixth—

Thou shalt not kill.

My career as a chef was not even budding while we remained in the United States. That was to come later, after we were settled or—alternately—wandering abroad. Judge Bracket's great force hammered at me, his voice hammered, his voice rang. The adjuration, the counseling, always the counseling. You must do this, do that. There was monumental reading for me to undertake, copy books to copy, even portions of the law to read. A dictionary to study. The piano; and Monsieur Menies' rapping away at me there as well, flying into rages, declaring that I hadn't practiced as he'd instructed. Though I had, I had! Monsieur Menies said that I must be lying, and my fingers were sausages, and could never do anything.

Through all this I was made to go to Mr. Drummond's school. Twas said to be a stylish place. I was entered as one B. B. Bracket, and the other lads called me Beebee. All I knew was that the work was demanding. I thought of young darkies down here at home on the plantation, and how their life had more of sport in it than mine. They could hunt possums, club them to the ground; they could take crabs, roast oysters, and—as they grew older—steal out to meet girls at night. They were field niggers to all intents and purposes, even though some were the children of house servants. They had a better time of it than I.

Then there came a flare in the school: word got about that I was a slave, the property of Judge Bracket. At which several parents withdrew their sons, and Mr. Drummond was piqued. But soon there appeared the two sons of some African potentate, and also a dark-faced lad from the East Indies, I believe. They were put into the school, attracting much attention. Then even the boys who had been withdrawn were put back.

I didn't care a whit for all this. What worried me was the grave amount of learning and performance demanded. If I was not gone to Mr. Drummond's or busy at the voluminous reading to which Judge Bracket set me, then I was working at the piano. So I grew hollow-cheeked and round-shouldered. The judge was smitten in his conscience now and then. On a chill evening he might come bursting into a parlor where I flailed away at the keyboard. He'd bang the folding doors like an angry giant, crying out, Ah, you're ailing, Beauty Beast. And tis all a fault of mine. Too often you're house-bound. We'll remedy that, and in this moment. Fetch me my cloak now, my boots. Fetch your own. We'll be off for a tramp. Then he might add, had he been drinking, A tramp, say I? A constitutional, you yellow—

Ah, *madame.*

Misty.

Misty, I was about to use the word he used.

So we would go plunging out in snow or rain or whatnot. Sometimes the night was clear, but winters can be chill in Washington— The judge striding ahead, holding his head high and his shoulders flung back, forcing along at a military pace. And myself, a tired hopeless yellow boy, fairly running to keep up with him.

You must have been an odd pair.

Misty. We were, we were.

You spoke of killing.

A great scandal at the time. That was when he gave a mortal wound to young Mr. Jessup. They were of opposed political persuasion, and perhaps of ethical persuasion as well. We all believed—naturally we in the household believed, and were speaking of it—that Mr. Jessup was of an especially vindictive nature, and became unwisely articulate in his utterance. This was shortly before the time when Judge Bracket decided to resign from the Supreme Court; but talk of his resignation was in the air. The word *bribery* was used by Mr. Hardaway Jessup.

Sidney interrupted. Beauty Beast, I remember. Indeed I do. That occurred while I was married to Mr. Tensley. There were accounts in the newspapers, and much accusation, much condemnation of Justice Bracket.

Beauty Beast said slowly, I feel that may have been his reason for going to dwell abroad. The two men met, of course. The judge, some thirty years the senior of Mr. Jessup, shot his adversary through the liver. The unfortunate man lingered for days in agony before he died. Judge Bracket took to his private rooms and would see no one. Not even Arnold. Only myself, and occasionally one of the maids. It was during this time that he first became possessed of the rather strange ambition that I should cook.

He declared that I'd progressed sufficiently in no practical direction— Not far enough to really earn my keep.

How'd you like to go marching along with a plough gang, hey? He'd ask this in his challenging manner. Or go to minding hogs? If not poultry once more? Or work at the gin? Have your fingers picked off by machinery, the first moment when someone grew careless?

I remonstrated, felt myself abused, thought that I was progressing well with my piano. Monsieur Menies had finally said—

You call that progress, hey? Praise from a beggarly Frenchman whose very wine is bought on extended credit, who has more debts than capital, more mistresses than piano students? You'd be hard put to make yourself important in any situation, on any plantation, d'ye hear me? Any household! With the few buttons you can sew, bits of mythology you can discuss— With those few gushes and trills you've learned, that bit of counterpoint or transposition? Beauty Beast, suppose that I were to die? Perhaps one day some scoundrel might be quicker with his pistol than I, and it would be one Pericles Bracket—d'ye hear?— instead of that wretch Jessup or his ilk, who's carried off to lie beneath the clods. Then you'd be sold. Wha' twould it be worth to any buyer to feed *you*, hey?

In a cavern at the rear, along the passageway— Place which was dormitory for young females—Linnet, Molly, Clemmy—and now little India growing into woman's estate—

Prattle went on.

Old mistress, she make him play that piano every night.

She do, she do.

She just make him.

Make him play by day, too.

Hear him play early, hear him play late.

I say, Beauty Beast, when you find time for cook? He just laugh, say he like play piano.

Somehow he get food cook.

Jittering laughter among rustics, loose chuckling hidden laughter running over whitewashed walls and boards, beneath beds (like palm rats finding their way inside in cold weather), out again. Laughter gossiping and guilty. Telling truth, telling lies? Nor caring.

Mistess, she make him set and talk.

Yeh-hah!

Talk and talk and *talk*.

Shapeless laughter running out to climb the Big House and peek again. But it is inky or mulatto and secret laughter also, not to be seen or heard if a white comes close. It is masked by an

145

innocent protrusion of lying glistening eyeballs when whites walk nigh.

She make that beautiful yellow nigger talk and talk.

And *play* piano. And *play*.

She know what she like.

Old Mist Irons. Reckon he want see mistess bout one thing or nother. He come up, look in, he see mistess and he see Beauty Beast, and they just talking and talking. And mistess setting right there, and she leave Beauty Beast set down to piano, and he setting on that bench, and she setting in chair, and they talk and talk and *talk*. Poor Mist Irons. He look in, don't have heart. No, he don't have heart. He up and go away.

Poor old Mist Irons.

Reckon old mistess, she knows what she want.

Yeh-hah!

She *do*. She want that nice big yellow thing.

Girl. She cut your heart out, hear you say that.

Linnet, you. You don't speak no word.

She surely don't speak no word.

Linnet, girl. Hear me now? Old cat got your tongue?

No. Old cat hain got my tongue. Cain you let poor girl sleep?

What you reckon they talk about? Mistess and Beauty Beast?

I hear them talk.

What you reckon they talk *about?*

Don't make no sense to me.

I listen to they talk. Don't make no sense *tall*.

Hih, hih, hih—

Cain you let poor girl *sleep?*

Beauty Beast carried a letter of resignation to the White House when Mr. Justice Bracket decided to leave the Bench for all time. Beauty Beast said that he wore russet Cordova boots which had been awarded him as a Christmas gift. He felt enriched at having those, there was snow in the tight damp dusk, he slipped several times and fell in sliding upon ice beneath loose snow as he approached the Executive Mansion.

He did not see the President, in fact had never seen him. Van Buren was no crony of Judge Bracket, as had been Andrew

Jackson. Some thought that to be a decisive factor in Bracket's departure from the judicial scene, but Beauty Beast said Nay. Twas the duel and a pillorying which followed, he was confident. Perhaps a sense of age and frustration? And also guilt, of which the judge must have carried more than the usual share (his sins were plentiful—often self-blazoned for the world to witness) .

The young Beauty Beast entertained notion that a gloom was removed from his own soul in the delivery of that letter; though he had no knowledge then of the contents. But he felt better than he'd felt in a long while. On the way back home (on H Street) he anticipated slippery places and slid on them as far as the brasses on his boots would let him skate.

He told Sidney, We were gone to France very soon thereafter, and remained abroad for many years.

Beauty Beast, in speaking of your going abroad, whom do you mean by *we?*

Judge Bracket and myself. (He spoke the unfamiliar word.) Misty.

But did not Arnold go? The valet?

Judge Bracket sold him off and said that he would acquire a French valet by hire, which he did.

So you were Judge Bracket's sole companion, in sailing to Europe?

Yes, Misty.

Pause.

But, did he not fear that you would be freed? There were laws of other nations to be considered. Was there not an occasion, back in the last century, when a negro slave fetched into England was automatically made free? A decision very like this Scott case which has been occupying America's great legal minds during recent years?

That was before the American Revolution, Misty. The negro was named Sommerset, and twas a decision by Lord Mansfield which freed him. The situation in France had blown hot, blown cold; possibly Judge Bracket felt uncertain as to what he might encounter. He demanded that I swear—

Beauty Beast came up as a toy, came off the piano bench on

147

high, a jack springing from box unseen, undimensioned. And as another jack—the jumping kind—he succumbed to tightening of nervous fibre. His hands turned into fists, they swept up and out and wide. Strike something, strike anything. Indeed he did sweep the candles. They flew, candelabra and all, from the piano, melted wax a-spattering.

O dark. With only smell of the wick-reek. Lady (Sidney inquired of herself on the instant), are you in terror? You stand alone with one of your colored slaves, man slave.

Of course tis Beauty Beast. Be reminded of that. It—is— Beauty Beast.

She had not been aware of rising, leaping up; but that was what she'd done when the arms tightened and expanded and fists went out and candles flew; and there sounded such sad thud and dissonance from the piano, as Beauty Beast had mauled the keyboard.

Then she detected an advance, long patch of deeper dimness stalking; and she receded through one door (lighter here) into the passage (why dog-trot? I've seen no dog trotting) and fading through the frame of another door. After her Beauty Beast came breathing.

Please, please to forgive. I am overwrought.

She made no sound, replied nothing, discovered herself on the east gallery, and it was lighter, lighter. Stairway revealed plainly at the southern end, the one rising outside her room; so she touched her foot upon the stair and then turned back and saw her musician looming.

(Ah. *Court* musician? *Queen* Sidney?)

Beauty Beast, I did not know what you were about.

Misty. Scarce did I know. Would you—please to overlook—?

You've done nothing, she said shortly.

Dear mistress, for the moment I had no control. Because of— questions— May I say this: Judge Bracket did not know what he'd find. He did not know what the condition might be, or whether twould change—perhaps even overnight—while we were abroad. He'd drilled into me a strictest attendance upon the truth, on promise or a sacred oath. Nothing could be more binding than that. I could not fathom anything more potent! Judge Bracket relied upon no uncertainty of European law. He was not about to be deprived of his control, not he. He set it down in writing and made me recite the oath, take it to my heart. Twill stay with me as long as I live or have pretension to a brain. Would you hear it? Misty, would you hear?

I, Beauty Beast, being an individual in the sight of God, but a slave by the laws of my native State and Country, and, according to those laws, being the property of one Pericles Bracket; and being about to be transported to distant climes and Nations, do swear on Holy Writ and by all else which I may hold sacred, that I shall not take advantage of any opportunity to terminate my condition of thraldom in any Land into which I may enter, no matter what my status may be according to the custom, tradition, rule or law of that Nation, no matter what pretense may be adopted or practiced; and that I will remain cheerfully in slavedom as the property of Pericles Bracket, yielding as heretofore to his will and direction, until such time as Pericles Bracket may, by deliberate act, and in accord with the statutes of his native State and Country, choose to set me free.

Once I ran away. It was in the town of Albi. I ran clean to the other end of town, across a bridge over the Tarn, and was out on the highway, rushing frantic and fast, and meeting with queer glances from people who carried stuff to market. And then I tired, and sat under trees for a while; and then went back. Judge Bracket never knew I'd been gone. He trusted me; knew I'd given my bonded word; trusted me through all those strange gypsying years. There were times when he was ill, and I needs must wait upon him hand and foot. We'd fetch in a nurse on occasion, but he'd have none of her contributions. He spooned up my little messes silently at first. Later he'd cry, Beauty Beast, you'll become a fable. D'ye hear me? A fable!—for your food may well become fabulous. The viands you prepare— I'll make you worth something to yourself, and to others!

What of my freedom?

I promised, he said. I've given my word. You shall be free. Once we're back to America I'll have it arranged. *Manumissio in ecclesia* or any other damned way that's needed. But right now you're here with me. And you've sworn—

You cannot feel all grief within the world.

Sidney compelled herself to go higher on the gallery stair and then she turned, looked back into gloom, saw Beauty Beast's shape now gone well below her.

She said, I think it was dastardly. To keep you dangling so.

Have you not heard, Misty? Slavery is a dastardly condition.

The spoil of it is vast and stands in stacks.

She told herself, Then I'll be cruel as Bracket. I'll keep him, keep him. Hold him tight!

She tried to haul her feet from that same step. What's this? They have adhered, are tacked or bolted there.

(O lean tan musician, pray light the candles once more, return to Chopin.)

Although may I confess, *madame*—

Sidney's lips quivered in the long corrective M-sound. Mmmisty.

Misty. May I confess that I'd discovered a new fascination, and used to wait with joy upon the moment when the judge would list his guests, and tell me that I must excel myself. Truly I loved that. Most beings welcome flattery, do they not? Even a yellow nigger such as I.

He said, as again she fought to climb— Said, When we returned to America we'd been at Shearwater perhaps five weeks when there fell the brain-stroke, with Judge Bracket soon unconscious, and dead in another hour or two.

So I remained—

Remained a slave in the sight of the laws of my native State and Country.

Had you not clung to that wretched oath—

But I'd been taught to do so. My father believed that there was no worse evil than a ruptured oath. Broken promise. A lie.

Your father? she repeated, and heard the brain within her skull yelling, *Let me out,* and she staggered against the balustrade.

From his lower level down there behind her he said, Misty, I thought you'd perceived. Judge Bracket was my father.

~8~

S HOULD HAVE been aware, should have been aware. Do I not recognize that some system of miscegenation prevails throughout the entire pattern of human slavery? Has always done so?

Back in Carolina. Take that repulsive Sohnfester. He owned a stately brown-faced housekeeper named Yulee; and Yulee's two elder children were black indeed, but the two younger ones were nigh onto white; and these were born long after Yulee became the property of Mr. Sohnfester, and she had no husband to be recognized.

My own overseer, Nathaniel Irons, lives in communion with Lora; she has children by him.

And frequently Pettey J. spoke (in crawling lascivious tone) of stud niggers. He found the term conducive to erotic stimulation, no doubt.

Why did I not recognize all along that there must have been a white father for Beauty Beast? Sometime, somewhere?

Recognition existed, but indifferently, easily acceptable.

(Bees sleeping in winter within a hive.)

There is a painful reversal of logic and what I might hold to be justice in this situation.

Come, who carried your own original seed?

One Philip Sidney Veck. In turn he and my mother were

descended from preachers and housewives, insignificant mariners and more housewives, throngs of persons who bought and sold commodities and profited thereby—or bought and sold them unwisely, and thus did not profit. Folk abustle over nothing, folk with meal in their mouths, or sometimes butter. Folk who might have enlisted your sympathy but never your trust.

Nobodies. Readily I'll admit it. Nobodies.

Mrs. *Shall*op. It is rumored that, through a series of pranks played by Death and Inheritance, you have achieved possession of a man who can fly farther than you can fly, walk with a better dignity than you can muster. And sing a more regal song. And pray a prayer which goes spearing into the ultimate, higher and faster than any prayer to which you might give velocity.

And suffer more than you might suffer?

Tis debatable. In fact I resent that suggestion heartily. As one resents being told that he was never a prisoner, when certainly he retains the memory of gratings and window bars. Or being told that he was never wounded, when he can uncover and show you blue holes in his hide.

But still, lady, your boughten slave may give more music to the world, in figurative fashion as well as literal, than any dozen whites you can name? Tell us true. You own the son of a rich planter, son of a soldier, son of a man who sat at the summit of the judiciary. An eccentric, but also an intimate of Andrew Jackson (himself eccentric). No doubt a rumored pillar or portion of the Kitchen Cabinet. Man of strength—if often misdirected strength. Man whose progeny should not come cheap.

Stud niggers, said you, Pettey J.? In local history we now study another form and color of stud.

Sold. To the lady yonder.

She writhed in an embarrassment which would not have prevailed had Beauty Beast informed her that his mother'd spent her young life in whoredom—say, in a bawdy house in New Orleans. Accident. His mother'd conceived. His father might be anything from a Creole fancy man to a boatswain.

Might be a skulking clergyman, a shyster, simple cotton-broker, a dragoon or fop. The fact that through Sidney's acquisition of Beauty Beast, and the compulsive friendship which she had allowed to grow between them (Allowed? Fostered) she'd won an afflicting but still impressive intimacy with the legend of Judge Bracket— It seemed that she waited now in plight for some sort of blow to fall. Some penalty to be paid, deserved or undeserved.

Early under clouds, trotting nervous to the lake, she sensed humidity and spectral coolness. Traces of rain rinsed against her face and said, Drouth is with you still. This is but a sample, quickly withheld. There'll be no decent rain today, so go on about the burying. Shivering more than ordinarily when at last water wrapped round her, not liking its taste, suspicious (was there some awful seepage up above? Impurity to come oozing down the stream?) — Back to the house again with a rapidity which was almost flight, hoping to meet no one, not ringing for Linnet at first, not wishing to see Linnet, dreading the moment when she'd be compelled to ring for breakfast.

Tug upon the gilt looped wire, at long last. Wire saws within its holes where it runs through floors and walls. The smallest bell goes skit, skit down where it hangs pendulous from its coil of spring. That's the one for Linnet, smallest bell of all.

Oh, mistess. You done rise already?

There's still slight rain a-blowing, and I'll breakfast in my chamber. I've rung the kitchen bell—

Strangely at this moment she could not say, The bell for Beauty Beast.

So please to fetch my tray as soon as breakfast is prepared.

He'd cut a slice of melon. She tasted it with apathy, thought it wasn't ripe enough. She tasted long, sat there in blankness, in what she termed to herself a meditation. Although she wasn't meditating, only staring plain, unthinking, a trifle bruised.

There were little eggs warm when she was ready for them, eggs neatly peeled, the yolks almost pink. She didn't know what nest they came from: some wild birds. Were plovers nesting near the shore? She played with the eggs, could not bear to eat them.

Pitiful robbed mother bird. I want no more of this sort of thing. I'll give orders—

You will, will you? And then all the darkies will take up birds-nesting, and enjoy the eggs themselves.

Toast, some jam, that was all. Strong black coffee served her well. Therefore to the infirmary first off, then go to shoot. No, no, go to ride. And I've not ridden in so long. But I'll not put on my riding-skirt at once, tis cumbersome.

She had Linnet fetch a simple gray gingham, also an apron complete with bib. Pink and white, almost as if designed to go with gray. She stood before her French pier-glass and knew that she looked well, but pale somehow this day.

(Concerned with my appearance before—my slave?)

Reluctant still to meet with Beauty Beast, but she must go. She gathered her weighty mass of keys and found the required basket, looked up a recipe, went below stairs.

He bowed when she came in, he stood holding down his head so long that the bow was nearly sanctimonious. Then Beauty Beast looked up, and she saw that he'd had miseries. Perhaps he hadn't slept a morsel, all night long. And with dinner guests to feed, that very evening. Though he'd prepared much in advance, she knew: ham in crust, sand cookies, stuffing for guinea hens—

Good morning, Beauty Beast.

Good morning—

She waited, then it came. He spoke the word, and in that instant something was forgiven, something mended. He said, Misty.

Little Coony, on the limestone step, grinning as he eats. Why, bless me, Coony's got my eggs— He's a good child—may he batten on them.

I must prepare an ointment, Beauty Beast.

May I assist in any way?

She lifted the keys, jangled them apart, found the old one with green paint on its ring and identified it. Turned the lock of the cupboard where medicaments were kept, it was a high cupboard, Sidney craned her neck.

158

Misty, may I—?

He fetched a keg, took her hand, helped her up on the keg. Rosin she found. The beeswax. Turpentine.

Here we are.

Beauty Beast helped her to step down.

Now fetch lard and honey. I'll need half a pound of lard at least. But only two large spoonfuls of the honey. Horse ointment, she told him. A receipt of DeGray's or Sloan's, I can't say which. We shall melt lard first of all, then put in the rest.

Misty, will you not permit—?

No, no, I make the medicines, such as are made at Apoxsee. This is for two: horse and man. Do you know Duke?

The blacksmith?

Recently he burnt himself at his forge. I spread on something else, but he complained. He likes this horse ointment, and he's used it several times before. Actually, tis very good for human flesh, though last I employed it when a horse was bitten in a fight. Ready now, she said. We'll take it off the fire, so. Now we'll slowly add the turpentine. This great cup, somewhat less than a pint it holds. I must stir, keep stirring all the while until it's cooled.

Beauty Beast rebelled. Misty, that's much too long a time. Coony, up and on your feet. Misty will show you how it must be stirred.

She yielded, she spoke pleasantly to the little boy, instructing; their heads were close together, she looked down and saw the wool.

Hair of Beauty Beast is straight. This must not be forgotten.

I shall trust you, Coony, not to spill a mite. You may rest your hand and arm between times, but then continue stirring until Beauty Beast shall give the word.

Up to the cupboard once more. There was another urgency: medicine left by Dr. Crampton perhaps a month earlier and many times before that. Professor Platt's Treatment, so termed. Twenty Years Without a Failure. Sugar of lead, ergot, opium, ipecac, ground and mixed. Twas given in a little honey. Sidney could not explain to Beauty Beast. This was for a girl named

Caramel if she was flowing still. She'd lost her infant at birth, there was all that wasting, profuse. Linnet had carried word this morning. And Dr. Crampton visited only once in a fortnight; sometimes it was three weeks and more.

Rain departed, worthless rain, not enough to lay dust. While the horse ointment was being stirred and cooled, Sidney sought the garden patches, to speak with Adam.

What was a-doing here? Snap-beans?

They're drying out, she said. All of these vines should be threshed.

Yes, mistess. Thrash em.

But see this Swiss chard—

White beets, mistess.

She agreed with him. White beets. (For that was what he called the chard, and he spoke of egg plant as Guinea squash.) In perfect condition, and we've had none on the table. Do you take up a basket to the kitchen. I'll tell the cook that it is coming. Adam, she warned him, the drowned child will be buried today. If you dare to drink rum, or any other spirits—

Great voice in an abyss a-promising. I don't drink no rum. Mistess, look. These hot-frames smash.

What has happened? All that glass shattered.

Oh, bad smash. That old bull calf, mistess. He get loose nighttime, get to running, dogs a-chasing.

Why, I didn't hear a thing. I must have slept so—deeply.

Oh, I did hear, I cover up my ears! But that old calf, he don't get cut too bad a-tall.

I'll need to dose him.

Tige already dose him, mistess.

Glass in these frames must be replaced. You'll have much to set under them later on.

Mist Irons say we ain got no more glass for cut for frames.

Then he must order more. It should be put upon the list immediate.

(List, the list. Mrs. Shallop, ma'am, we need some bagging for the picking-bags, we're short of it. Short of rope for bales as well. Salt: perhaps a hundred pounds. And a band sorely needed for the gin. We must have plough-points. The cook begs for cinnamon sticks, next time anyone is to the store. Potash needed. At least four new axes. Mustard, ground or unground, we can grind it. Always the list, list, list. Twill soon be cooler, and some blankets must be given out; the carpenter asks for hand-saw files; the blacksmith asks for nails. I am moderately low on ammunition, and must have bullets run for both pairs of pistols, but there's no lead. Keg of vinegar next trip. Should dicker for a quantity of rice since we raise none. Buy cayenne pepper.)

Sidney considered that her horse ointment must have been stirred and cooled sufficiently, she could take it along. (Coony was safely supervised by Beauty Beast, and the vessel had been placed in a flat bowl of water to speed the cooling.) Sidney held that she must lose herself in domestic event and demand, would have no right to go target shooting, no right to ride again until she'd proved herself a fully competent Mrs. Mistress to the limit of will and vigor.

She went away from Adam, pleased to have found him tractable and not a hoarse frog exuding peril and stench. Sidney thought of reassurement he gave the shoots he planted. She'd even heard him apologize to those which he must trim or dig up, heard him rumble out such licit chatter more than once, unheeding of her presence. She thought that surely he must have felt or seen her there; yet it was as if he spoke a separate tongue, dwelt in a state apart, was necromantic and should be recognized as Philosopher by all good growing things and green growing things, if not by men. He called them He, never She. Called them boys and brothers. You little boy, you get in there and grow. Grow now. You little boys, I put this chicken-shit round you, make you grow so high, high, high. Now, brother, you, I got to shave you down to just about roots. Just above. Don't aim cut you roots out. No, just make you well again when you is sick. Lil old men, I bring black soil in here. Yes, surely, bring black soil for lil old boys. You catch you breath again, you get black soil.

Suddenly Sidney halted, motionless. She recalled how Beauty Beast had uttered his chant for the child who was drowned.

Poor little black girl.

161

Run and play, running in sun.
But escape so much.
Poor little slave.

Sympathy and understanding, with their attendant poetry, went through her like electrical shock. Laughing, in Germany, she'd been challenged to pick up two metal poles and hold them in her hands while a young professor did mysterious things with apparatus at the other side of the table, and he set electric juice to tingling, till she squealed and dropped the poles.

Shock again.

Black soil. You catch you breath.

Not the voice of Mr. Justice Bracket, or any of the other whites who'd marked his mother's line. Never. Black soil came from black.

She spoke to Mr. Irons about the body. Wisely preserved, he told her. Always he kept coffins on hand, large and small. Once there had been somewhat of a disaster, when no coffin was immediately available, and one had to be made. And—

I don't like to talk about that, ma'am.

Then we shan't. You say the body is already—arranged?

Yes, ma'am. Just a little box. It was set up on rafters in the shed next to the carpentry shop.

He gave his sparse dreary smile and said, I can't scarcely get any hands to go in there. Cause they knew there's empty coffins.

And where have you kept her?

Had some women lay her out, ma'am. Lora took charge, Tickle's neatly fixed, and the coffin nailed. Up on saw-horses in the old root cellar where it's cool. Cool for weather like this.

(Far from the past: *Mind, tis hot weather.*)

Have you kept the corpse—guarded?

Yes, ma'am, there's still some conjur niggers hereabouts. I know of three at least who might have— Well, a lock of hair or—

We shan't discuss that either, Mr. Irons. What I wish to do is this: at noon the bell will ring. Drivers will see that everyone comes in from the fields. All the pickers, everyone out of the corn, everyone up from the gin. Only those needed by the animals are to remain working.

I understand, ma'am.

And they shan't go back to work afterward.

Irons became distressed. Now, ma'am, the cotton's all broke out so far, it's all so open. Never saw so much open cotton in the fields right now, this season, as we've got this year. True, it's a little dark in cast, but— Sent my first load off, I guess it was last Monday. I've marked it in the journal; and maybe there's another dozen bales gone since; and I expected to send more, come Saturday—

She said resolutely, Mr. Irons, I will not observe a funeral service and then send the hands back to the field to pick. Leave them to their half holiday. Gloomy enough it is.

Thin sun came through loblolly pines and found a corner of Tickle's grave, open, sharp cut, new-dug, waiting. *Small body, come, I need to be filled.* Thin sun lay mildly on soil thrown loose, sun found the hands as they gathered, illumined faces black and brown. Jays reviled a loutish crested woodpecker at the other end of the grove. They flew high over the sandy entombment of slaves long put there; past tilting wooden grave-boards; past rocks which in some cases had been used for marking sites—rocks, or large shells fetched from the sea. On more recent mounds wilted flowers had hardened into brown relics. Fresh purple pickerel-weed grew from a bottle set into dry earth at one sunken spot. There rested the skeleton of a woman, Dorcas. She'd been dead for many years. Her son, the driver named Madison (called Maddy) — He counted the season doleful when he found no blooms to put above his mother. In deep winter he gave her holly.

Some of the elder children had assembled bouquets. (Sidney'd bade them do this.) They watched with chalky glaring eyes. They could remember a number of infants dying but only the eldest might recall when another child of their own group had been put there.

The mistress of Apoxsee confessed to herself that she felt

163

removed further and further from Presbyterianism. She observed that the young Reverend Mr. Fortunatus Stephens failed to personalize any element of a rewarding religion—failed to make it beat its heart, breathe, walk in wisdom and pride. It had nothing to say of or for a child tragically and quickly dead. The tenets he retailed offered but a stinted balm to the grieving. Consistently he sought to spin a web of church law and hypothetical discussion. Coldly ethereal at its best, Pharisaic at its worst.

The Directory stated, *And the minister, if present, may exhort them to consider the frailty of life, and the importance of being prepared for death and eternity.* Sidney had found what seemed to her a much better "Order for Worship" in *The Book of Common Prayer* as observed by Episcopalians. Pettey J.'s ancestors lived in that faith long before their descendant swaggered withdrawn from it; and there were two or three such little books about the house. Yet Sidney found herself irked by a direction in tiny italicized type: *Here is to be noted, that the Office ensuing is not to be used for any that die unbaptized.*

What's it to them if Tickle was not baptized? At least she was *immersed.* Grievously. Then may we not read liturgy for her?

Sidney quoted to the listeners, *I am the resurrection and the life, saith the Lord: he that believeth in me, though he were dead, yet shall he live: and whosoever liveth and believeth in me shall never die.* At the other end of that grove the molested ivory-bill took wing and went swooping into thicker adjacent timberland, bluejays following, their harsh voices becoming almost smooth as distance polished off the sour angry edging of their screams. Here in the cemetery people swayed, closing their eyes and humming in rhapsody of bereavement. Sarah, the mother of Tickle, crouched with her head drooping forward. Sometimes she would lean far over and rub her forehead on scant grass and leaves, then someone would pull her back, haul her into sitting position once more.

Coot, husband and father, was nowhere in sight. He'd remained at home in the family cabin. Everyone knew the story by this time: during the night some member of the Holy Family

164

or Holy Trinity had appeared unto Coot and informed him that Tickle would be brought back, rejuvenated, resplendent. Child come alive, yeh, yeh. Lord put spark in her again!

At earlier funerals Sidney'd contrived her own offering for graveside use. Little readings from the Psalms, verse here, verse there. Why not?—what was done by clerics long ago when they built the prayer book? They derived from the book of Timothy and the book of Job in the same breath.

So may we be comforted by fragment Psalms.

I cried unto the Lord with my voice and he heard me out of his holy hill.

I laid me down and slept; I awaked; for the Lord sustained me.

I will both lay me down in peace, and sleep: for thou, Lord, only makest me dwell in safety.

Who shall ascend into the hill of the Lord? or who shall stand in his holy place?

He that hath clean hands and a pure heart.

Interruption. Coot ran rapidly from the quarters, sending his voice ahead of him, yelling, waving arms as he came, stopping now and then to turn in a circle as if seeking guidance; and then recollecting where the service was, and the people, and coming on over a slight ridge to the pines. A brother of his, Shepherd, stood among the hands; also a sister named Queenie. Brother and sister hastened to meet Coot and lead him among the mourners. The field hands were torn by curiosity. Some wished to venture to greet Coot and learn what ailed him, learn what he had seen or heard. Others, more docile, obeyed the injunction which their mistress had put upon them only a second or two before Coot came capering and emitting cries: *Let us pray in silence.*

Coot howled that he had just seen his daughter Tickle and she was transfigured. But no—she would not be poured back into her body to play about the plantation once more, running with packs of children. The Lord had dressed her in fine raiment, and Coot witnessed Tickle wearing gold and silver, everything shining.

165

Angels done took her away, done brung her back! Child had *wings!* Dress in gold and silver. Wasn't nothing bad could get her.

No devils get her.

No, no, no.

No spirits get her.

No, no, no.

Many began to weave, stamp, clap their hands. Even Basil (house servant all his life, and scorning field negroes for the most part) was nerved to begin singing. He acted as chorister at any Divine service. Sidney considered those obdurate whites who still resented the notion of music mingling in worship, and mentally she turned up her nose at them. O freshness, eagerness, complete surrender in the grief of these creatures. She wished that such ardent raw potion might be swallowed by her own kind.

But it is not contrived for us to take, cannot be stirred and strained and administered. One has to be—

Born to it, she murmured, and started toward the Big House. Soon she discovered that Beauty Beast followed a few steps behind, much as a trained footman might have done.

Among trees pestering of bluejays could be heard no longer. Only song arising, old Basil's utterance soaring clearly to line the song.

> Peter say to me—
> Why you no pray?

They roared back, some bellowing, some making a kind of chitter with their voices (mostly these were female voices). Ring and swing of tone, as if they danced to a melody intended to be wept.

> Oh, long time, long time,
> Long time weary.
> Mighty hard to pray.

Sidney halted to watch and listen. Beauty Beast remained at a discreet distance, but still as if he attended her. Other house

166

servants drifted behind—India, for instance, and another maid
or two— Sidney did not notice just who they were. When they
saw the mistress stop to turn and take note, they did so as well.

> Saul, he say to me—
> Why you no pray?

Mutter of deep hot hollow midday thunder, the horizon
shook with it. Mr. Irons would appear presently to say (as it
were personal aggravation offered by Sidney, as she had been
keeping rain back from him) : Ma'am, I tell you this. If we
don't get rain them small bolls are all going to go short. Won't
grow, won't open at all. The new fruit coming on, I mean. If we
don't get rain—

She shook her shoulders impatiently to rid herself of a nuisance, a Mr. Irons who clung and bothered her. Singing rose
untamed, more disconsolate, more punctuated by wails and
yelping with each fresh-sung verse.

> Mighty hard to pray.
> Oh, dear Jesus, Jesus,
> Long time weary.
> Mighty hard to pray.

On impulse, when Sidney neared the Big House back door,
she turned and spoke to Beauty Beast, called his name. He came
in courtesy, donning an invisible coat as he approached, costume of the servitor.

She said (no others close enough to hear) , Their music. The
spontaneous quality of it. Is there not a strange rapt wonder?

Misty, a primitive thing. Entirely too primitive. One might
say even— The outcry of *cannibals*. I want none of it.

The mistress spoke in reproof (other servants advancing the
while) . I do not think you felt that way when you yourself were
reciting, as of last night. When you played the Prelude in E-Flat
Major, composing your own ritual. The things you said about
little Tickle. *Poor girl in— In bright clean water.* Phrases of
that sort. It had the same rare worship, and wailing. Yet a

bright splintery tune underneath. It was immediately before you played the C Minor, which is nigh to being a funeral march.

Beauty Beast replied, snapping the words, That was the nigger in me, coming out. Rudely, without waiting to be dismissed, he dived into the kitchen, plunging on to his own room beyond. Door was slammed.

The notion of all Africa prevailed, and possessed her, and struck like a blow or mud-ball spattering (as thrown in a fight. Countless times she had seen them do it: the children on the place warred with mud-balls; and some of them, plumper ones, looked like mud-balls). What she saw was Africa as she knew it or rather knew about it, or tried to conceive from what she had read. There were books of exploration, especially the one by Mungo Park. Sidney was aware that she understood Africa sketchily, but that lack was a fault also with the rest of the world. Her imagination might supply and fill the interstices.

In illusion she watched outlandish tribes lifting from the jungle, laden with clubs and claws and white ash-marks and paint-marks and chalk-marks to make them appear skeletal; and bones were piercing their noses, and trade wire hanging from their ears, and adorning arms or wrapping necks. They were grisly as vultures, and stank of feral musk. Whites of their eyes were oh so white, lips were oh so full and blobbered. They uttered the coarse African words—Geechee words, Gullah words, words spewed by Susu and Ashanti. They came adorned and unadorned alike, came naked and shiny as reeds.

So often she'd watched Goosey, and later watched Beauty Beast, slitting the dead firm carcass of fresh-netted mullet. When the guts were pulled loose, what a sheen lay like silk across flesh and ribs in the body cavity.

You get rid all that black, Goosey had said, or it bitter up your mouth when you eat. So she'd scrape until the black was gone (but still it was recalled as black, it was shiny, it was silk, was so black).

Terrors arose from mire and out of Niger and Congo and

such wet places. Terrors came with hyenas, Terrors fought and hooted at each other, threw spears, wielded knives or slings, they bludgeoned and gouged and slit. There were many dead who were eaten. They cooked them in pots, huge pots, and the pots were black, and cannibals danced in their cooking. But those who were conquered and not dead were sold for slaves. Then the dealers marshalled them on to the oceanside, they had them chained in inevitable coffles. They put them into barracoons or whatever they were called—places where slaves were kept and scouted out by traders who touched that coast in ships. The Africa which they were leaving oozed and groaned in the dark.

They would not be leaving all of it, they would be fetching some of it along.

Much they would be abandoning: lion and tusk, the big growl as made through a nose, haunting horse-wail of a beast, a beast— Was it elephant or camel? (Sidney'd seen them and heard them grunting or making snort sounds in menageries abroad.) So that was what they were relinquishing: a society of zebras galloping in stripes, and crocodiles which slid and grabbed and snatched with their immense mouths, carrying off swimmers or victims who'd tumbled in and had no fortune: infants, and women who were washing clothes. Clothes? Ah, they *had* no clothes. But women who were down by the dusky water—washing, washing something— And crocodiles snagged them and carried them off. And it was peculiar about crocodiles: the same offense one found in gators. That was their storage of food, the way they let it rot until they were ready to feed. They'd bury it, put it deep and let it spoil, and then come smelling, to reveal the corpse, and then they'd feed.

That was the crocodile of it.

Following the pattern of crocodiles, that would be the Africa of it.

Good thing for the blacks' sake that we've got the gators here. Make them feel at home.

But there was still the flaunting Africa they had left, marked by head-dresses of Moors who'd sold them—garnished with flapping insects and eerie birds, and mighty apes who hammered their breasts in the mountains (twas said) and carried off women, and abused them lustfully (twas said).

Tell me, O apes. Did ever you visit Venice?

And were you buying glass?

There ran ostriches supposedly, and that immense slobbery pig in the water: the hippo. Hippos' mouths could swallow boats—whole canoes filled with natives would be welcomed between wide red-and-white jaws, and— Hey! The screams would resound.

There was the dromedary, she thought, and certainly there roved panthers and leopards without number. And again the apes, ones with scrolled blue faces and raw hindquarters, and again miniature monkeys swinging by their tails, and once more black children—it seemed that they were swinging by their tails as well. The whole place was a quagmire and it smelt of sweat, smelt of grease and pitch, smelt of skunk oil perhaps. Fluid was there, and ebon gleam, and thick darkness, the grunt again. And jabber, coarse word, ugly-sounding word, the Simian word.

And mud in the marsh.

With iced-purple butterflies a-flitting.

And then slavers, evil ships (let us genuflect before Calvin Tensley and his kind). The vessels blown along from Africa and Cape Verde Islands, and all the way to America and American islands which were not so monstrous and muddy and thorny, not so crowded with jackals (Mungo Park said they were wolves) and drums and dancing, and not so overflown with birds with gaudy feathers; and with no lion sound or flourish of a rubbery trunk.

What of tigers?

No tigers.

She did own three males named Tige: Old Tige and Little Tige, and just plain Tige.

In her room Sidney thought, It is requisite that I forget Africa directly. And Africans. Forget the nigger in Beauty Beast a-coming out. I'll go to ride, ride headlong.

Sly voices inquiring, What is distinct within your life, Fair Lady? Tell us now.

This Shallop woman. What owns she? Beauty? Some have so designated. Cultural attainments? Obviously (so zealous was she in their acquisition). Her ways of walking and speaking, her pistol shooting and fierce riding? They say her husband was something of a fine horseman as well, but rambunctious. Well, so is she.

They say, they say.

Why, burn them all. I sold off that Watson horse after Pettey J. died. But Cinna is almost as hard-mouthed as Watson ever was, and completely unpredictable. And I have not been mounted on Cinna since early this week, nor have I ridden any other horse.

What has come over you, Mad Equestrienne?

Take this uncurbed riding. Could it be that in your life such sport has served merely as substitute for an entirely different preoccupation? Perhaps one more comely in your sex and breed?

Sidney ordered that Cinna be saddled and brought round. She told Linnet to lay out her riding habit, but early afternoon was far too warm for a jacket. Sidney donned the dark-green skirt and a high-collared pleated blouse (German women were wearing such, years before, when she rode with Pettey J. along bridle paths adjacent to the Black Forest). She found the gloves she wanted, caught up the loop on her skirt, walked below stairs heavy in boots; and found Cinna stamping and angry-eyed because he'd been made to wait. The stable boy aided her to mount; but while she was adjusting her knees over side-saddle crutches, fumbling still with skirt and all, there sounded the remote clinking of silverware on glass, on china. Sidney did not turn. A sidewise glance showed that Beauty Beast had walked into the roofed passage between kitchen and Big House, and was bearing a luncheon tray. He halted indecisively. Sidney gave him no heed, she swung toward the rear gate. Off now. Down the lane beside Divide Field she went at a gallop.

171

So the nigger in him is coming out, is it?
None of my people shall dare a discourtesy.
Let him fret.

Lane narrowed into wood road, and then dissolved and lost itself in forest toward the northwest. This was called the Big Woods, where gangs cut firewood against winter and stacked the logs to be hauled. Cinna was in a shying mood: his rider found difficulty in guiding him wherever piles of cut timber loomed. He capered, stiffened his ears, regarded the stacks as enemies. Sidney patted, petted, assured him that there was nothing to the woodpiles, they were benign. Cinna snorted, shook his head, refused to believe. At last she headed him along a path bisecting this triangular tip of forest, and then went into a public highway. The road was well maintained, Sidney was able to let her horse out. She pushed him recklessly until Cinna's energies were abated and he was willing to loaf. She turned back then, entered the Big Woods by a different path.

Creek margin here, mats of satin mud caked and shiny and split into curling sections; but still a handsome clump of pickerel-weed blooming purple. *What's this, what's—?* Horse springing up and out, twisting his rear like a fox-squirrel, whinny rising to a shriek. *I see it even as I'm pelted into the air: a turtle, big one, call them gator snappers, gator turtles—*

As always when being thrown, she heard the sputtering syllables of a German word, one drilled into her by a ferocious old riding master. *Körperentspannung.* Body relaxation. Sidney managed to loosen her joints before she struck the ground.

For a few minutes she lay dazed. Then she was able to sit up and make faces, even though no one stood nigh to see them. She found herself bruised and shaken, but not seriously injured. Her fall had been cushioned by sand, reeds, the mud platters. That scaly turtle was nowhere in sight, neither was Cinna. Other mounts at Apoxsee might have stood after recovering from first fright, but he practiced no such civility. Untied, with no one up, he always raced for home.

Sidney followed on foot, and at the next branch she managed to wash her face, and giggle to observe the sordid state of her attire. She tramped away past oaks in the general direction of Divide Field, glad not to be lying with broken bones.

There sounded rapid patter of galloping. Beauty Beast, bareback on Cinna, charged from the lane beyond. Sidney hooed; he came bobbing toward her and dropped to the ground.

Misty. Are you hurt?

Sweat stands out on his face like jewels, small stones, pale wet topazes, and his eyes glow with concern— Ah, sublimely sweet, he feared I must be hurt or—

If it was nigger in him coming out, before, then now appears gentility and all the doughtiness and sympathy which any gentleman might show.

Bless the critter.

Cinna shied at an enormous turtle, and off I went, and off he went! I was merely a mite shook up, as Mr. Irons says.

Beauty Beast, she warned, do you tie Cinna or he'll put for home again.

He knotted the reins around a sapling. Oh, Misty, we've been alarmed. I heard Coony yelp, so rushed out of the kitchen. There was this horse, with saddle slipped down, and dirt— I sent a boy to tell Mr. Irons that he'd best come searching. Then I pulled off your saddle and hopped up bareback.

You bestride like an Indian. You've ridden often without saddle?

Long ago, Misty, at Shearwater. When abroad with— We used military saddles. Twas his preference.

Explosively. My dear mistress, you had not ordered your luncheon. But I did put together a tray, for it was growing late. When I came out I saw you mounting. You rode away.

Sidney examined the ground and crushed a tiny slab of cactus with her boot-toe. Said, I was indignant because of your rude behavior.

She was surprised to look up and see that he blinked back tears.

I do apologize, Misty. Deeply, from my heart of hearts. Should you like me to— Kneel, and beg pardon once more?

Twould be unnecessary, if symbolic. The fact remains that you are my property.

One tear crawled the smooth gold cheek, he brushed it away. I rode in great dread. Didn't wish you to be hurt.

Big Woods became enriched by his words. Previously glades stretched tasteless, dried and wounded, not enough rain, thickets aloof and worrying about fire. Instantly they had blossomed in an out-of-season spring. Sidney imagined more birds than there were truly; and small animals flirted, there might even be a Robin Goodfellow posturing. Clumps of stiff cactus had turned succulent.

I must go seek some dewdrops here.

The error should be charged to me, she told him. It was I who permitted the distortion of normal relationship between lady and servant.

It gnaws, Misty. Eats.

I can believe.

Last night when I—leaped up—

She gazed at him steadily. It must be hell.

Beauty Beast bowed his head. Nigger hell. Deep with sulphur, no doubt. And— Hotter? He lifted his face and tried to smile.

Sidney cried in hurt, Please to remember that I did not originate the institution of human slavery.

But you would buy me.

More gently. Are you sorry?

Ah, I'm pleasured to have music again. Grateful for many things. But, had I been bought by someone else, I should not have raked forth the details of my peculiar life. So doing, I was burned. Like reaching into a fire, drawing out pink coals with bare hands.

Misty. In change of tone. I hear horses approaching. The overseer—

He's meticulous, and in likelihood is bringing a led horse and my saddle as well. Do you give Mr. Irons a halloo.

174

Beauty Beast sent a cry keening off through mosses, needles, oaks, pines. Woodpeckers and other birds were disturbed by it, they flew. Old plantation cry, imitative of horn or conch-shell blown. To build such sound a man pushed his mouth out in a protruding cone, lips squeezed. He puffed as on an instrument, long as his breath would let him. The wail was high, protracted, *sostenuto*. Twas related to ragged fields, coons in hollow trees, coons stealing corn; related to dim hounds hollering in swamps where people never went at night. This was a call which could be spelt upon a page. It read as *Whooooo*, a single blowing tone. When you heard it you recognized a yell which plantation men might carry into battle, were they to go. It had been bayed by ancestral warriors in other centuries, and might still be soughed in perilous years to come.

Labors to be performed in this afternoon, every requirement put upon Beauty Beast, quaint domestic challenges assailing the hostess. Funereal breezes could blow sad or contrary across the hedge, but here was to be celebrated the first Apoxsee dinner party since Pettey J. died. Sidney had entertained her neighbors the Wilkeys on a few occasions, that was all. Now were to come the Wilkeys again, with their daughter Eleanor; also the Reverend Mr. Fortunatus Stephens and his young Yankee wife.

Pleasantry arose from the fact that Senator Ledge sent out a note, requesting his own inclusion.

Mrs. Ledge having gone to visit her brother's family at Pensacola, I am solitary, and should like nothing better than to hand the young Reverend and his Mrs. into my carriage (they have none) and dine at Apoxsee, on Saturday next, along with them. Child, these elder orbs are eager to observe you. It has been a while, so pray grant indulgence to my whim. I shall consider that I am in favor if no reply is forthcoming, and promise to award you a nosegay. Ever thy retainer and friend, not to say Uncle, F.L.

Shepherding of house servants, setting each wench to her task, being shrewd and observant, saying, No, no, these candles must be replaced. No, no, the *couverts*— Wrongly set— You pay strict

175

heed whilst I arrange this once again. You heed me, India: watch with care. Spoons *so,* forks *here.* And glasses ordered *so.* Turned *up,* not down.

What of the crabs, Beauty Beast? Did Flash and Eddie fetch them, and in sufficient quantity?

Misty, they are fine fat fellows, not large enough to be coarse-grained. I'm keeping out two for you—they've freshly lost their shells. You might wish to breakfast on those, come morning.

Thank you for the pampering. But your receipt for serving crab salad this evening—?

My dressing is fresh-made. I've set Coony to picking out the flesh. He's to include no bits of shell, under most severe penalties. Do not be alarmed, Misty. I'll examine the picked-out meat with care.

Senator Ledge owns a parlormaid who has a way with flowers. His nosegay offered to the hostess (packed carefully in a leather hat-box for safety's sake) turns out to be a Colonial bouquet composed chiefly of periwinkles, plucked-off geranium blossoms separated into tininess, white wildflowers unnamed. Sidney suspects that the starched lace edging had its inception in a handkerchief plundered ruthlessly from the kerchief-box of Mrs. Fenton Ledge. Wicked glee in the notion.

It is gay beyond description. How gracious of you.

Ledge's face is lined with smile and patience. I followed you into this hallway purposely, for the briefest of words. Eleven days ago I would have counted you as seeming weary. Now you're blooming.

Only pleasured at the notion of having you to Apoxsee once again, dear Senator.

Child, you are the talk of the town.

That was to be expected. I've already been censured as a mannish and extravagant hussy.

Perhaps not mannish. But with a deplorable fondness for firearms and such. Did you know?—you paid five thousand dollars—or six, some say—for a near-white cook. The *near-white* is emphasized.

Mrs. Shallop feels her face a-growing warm, but she can smile. I take it, then, that the minister's new wife has— The ability to repeat idle gossip? Tis eminent among her churchly virtues?

Child, I'll return to the parlor. I informed the Reverend and his Mrs. that I should retreat with you for a few words on some legal matter. But here come the Wilkeys in their buggy, and you must hasten to receive them.

As Sidney turns toward the gallery door, he adds in the barest whisper, Employ caution when you converse with Mrs. Stephens. I'd consider her a scratch-cat.

Potage à la Bisque
Petits Soufflés de Poisson
Jambon en Croute
Pintade Farcie
Purée de Pommes de Terre   Carottes à la Crème
Salade de Crabes
Compote de Melon
Sablés Fondant
Café Noir

Keys not turned in locks for oh so long, and thus the mechanism of the locks is stiff with rust, twas hard to turn the keys. But when our treasure was lugged forth, and all the spider-webs rubbed off: a prize Chablis, claret from the Bordeaux region, the '47 port, the Pommery. A choice of rum or brandy for the men. Cigars from Pettey J.'s cabinet—first time that any raid's been made. And mildew formed upon cigars; I said they must be thrown out; Beauty Beast was laughing (threw back his head and closed his eyes).

Still gone to Texas, Joel? Or gone— Farther?

Misty, a connoisseur of cigars would shudder to hear of such suggested vandalism! But look, the slight deposit here— It signifies the *ne plus ultra*. But see these tiny holes, they're made by very special worms! Connoisseurs would sit and fairly drool with satisfaction, even though they had to put their fingers over the holes.

He chuckles more and tells Sidney, As they were playing piccolos.

The hostess's right hip informed her that she'd endured a fall, so did her elbow and shoulder. A bruise was displaying itself along her right cheekbone, enough so that sharp-eyed Mrs. Wilkey inquired about it while they freshened themselves above stairs after the dinner. These were minor woundings, counting for naught. Sidney had Linnet seek a certain vase and bring it, water-filled, to the bedside table where her bouquet might revive. She looked at it in comfort.

There sits my heart. My heart is a shapely vase filled with tranquil flowers.

How can this be, when so often I have felt ferocity?

Tenderness is sweeping, and with it I anoint all within my range. Gratitude flavors my dominion.

There are secrets so deeply buried that they may not be told, may not even be tongued by one portion of the soul into the ear of another portion.

Once again I feel powerful and wise. In this I bask. But I shall not permit wisdom to become abrasive; and power shall be housed in the wrappings of gentility. Twill be power still.

For the three Wilkeys she felt love without admiration, defensive love mingled with sadness. The parents were simple souls, respectively boyish and girlish despite cottony white hair which puffed in curls on their heads, and made out that they masqueraded as brother and sister instead of being husband and wife. They were not aware of much evil in the world, but what they recognized puzzled and hurt them, and sometimes annoyed the woman, who had more pepper than did her spouse.

As for Daughter Nell: the only bounty which one might offer her would be distilled pity, and the desire to wield a good fairy's wand and make over the little spinster's face. Her dark-blue eyes were sunken and tragic, her mouth a twisted mass of fangs grown every which way. Since a child Eleanor Wilkey had attempted to keep her lips drawn to cover ugliness; such distortion of her mouth resulted in deep lines, visible strains and tensions leading into the lips themselves. Besides the mere fact of a physical blemish to which she could make no adjustment, the more profound misery was that she'd gone unsought year after year. Few men had attempted to court Nell. A sickly widower with several children; a handicapped youth from an old and well-to-do family (but he flopped his hands when he walked, and held his head on one side); a handsome cruel young doctor, lately come to town, whose reputation for malpractice caught up with him (eventually he was shot down in the street by the husband of a woman who'd died under his knife). To such rag-tag-and-bob-tail the senior Wilkeys offered scant courtesy and no encouragement.

Once Sidney Shallop had been shown into the Yaupon house at an unusual hour and on an unexpected visit, to hear Eleanor shrieking above stairs.

Oh, oh, if you'd only let me have em all pulled—pulled out of my jaws! *All* of em. Then I could have *false* teeth, oh-ho.

Stop it, Miss! her mother was chiding. I say *stop* it! False teeth are of no worth whatsoever. Look at Aunt Annie Jay. Nothing but misery all day long, with hers. And all night too, I vow.

But if I could get rid of the dang things whilst I'm still young enough to have a *chance,* oh, oh. I could live on milk, I tell you. *Milk.* Wouldn't need *teeth,* oh, ho, ho—

Maid's voice, giving news that Sidney had come. A door slammed, hysteria was subdued or escorted away. Mrs. Wilkey came down red-eyed to greet her guest and say, Daughter Nell hasn't felt very peart of late.

Thus to my neighbors: affection, the warmest to be mustered.

Thus to the Reverend Mr. Stephens: a gift of tolerance, which might not be alive for me to offer it in other season or on another evening. His bland pink infant's face, his smug tone! So must be his spirit. But perhaps there are values which he can offer nevertheless?

Newspapers have been concerned with the Dred Scott business once more, and folks are bound to speak of it. These court decisions, says the Reverend, must reflect the honest consciences of those who make the decisions. Are they not worthy men? How else might they be projected into such position?

Senator Ledge ventures cautiously, I suppose we have all seen unworthy men projected into positions of trust.

(He and Mr. Wilkey begin mentioning openly such of the judiciary as they've known who won to the Bench without being properly equipped in conscience *or* intelligence.)

Ah, our Reverend Stephens believes that perpetually he is delivering a Sermon on the Mount! Every audience, however small, becomes a multitude. But—

Tolerance, Mrs. Shallop, tolerance.

We must remember the very rudiments of our teaching, both in the Presbytery and out of it. Are we not told that God alone is Lord of the conscience? Conscience is believed to have been left free from the doctrines and commandments of mere men. At least those which are in any thing contrary to God's word. We should quote: *So that to believe such doctrines, or to obey such commandments out of conscience, is to betray true liberty of conscience.* Or, in the words of Paul: *For do I now persuade men, or God? or do I seek to please men? for if I yet pleased men, I should not be the servant of Christ.*

Senator Ledge winks openly at Basil, and the old servant comes to fill up his glass.

Mr. Wilkey's glass as well, warns Mrs. Shallop in undertone.

Senator, asks Bonaparte Wilkey, was it the Federal Circuit Court which ruled that Scott remain a slave, out there in Missouri?

That little drama, sir, was played first in the Missouri *State* courts. I think it began some five or six years since; but Scott— or rather, his Abolitionist lawyers—eventually carried the case to the State Supreme Court.

Now, I declare, says Mrs. Wilkey. What a thing to do.

And Daughter Nell mumbles through the awful cutlery within her mouth, Why, I declare as well. Those Abolitionists— They'd just like to ruin us.

Hush, says The Foot which promptly kicks Nell's own foot beneath table. Do you not know that Mrs. Stephens comes from Maine?

So then, the Court's decision was—

The judge ruled that Dred Scott had legally reassumed his condition of slavery, on returning or being returned into Missouri. But enough of the Scott matter, says Senator Ledge in a ruling of his own. Twould be more appropriate to discuss another gentleman of color, one who is not bent upon making noises in the courts. I refer to Beauty Beast, the new cook acquired by our lovely hostess. It is he who has prepared this feast. We shall alter the name of Apoxsee to Olympus forthwith. I never felt more like a god.

Hear, hear! cries Mr. Wilkey.

Sidney, lamb, says his wife, I've eaten crabs for most of my born days. But, tell you now, I never tasted crab like this before.

Sidney explains, Tis prepared with Beauty Beast's own sauce, one newly used in France. He calls it mayonnaise.

Mayonnaise? they wonder. And Mrs. Wilkey adds, I never heard the beat.

The counterpane of my benevolence is wide and fair. Also elastic. It can be pulled and stretched like knit-goods to cover anything, to cover even Mrs. Stephens. Her *eyes*. No leniency about them, they're hard and green, she sits up nights a-polishing them. Her pronouncements are short and to the point, or so she must think. Says to herself, each time she's spoken: There, that's that. Settles everything.

But I dare not despise her, not this night. Too many jewelries do I own. Possibly I'm addled by them, and thus made munificent?

Mrs. Stephens pries, pokes, she peeks about. Went snooping round my chamber when she and Eleanor were there. Oh, Daughter Nell is loyal to me, and managed to get my ear before the menfolks even left the dining room.

Land sakes, Nell said (upstairs). Where on earth did that darkey learn to do such cooking?

Ought to be good, says Mrs. Stephens. She paid enough for him.

I don't know what Mrs. Shallop paid, says Nell. But no

matter what it was, he's worth it. We hold our own cook, Dolly, to be right fine. But—

Folks say Mrs. Shallop's cook is almost white, says Mrs. Stephens. Have you seen him?

Yes indeed. He came to Yaupon. Dolly gave him spices and artichokes and such. He's fine-figured, seeming very bright. He's gifted musically—plays the piano mighty well. We're to hear him play tonight.

Heh, says Mrs. Stephens. I couldn't live alone like this. What's she thinking of? Aren't there any ladies in her family, to keep her company? Maybe an aunt or cousin? So he's almost white. Heh.

Buggy and carriage went away under drooping plumes of moss. Goodnights coming back to the hostess in their variety of voices; and she stood waving on the gallery, waving at receding jolting lanterns of the vehicles, waving at hoof sounds, wheel sounds, but hearing louder and in wealthier reward the strings touched by hammers.

It persists. As if he were playing still.

Beauty Beast walked from back regions. Lingering at the foot of her stairway, Sidney heard the piano lid put down. She called, and quickly he came out on the gallery.

Misty?

I wish to thank you, Beauty Beast.

How can you, Misty? I felt such shame when flummoxing that minuet.

The guests were lyrical in their praise.

He stood like a soldier at attention, hands at his sides, light from the front parlor blending in pale colors on the sprigged shirt.

How does it feel, she asked, to be able to feed both body *and* soul, as you do? I believed during the last half-hour that my name was Esterházy and I owned a Haydn. But after all you've done, you must be exhausted. Sunday shall be an unsullied holiday for you.

He said, On Sunday as on any other day, Misty, you must be fed. So must the house servants.

Pother. We'll all piece out, on tonight's leavings. There's the ham-in-crust—

Misty, that's what I'd planned to offer. Except, of course, for the two soft crabs. You are to have those at breakfast.

He told her that the wench Clemmy was fast asleep on the rear stoop, and might not he douse the lights in Clemmy's stead?

Of course. Nor shall I call Linnet, but put myself to bed. Goodnight, Beauty Beast.

Goodnight, dear mistress. Rest well.

I shall, she told him. Thanks to you.

He bowed, he went away to snuff candles, blow out lamps. Sidney climbed the stair lamely, she'd been up and down so many times. But very soon she was asleep and dreaming vividly.

Through a transcendent existence she trotted from room to room, hunting for a certain book. (Actually there were jam-packed bookcases in nearly every room of the Big House: elder Shallops had been bookish people, but not Pettey J.—he'd acquired only a superficial store of classical quotations which he could brandish at will, and thus delude strangers into thinking him erudite.) In the downstairs northeast room—this was called the library because it had more bookshelves than the others, and also it was called the House Office—Sidney found a thin volume with calfskin spine and marbled covers. It bore a crest, and was entitled *The Bracket Family*.

At last, she heard herself saying, I've found it. Searched so many other times, in vain.

For apparent decades she studied the history, salting it in memory, it must never be lost. Henri de Braguette had been a Crusader, Louis a favorite of Charles VII the Victorious; another Henri had died fighting under Coligny; and his Huguenot son fled to England, where the name was duly Anglicized. Two Brackets came to America with Oglethorpe, and one was with him in the abortive expedition against St. Augustine. Their progeny went on to become generals and jurists. Leonidas Bracket, father of Pericles, served brilliantly in the Revolution, and became an intimate of John Marshall. Pericles Bracket was born in 1786—

Say, to a dozen mantles.

Beauty Beast Bracket, his son.

How the line glitters!

But please to remember that Mrs. Vile Horrid Dowson, who considers me no lady— (*why?* in pain) — Mrs. Dowson is in actuality a *niece* of Beauty Beast.

Half-niece.

Everything is whirling. Away, away—

Let me ride, and be thrown.

Ouch. In mud and weeds.

During her last furtive clutch on slumber and on illusion, Sidney reasoned that perhaps she should call him Beebee as the boys at Mr. Drummond's school in Washington had done. She awakened to the sound of heavy thunder, but no rain fell as yet, and she returned to sleep. This time she dreamed of her nephew.

9

JOEL came to Willowhurst again on the Sunday following his first visit, and twice afterward he walked that way of evenings. Chill weather descended, the fireplace became a felicity. Joel brought along a bag of chinquapins the first evening, a bag of Northern chestnuts the second. These he and Sidney roasted on a shovel with flurry and bustling, they screamed when precious nuts fell off and were lost to the blaze. Sidney baked gingerbread men, whole rows of them holding hands. She discovered a receipt for Turkish coffee, they tried that, didn't like it, made exaggerated gestures of repugnance. Maury the hound came seeking scraps which Sidney kept for him, and he went to sleep across Joel's boot.

Well, read on, Aunt Sid.

We're come to Act Five. Scene One. This is before the cell of Prospero.

> And you whose pastime
> Is to make midnight mushrooms, that rejoice
> To hear the solemn curfew—

Scuse, Aunt Sid. But that's the *limit*. Mushrooms *couldn't* hear any curfew.

Hush, and do not interrupt. The entire play is concerned with magic, is it not?

Reckon so. But between Prospero and Caliban and Ariel, there's maybe *too much* magic—

This play fretted him. Sidney had read some scenes from *Julius Caesar* at another time, and Joel said flatly that *Caesar* was more to his taste. But he pricked up his ears when Ferdinand and Miranda were discovered playing chess.

You play chess, Aunt Sid?

No, I've never learned. No one played at home. Nor did my late husband. He—didn't play at anything.

Mr. Grempel taught me. We spent many an evening at chess, before he took sick. You'd enjoy it or I miss my guess.

Then I'll order a board, and chess-men, and you'll teach me.

That'd be the ticket, he said with enthusiasm.

The only heartbreak came when Joel said, Late. Got to go, and went away from her, hat pulled down against the night's wind, muffler wound tight, gripping her small hand in his bony paw when he spoke the farewell; and he'd look back through milky mist and moonlight, calling again before his feet struck loud upon the bridge, but going away from her just the same; very tall figure now claimed by shadows, striding off; and she fancied that he took along the string by which she kept him attached, and that string uncoiled within her (tight-wound upon a kind of reel or bobbin) and ran out farther with every stride; but the string was there, was there, and so the two of them were fastened together no matter how far he went or might still go.

Mrs. Tensley. Respected Aunt, I send a nigger boy to carry this Sunday message to you, trusting that your in good health and spiruts. We are here rushed to deth, and there have been complikashuns all week. Mrs. Hendry, wife of my employer, has been ailing pretty bad. Mr. Hendry therefor has been much conserned with his wife, and scarse able to give the business attentshun it needs. An ill wind, however, etcet, because some good has been blown my way through his misfortun. This week it was nessary that two bids be made in our capasity as chandlers, regarding two diffrent vessels, and Mr. Hendry said, This

must be in your hands. There is no one else, Joel. I set up the
most of three nights, going over my figures, but made the orders
complete from stock at hand, since there was the elument of
time to be consider. Mr. Hendry, on examnashun, has said kind
words and awarded me an increas in my wage. Mrs. Lavinia
Hendry's cousin, who bears some reptashun as a nurse, was
expected to arrive last night from Fayetteville but has not yet
put in appearanc. Therefor it is impossible for me to come your
way on this day. This I regret, since I have been cozening myself
with dreams of pleasant Sunday spent in your company. When-
ever matters are straitened out and some degree of sanity
prevail hereabouts, I shall take the Blackwater Road once more
with alakrity. Advices from home are pretty poorly. We are
conserned with my father's health. He does not recover from his
indiskreshun as rapid as in years past. This should be warning
to all who persist in drinking to exsess. But you know the story,
so I shall not go further into the subjeck. Your affeckshunat
Nephew, Jo. Airhart.
P.S. Should the hungry hound appear, trust that you will
remember he has just been found gilty of forgry, and reward
him akordingly.
N.B. The last time was exseedingly pleasant. J.A.

There shone no visible sunrise on the day when Joel Airhart
arrived at Sidney's cottage for his final visit. Merely reluctant
lightening, a gradual change from utter blankness to the curling
gray-and-umber of low clouds. Wind chased in gusts, abated
slightly, twisted in another direction, dissolved to nothingness;
for minutes an uneasy quiet ruled the reaches of sycamore or
gum. Dead leaves, not desiring to be disturbed, pine needles not
wanting to blow— Yet all knowing that they might be twisted
and flung, the very branches grating against each other and
wailing when worst gusts came. Were it summer or the beginning of autumn, people would have thought in terms of hurricanes; but now a tropical storm staggered north in earliness of
winter. Shipping was certain to be pounded, some carelessly-
handled shipping might be capsized or shoved ashore. Rivers

and bays would swell a-plundering, signs and roofs fly, fences be swept down, trees crush across shingles.

Sidney had arisen briefly before light came, she roamed below stairs, unbolted the kitchen door, stood on the roofed rear piazza (she liked this place better than the stoop in front, because this was where she and Joel sat or stood and talked, the first day he came).

Fitful breezes. That's what they are termed: fitful. Odd word. Does it mean full of fits? Surely.

High above the uncertain march of winds which touched her terrain, Sidney was conscious of vast restlessness, a contortion at incredible heights. It called to mind old superstitions, myths of valkyries. *Saint Walpurgis, protect us.* No wonder ancient peoples believed that Furies went aloft on their sticks and rode howling.

Sidney was reawakened when Joel signalled her. *Gah um,* he called in muted falsetto, dragging out the vowel-sound and the M-sound, repeating it over and over. He'd explained that this was a selling cry off the Charleston streets, uttered by one of his favorite peddlers. She used to go by Mr. Grempel's place with a huge withed basket on her head. Sometimes she'd be holding to it with one hand—if it were extremely heavy and the way seemed crowded, and she felt uncertain, and thought she was about to lose it. But usually she'd be holding both hands before her mouth to make a trumpet, make her cry ring farther.

Gah um.

But, Joel— *Gah um?* I don't—

Twas her way of saying, *Got em.* Her way. And then, every now and again she'd sing out, *Fray fee.* Know what that was, Aunt Sid? *Fresh fish.* I could never make out whether it was her Gullah talk or some kind of other nigger talk or whatever. Or whether she was just plain tongue-tied. But her tone was most melodious—even old Mr. Grempel liked it. He used to laugh, and shake his head when he heard her, though he wasn't up to observing most things that went on beyond his bench.

Gah um had become Joel's signal whenever he drew nigh Willowhurst. Sheer joy, to hear him sending out this call while still down the road, before he'd even crossed the bridge. Had she owned a piano, Sidney would have sought the proper keys; had she a penny whistle she would have attempted to blow the notes in private. Truly it was In Private that they were called. Few people traveled that road, except for the drifting children, or old Aunt Sedalia limping there—talking to herself, fetching something in a basket, something to sell or give. *Gah um.* First note so high, second note lower, the M-sound a harp-string in vibration.

Joel's plaint reached through sleep and touched Sidney's ears as a lover's kiss could have touched her lips and brought her lingeringly awake. She sat up blinking, heard the cry again, asked if one of those tricking witches in the sky had ridden down to offer that cruelty of all cruelties—gift pretended, gift seemingly offered and then jerked back (as a boy twitches a wallet off the path with his string on All Fools Day).

Then she leaped awake, alive, oh yes, intently. Air was chill if blowing and damp; but Sidney scrambled fast from her warm bed and ran to the little window pressed by eaves, thrust her head up into dormer space, looked through panes, saw him walking. Twas he, Joel, Joel, once more he strode the Blackwater Road.

Sidney's preference was to sleep without a cap. But one look in her mirror— My hair, my *hair*. She found a cap, hoped it was her prettiest. Not this wrapper—another—gad, where can it be? (Whilst she sewed it, Mrs. Utt the seamstress prattled about the harlotry of Lolly Tripwood.) Ah, here, here upon *this* peg! And there's the high shriek of roadside gate in picket fence. You can hear it even with quick wind making a growl and pounding the shutters.

Joel came to the rear door naturally. *His favorite porch as well?* She met him there.

Forgive me for arriving at such an early hour, Aunt Sid. But we were working all night. Tying things down, getting gear in from the loading dock, making doors and hatches tight. Mr. Hendry's warehouse is kind of exposed, as you know.

He told her that this was a weather breeder for certain—the

whole town said so. Certain vessels had been moved up the river and others down toward the bay, according to individual masters' notions as to where best to ride out the storm. You'd think twas August or September, Joel said. But of course a December storm can blow mighty bad. I mind one time we lost our kitchen roof, at home, and all the window-lights busted out on one side of the house. As for water—

Sidney stood looking up at him in bliss; and then he realized that he still held her hand, the hand she'd given him in greeting. His face flushed slightly. He dropped her hand.

Joel said he'd planned to come later in the day. But Saturday evening was spent in putting together an order which had been promised and was necessarily hastened by weather conditions. Then all the dark hours inside and outside the warehouse— Sakes, he said. Realized I might as well set out. Desired to get with you before the storm struck, or likely I couldn't have made it along Blackwater.

Joel, I've a bed already prepared. Isn't that fortunate? In this little bedroom, downstairs— See, right in here. Now you go in, take off your things, and go *right to bed*.

Why, Aunt Sid—He yawned prodigiously, and they both burst out laughing. I'm not really sleepy yet. Later on— Well, maybe I can take a nap. Just lay down a while.

No, no, she wished he'd really go to bed. No, no, he wouldn't go. They kept a-fussing until Sidney ordered, You quicken the fire a trifle. I must run upstairs and make myself more presentable.

Long time a-dressing, no gown seemed right, nothing would do. Her *hair*. At last she bound it with blue ribbon. Her figured blue twill, blue slippers to wear with it. She crept down the narrow closed stairway, opened the door, peeked out, heard nothing. She went softly into the kitchen-living-room. Fire in the stove roared. Joel lay stretched on the old sofa, fast asleep, snoring with his mouth open. A sudden smother of wind outside, strongest gust yet. A wooden bucket was blown across the porch, it clattered and rolled. Sidney stood looking down at Joel. She experienced that almighty choking tenderness in which women hover above loved ones who are sleeping. Profundity, maternal realization.

He is in my charge. I must take care of him.

Tiptoe.

From a press in the front room she brought a knitted coverlet. Joel did not awaken when she spread it over him, but he turned his head and lay in innocent profile, no longer snoring, a baby Joel again.

Will he bawl for his chosen dress in the hamper?

Grown so long and firm and— Hard—

She turned away hastily, rescued the violent coffee-pot from splashings and scorchings, settled the grounds, poured a cupful.

Aye, refresh yourself. Then come see: shouldn't his coverlet be drawn a trifle higher? A cold draught is racing in under the door. But how neatly he removed his boots and placed them side by side! He'd not lie down upon your sofa with his boots on, not he. But, dearie me— That oily hair. Why was there no doily on the upper part of the sofa? What became of it? None there to begin with? I should have thought of Joel and his hair and macassar oil. Still, what matters a spot or two? He's here, he's come, he's back again. He worked through the whole night and then walked to be with me. He knew that I stood in need of him.

She was inclined to open the door in a paroxysm of gladness, and stand welcoming the storm, speaking Thank You, being intimate with its undirected force. Yet the way that loose rag rug was rolled back by currents of air—

Here's rain, the first. It's scouring the windows like sand thrown in spite, it snaps and pops and fairly sparkles. Welcome, welcome. But I dare not open the door: things would be whirled on high, the unlit lamp blown from its perch. Thankee nevertheless.

Pressure of daytime darkness, gale-induced darkness closing with its ordinarily baleful clutch. Why should this be? Natural darkness of night is an easy and needful thing. In any season we gratulate the kindly night. Welcomed in spring and early summer by chuck-will's-widows, welcomed in winter by the sound of voices in frosty air— Dog barking off somewhere, steam whistles sounding where there are modern men and modern steam and industry. But Mrs. Tensley's Darkness of This Early Morning is joy in its own right. Because all living things must feel a threat, and so withdraw, go into their burrows. Joel and I lie in our own burrow. Here at Willowhurst. Together.

Cook-stove flames burned lower, yet Sidney hesitated to go banging about with wood. She looked into the front room to remind herself that the fireplace was ready, fire laid neatly. Even to fat pine kindling, you could smell the pine. But no blaze until Joel was awake and in attendance, it would be a beacon flaring to warm and honor him. Racing air outside had turned cooler, the rain intensified. Sidney found her own black shawl hanging with a cape and a bonnet or two, next to the kitchen door. She wound the shawl around her, and went to sit close to Joel on a stool, discovering new qualities to admire in his face. She watched his breathing, watched the occasional flicker of an eyelid, motion of the mouth, she listened to the light sleeping sounds he made. She felt extreme pervasion, encompassing quality of her love for him.

I did not know, she told herself in excuse of apology.

Apology to whom? But apologizing still.

Did not know that it could be so. There is so much which I have never learned.

Must sit humble.

When fiddling with absurd conceptions of immaculate love— pageant of cupids, lambs, lilies, dairy-maids and the rest—she had never entertained the briefest straying notion that the more deeply and sincerely one loved, the wider went her range of thankfulness and thoughtfulness. She longed to contrive a charity which would benefit the entire world, and all in it, and all persons and birds and animals who'd lived in the world before, and who might live in the world in times which only the future could annunciate. She wished to pet (and be otherwise generous to) all living creatures, even noxious snakes. Who were those folk— Was it in far-off India? Those who would not step upon an insect, and must have the way swept clean ahead of them.

194

I couldn't kill a fly at this moment. Couldn't. Were I to hear a mouse squeaking in the trap now set, I'd scream with grief.

Where is Maury, why hasn't he come a-begging? He must need something to eat.

Sidney became possessive of the tempest's strengthening. She called it *her* storm, suffered the whimsy that perhaps some other storm (unaccounted, unseen) had blown Joel away from her and now this storm had blown him back. She scrutinized a big hand thrown loosely on top of the knitted yarn wrapping him, she frowned because one finger had been cut. But then bent even closer and gave thanks: the cut was healing nicely.

Ah, glad for the roof above her head. Roof over *both* their heads. Walls keeping out the wind. Thankful for fuel, thankful that there was food in the house. Nay, they'd never need go begging for their suppers, not if they were to take supper together for the rest of their natural lives. Or breakfast—

Breakfast? He'd wake up soon and be ravenous. What to offer him? Beefsteak? This was a season of fresh meat. Also she had sausage, newly chopped, Aunt Sedalia made the best.

Thankful for brain and body, thankful for whatever beauty I, Sidney Tensley, have been given.

(How soon, Lord, am I to share my bodily beauty with him, and take his amplitude for my own?)

I love the whole place, sweet gums, willows. Stream beyond the dooryard and fish swimming there. I love spring and fall and all seasons. Love my books. And so many more books to come, many to be read in the future! I shall never get to the end, but I love them. Beyond that there's much more, so much. I long for music, I've heard but scraps, I shall go where good great music may be listened to. *We* shall go. Somehow. And later there'll be laughter rolling which has never yet been heard. And no one can ever kill all the birds, and surely no one can ever spoil all the grass and viny thickets, or chop down all the trees. No one must ever drink all the water, or dirty that which isn't potable. And surely not all the springs will ever run dry.

May I not now fondle my own heart?

There'll come frost again, lightnings again, humanity will be the happier for it. (Perhaps not that immediate section of humanity who'll chill to death in frost, or who will be hit by lightning; or people left to mourn them. But even those shall be privileged to participate in intense adventure, from which there are bound to fall a few hurtings and woundings. And of course some will be slain—along the edges, as it were. But the adventure *was there*.)

I would do anything, anything. Offer, give, sow.

To and for the world. For everyone.

I love him so much that I would worship all things which live, and the God who made things live.

How silly can one be? How demented was I, to declare that there were witches riding up above? All the time twas only God, exercising Himself among loftiest winds.

Sidney sat for long, watching Joel, loving him, loving all else; and in fortune she realized that she was doing so.

All that brief dark day she worshipped the activity of nature which had drawn (and was maintaining) them together. How thin, she thought, the veneered shell holding weather away from Man! At lightning stroke or thunder-clap, Man cringes back into caves, eats raw meat, peers forth in awe at unruly stress which has rescinded his advancement.

She spoke to Joel hesitantly on this matter, and he said, Must be true. I've noticed that even animals get frightened. But he and Sidney were young enough to find lively agitation in what could be witnessed. They ran from one room to the next, peeking at rumpus beyond, hollering when rain sprayed in around window-frames. Sidney hunted out rags, scraps of rugs with which to sop up. The low kitchen roof sprung multiple leaks, water *tunk-tunk*ing in pans set beneath.

I'm so happy.

How come, Aunt Sid?

Because you're here.

Glad it didn't hit when I was halfway out from town!

196

Long at table.

Joel, let me help you to some more sausage.

Afraid I can't— Well, thanks. Just one more piece.

Another biscuit?

Well—

You finish the gravy, for I can't eat another bite.

Tell you, Aunt Sid. I'll divide that last spiced peach with you.

You shouldn't like me if I were *fat*.

Here now. You take *that* much. There. I'll take the rest. Everything's so good! We haven't been faring too well lately at the Hendrys'.

Isn't the cousin from Fayetteville—? Isn't she a good manager?

Excellent nurse, they say. But as for the household— Suke and Patchy, they just go slopping around the kitchen. Need to have a firm hand a-driving.

I know. When things are at sixes and at sevens, they're apt—

Breaking off suddenly. Joel, wouldn't it be nice if the chessmen and board had arrived? But Mr. Caddy feared it might be some weeks.

In vigor they were discovering their mutuality. I must tell you everything, you must tell me. There are so many trifling matters to relate— The bones of our lives are fleshed with the nondescript. But This I feel drawn to impart to you, and That you must impart to me. I remember, I remember, what do you remember?

Will you understand? You may not, because I'm older, and so much more has befallen me.

Will you understand? You may not, because you're female, I'm male.

Whether clinging before a window (windows on the south and east were plastered with leaves and husks) or hovering by the fireplace and seeing flames alternately sucked up the chimney by giants, or whipped into the room— They tattled on. Must tell you. What about this, what about that? Have you heard? Do you know? Did I ever tell you?

Man came into our place of business the other day and he'd

197

just brought a small vessel around from Texas by way of New Orleans, way of Havana, and then up here. Huge powerful fellow, name of Kemper. Taller'n I am, and about three times as broad. My, the things he had to say about Texas. It really got my fever up. Had half a notion to throw everything aside and put out for Texas.

I'm delighted that you didn't.

So am I, at the moment. Because I would have missed being here today. I'd miss lots of things, naturally, were I to go.

Would you miss me, Joel?

You more than— He said softly, More than anyone else, I guess, and Sidney closed her eyes momentarily in ecstasy at his mild declaration.

But, honest, I was steamed. Like the Henderson brothers' boiler, time the valve stuck and we thought she was going to bust. Texas must be prime. Twould be something to be part of the very newest State.

She said, Often I've dreamt of going to older countries.

I'd like to see those too.

You're so young, Joel. It's natural enough. Newness is a magnet. It shines, and pulls you.

Aw, you're not so much older than I am. Only seven years.

There are times when I feel very young, like yourself. And in other hours, looking back, age creeps and chills, even though I'm only in my twenties. Why, she exclaimed, I never said that to anyone else before, not in my life. Confessed to being *elderly*. What have you done to me?

Wind shouted, near at hand there was a sundering, groan and splash to make the cottage quiver. It's gone, they cried when they'd hustled outside and were wettened and pushed. An immense sycamore which had towered on the other side of the creek was down, shaggy head nodding. Blackwater lost identity as a stream, there lived instead a lake which rushed this way and that through bowing willows. Rails of the bridge, built of saplings with bark still on them, were all that could be seen, and waves ran through the rails. Soaked ropes of Sidney's swing trailed and lost themselves in currents.

198

Never expected this, said Joel. Two or three foot higher and it'll be in the house. We may have to leave.

I wouldn't think of it. If worse comes to worst, we'll put things up on top of tables, or carry them upstairs, or—

He stunned her by quoting, *The wills above be done! but I would fain die a dry death.*

Joel, you baffle me. I thought you didn't like *The Tempest.*

Just happened to recollect that shipwreck. I'm going to set a mark, then we can tell whether the water's going up or down.

He took a sharp yellow kindling from the woodpile, drove it into earth at the margin, then fled to join Sidney in the kitchen.

You're soaked, my boy. Here, take off your jacket and I'll dry it above the stove. What of your shirt?

No, that'll do, twill dry on me. I'll just put this scarf round my shoulders.

Joel—

He looked down questioningly.

You won't be able to go home tonight.

Black eyes flashed as he considered. Certainly not on the Blackwater Road—that'll be under water most of the way. I can walk up past your darkey woman's place, and take the Old Plank Road into town. It'd be several miles farther, but there's high ground all the way.

Do you think Mr. Hendry really needs you?

Clock ticking. Louder.

Can't say he really does. Everything that needed to be tied down was tied. Far as water's concerned, no floods ever got into his warehouse yet, not since twas built. Thank the Lord he's been able to take charge again, ever since Cousin Net arrived.

Came one of those visible changes in color and measurement of light, as one said, I'll make it dimmer for you, not by degrees, but now. An increase of darkness shall be visited this very second. I pass my hand before your eyes and you witness thicker darkness after the hand has gone by. See, see? Quick it falls.

Again mechanism of the clock tapped on their ears.

Can't you—spend the night?

Joel cleared his throat. His voice shook slightly as he said,

199

With this storm and all. Though I think the wind's slackening, and it's not raining hard as it was.

Course, Aunt Sid. I'll stay.

Through the evening they were disconcerted by advance of a flat black ocean which bordered Willowhurst on two sides, rising until lantern light discovered it slapping at the steps which led down from the piazza.

Isn't it time to start moving things, Aunt Sid?

Stubbornly. We'll wait and see.

In another hour the water seemed falling. Rain had ceased with coming of darkness but winds were reluctant to die.

Shall I read? she'd asked earlier.

Yes, please. Something funny?

Sidney read him to sleep with "The Spectre Bridegroom," and would remember always how he grinned at the name of Katzenellenbogen. Joel sprawled on the sofa, Sidney sat in a rocking-chair beside the lamp. When she became aware that he slept, she took up her lantern and crept outside for another inspection. At last: going down, down rapidly. Old corn-stalks and clay scum proved the truth. She tried to reënter the house as quietly as she had gone out, but a breeze, obdurate in its dying, tore the latch from her hand. *Slam.*

Joel's body jerked, he was sitting up.

I'm so sorry—

Gol, I did go to sleep. And whilst you were reading! Let me beg pardon, Aunt Sid.

(How can a throat be dry as mine? Someone else, someone scrawny, doing the talking.)

Joel, you're still weary from working all night.

I had a nap. Can't understand why—

You're to go into the back bedroom immediately, and take off your clothes, and go to bed. It might be difficult, tomorrow, reaching town, even by way of the Old Plank Road. There may have been some flooding over Coon Creek way.

Don't reckon so.

(His voice dry as mine, stranger's voice. We are croaking like monsters. Queer birds, crows in a tree, cawing at each other.)

But I ought to start off by daylight.

That's why I'm telling you to go to bed immediately.

How about the water in the yard? I'd better—

Just looked, she said. That's where I'd been when the door slammed. It's still receding: halfway across the lawn now, and a pretty mess left behind.

She said, I have no sleeping garment to offer you. I fear that a nightdress of my own—

Wouldn't fit.

Laugh.

I'll leave you the lamp, and take this candle.

Won't you need the lamp, upstairs?

Silly, I've *two* lamps in my chamber. Now go to *sleep*.

She forced herself to turn away.

Good night, Aunt Sid.

Coarse brittle syllables. As if mocking himself.

Good night, Joel. Coarse, brittle.

Sssleep well.

Sidney went away with her candle, closed the stair door firmly, trotted up with great clacking of slippers. In the bedroom she puffed the candle out and flung herself across the bed. A while she trembled in nervous seizure, arms and legs shuddering beyond control. She heard herself mewing into the quilt which served as bedspread.

You want him, you ninny. You desire him, can have him, he's there for the taking. You could be lying with him now. If you'd only—

Love, great love, I tell you, though everyone else says it's evil. But whom do you fear?

Convention. And what is regarded as Christian decency.

Christian only? Tis a fibre in the moral structure of almost every tribe.

Omit the ancient gods, they were busy with incest.

Who'll know? You're a grown woman. Haven't you sufficient will and purpose to seduce a seventeen-year-old *child?* Ahhhhh, and she chewed the crushed stuffed folds.

Perhaps not true sleep in time, but at least some form of removal and suspension. Sidney heard words repeated in monotony. One phrase kept dinning. *They are too many, and they would not approve.* As, when she'd first considered sacred love, she fancied later a Holy army coming to menace her, and tried to hold ground. Finally she caught up her skirts and ran away. *They are too many, and they would not approve.*

Heard it called from pulpits, read words in newspapers flapping past.

Too many, and they—

Don't say that again. *Don't say that again.*

Then we'll play it on instruments.

A bassoon booms. *They are too—*

Never again. Speak new words now.

Entire colony of folks guffawing at the idea. They gathered in a tight bunch, the inner circle pushed their heads together, whispering. They came forth with a word. *Demented.*

Oh no, someone objected. Should be simpler. Call her *crazy.* Then they took up the chant and began repeating, Crazy, crazy, crazy.

Joel lurked in a corner of her bedroom, and fired off a tiny silver pistol. It went *ting.*

Awake. Aching in joints because she'd been lying fully clad, corseted, in an unfamiliar position. With her waking, people and spirits drifted away through bent walls of the chamber and left her staring. There was not a visible ember glowing in the grate of her fireplace.

Sidney fumbled for the match-block and ripped off a match. Phosphorous flare and stench, she touched the candlewick, yellow flame serene. She took up her watch. Nearly three o'clock in the morning.

Suffered too long, I tell you.

Don't start that again. Those mobs and herds who talk—

Yes, I know.

Best to see about the flood.

Sidney's slippers had fallen off during the night, or perhaps when first she hurled herself at the bed. She put them on, thought a moment, took them off. The sound of her walking might disturb Joel—she should go in stocking feet. She lighted

202

the lamp, twould be ready against her return. Took out all pins from straggling hair, let hair hang down.

Take note, however, that you are in your heart both witch and bitch. Witches wear hair long though tangled.

Go tangle your own.

She moved quietly down the staircase and opened the door with no creaking. A draught snapped her candle flame away. Sidney felt with her foot, closed the door.

Pale whiteness coating the parlor. Windows larger here, and winds had scrubbed off most of the debris which coated previously. Sidney recognized a condition unperceived when still in her own chamber. Clouds had vanished, a high chunk of leftover moon illuminated the world again.

Panic here? A man stood dark, looking out at the pale landscape. He heard her and turned. Man was Joel, he was fully dressed.

They met in the middle of the room, colliding with force. Their arms belted their bodies together.

So neither of us was able to relax, so neither removed clothing. But did I rush to lay my hold on him, or did he pounce at me?

No answer. Never know.

Against me, against me, against me. My God, I can feel it. Feel it through our combined clothing. So tumid. He must have been that way for hours.

Faces together, mouths mashed together *Oh, Joel*. She tried to utter her lover's cry. *My darling*. But with their lips spreading— Like the flood of hours ago, she thought, flood in the yard. We're Nature, give us remission, tis uncontrollable, can't stop it. She could only growl in her throat, and squeeze against him the firmer, and feel—

Feel that—

Please, *God*. It isn't happening. It isn't *happening*.

But it *is*, already, within his clothes, and we haven't even—

Pulsation turbulent, extended in spasm. Joel was gasping, his face slid across her cheekbone down into her neck. He asked

203

only, Aunt Sid, for God's sake, what are we *doing?* His voice went high as the last pumping of his vigor spurted.

Ah, dear Joel. You couldn't wait, you couldn't wait, you waited too *long.* I made you wait too long.

He pushed her away so roughly that she nearly fell. Aunt Sid, he howled. I couldn't marry *you.*

An unacceptable pack of eavesdroppers jeered through the house, the soaked countryside derided them, Aunt Sedalia was hee-heeing up the hill.

Entire countryside and town beyond.

Aunt Sid, I got to go. Joel blundered in stark moonlight and shadow, seeking out his hat and the knitted scarf to tie around his neck.

Please, Joel. Don't go.

I'm heading out of here, far and fast!

We could go together, she said faintly. Go somewhere else, where people didn't know.

Yeh. In ridicule. And raise a gang of idiot children, the way niggers do when they get to cutting up like this. Goodbye, Aunt Sid.

Then kiss me just once more.

Don't dare. He drew in his breath and said, Far, far away. I'll be gone to Texas, quick as I can manage.

Dear moon, she prayed as he marched up the rutted road and blended for Eternity in patches of half-light, patches of chill emptiness—until he, Joel, was only an anonymous author of sundry footfalls and splashings—

Maury the hound challenged him, baying.

Dear moon, cruel moon, piece of moon with such detachment (because you have seen so much of love and attempted love, and the weeping which follows) —

Guard him, she said aloud through clenched teeth.

Four weeks to the day after Joel departed, John Airhart fell off his chair at a wharfside tavern and was carried home in a wagon. He lay unknowing, unrecognizing, dribbling broth from his mouth when they attempted to feed him. In desperation the doctor tried a form of revival with brandy and water, but for the first time in his adult life John was unable to swallow down spirits. His bloated face could be dented when a finger was pressed upon it. He lingered until the end of the week, death rattling in his throat frequently before the final clicking came.

Twas Joely's going did it to him, Emma told her sister. John was deep in drink most of the time afterwards.

Emma, please to remember that John was deep in drink a hundred other times, and had a hundred other excuses.

Oh, sister, don't be cruel, not right now—

I'm not being cruel. Nor are you to worry about finances, Emma. I'm better off than people might suppose.

And we've not had a line from Joely yet! Here's his father laying dead, and Joely don't even know. We've no address for him.

Aunt Sid, I got to go.

Emma, everything must be disturbed in Texas just now. Coming into the Union and all. Dearie, I'm riding to town with your Neighbor Tate, so I must run change my gown. There's dealings to be discussed with Mr. Hearn.

Lawyer Hearn was a son-in-law of the late Mr. Ashford who had served the Widow Tensley two years before. He'd been approached by many would-be buyers for the two business properties Sidney owned. Both lay in areas where real estate doubled and redoubled in value; and Mr. Hearn surmised that prices were come close to their peak—there'd follow an inevitable decline.

Sold. By the lady yonder.

Mrs. Tensley, I congratulate you. This amount in cash, put out at the same interest rate as heretofore on the other monies which you possess—

Half the principal only, she said. The rest is to be deposited in New York, subject to my need for withdrawal. Might you be so good as to arrange for foreign exchange, Mr. Hearn?

Willowhurst was boarded up, she could not face the act of

selling her cottage, not yet. Or of permitting tenants to occupy the space where she and—

Mrs. Utt was called in, and sewed morning and evening for the two women and Mamie. Mr. and Mrs. Veck heckled in the background: it was almost more than her father could bear, to observe Sidney squandering (as he declared) large sums of money on a lengthy stay abroad for the bereaved Emma, Mamie, and herself.

It's what I wish to do, Father.

You've no proper respect for your parents, or the guidance we can offer you! Now please to listen whilst I explain once more. There awaits a golden opportunity for one to become co-owner of controlling stock in the initial phase of the Wilmington, Chattanooga and Western Railroad—

Father, Emma and Mame and I must to Mr. Levine's rooms for our lesson—

How much are you paying out, Daughter, for lessons in *French?*

None of your business, sir. You imposed your final guidance upon me when you thrust a sixteen-year-old girl into matrimony with the late Mr. Tensley. If this is your own private whirlwind, well may you reap it.

Mr. Veck, cried his wife, let us go *home.* I refuse to stay here another minute, and hear ourselves just plain *ridiculed—*

Emma began weakly, Now please, Sidney, don't go to upsetting Pa and Ma—

Allons, ma chère soeur! Allons, ma belle nièce! We'll be tardy, and our precious little old Mr. Levine'll be in a rage.

Aboard ship for Liverpool they became acquainted with an elderly couple who spoke highly of a convent at St.-Germain-en-Laye; their granddaughter was in school there. Again fell kindly shadowing of the late Lawyer Ashford: old Mr. Dobson was his classmate in college, and they'd kept a lifetime's friendship. Neither the Widow Airhart nor the Widow Tensley could but believe that this was indicative of some Superior guidance. On arriving at St.-Germain in April they found the convent walls festooned with lilacs in full bloom; Miss Mamie soon gabbled and squealed with several English and American girls; at tea the Reverend Mother told in her gentlewoman's voice of how she'd gone nursing wounded soldiers on the Waterloo battlefield while still in the novitiate.

When bells rang at this convent they spoke with mature reverence but bore leisure and confidence in their tone.

You'd like it here, Mamie?

Sure enough. Did you see all the rabbits, Ma? Great big white ones—bigger'n any bunnies we got at home—and the girls have em all named. All the same family: *la famille Lapin*. Pierre Lapin, he's the father; and Celeste Lapin, the mother; and André, he's a kind of uncle—

At night in Paris there was sobbing by Emma, the unhappy reiteration of bereavement and dependence.

But I *do* wish to have you with me, Emma.

Can't see why. If I needed help from you—and looks like I did, with most of Mr. Airhart's property mortgaged away— twould have been cheaper just to let me *set*. Mamie could have kept going to Miss Oakes for her learning. Only a dollar a week. And then, maybe Joel might have come back from Texas to help out, once he knew his father was gone—

Sidney told her (far away when she spoke), You'll remember I offered to send Joel to the Academy.

Yes, and John wouldn't hear to it. Nor Joely. Tain't right for a mere aunt to be saddled with—

Emma, cease your utter nonsense. You've made it possible for me to come to Europe, something I've always longed to do. I couldn't come alone. No woman can go gallivanting around by herself, especially abroad. Tis unfortunate, but it happens to be the way of the world. I had need of a traveling companion. Did you not accompany me, who else would there be? *Ma?* I'd have been guilty of matricide the first day out from harbor—

Weakly, but somewhat mollified. Matri—?

Matricide. That's when you slay your own mother, and assuredly I'd push mine—*ours*—overboard. I needed you and still do need you, and you're not to fume at what I spend, nor at accepting pocket money. Now go to sleep. Like a— Good girl.

Sidney—

What is it, dear?

You're so sweet. I tell God about you, every time I pray.

Aunt Sid. For God's sake, what are we doing?

Instructions had been left for Airhart mail to be delivered to Mr. Hearn, so that Joel might be told of his father's death. Thus he was informed belatedly, and two letters from him reached Emma in June. Joel said that he expected to join the troops, and fight Mexicans. *You may recall how conserned I was with this idee, ten years agone when only a little tad, and first learnt about the Alamo. Tell Mame that I will save for her some milutary brass buttons if I have any extry. Please tender my affeckshunat regards to Aunt Sid.*

Why, Sister, where have you been so long? I was in a real fidget, so was the *concierge.*

Just taking a stroll, Emma.

But it grew so *dark.* And raining too. Why, you got all *wet.*

If earth trembled in America, it shook on the Continent as well. Sidney'd dreamed of Switzerland, they were advised not to go: bloody riots and pitched battles recently, a civil-political-religious quarrel which few outsiders might understand. What of Italy? Talk of revolutions, of war with Austria, head-shaking because of the new Pope Pius and what changes he might instigate. In Paris the ladies watched from their carriage while two ragged fierce-faced young men were dragged off by soldiers. *Assassins! They declared that they would murder King Louis Philippe!* People muttered about the threat of impending famine. It was said that many German states were in a ferment of differences with Prussia.

In the end Sidney told Emma, We shall go exactly where we please, looking only to convenience and comfort. They were in Baden-Baden in 1847 when Pettey J. Shallop came riding.

∽10∾

ON THE DAY following the dinner party Sidney was true
to her word: she would not permit Beauty Beast to prepare food beyond the setting out of biscuits, cornbread, cold
meat. An elderly hand belonging to the Wilkeys, one who'd
borne the appropriate name of Parson from birth, fancied himself a lay preacher; once in every month or two he contrived a
lively sermon. At their owners' discretion, negroes from adjacent plantations were permitted to walk over to Yaupon and
hear Parson exhort at the quarters there. Many Apoxsee people
went on this day, and an air of Sabbath lassitude settled over
the place even more discernibly than usual. The mistress kept
faith with herself at pistol practice, and was amused (tenderly)
to find that Beauty Beast was keeping his own brand of faith
when she returned to the Big House.

He sprang from the bench as she entered the back parlor.

Sidney said, A familiar minuet. I could hear you in the drive.

Misty, I'm still chagrined about my performance—

The guests of last evening were all applause.

He shook his head. Even a slave can have pride.

Now, no more of *that,* she thought. To him she said, Beauty
Beast, I wished you to enjoy a holiday—

This is holiday in sufficiency, Misty. Do you not recollect—? I
need time at the piano. I'd like to ready Gossec's *Gavotte
l'Antique* and several— But will it disturb you in any way?

211

I'd term it a blessing. This, unfortunately, is account day. Mr. Irons fetches his books every fortnight and offers full report on Apoxsee affairs, and he'll be here soon, and the door'll be closed necessarily. Still I can enjoy these scraps of music at a distance.

Beauty Beast said, Scraps indeed! and was sad. But once above stairs Sidney found herself humming. When the maid announced Mr. Irons' arrival, she went to the interview willingly.

I brung the drivers, ma'am. Want they should offer you evidence on a certain matter. They'll be out on the gallery step until called for.

Sidney's overseer had come into her employ two months after Pettey J. died, at which time an existing contract with a man named Hafflin was terminated. Hafflin's idea of operating a plantation was to brutalize the hands past reason. He thrashed field negroes mercilessly for urinating in their picking-bags, exemplifying his private notion that the act was debased and unusual, and performed expressly to bedevil him. This, in face of the fact that every cotton grower in the South was aware of the practice. It had been carried out since the first boll puffed white. Moisture increased weight of the cotton, and weight was what counted.

Also Hafflin was given to low conduct. He sneaked about the region by night, seeking carnal knowledge of black women belonging to various households. Gossip had it that this was a personal exploration performed at the behest of Pettey J. Shallop. Sidney was positive that both Yellow Martha and Jiggy had been purchased on Boyd Hafflin's recommendation. She'd sold the wenches immediately when she came into control, even before the Shallop contract with Hafflin expired.

Senator Ledge told his client that she must be of good cheer, he'd put out feelers. This he did, and in another week Nathaniel Irons appeared for an interview. Recently he had been employed by a patriarch in an adjoining county, but now Mr. Dexter was dead, and Irons pronounced the heirs—a trio of nephews—to be quarrelsome and improvident.

Told em I wouldn't continue.

He rode his claybank horse out to Apoxsee, rode round the plantation to view with critical open eyes. He said to Sidney and to Senator Ledge, I can run this place better than she's been run heretofore. But I'd like a slight increase in wage, sir and ma'am.

What did the Dexters pay you?

Five-fifty. I'd like to get six hundred. And one other thing: you'd not need to supply a housekeeper or cook. I got my own. Her name is Lora, and I bought her right after I come back from the war down in Mexico. I'd been wounded in the belly; she's right peart as a nurse too, and helped me to cling to life.

He said, Not many folks get well of a belly wound.

He said, Lora's got two children.

Nat Irons was engaged (Fenton Ledge: I think he's your man) and came in caravan with his colored woman driving a wagon filled with possessions. The possessions included two tiny mulatto boys, each with the long bony pinched face of Mr. Irons and the same wistful gray eyes. Lora was squat, taciturn, and held passion for floor-scrubbing, and an overwhelming fear of house-spiders. She emitted whoops on entering the overseer's cottage behind the plantation office, and seeing spread-limbed insects which hung on the whitewashed ceiling.

I just plain can't stop her from yelling, Mrs. Shallop. Sorry you was disturbed, and come to see what was happening.

Tell Lora that she is not to crush them with her broom! No one is permitted to kill house-spiders at Apoxsee. They are harmless, and eat skeeters and other plaguing things.

I'll do my best, ma'am. But the mistress went away with the feeling that any house-spiders in the overseer's *ménage* were doomed.

Progressing with the seasons, Sidney realized (I should not be a female did I not see and feel it) that Irons grew to adore her in hopeless rustic fashion. His musing gaze said clearly, I never saw such a critter as you before; I guess there ain't no more such; land, I'd like to whisper pretty words in your ear; but I hain't got any such pretties, wouldn't know how to utter them.

His workaday conscience was hurt continually by Sidney's unwillingness to discover joy in the lists he set before her.

Might have said, See how hard I'm working for your sake, ma'am? All for you. Wouldn't toil like this for anybody else.

Mr. Irons rode with hooded stirrups, Mexican style, which most riders thereabouts did not do. When he had grown weary from traversing acreages of cotton, patrolling pastures or corn-fields or stables; going back to the gin again, going to the hog lot; directing people who built a new shed, people who ditched, hauled, delivered; riding to see the sawyer, to criticize the mason— What's with the nigger shack roofs, what's with the granary and stacks—? Give out rations today, an ox is down sick, I'm scairt we're about to lose another mule— When tired thus he'd learned to loll, as when he wore a uniform and bestrode another horse. You'd see him resting so, one leg draped over the pommel. He spoke of buying a Mexican saddle, having it freighted in by one of the local traders. There was a rocking chair for you!

Nathaniel Irons' illusion of himself was as being indefati-gable. He kept trying to prove that this was true. Habitually he sat up late of nights, going over accounts and always finding errors, places where he'd made mistakes and needed to rub out betraying numerals and indite fresh ones. The only holidays he permitted himself came with cooler weather in autumn when possums and coons could best be hunted. With rarity he'd take his shotgun and fetch home some partridges, and then only if requested to do so by the mistress.

Too much to be seen on, on the place. But— Since you ask, I'll oblige.

Perhaps one of the hands—?

He was appalled. Niggers can't bear firearms. Gainst all laws. You should know that, ma'am.

Oh, I do. But folks make exception—with due intelligence, I mean to say. The Wilkeys have a boy named Lucifer who is a crack shot. He fetches in doves, turkeys, iron heads, ducks—

Gainst the law.

Any single page of Mr. Irons' journal might have been a pattern for the entire year.

Thursday, 7 of September, 1854.
Wind south, hot, no rain yet.

3	In sick barracks. Duke, Carmel, Dulsy.
4	At the gin.
1	C.A. making shuck collars.
2	Haul leaves.
1	Tod, mind mules.
40	Pick cotten.
2	On waggon repair.
2	Lenten and Delia cook for hands.
3	Minding other stock etct.
2	Coot, Joseph work on stable roof.
3	In gardens. Adam, plus 4 haff-hands.
2	Driving. Maddy, Honga.
2	Minding sick and children. Jen, Sarah.

———
67

He was impelled to the preparation of peculiar inventories and statistics at odd times of the year. Pages would be filled with this information, and he'd tell Sidney that he was grieved at being behindhand, but there'd been such claims upon his time. *Turn ploughs 23, horse ploughs 2, shovel stocks 18, wide shovels 16, solid sweeps 31, scooters 9, narrow shovels 19.* Sidney wondered why he didn't list every fence rail, every pine cone. *Cotton plantin small ploughs 5, single trees 23, clevises and pins 16, sugar furnace 1, sugar skimmers, a set, 1.* When she praised him for attention to detail, his lonely face might relax briefly and his rapt gaze tell her, I do this for you, my lady. No other.

Carridge 1, shay 1, freight waggons 2, ox carts 1, horse carts 1, set of blacksmith tools 1 (in care of Duke), set of carpenter tools 1 (in care of carpenter), grind stones 2—

Mr. Irons' obvious infatuation was apparent to Senator Ledge. The senator teased Sidney, said she'd have Lora pulling out her hair or manufacturing baneful charms.

215

Pshaw.

Hell hath no fury, child.

Lora's far from scorned, I can assure you! In any event, Mr. Nathaniel Irons is of such shyness that he'd never offer his affection, were every difference between us to be planed down.

Nat Irons rode among oaks and he saw oaks. He ventured into palmetto scrub: he saw palmetto scrub and perchance wild pigs. He traveled his route to the gin, and thought, There's much cotton blown away from loads now. Lining the verge of the road. I must put a raft of children to gathering it.

Sidney became acquainted with trees and asked them, Whence your unstudied geniality? Always you are obliging. From what polished green acorn grew your comfort, are you offended by red lichens? Truly not—they are no disease making a scab, they become chevrons worn by old soldiers with esteem. Might not we be happier if all males owned beards with your beauty?

She'd heard Yankees, viewing the vestments of moss for the first time, declare them funereal. Ludicrous. She thought them to be gentle banners.

Palmetto scrub acrawl with serpents, one should not walk through it. Niggers teach their children so, and justifiably. Furthermore it is harsh and pliantly knifing, can draw blood, does. But consider miniature melodious life therein. O warm little nest, and young partridges come walking a-twitter.

Cotton festooning the roadside grass and burrs—what a snowy treasure! Wind wisps it away from the load, it is gossamer and fine, comes down lazily reluctant in settling air, joins other fragments there. The truant snow thickens with each day of the picking season, soon the roadway is rimmed fuzzy white on both sides.

Difficult it must have been to handle the stuff, before the first gins were built. But now great mills in England and at the North, with pale multitudes going to the spinners and coming tired from them. Would it have been something else, some other enduring weariness and economic slavery, had we not produced the cotton? We, who have our people plant and plough and make it grow?

Verily.

And the fields lie in uncertain variegated color when a crop is at its first picking, never knowing whether to be green or brown or white. Puzzle in the cotton, in virginal fuzz.

The two drivers had been painstakingly evaluated and selected for their task by Mr. Irons (neither had been a driver when Pettey J. was alive) . Madison, the younger of the two, was wide-faced, wide-shouldered. Sidney looked at him and recalled Mungo Park. *The Foulahs are chiefly of a tawny complexion, with soft silky hair, and pleasing features.* It was Maddy who nurtured the memory of his long-dead mother and left posies on her grave. He had an excellent way with growing boys and girls. These half-hands were transmuted under his direction into capability, into the drudgery or craft toward which they seemed best inclined. From time to time some scallawag attempted to take advantage of Maddy's fundamental geniality, but did so to his own confusion. If he had half a brain (many seemed but quarter-witted) he never tried the same thing again. Madison was capable of recommending a whipping when he considered a whipping to be necessary, but in accord with plantation edict he preferred to let Mr. Irons wield the lash. (Some overseers did not whip, nor would the masters; then malefactors were carried to town and got their beatings in jail.)

Occasionally, there came about an insubordination somewhere in the fields, and Madison had his own select way of dealing with such situations. When rebellion or other naughtiness was demonstrated, Maddy owned the power of body and clearness of mind to administer immediately an effective punishment. (Alone he could have handled any man on the place except Adam the gardener.) He took the wicked by their shoulders, grasping them under the arms, the while they squeaked, squealed, kicked, tried to bite. He lifted them off the ground and banged them down again, whirled them back into the air, swung them, twirled them, spun them until they could scarcely draw breath; shook, whisked, hustled them, sometimes turned them completely upside down.

Now then. You pick up you hoe and go to hoeing *right.*

217

Now then. You get back to you picking-bag and you *pick*.

Now then. You never leave bars down *again,* so cattle stray. You do, and I really *trounce* you.

Both Mr. Irons and Sidney had been first-hand witnesses, and with justice they granted this driver latitude in his discipline. He scaled these chastenings up or down in severity in accord with the culprit's size, age, sex, general physical condition. Basically Maddy was a considerate soul. Often he observed the weariness of the pregnant, even before she who was pregnant might complain; and he'd beg leave to tell her off to less demanding chores than those of the field. Maddy had been born at Apoxsee in the days before elder Shallops built the Big House, days when there was but a log house, and Indian *chickee* structures for the hands, and a lurking sense of feathery danger.

Sidney had said one time to Mr. Irons, Our driver Madison— Tis unfortunate that he's colored. I know little about the army, but might not Maddy have made a good soldier?

Irons caught this notion in his mind, rolled it around (some kind of fruit tossed to him, he found it fair). He smiled, compressing lips, turning tight lips inward. His smile was private, secret, he dared not share.

Now that you say so, ma'am, I can't help but agree. He'd done good at Contreras.

Are there ever free niggers—colored troops—in the army?

I never seen none. Cept officers' servants. But the Mexicans appeared to have a quantity of niggers— Mr. Irons scratched his jaw. Come to think of it, they must have been some variety of Indians instead.

Honga, the other driver, was born in Africa. He might have been forty, might have been fifty. Long time Apoxsee. Long time belong Mass Ramsay fore that. Long time belong Mass Mercer fore that. Fore that belong Frenchman in Sugar Islands, he buy me off boat.

Honga's early years had been a succession of barracoons and caffels. Honga said that he was taken in war. Oh, far, far away. He'd been sold to Arab dealers, sold to Moors, sold to blacks, sold back to Moors again, sold again to other negroes. He was a little boy when first dragged off into slavery after his father and his mother were slaughtered at his side.

All my people very tall. Like me. Some more tall.

He'd hold up his hand to show how tall they were. In maturity he himself stood at least six feet five or six, he was built of reddish-black skin and bone. His long legs looked to be thin as cane, yet tendons were tough, muscles made of wire. At merry-makings amongst the hands, it was a gleeful moment when they might persuade Honga to dance like Africans. He would leap so high into the air, shaking his head and yelling, pretending to have a weapon in his hand when he jumped. And then he'd be pretending to strike someone dead with the weapon.

It was told that he had enraged previous masters by indulging an original taste for savage fare. This was milk of cows mixed with blood of cows. Honga would creep out at night, open veins in the necks of selected cattle, draw off a small quantity of the blood, stop the bleeding with care, leave the cattle to graze, go away to shake milk and blood together in a gourd. Sidney had heard Pettey J. telling visitors about this. The story went that Honga was caught literally red-handed in such an experiment when first bought by the Shallop family. He was considered far too grown and disciplined for such primitive pranks. The overseer flogged him brutally, scars still showed on his russet-bronze back. Other negroes looked at his scars with big eyes. Nowadays almost no one was ever whipped so viciously, not anywhere in that neighborhood, although ugly stories could be heard about rice plantations in distant coastal regions, and what went on there.

You pray, boy. Pray you never get sold to rice.

Oh, bad, bad.

Right bad, get sold to rice.

If Honga's original appetite for blood-and-milk sometimes got the better of him in modern times, evidence was never produced. He loomed importantly as a grave conductor of laboring affairs. A stolid disciplinarian, he appeared to have little of Madison's humor and compassion. But he recognized steadfastly any law laid down for him or for others.

Old Honga, he make folks mind.

Yeh-heh. Make everybody mind.

You mind, boy. Or he drink you *blood.*

Mr. Irons reported, We hauled seven bales a-Thursday. If we get a good pick tomorrow and have no gin trouble, I look to haul seven more.

Have you the weight listings?

Yes, ma'am, first seven right here. Number One bale run five hundred and thirty-six pounds; Number Two, five hundred eight; Number Three, five fifty-four—

Just so you have them all, Mr. Irons.

He recalled with delight, Last year we shipped one hundred and twenty-eight bales. Do better this season—with rain. But twas thundering again, while ago. Now, ma'am is there anything else I can—? No? If not, may I have the drivers in, or would you go to the gallery?

Do you tell them to clean their feet. Then they are to come in. I wish to hear the story in their own words.

Adam, Sidney thought. Will there never be an end to the unhappy saga of Adam? A few minutes later Honga and Maddy followed Nat Irons into the dog-trot and through the doorway of the House Office. In the back parlor Beauty Beast had been paying grave or gay respect to the selections on which he was at practice. Reiteration of a bright tingling phrase, inevitable pause and silent study—then unexpected stripping of the left hand to its chorded essentials— These induced a nervous claim upon attention. Now he went into stately clarity of another minuet. With half-closed eyes, Sidney listened until the slapping tread of big bare feet came close, and Mr. Irons cleared his throat. Then she sat more erectly in the desk chair, and motioned for the door to be closed.

Good morning, Maddy.

Morning, mistress.

Good morning, Honga.

Morn, miss.

Sit down, Mr. Irons. Now then, let us hear about Adam.

They offered unpleasant news. Adam had been cruel to two of the half-hands who were told off, during seasonal needs, to assist him with vegetables and fruit. On Saturday afternoon (sometime after the burial of Tickle, and after Sidney's ride and fall) Madison ran to the potato patch in response to outcry. He found Adam belaboring a boy named Flash with a strap. Another boy, Eddie, was already sobbing on the ground, bare legs striped by the beating he'd received. Maddy commanded Adam to throw down his strap, and the gardener's answer was an attempted attack in Maddy's own direction, which the driver managed to avoid. He sent another boy to fetch Honga, and the two drivers subdued Adam; but only after knocking him senseless with the handle of a spade.

Maddy, gave he any reason for his attack on the boys?

He say, mistress, they try to take holiday.

That's absurd. Both Eddie and Flash were sent to the shore by my own direction, to net crabs for the dinner party. Adam knew of this.

Told him myself, said Mr. Irons.

Honga said, He not make sense, miss. Drink.

He drank?

Eat onion—

Maddy declared that Adam's breath reeked with the smell, and when he was struck to the ground a half-munched onion fell from his pocket. The overseer himself found a shattered bottle near the entrance to the root cellar. There must have been another bottle somewhere around. For Nineveh, the coachman, reported to the overseer that someone had taken two bottles of muscadine wine which he'd concealed in the root cellar.

It's all pretty clear, ma'am, said Irons. I set Adam to guard the cellar whilst the child's coffin still lay there, count of he was working so nigh. Also he was the one carried it out, when the hour come for the burying; and then Tige and Joseph toted it up to the grave. One way or another, Adam must have come across that wine in the cellar. He bided his time until most all the hands were gone up the ridge. Then he got holt of the bottles.

Maddy asked of all, How come that old Nineveh, he get to have *wine?*

The mistress explained, Because he can make better wine—scuppernong or muscadine as it may be—than anyone in the countryside. He's been permitted to do that for years, long before I was ever married to Mr. Shallop. The doctor prescribes wine as a dietary for Nineveh, and thus he's allowed to save out part of the batch for his own use. He's sober as any deacon, and never abuses the privilege.

Sidney thought that she wished to be rid of incessant responsibility. She saw and heard herself as a worn schoolmistress surrounded by prattling nincompoops: boys who fired squirts at each other, naughty girls who put ink into the waterbucket (she'd done such wickedness herself when small, and got laced with a switch for her pains). Twas like being proprietress of a troop of puppies which had to be fed, housed, rubbed dry when they were wet, covered or basketed when cold—spanked and flung outside after they'd made musses on the matting, restrained from gnawing bones on the bed. (And some were a bane, and treacherous—might go for your throat.) And they would never grow to be sedate and principled, would always be ragged pups a-slathering.

Beauty Beast has tired of intricacies, and taken refuge in a jolly novelty. Oh, that I might listen unannoyed! What's the selection, who's the composer?

He's mine, and he plays for me, and it's only just that I should be allowed to enjoy him.

She thought, Tonight. Do come soon, please, Night. Then I'll not be feeling Apoxsee like a weight around my neck.

What of Adam, Mr. Irons? After the drivers quieted him down?

I sent him to the quarters, ma'am. Told him to stay there and sleep it off—we'd tie him up and give him a real bullying if he didn't. But today he just let in to work, even on a Sunday.

Sidney told the drivers that they might leave, she and Mr. Irons would decide what must be done. I like whip Adam all lone, miss, said Honga on the way out.

222

Irons grinned wryly. He couldn't never make it, ma'am, but he'd be spoiling to try. He's a real African native.

I know.

Kind of like those Indians I spoke of. Mongst the Mexicans.

Adam must be thrashed again, Mr. Irons, if we're to keep him.

On the whole, Mrs. Shallop, ma'am, I don't know where you could buy a gardener half as good. Want we should drive him to the calaboose tomorrow?

No. You've all much to see to, after yesterday's delay. Twould disrupt the picking. There's that big post in the stable. Tie him tomorrow morning and give him twenty-five lashes with— She hesitated.

Cattle-whip, ma'am?

Yes. He's stronger than most oxen, and I'll warrant you he won't even be lamed up. But it'll hurt, most horribly, and—

And— Oh, *gad*. I hate to have people whipped.

Me too, ma'am. But sometimes it's necessary. Reckon that he'll submit in peace. But, if he doesn't, he'll have to be clouted on the head once more.

Then Honga can lay on the lashes, Mr. Irons.

Ruther not have to do it myself, I swear.

When he was gone Sidney went to the doorway of the back parlor. She stood watching Beauty Beast at the piano, listening in tired relief. It was several minutes before he discovered her there. Then Beauty Beast rose quickly, calling out an apology.

You must rest now, she said, and play for me again when it grows dark. I need you.

Misty, I'm glad.

In a very low tone, but affecting her heart when he spoke.

Because I like to feel needed.

Blessed rain was wettening at last, a perfumed comfort through the calm gray afternoon. Palms seemed reaching up their scissored fronds in salute, the live oaks smiled at moisture soaking into rough bark and letting blowing whiskers of moss turn greenish. Two maids idled in the covered corridor at the rear, blending voices in a remembered hymn which had been lined out at the Yaupon service. *Jesus, the friend of sinners, calls, with pity in his eyes, and warns them of the dang'rous foes that all around them rise.* Sang in calmness, disturbing neither rain nor mistress, altering old words into a mish-mash acceptable to themselves, altering old melody as blacks always did. *Jesus, yes, O Jesus, he friend of sinners, call, yes he call, with pretty in he eyes.* When Sidney went to her chamber to doze, to appreciate steady tap of rain on a welcoming roof overhead, she looked out and saw a parcel of children strayed to the south lawn, performing a ballet of their own design. They turned and twirled, holding up hands to let rain strike freely, bending back with open mouths to suck the droplets. Their play was a manner of worship, they must be feeling that a generous soaked God stepped over and among them.

So grateful. Grateful.

Sleepily. Grateful for—?

Grateful for gratitude.

Sidney knew a long peace, rain spoke until she heard no more.

Again. *There sits my heart.*

Rain ceased with the coming of darkness, and warm-weather humidity folded the Big House. Tiny green frogs, seemingly translucent, spread themselves on glass, and pulsed visibly if you came near with a candle. Beauty Beast had transcribed more than the single movement of Telemann: he brought out another portion of baroque and offered it to Sidney with almost impish satisfaction.

Did you enjoy it, Misty?

Of course. Whose?

Woodcock.

As in—the bird?

Woodcock, as in the bird. I think that his first name was Robert. He's nigh to being forgotten now. But that was my pianoforte rendition of the *allegro,* from an oboe concerto which he wrote.

Please to do another of your transcriptions, Beauty Beast.

224

He leafed through his music eagerly, wide smeared pages fanning between busy tan hands. Boieldieu, Misty? Of course he did write for the piano directly; but I've my own interpretation of orchestral passages from his Concerto in F—

A mockingbird struck up private melody beyond the front gallery, and they waited together without speaking, sharing listeners' joy. Within Sidney's own perception, however, began to ring a tenseness unnoted previously. She sat rigid. Once the mocker was gone, she rose to say, We'll save the Boieldieu for tomorrow evening.

And, more abruptly, I must retire. She felt that he watched her with musing speculation as she left the room and climbed the stair.

In windless night there was still much of summer. Insects conversed, bullfrogs disapproved in steady negative parliament beyond. But also prevailed, especially noticeable in humidity out of season, the awareness of a multitude of human beings and domestic animals and poultry—living there, respiring, sustained in heartbeats actuated by the soft machinery within their bodies. You could never reckon, never separate and say, This sound constitutes the breathing of a cow, that is surely the blat of a calf, there a horse whickered, there a hen croaked, there a skunk ran. The dog scratched himself—many dogs, all wagging and lounging and scratching, or going off to give voice in the brush.

That is an infant yelling. One of the black children in a tantrum? Nay, they are not given to tantrums, the little thing is teething. And one slave banged a door, and one dropped a jar and one went out to a privy. Difficult to manage a sanitary conduct, you had to discipline them into using privies. In carefree woods fashion they were eager to go almost anywhere, and then you'd be stepping in it and— Who knew? Coming down with a disease? How'd you enjoy the affliction of Calvin Tensley?

If you walked by night—as on prairies, suppose—and someone conducted you in order to two places of grotesque blackness—

225

As if you were blinded, seeing no shapes and hearing nothing consciously—

Yet your guide told you, In this one spot there are many sleepers, or at least many organisms resting, animals and humans alike. They are around you. Then, in this other spot, there is no one: no people, not a snake, a bunny, a bird. No one.

Now—which place is which place?

You'd be able to tell them. Correctly. Never go wrong.

Because the mere activity within their bodies (and addlement ensuing in the minds of many) would be transmitted, become a fact to be sensed. You'd know that they were there.

So lived the world of Apoxsee at current midnight, but there came to be another titilation. Twas the bird, mocker come back again, saying aloud, There is not much season longer for me to disport myself. Still I think of the love I had, and perhaps more perfection tomorrow. Must tell you.

Sidney heard him. He went high in a pine, came down to peach trees a little farther away. Odd, odd, she said. Seldom do the mockers busy themselves among oaks. They fancy pines and palms, high open perches, and often they'll flit to a dead tree and be enthusiastic there.

He sounded open and nearer now, must have floated to a tip-top of pine.

Sidney thought— She writhed physically in shaping the words, in birthing the notion. She thought, It is a merciless beauty. So great a beauty that you fairly die of wanting to capture it. But how might that be accomplished? There's no way we own, to catch those warbles and hold them. No one might ever reduce such gallantry to a series of stiff dreary notes, climbing or descending the scale like ignorant blank-faced children annoying on a five-barred gate. Neither song nor singer can be prisoned and held. They'd die if you tried to make the capture. Who'd desire to slay an angel?

A few words came to her, remembered. *Darkling I listen; and, for many a time I have been half in love—*

Sidney twisted on her coverless bed, stared up and sought to see the canopy, make out its arch in gloom.

A few more stray phrases did come to her. *Do I wake or sleep?*
Deceiving elf. Tasting of Flora and the country green.

Useless to put it off. She must rise and seek the reassurance of
Keats. He had come nearest to capturing such grace, no composer could do better. Sidney lit her shielded candle, went in
search of the book, found it. Well she remembered the day
when she bought that 1820 volume.

She tried to calm the struggle in her body (Against whom am
I contending?) by tender washing of a young man's words.

> *That I might drink, and leave the world unseen,*
> *And with thee fade away into the forest dim.*

She stopped sometimes in reading, and remembered nightin-
gales she'd heard on steep hillsides behind tile-roofed towns.
Her mocker went away, or died of his own pure exultation, before she'd come to the last lines, and the world was poorer for it.

No marvel such as the bird, or the poet's marvelling at the
bird, could soothe her now.

She thought of herself as being bound tight as a cotton bale—
banded, burlapped. She could not get loose from—from—

There was no release.

You speak in error, Mrs.

Ah, there was release, and she'd sought it many times. But
there was a shame to follow: the idea that she embraced a
wickedness completely secret, never tolerated or practiced by
other lone women—

Well, yes, she had heard—

She'd heard her elder sister speaking with some others. And
they said—

Had I not been bashed so cruelly, why—

Again she drew aside the net hanging round her bed, and
went out through that other net which blocked the doorway
none too tightly. It discouraged if it could not completely
eradicate the plague of mosquitoes humming in a dozen keys
and dozen areas. There was the illusion of more of them,
billions beyond, stacked in a solid droning mist.

Sidney stood on the high front gallery with hard fists against her temples, stood with eyelids squeezed tight, hearing naught except her own breathing for a time. And then hearing—

What came first to the ears? Was it laughing, or the plashing?

Someone in her secret pool. People in Lake Tannin.

Ah, ah, curse them, they wouldn't have needed to pick the gate lock! There were several places along the fence where they could have clambered over with ease. One spot where they could go up on a long low bough above the fence, and drop readily on tother side. Even a woman wearing skirts might do as much, and for the athletically inclined twould be no trick.

All Sidney had relied upon was a matter of edict. If not edict then a matter of rule, matter of custom. And of course the dread of penalty.

How *could* you, how *could* you? *Whoever* you are!

Saying these things, and feeling rages rushing inside her head like bats in a closed room, bats swooping and being struck at by a broom, and squeaking as they were crushed and swept.

Should you cry to yourself, *I know* who it is, *I know* who it is? When in fact you don't *know?*

Gator? No way in which a man-sized gator might enter the enclosure, and at least one trespasser was man-sized. So that excluded night birds and also the race of mink and otters and other weaselish critters churning waters in a chase for fish. Nor did such beings give vent to laughter high or low, and surely she had marked the laughter.

One of the hands gone mad? Such as Adam, again in liquor, not knowing what he was about, and possibly now he drowned one who sought to restrain him?

Ridiculous. Field hands would fear to come there. The penalties are obvious.

One has strayed this way from a neighboring plantation?

The while Sidney hazarded for answer she was donning slippers, folding herself in a shawl, feeling through gloom for reticule and the revolving pistol contained therein. She'd bear no lantern, it might identify her approach. She moved as in an act of levitation, without wing-flapping, but still with no treading of the gallery outside, no touching of the straight stair as she went down. Then here, then there, then passing cleanly but without a rush to be felt. She had pressed steadily through the air and was now on that path which led from the drive, and again she heard snickering ahead of her.

(Long since, Sidney had summoned herself into a census of house servants and traced out their abode in every case. Beauty Beast's bedroom was that one-roomed log affair built against the kitchen at the rear. Along the covered passageway which led to wine-cellar, larder-shed, smoke-house, and all such domestic offices, stood three more cabins. In one of these dwelt Basil and his wife Fairy who served as principal laundress. Beds in the next cabin were occupied by little India, Linnet, Molly the chambermaid, and Clemmy the housemaid. Occupant of a cabin beyond that was the seamstress whose name was Trudge. She shone neat and agreeable, a pleasure to have about the place except when she slept. Then, owing it was thought to some malformation within the nose or throat, Trudge snored so terribly that no one could abide to be near. Thus she had this place to herself. Excepting for small fry who served their variety of apprenticeships underfoot throughout the establishment, these were all of the house servants. They became enumerated and located, and were put back into their beds by the mistress' mind as fast as she took them out.)

She felt and heard an airy rush of bodies speeding toward her up the incline from creek and dam and fencing, and in unreasonable terror she fell back through vines as if she herself were the wrongdoer. Twas not her sin, twas theirs! She felt them approaching, heard the wet rush they made, and so she toppled among jessamine, and wondering why and how, and then making out, in a nearness to physical nausea, that it was Beauty Beast and Linnet who raced upon her.

They chuckled cunningly. Nor could she tell whether they were clothed or danced in nudity: maybe they had some sort of rags about them, some frippery of garments brushing the tunnel in herbage where Sidney Shallop huddled. Opposite, so close that she could have struck him as he ran, she heard Beauty Beast exclaim in softness, Oh, a pretty sport, Miss Linnet! A pretty sport! And the girl was all ascamper as she laughed back at him, and you felt that she was tossing her head while she ran.

Far-spread Keats, persevering constant Keats.

> What mad pursuit? What struggle to escape?
> What pipes and timbrels? What wild ecstasy?

You could hear, you could feel, know that they were there, mark the identity. You now surmised, in shock at their implied insurrection, just what they might have been up to.

Just what they *had* been up to.

Nor, she was sure, did they hold any idea that their mistress was become alert. They considered her as salted down in an inviolable bed, in inviolate dignity. There lay Mistress, lay Madam, lay *Madame,* lay Misty—apart, immaculate, built of the white stuff of God and hard iron stuff of mastery, and of braided leather of the Law itself (as a lash is braided).

Sidney stood aghast at their craftiness and intrepidity, the while in equal fascination she sought to reconstruct the merriment they'd been pursuing. She thought of them as shiny and leaping, satyr and dryad (Beauty Beast a satyr? Come, say faun).

Linnet the dryad.

That nigger bitch.

Come. Say nymph.

All so golden, and mashing the water in dark of the moon, speaking cuteness, running from each other, swimming from each other.

Swimming *to* each other.

As imaginary painted Beings ran through an eternal extravaganza of Brueghel and the wickeder Bosch, in museums where she'd gone to walk and stare, sometimes to recoil and sometimes to worship. But also there was menace not to be disregarded when those creatures got out of hand and came trooping like ugly ants all bloody-mouthed and disembowled. They were overwhelmingly evil, no matter how flimsy of limb and tenderfooted, and speedy in their gait, and possibly lilting with their voices.

They were Menace. Could take over the world. Might do so in time.

What shared Linnet and Beauty Beast that she had no part of or in, could never share?

Tar. Black matter underneath.

They've violated your precious little Lake Tannin, Mrs. What now, of theirs, shall you choose to violate in turn?

The cream is there.

While she lay fuming. Covered cup on drum table near the window where breeze might preserve it and keep the stuff from souring.

Hey. *The cream—*

Let us be deliberate, and consider only facts. Cream is a fact; that yellow glass thing is a fact (once a tool which might have been employed in locked brothel chambers while the little girls shrieked, and older women too; but now, at times, Mr. Glass your lover, the only one you have).

Proceed wisely therefore, endorse solely the proven events, make no claim to a knowledge unpossessed when it comes to those erring servants.

Hold you evidence of copulation? Who swore to it? The mockingbird?

Well you know that they are jungle-blooded, both of them, they share that common stain somewhere back beyond, and all the white injection in the world may never wash it away.

They're niggers.

Say for the moment that they're nigger children. And you are fond of children, and have been a bountiful nurse to many of the little blacks. Or say a rich relation, say a goddess or fairy godmother, or brownie bringing gifts. Say that you've been pastry-cook to the darkies' young.

Nor did you then perish of rage and loathing when they kicked up their heels.

See? Blacks are children.

See? Beauty Beast and Linnet are darkey children because— Aye, because they're darkies.

Simple.

Therefore let it be said that some slave children stole a toy of yours, or maybe borrowed it, and have now given it back to you undamaged. What will you do—have them flogged for it? As Adam will be flogged tomorrow?

Children, children of course, with hair tied up in kinks and knots, and looking very droll if they're scrubbed clean. (Like Little Mag at the auction.) And if they're naughty, you award them shaking or cuffing, and then perhaps a peach in the end.

These things you know well, so why lie a-fussing? Linnet? Who's Linnet? The girl who lays out your clothes, girl with the hairbrush, girl to bring intimate things to you when you're *en déshabillé,* the one instructed cleverly to do up frills which not even laundress or seamstress can do. She's a lady's maid, is Linnet, and valuable accordingly. But she has the brain of a quail, and not one comparative ounce of heart (as when you might consider, say, the hundred-pound heart of a mocking-bird). Nay, not one ounce. She's trivial, she's nothing. Not even the peeling from that same peach, not even the fuzz on its rosiness.

And you've been behaving as if she were a *rival* of yours? A rival for the affection of— A nigger?

Damn that wench to hell.

I'll *have* him.

You cannot.

I can, I will.

No, you shall not.

I shall.

It is against all laws.

So?

It has not been done.

What has been done?

White men and *black* women. From the dawn, the very dawn. You know of that, everyone knows of it.

White woman and black *man?*

He's not, he's not black. He's also tawny.

All? How do you know?

I think he'll be tawny, and there's a kind of ginger and other condiment in his smell. It is not heavy, his smell is not thick, like pitch.

Other niggers have that smell.

Not Beauty Beast! Oh, you beautiful, you beautiful, *you resemblance of Joel.*

Now look you, woman, you know well enough what's ado. Beauty Beast is crocodiles and coffles. Coffles, caffels, *cafilas,* strings of slaves bolted together. There are camelopards beyond Beauty Beast, and lions and pigmies and varieties of desert and jungle. Thick jungle, monkeys swinging, rare odd flowers which eat insects, and flowers eating birds, and flowers noxious, and flowers smelling like rot. And worse than rot.

Field hands' quarters?

You freak. He's a nigger.

Remember what they are: sing bizarre songs, have bizarre practices. They sway and grunt and stare. The thin ones own an especial thinness of the shanks, and fat ones are especially oily and sweating and grotesque. They mess things about. Mess in corners, sweep dirt, hide it. They roll their eyes as in lunacy, show the whites. They grumble, they lie.

God help, God help. I crave him.

The cream—

She trod slyly, trod slyly as certain men might go to ravishment, or certain women simpering to assignation. She knew the way. Cream was on the table where it always stood. Sometimes she sipped it in the morning hungrily whilst dressing, if it had waited unused and unsoured, as in colder weather. Often also it went into the chamber-pot, or over the rail into beds of transplanted lilies.

Sometimes it was employed.

What's that, Linnet? (She'd come a-tapping.)

I come bring mistess her cream. Done forgot cream. Sorry, mistess.

Once Linnet was gone back below stairs they all might be talking about it, saying, Mistess do love have cream to drink at night, yet it ain build no fat on her frame.

233

Viennese desk waited against the north wall of that wide room. Sidney could find the magic compartment in darkest of nights, had done so.

Up rolls the top, there is such meaning in the smooth promising sound.

Now two little drawers are removed, upper right; now the third one out. Press against ancient paper which dresses the interior: an entire frame which had held the drawers slips out. A secret compartment is beyond. Press on this side; compartment door slides open, and your hand can explore the space. A beloved silk sack is contained there, with weight inside.

Why didn't they make it hollow? It's so very solid.

Had they made it hollow, hollowness is a synonym for fragility. Pettey J. would have snapped it with crushings and proddings.

Strange that the same instrument which brought such misery before may now effect a fleeting joy. But that might be true also if the object were alive, and formed of flesh instead of elderly silica and— Carbon? Lime? How the fires must have blazed to melt sand, build glass when it was new and pungent and malleable. Color— What wizards they were. Somewhere I've read about materials they mix to make the hues. Yellow? Silver, or uranium.

Joel so tanned, and naturally swarth to begin with.

Beauty Beast is— Is a gentleman.

A gentleman of color. Yah, yah, yah.

Back upon the bed, and cream is brought to hand. Loose fragment of Shakespeare adhering, as if intermingled with the fresh sweet clots. *Now is she in the very lists of love.*

Not now. But soon.

(Odd comes the notion. A cow is lowing in this lateness of night—perhaps that Dinah cow, her calf's just been taken from her, possibly she gave the cream.)

And Shakespeare wrote of man and girl, both vigorous. No lorn woman lolling in enforced chastity, with nightdress taken off.

Delicately as one might. How delicately can that be?

Thank Heaven for the cream. Delicate also. So rich. Oily.

How dare I invoke the name of Heaven? Would Heaven not be agog at an antic such as this? Moneyed woman, nigh onto thirty-three in age, twice married, twice widowed, woman alone and aloof, making capital out of remoteness and conscious dignity. Herewith she performs that trick which her mother used to term a Secret Sin.

No daughter of mine must ever be guilty of Secret Sin.

What care you, Mrs. *Shal*lop? You're fabricating your own private disgrace.

Disgrace indeed! I have become heiress to an endowed plaything. I am so fortunate, so very fortunate to feel this way, and to know that—

I can see him now. Him, him. See *them*. Them, them. They are fused: a Joel-Beauty-Beast at first, but can it be that I am losing the Joel? Astounding! It was as if they were moulded together for a while, but surely Joel is fading. Beauty Beast haunts alone. I'm all confused, but this is—

Adoration.

Ha, stop it. Stop for a moment. Cease.

For if you don't, you'll not partake of the long salacious value of it: reflection, jolly wrigglings in between, riot that comes when you hear your own voice soliciting aloud. Twill be wasted, wasted, going too fast, too fast, I say again too *fast*. Must be slower.

Slower.

That's better.

Ah, nasty little Linnet! Dear Beauty Beast, you have her, have her, have her. What care I? What care we?

Not *possibly*. I could never stand idly by and—

You could never stand idly by.

Desist. I declared them to be, and identified them as, nigger children. All is forgiven. I forgive you also, Beauty Beast, for being blackamoor.

Ah.

Because I thought the long shiny arms were tight around me, I was confident that I felt their squeeze. And smelt them also, smelt the juice of armpits, felt treasured weight upon me. Weight which should have been a gay abundance, long ago, and never could be with that grisly Calvin, and his dry jamming and jerking; or with Pettey J. oh poor Pettey J. His Venus' curses left him with nothing but a worthless tendril hanging as a root might dangle from a dead stump. Yet he owned the grim desire, and so he loved to hear a plaint of women. Or sometimes, I suppose, marshalling the two together and forcing them to—

One way or another. Both Jiggy and Yellow Martha were involved, involved together. I heard them.

What mad wonder works, possessing me again?—I fear too frequently. To think that the very instrument, the very weapon, very torture tool which was a dread has now become a momentary salvation. Ah, more than salvation.

A bliss, a bliss.

Wild we enter the tourney (what was that The Bard set down about *the lists of love?*). We are so able and prancing and chewing well. My mouth is open, I feel it open, gulping air, the moisture flying. The rest of me open, open, open to receive. And how that thing is *plied*, it's plied so well, I know because I'm *plying it.*

Oh, hot sliding Fate. Someone gave dictation, twas ordained, this was the night, the night for— Began so tenderly and ordinarily with music he touched from the pianoforte. I slept, I was awake. And then the bird, the mockingbird, and Keats, John Keats, and then, what was I hearing in my Lake Tannin, I heard them, and so I sped, I knew.

No, no, I didn't know. But so I felt and so I—

Cream was here. The Thing, the glorious Thing was in its nest. What other relic did that Viennese lady, who owned the desk before, put there? Shall I ever know? Perhaps she kept another Thing of glass. Perhaps she had *the same one.* But now it's mine, and it is his as well. All in my fancy he is wielding it.

Ah, yes, now *rapid.* Now it can be *rapid.* So very fast indeed. But not quite—not quite *that busily.*

Now easy, easier. And then— Oh, just like *that.*

Again, again!

Ho for the clouds, and we shall roll among them, they're stuffed with silk and satin. They are piled higher than the most ultimate shiver of the night bird's song, the nightingale of Keats, the mockingbird of Sidney, haha. Am I now laced intimate with Keats? Ah, was he tan and hard, yellow and hard? Oh, was he, was he? No, poor thing: consumptive. But still I feel as if I were akin to him. Because as well I am akin to all the clouds, and kin to you—you— O my enchanted darling, I am all of this: your wife, your mother, yea I'm your angel and your aunt, and let me screech instead of sing. For we are representing the entire fund of lovers' agony and lovers' madness which has ever come about. Twas saved for us, it flows right here, here, there, there, oh mercy, mercy, mercy. We've done it, we are doing it. I feel your breath on me, I feel your mouth about my breast. Ha, quick the other. Here, here, here, You Other Mouth. Invent this happy ravishment instead of force, yes, yes, most gaily-plotted rape that ever came about. Propelled upon the clouds again at last, at last, the clouds of satin and velour, and I am rolling there, and you are rolling too, we roll together, limbs around you, my small feet a-beating out their vulgar fury on your hide.

Danger, danger, danger bristling. Danger! However can I say another word? Just mumble, mumble, gulp for air, and mumble, mumble, here we are, we are, as lovers always were we are, as lovers, lovers, over, over, more and more, you're in me all the while, you're out, you're in, you're with me, I am giddy, you are plunging fierce. And *we,* and *we—*

Oh—

Christ.

~11~

MONDAY MORNING, Sidney rode to town as speedily as Nineveh and the team could take her. Fenton Ledge had spoken of an appearance which he must make on this day, and she hoped to find him at the office before court convened.

Only young Mr. Buck Heyward was present. Senator Ledge went directly to the courthouse from his home, madam. But there may be a postponement, it was rumored so. If you choose to wait, perhaps the senator will be back within the hour.

It's only that I wish to have a letter drawn and signed by him.

I'll be glad to draw it up for you, Mrs. Shallop, if you'll offer the details.

Very well. It is to be directed to Mr. LeRoi Cuzzen, whom I should not wish to address personally. But if Senator Ledge, acting as agent and attorney-at-law—

I understand, madam. He limped nervously, eager to please, settling the caller in a comfortable chair, laying out writing materials, reminding Sidney of her father in gesture, expression, intonation.

Twill take but a few minutes, Mr. Heyward. The letter will be brief. We should address Mr. Cuzzen at his home. What is it? Some flower. Dogbane?

Myrtle Acres, and the youth went into a fit of giggles.

Brief as the letter might be, it was a considerable time in the writing. There were frequent interruptions: several other clients appeared, seeking Fenton Ledge, but all withdrew at not finding him in. Mr. G. Wash came by, fetching his son's luncheon in a basket with a red napkin over the top, and said that he was Red Riding Hood.

Of course Buck *always* totes his lunch to the office, so that he shan't have to walk home at noon. You know, Buck is *very* lame.

This in immediate presence and hearing of the young man, who kept his face turned down.

But our old nigger woman is a dreadful lazybones, and this morning she claimed to have a toothache—sheer pretense, you know how they are—and claimed that she couldn't *possibly* get out of bed. Well, what with one thing and another, the lunch wasn't ready until *now*. So I'm on my way to the Porlock place, I'm doing their youngest granddaughter, she's here a-visiting. And the most *divine* little creature, with delicate pink cheeks and delicate pink hair, if you can call it that. There's a *great* delicacy about her, she should have been painted by Fragonard or Boucher. But as it is, I'm doing my best. Yes, in oils, not *too* large a canvas. And oh, Mrs. Shallop, how is that *wonderful* quadroon or whatever you call him? Your boy who plays so excellently. Black Boy, isn't that his name? And *is* the Broadwood standing up under his attack?

Once the elder Mr. Heyward had gone winging across town, they settled to the letter again. Buck was revising the last lines according to Sidney's preference, when Senator Ledge came in.

My eyes are keen, for those of an old man. All the way across the courthouse square I could see Nineveh with the carriage, here at the rail. I trust that Mr. Heyward has given a good account of himself in taking care of you? Come inside, my dear.

Why, what's this? he asked sharply, once they were settled in the inner office, and young Heyward had offered him the sheet, and had gone out and closed the door.

Mr. LeRoi Cuzzen, Myrtle Acres, Holgate County. Sir: It has been brought to my attention that, not too long since, you expressed a desire to acquire—

This much he read aloud, and then went on reading to

242

himself, at first with lips moving, and then with his mouth squeezed shut in obvious disapproval.

He put down the letter and said simply, Child.

I intend to sell her.

But what will you do for a lady's maid?

My dining room girl, India, can be trained.

But Linnet's trained already.

Senator Ledge, sir. Is it essential that I go into domestic details which I had rather not discuss?

Of course not. But—

Then allow me to say only that there are certain things which cannot be tolerated. I recalled that Mr. Cuzzen, before my husband's death, often expressed a desire to acquire this property. No doubt he will be willing to pay the going market price for the girl. If not— Then let him have her at a lower price. She shall leave Apoxsee, and immediately, that's all there is to it.

Fenton Ledge arose (in that moment he gave the impression of being weary, and it was still nowhere near noon) and looked down, studying Sidney's face. I never saw you so. Repeated musingly, as if searching for reassurance. Never saw you so.

Sidney tried to turn herself into brass. Soon there fell discomfort, soon her gaze ran from him. Spasmodically she clutched one hand upon the other, mashing gloves between.

Rich steady voice said presently, Whatever occurred has occurred since Saturday evening. Am I correct in that assumption?

Twisted gloves, felt sharp edge of button cutting into the ball of her thumb, let it keep grinding deeper.

Tell him nothing. Not—one—word.

Ledge moved past the corner of the wide table. To Sidney's surprise he reached down with his great left hand, put the hand under her chin, and tilted her head back against the rocking-chair where she sat. Graven face came down, his amazingly soft lips touched lightly on her forehead.

There, he said. Never did that before, did I?

You've kissed my *hand*.

Often. And I'd like to kiss your lips. But nothing could come of it. Not a thing. So—

He walked restlessly to the window, stood looking out for a

time, though all anyone could see from that window were a high board fence and a rainwater barrel. Then he came back and stood beside her.

Once and for all, you must know how it is with me. Were I a much younger man, and you'd have me, I'd call it quits with Hen. One way or another.

(His nickname for his wife Henrietta, and several other people's nickname as well. Cruelly appropriate, Sidney believed.)

Call it quits, buy her off. She loves money too well, Ledge burst out in a rare flash of anger and disgust.

Then once more in control.

Often I've thought this, never have I said it to you before. If you choose to forget that I've spoken so, tis just as well. But do remember that anything which I may suggest or advise is prompted by solicitude and affection.

Thank you.

Two words nearly lost. Then it was like a sneeze, like orgasm, she felt it coming. Tears. Sidney sobbed convulsively for several minutes. She heard her own muted mewling, Don't like to cry. Why, I never cry. She was dabbing at her face with tiny kerchief, then started to mop with the gloves. Ledge's handkerchief served better.

Child.

I'm all right now.

Dear Sidney, you gave the impression that there were certain things which you chose not to discuss. Your motive or purpose, shall we say? The impelling factor—whatever. Now then, am I correct in my assumption that you detest Mr. Cuzzen?

Can't abide him.

You'll loathe him even more if you hear me out. There are things which men— At least, those who pretend to the state of being gentlemen. Perhaps only a few stragglers left in my own generation. God knows. The changing attitude of the times— Ah, well. I mean to say: things they do not discuss with ladies. Not even with their wives. But in this case it is essential that I tell you. This is a thing I know for a fact. Cuzzen had in his household a little maid named Gwenny. Twelve, thirteen, somewhere in that category. Kitchen-maid, parlor-maid, upstairs girl? Cannot recall: this occurred some years since. Mrs. Cuzzen was ailing, as she still is; and she had been taken on a sea voyage to New Orleans by Dr. and Mrs. Carrington, who hoped that the change might do her good. So Cuzzen, as many will do, declared bachelor's hall. One night he had four guests. They were busy with cards—cards and bottles. You've had some experience—

Sidney closed her eyes and nodded.

Later the slave girl, Gwenny, was brought in for their delectation. They took her, child, five men, one after the other. Including the master.

Grateful for the glass of water which Ledge poured from his carafe.

I don't blame you for feeling ill. I grow sick myself, every time I think of it.

My dear late husband—?

He was one of them. It was before he lost his—powers. Well, then. Gwenny was rendered pregnant as a result of this business. But she miscarried and died of hemorrhage.

Child. His voice rang. You'll not sell Linnet to LeRoi Cuzzen. I'll buy her myself first. Though I can't well imagine what Mrs. Ledge would do with two personal maids. Sell her off in turn, I suspect. If she could make a fancy profit.

Sidney kept motioning dumbly, and finally Ledge understood. He went round and got the letter, passed it across to her. She tore the page to bits. Ledge hunted amid debris and came up with a pottery vessel in which several cigar butts mildewed. He dumped them into his waste basket, and produced a phosphorus match. Crackle and smell, they had their paper bonfire, sat watching it.

What of young Mr. Heyward?

He's well on the reliable side. I've found this true in the past, and do not expect to be disappointed in the future. For all his girlish whimsies, Buck's not a blabbermouth like his parent. He holds his tongue very well. I'll simply mention that we arrived at another decision insofar as this property is concerned. He'll forget the whole matter, or at least pretend that he has forgotten.

The Wilkeys, she said.

Wilkeys?

They shall have Linnet.

He smiled and began to shake his head. Child, I'm afraid that you're due for disappointment there.

By no means. We are good friends, and I'm almost as conversant with their financial status as you yourself. I know all about Mr. Bonaparte Wilkey's purchase— That big piece from the Iversons. Know that he refuses to sell off any land, and always succumbs to a mania for buying more. Know that there are times when they scarcely have one dime to lay against another. Know that at this moment they're strapped, and shan't have any money until they've sold their crop—

Senator Ledge held up his hand. Enough, enough! I'm often hard put to pull him out of the scrapes he gets into. The specter of bankruptcy stalks forever! What'll you do, then? *Give* Linnet to Mrs. Wilkey?

To Daughter Nell. She has no maid of her own, and she's a dear sweet thing, used miserably by Fate. I think it might hearten her, to have her own maid. Old Juno does for the two of them, and Juno's becoming infirm, and her hands shake—she can't even brush Eleanor's hair decently, or do up a frill. So will you please to have a Deed of Gift drawn?

Not that. A regular conveyance shall be made: a true Bill of Sale, in standard fashion, just as you'd sold her to the Wilkeys at whatever price she would normally fetch. We'll say, *The sum of One Dollar, to me in hand paid, and other valuable considerations.* Printed forms are available, only needing to be filled in in the proper places.

He pulled the soiled silk rope above his desk, and a bell made solemn tone in the outer office.

Bill of Sale, please, Buck. Personal property, goods, chattels.

With a mortgage also, sir?

No, this is strictly cash. *And other valuable considerations.*

When he was gone, Sidney whispered, Wish I were a Catholic.
Why so?

Because I could go to confession. I feel soiled. Self-smeared, grimy. At my own instigation.

Then I shall be your priest, and pretend that already you've confessed to me. Bald enough, am I not, to be a Franciscan? Aren't they the ones with shaven pates? But pray don't neglect to tell me what poor Eleanor Wilkey says and does when you inform her of your generosity.

He added, in a different tone, There is only one thing—

We have three types, sir. Step-thud, step-thud, Heyward came in and placed the forms before Fenton Ledge. You'll wish to examine them, and make your own selection. He went away, closing the door with care.

Sidney was standing. One thing?

Perhaps Yaupon is a little too close to Apoxsee?

Linnet's Aunt Eve is owned by the Wilkeys, and her mother used to be, when living. Linnet is devoted to her Aunt Eve.

She's known as The Elephant? He began to chuckle.

I fear you're correct. She's the laundress, heavier and blacker than her kettles. But forever Linnet is begging to go to Yaupon. And—

Crisply. There's no night-wandering on the Wilkey place. Every darkey in the country is mortally afraid of Peg-leg Paul. He's their watchman, and comes on duty at dusk, very proud of himself. Goes about with a club and pistol. The pistol won't shoot, but the colored don't know that. There may be some hanky-panky at other plantations, but not at Yaupon. No slave, male *or* female—

Sidney stressed the *or* unconsciously.

—Goes off that place at night. Nor does a stranger come *on*.

Ledge stood squinting for a moment before escorting her to the carriage. Child, I think you've made a wise decision.

She spoke softly. So do I.

Dear Sidney, I declare, just look at my hands, just a-shaking so, I can't get over it, I'm all atremble. It's just the most lovely splendid beautiful thing that ever happened to me in all my born days. I know Mother said I shouldn't, and probably I *shouldn't*. But if it's what you want to do, and— I'm mighty glad Mother went back to supervise that soap-making, cause she's already made a meal, and I hadn't yet: was out doing a little supervising my own self, whilst she et. And Father's over to the Iverson place—something bout drainage on that new piece of property. So you couldn't have dropped by on a better day. But when you get right down to brass tacks, why, I *am* over twenty-one— Well, and then some. And I got perfect right to accept a gift if I want to, hain't I? Oh, I know you got your reasons, as you said plain enough. But at least the old folks aren't around right now to *meddle,* and we can just set right here and eat our biscuits and preserves and cold duck—have our little old snack all by our lonesome. Law, Mrs., I just break right out in a glow, every time I think of it! To have a maid *all my own*. And Linnet, of all critters. I'll be bound. Well, I just judge from what you said that there's been some kind of carrying-on over there, and I'm not going to fret you bout it; but I just wonder if it isn't that yellow darkey that does such scrumptious cooking and plays piano like a little old lamb. Fact is, Linnet'll probably get to cutting up some kind of high jinks over here. You know, we got a boy name of Lucifer, and Linnet *lets on* that she comes a-visiting her Aunt Eve, like she always tells you; but I do think Lucifer's just about the chief attraction, far as Linnet's concerned. He's a big brown fellow, real expert at plastering and masonry and such arts. Oh yes, and he's the one that Father lets take an old fowling-piece and go out for birds, and he just plain *fetches* em in. Course, we try to keep that kind of quiet, cause Father says it's not cording to the law. But— I think your Linnet— Sakes, she's going to be *my* Linnet now— Is just honing for that big brown boy. So she ought to be happy over here at Yaupon, and I reckon she won't have the sulks *too* long, if she didn't want to be sold to me. Now, I know that's what you said we were to tell her, and what you'll tell her: that's she's sold, not gifted. Well, I declare. When I think of having her do my hair at night, and then— Instead of old

248

fumble-buttons Juno shaking all over the place, and breathing just like a railway engine. And Sidney, her *breath* is so *bad*. It's got so I just can't abide having her do for me. Now— To have *my own* ladies' maid! Why, I'm so set up. I got some precious savings all hid away in a china powder-box— Did I ever show you that box? Twas a keepsake from Grandma Mansinging. And I'm going to set down right today and start going through all our *Lady's Books,* and just see what to get. Very next time we drive into town, I'm going straight off to Cousin Willie Ann Merrill's place and decide what she should stitch for me. You know, I hear tell that Mrs. Dowson is going to give a ball for some niece of her husband's who'll come a-visiting soon. Word's gone round and— Oh, Sidney, I'm sorry, I know you're not on good terms with Mrs. Dowson, and I'm not really, either; but if we *do* get asked, and I suppose we shall be— And then, to have a new gown and to have my own maid to do me up! If satin didn't come so high, I actually believe I'd— You know: the skirt very plain and very *very* full, with a little kind of train thing, and then a fall of lace up round the neck. But I reckon satin would be too costly, so I'll have to be content with something less expensive, cause I haven't got *too* much saved in that pink powder-box. Sidney, lamb, how do you really feel bout pagoda sleeves?—I know you don't *prefer* to wear them. But oh, your gowns are just so beautiful. And Linnet—she does keep all your marquise waists and chemisettes in such downright *beautiful* condition. Well, it just takes my breath clean away. Sidney, are you sure you're not going to be regretful? I hope this isn't too much an act of impulse or—or— Cause you can always have her *back.* You know that. Just any time you *want.* But I suppose there'll be— Isn't there some kind of paper that folks have to sign? I don't know a single thing bout such matters. Course, Father always looks after all our affairs and accounts; but he won't always be here, so doubtless I've much to learn. A Bill of Sale? Oh, Senator Ledge's drawing it up? Isn't that wonderful? And—Sidney— You spose it could be in *my name?* I mean my *own* name, not to Father. Goodness sake, that's what you had in mind all *along?* And it's being done? Darling Sidney, I can *kiss* you for that. I'm just going to give you a little old kiss, right *now*. There! You know, Linnet'll be the first darkey I ever had for my very own. Oh, there was a little nigger gal when I was young, and she used to run errands and such—do for me in little ways. Course, we'd *play* together, too. A lot. We played dolls, and we used to play at horses, too. We had a great big stable just plain *full* of horses. They were just sticks; but we fixed kind of little bridle strings on em, and had em all named. Her name was Zoë—the nigger gal—and she was just the smartest brightest thing. And then— I guess it was when I was bout thirteen, Zoë fell sick. Yes, twas dyphtheric fever, and oh she was *so* sick. And then she *died*. Poor little old Zoë. I felt so bad off that I cried night and day. Cried like I was *possessed*. Imagine crying like that bout a nigger, but I *did*. Never did have another nigger of my own. Goodness, I just had I don't know *how* many cats. But Mug run off somewhere or other— You know, he was a regular *tom*cat. And Martha died whilst she was trying to give birth to a litter of kittens, poor thing. And then Tippy got stepped on by a horse, and— Sakes alive. Something terrible just seemed to befall *all* my cats, and the kittens too. One of em got et by a *rat*— ain't that awful? But— Sidney, to think of having *my own maid*. I got to weep a little, I just can't *help it*. Oh, look, it's *raining* again. And there's Mother, coming back to the house. She'll make a lot of talk bout how I hadn't ought to accept such *munificence,* and so on and so on. But I don't *care*. I'm going to *accept*. I'll just put my foot down, and tell her that the gift is to *me,* not to *her*. You know, a girl's just got to put her foot down with her own mother sometimes. And— Would you mind terribly if I asked Linnet to do my hair the *identical* way you do yours? Would you mind, honey? I'd just *love* to have it like yours. Twould make me feel so good inside.

It had occurred to Sidney, when struck with remorse at Fenton Ledge's revelation concerning LeRoi Cuzzen, that it might be well to give Linnet to Emma or to Mamie. Emma was remarried years before, to Mr. Chat Hendry. (Lavinia Hendry died of cancer shortly after Sidney went abroad with sister and niece.) Emma was well supplied with servants. So was Mamie, wed to a young tobacco broker and busily bearing a succession of fat-faced babies. A long way home to Carolina, and how might Linnet be transported there? The idea was rejected in the same instant it was born. Eleanor Wilkey stood as the proper solution. Her pathetic—well-nigh hysterical—acceptance lingered in Sidney's memory.

(Nobody'd heard from Joel Airhart during recent years. He'd survived the fighting in Mexico and some affrays with Comanche Indians which followed. His description of these incidents, as included in rare letters which came to his mother and were passed on to other relatives, was, *Intersting*. He spoke of commanding and directing a small fleet of freight wagons operating on the frontier, but whether he worked in the role of owner or part owner or paid employee he did not say. In his last letter, in 1851, he'd spoken of a journey to California, followed by return to the New Mexico country and Texas again. Joel wrote in concentrated enthusiasm, describing men with whom he'd journeyed or worked, or whom he'd fought beside in wilderness encounters; but he did not speak of marriage or indeed of women in any way. He wrote nothing about his financial situation, nor did he ever send any money home; but no longer was there need for that. It was Sidney's relationship to Joel and her passion for him which put him to wandering in the first place, but she now supposed him to be one born to the wandering. Forever she'd remember that glint of suns and stars when first he spoke of Texas. There were certain insistent travelers across unrecorded deserts, she knew, who found themselves irked by bare consideration of family ties; they stripped themselves clean of any such harnessing. Oftentimes there'd been hatred fouling the home; but often too there'd been only respect and even admiration along with every other affecting exchange. Still the dissolution of any liability of kinship might be hankered after, and obtained. In solitary orgy of the preceding night, it became clear to Sidney that the illusion of Beauty Beast had supplanted the illusion of Joel, both as symbol and as treasure for future embracement. Contemplating the nephew, she saw him as a figure to be visioned without either longing or regret. He walked off with agility and in confidence, wore rough romantic clothing, was armed adequately, ate wild flesh, drank from purest streams in azure mountains, turned to salute her and others in farewell. At night when the moon was on him, he heard coyotes howling, and only rose up on one elbow and said, Listen to that, now. Then he relaxed in steady assured sleep of one loving lonely earth and the cliffs and sharp cactus or giant trees that go with it.)

Nineveh brought the carriage to the door at Yaupon. He'd got the top up, side curtains were in place, he'd wiped the cushions dry. Mrs. Wilkey demanded that somebody fetch an umbrella. Sidney said that she needed no umbrella, and dived down the steps and up into the carriage in the same breath.

Daughter Nell cried, Sidney, lamb. You're going to send her over *this very day?*

Nineveh shall bring Linnet, soon as she's had time to pack her duds.

On Apoxsee soil beyond the Big Gate they encountered Mr. Irons, who rode out in poncho and oiled hat. He'd been to examine corn in the Far Field. He brought his horse to the nigh side of the carriage and Sidney opened curtains to speak with him. Irons complained about the rain, said he'd have to take the hands off cotton.

But you insisted that we needed rain so severely, Mr. Irons.

Not *this* much, ma'am. Everything that's open is getting down and wet. If we don't have some bright sun to dry it—

But only two or three days ago—

Yes, I know, ma'am. Truth is, we're better off than some. I've got around the region a little, and some of the neighbors won't make more'n half a crop. They've got fine weed, but no fruit on the stalks.

And in my innocence, I'd thought these rains to be a God-send!

Well, ma'am, they come a trifle late. Our pea crop, and

potatoes, and the little bit of cane we got, are all bad hurt by drought.

She thought emphatically, I never heard a husbandman—a planter, farmer, call him what you will—who didn't complain about the weather. She envisioned a new page to be toilsomely inscribed in the daily journal.

> Tuesday, 12 of September, 1854.
> Un settld, more rain, wind N.E.
>
> | | |
> |---|---|
> | 2 | In sick barracks. Carmel, Dulsy. |
> | 4 | At gin, 2 work on screw |
> | 2 | Haul fodder. |
> | 1 | C.A. repare ox cart. |
> | 2 | Delia, Lenten cook for hands. |
> | 3 | At gardning. Adam, plus 4 haff hands. |
> | 1 | Coot, to town with 7 bales cotton. |
> | 1 | Mind mules. Tod. |
> | 3 | Mind other stock. |
> | 3 | Split rails. |
> | 2 | Driving, Maddy, Honga. |
> | 1 | Mind sick children. Sarah. |
> | 42 | Pulling corn in Ridge Field, Far Field. |
>
> ———
> 67

Of Mr. Irons she asked, Did you have Adam duly flogged?

Yes, ma'am. Twas done early.

Was there any trouble?

Mrs. Shallop, he was sober enough by that time, and he plain walked in there and put up his hands to be tied. Barely grunted, spoke a few cuss-words. Honga might of been beating the broad side of the barn, for all the fuss Adam made. Honga was willing to really cut him up, but I drew the line. Lashes were laid on in regular fashion, no sense in being mean about it. After all, there's small profit in carving a good stout able hand to ribbons. Don't you agree?

I do. Is he at work now?

Can't say as to that, count of the rain, it's come on so heavy. But I tell you, he was back in that garden—tweren't more than an hour after he was whipped. Most hands couldn't bear with it but he's built like—

Thank you, Mr. Irons. I hope this flogging's saved the day. I should not like to dispose of Adam.

As the carriage started, Sidney put her face to the curtains again to tell him, I have sold my personal maid to the Wilkeys. Incredulity marked his face at her words. (Account-wise, in the matter of plantation records, there was no reason to discuss this matter with the overseer. He had nothing to do with house servants, with their acquisition or sale. Such doings were concern of the mistress herself, and of her attorney and banker.)

She realized in distaste that she'd informed Irons before she'd even told the subject of the sale.

Nineveh—

Yes, mistress. As he was handing her down.

Did you eat at the Wilkeys'?

Dolly, she give me good meal.

Did the team have their nose-bags?

Yessum. Well fed.

Very well, keep them in the carriage. Linnet is to go to the Wilkeys' in a very little while, and you will take her. She'll have her things, box and bundles.

The loose seamed face gaped at her. He'd heard her mention Linnet to Mr. Irons as well as to the Wilkeys, yet the fact had not sunk in. White folks talking to white folks. But in this moment, addressed directly, he understood.

Linnet, she *sold* to Wilkeys?

Yes, Nineveh.

Soberly. Nobody ain been sold off this place in long while. Cept that Yellow Martha. And what they call that other girl? Jiggy?

You'll be summoned as soon as Linnet's things are ready to be put into the carriage.

Sidney went directly to her room, and rang for Linnet. When the girl appeared, the mistress asked first that she arrange bonnet and shawl for dying.

I do not think twill be necessary to put them near a fire,

they're but mildly dampish. Also the skirt of this gown is wet—come now, undo me, then fetch my flowered wrapper—the tan and gold—

Settled at her dressing table, Sidney looked into the mirror, gave long scrutiny to Linnet. The girl moved about, spreading gown for drying, rearranging shawl, fitting bonnet on its block. Sidney had thought to be direct and rudely severe, she'd gloated earlier about the sale to come. She'd typified the creature as Nigger Bitch, and anticipated Linnet's frustration at recognizing there would be no more clandestine revels in the mistress's pond. But in these minutes Sidney experienced that unnerving deflation of wrath, almost apologetic in intensity, which overwhelms those who are by nature charitable of heart and unaccustomed to practicing villainies. Still Linnet must go. There was Sidney Shallop's peace of mind to be considered, her vital if covert female jealousy. Lady, she informed herself, the whole matter's painful on your mind, so best to get it off.

And you could not help but be relieved when you heard about the boy Lucifer.

Linnet. I have news for you.

Mistess?

You like very much to go to Yaupon—

Linnet grinned. Mistess, I does surely. My Aunt Eve—

This day you go to Yaupon, and you will be living there from now on.

Jaw sagged, full purplish lips seemed to pale and collapse and widen. Hazel-brown eyes held on Sidney sleepily.

Wench is dreaming. She does not understand what I have said.

I've sold you, Linnet, to Miss Nell Wilkey. You will now be her maid instead of mine.

Tinted full mouth opened further in effort to speak. Demand was too much, words could not be uttered, eyes still stared from under lowered lids.

Go over Yaupon with my Aunt *Eve?*

Not with your Aunt Eve. With Miss Nell, Miss Eleanor Wilkey. You will be her personal maid, just as you've been mine these several years. You have been sold, Linnet. Can't you understand? I've *sold you* to Miss Nell, and you will be living there.

She must grasp it at last, but is still tranced in some fashion.

But who going *do* for you, mistess? You gowns an all? You room. An—hair? An—

India shall be trained up in your stead.

But she dining room girl.

So were you, to begin with, until I came to Apoxsee. Then I selected you as my personal maid. Just as I have now chosen India to replace you.

Linnet asked only one more question, feebly. Mistess. How come you sell me?

Because Miss Wilkey has long desired to have a maid of her own, and there's no one at Yaupon who can serve. Miss Eleanor and I are both satisfied with the transaction as it has been made.

Sidney's voice lifted. You will go down now, pack your things, and Nineveh will drive you to Yaupon. That gray valise in the closet yonder, I'll give it to you for your own. Take all your little belongings: combs, scent, soap, kerchiefs and the like—everything except your Apoxsee frocks, the ones such as you are wearing now. Leave those behind, they'll be made over for others. Do you take the light-brown linen out of the press yonder—one with blue ruching—

Yes. That.

You may wear it today. You'll wish to look nicely dressed up as you first come to Miss Nell, won't you?—so it shall be yours as a parting gift.

Take the valise now, and the gown, and go down and pack. Your own gowns—Sunday best and all—should not be bundled or crushed, but folded carefully to go on the carriage seat, with something over them to keep off the wet.

You may tell the other wenches what has happened.

Wenches?

Beauty Beast.

Ha.

Then have India come up to me. I must talk with her.

Do not dally about your packing. Tis already well into the afternoon.

Linnet breathes, the slender bosom vibrates in breathing. It was outer air, owned by no one, but now that she brings it into her chest the air is become part of her body, and thus an addition to the owner's moiety. Then expelled, out the air goes. Her owner is again the poorer by lung-fulls.

Property in a process of transfer at the moment. No papers signed yet, they will be signed.

Sold. To the lady yonder. In this case Miss Nell Wilkey, overcome with nerves and fangs and loneliness.

You occupy your room now, mistress, listening to rain dripping, hearing the occasional far hoot of a darkey, yelp of a child, brayings made by stock. All of these you own (Sounds as well?). Wet roofs, wet trees, wet cotton, puddles in clay driveway, you possess them. You sit here—soon you'll lie relaxed, resting—and you are aloof. You recognize the suspended quality of your abstraction—no directed energy in limbs or flowing out through fingertips. You know this cool eminence, tis immediately premenstrual, it comes upon you with every moon.

But what if someone were to address you, as you just addressed yourself to Linnet, and say, Go pack your duds, I'll give you this box and that gown, you are to live elsewhere. Because I've sold you.

Suppose?

Suppose what indeed? I suffered it long ago. Felt an anguish worse than Linnet will ever feel, because I had more sensitivity.

And— And— I was *white*. I wasn't a nigger. And— And—

Dear Father. Dear Philip Sidney Veck. Announcing it. Daughter, your mother and I have arranged that you shall marry Mr. Tensley. No, no!—that's all there is *to* it. No vapors and megrims on your part. No fume and fussing, young lady! Your mother and I know what is best.

Damn him. Damn the dry ghost of Calvin. Damn Mother. Damn em all. I was sold peremptorily. Again I'll give you the amount fetched at the sale: eleven hundred and—

Bitter Mistress, Water Hickory Mistress, Bitter Pecan Mistress, what wrong did you intend to effect? What devilish trade would you have indulged in, had it not been for the stout soul of Fenton Ledge who loves you? You'd have sent the girl into a bed more vile than that of Calvin Tensley. You were all for ordaining it.

Rail if you will, then, about grotesque young years when you went stony or cringing in your attempted enactment of the role of matron. But rejoice that you made not your own miseries an excuse for visiting additional anguish upon one whom you know to be guiltless of any crime except that of exciting your own dudgeon. And in the alternative, the substitution which actually was brought about, you evoked a quaint little-girl delight in one soul long dried for the lack of it. Rejoice!

You've owned Linnet, thus you can do this to her. It may be for better or for worse, in her heart, in her miniature mind. But a point must be made: the choice was not hers. Twas yours.

An owner owns, has the right to do what she may select to do. An owner owns more than pea-pods, straw, mules. Owner owns more than trumpet-honeysuckles in their season, more than cut timber waiting to be burnt in winter, more than bells sending jangles through a kitchen passageway, more than that roofed passage itself. Ah, dainties other than Lake Tannin, other than house-spiders, *baa*ing sheep, elderberry lace, graves where bones of slaves lie near the higher pines, and where woodpeckers with arched necks go ramming with their beaks and crackling with their voices.

(Same woodpeckers: portion of the owner's flock, Bill of Sale signed by God.)

It has now been noted that the owner owns the respiration of his properties, their heartbeats and their thoughts. Owner owns every spermatozoon of the male slaves, and the eggs which black women put down for mating; and emerging babies which follow.

Slave, cherish you a special hope, cherish you a desire? They are mine. *Mine.* Bring them, unfold them, lay them out for me to see and decide. I am mistress, and I will have the skin of your palms if I choose, the quivering hair of you. The song: I'll make you sing it as I decide, and make your feet go dancing to accompany, or insist that you hold them motionless so that I be not annoyed. By exchange of money, by inheritance, by gift (as witnessed) you may be acquired, dispensed with, parceled out, reidentified on a new list. That is the law of the land. Not your land, *my* land. You are a chattel, and can be shunted, hunted, mortgaged as the yield from the fields. I own wells, own an ash-hopper, own ploughs, hogs, magnolia trees arustle like taffeta. I own you, you, you, and we'll have no nonsense about it. Machineries at the gin, blades, press, screw, they are belongings of mine. Corn is a belonging, any meat which hangs in the double-locked smoke-house, any wine in the cellar. And your big toe, little toe, your cough, shine of your eye and tremor of your pulse, juice of you, temper of you, your very ejaculation. They are apparent among my holdings, a logical part of them. Just as I am invincible proprietress of potatoes, fat-back, house furnishings, fence rails, plough-points, jasmine and willows, so am I the invincible proprietress of yourself and Basil, Nineveh, India. Name them: Dulcy, Goosey, Coot, Coony, Sarah. The very inches of earth wherein poor Tickle is ensconced in first decay. Meadows, mongrels, clothing in hamper, fire in the stove, meal and pork measured for rations. So do I own Maddy and Honga and Flash and Eddie. Fetch out the names, present them on the list, there are Caramel and Duke, there's C.A., there are Lenten and Delia, enumerate them. There are Trudge, Molly, Clemmy, Adam. *And you.* You're naught but another penny in my purse until I choose to dispose of you.

Correct, according to the plan of God? Many so affirm.

Privately I think it wrong. In secret I hold the conglomerate to be a horror; yet I'm too weak to dispense with it. Ownership has been awarded to me, I'll cling.

You are mine, or were mine. Mine, to be gifted away as I elect, according to mandate.

Beauty Beast also. He should know that.

Oh, he does, he does! All too sadly.
But did he not know, I'd make him learn.

There ensued an interview with India, rigmarole to be gone through again, along with impressing on India the import of her new assignment, every heed which she must pay—
India, are you chewing something?
Yessum.
What?
Sweet ellum.
What?
Sweet ellum.
Go get rid of that mouthful immediately. And you are to chew no more elm *at any time in the Big House.*
Yessum.
Tomorrow morning you will go to Trudge and she'll arrange to make new frocks for you. What you're wearing has become too childish. You are no longer a little girl.
Yessum, said the maid with enthusiasm, well aware that she was no longer a little girl.
At the first opportunity I'll carry you to town with me. You are to be fitted with shoes, supplied with stockings. No more barefoot days; you're grown, and able to be a lady's maid.
Yessum.
(Mercy me, what have I done? Must teach you to brush, fold, press, lay out, hang, freshen, draw a bath, turn down a bed, fetch things strictly personal, spread a night-rail— Gad.)
Mistess, I come say Goodbye. Linnet's small voice, bird voice directed by its sparrow's intelligence.
Sidney went down to see her off, to make additional gift of a few ribbons and such. The girl beamed with animation, won completely by unprecedented adventure. She giggled in the carriage, peeping out and flapping her hand, crying thinly, Bye, mistess. Bye, Injuh, Bye.
Imagine.
How could it ever *be?* Who'd have thought—?
That nigger at *Yaupon.* Lucifer. When she—

260

When Beauty Beast is *here*. When—

Nevertheless Sidney felt a sense of elation and thanksgiving. She said to India (something which she had never said to Linnet) , Be it understood from this first evening, that there are many times when I do not wish to be disturbed. Unless I bid you, therefore, you are never to come upstairs after I've retired. Any time I need you, I'll ring. Never, in the night, are you to come to my chamber unless I do ring. Do you understand?

Yessum.

Never.

Yessum.

~12~

DURING remaining days of September and on through October, Sidney found her life shaped with cordiality and smoothness unknown since Willowhurst. She experienced no turmoil when she regarded Beauty Beast, no conflict with established rule, mores, morals. Her intent was clear to herself without accompanying confusion. She recognized that the presence of Linnet at Apoxsee would have compounded resentment (I know, I know!—often distrust can be more hurtful than a proven fact). Now it was unnecessary to fry herself over a fire of daily suspicion. If those two had actually indulged themselves in what was most politely termed Nigger Nonsense, at least they did not longer intrude, either within her pond or her fretful spirit. (As for Lake Tannin: water grew increasingly cool, Sidney gritted teeth before she plunged.) Neither by gesture, glance nor by implied question did Beauty Beast display any reaction to the banishment of Linnet. He exuded cheerful vitality, ardent desire to please, whether at the piano or at his cookery.

Evenings extended into perennial delight.

Beyond voicing a desire for little luxuries difficult to obtain, with which to augment larder stores, Beauty Beast came forward with only one request. That was for music. He'd possessed previously a greater library than was represented in the parcel of sheets fetched along to Apoxsee. Through carelessness of a new overseer at Shearwater, this treasure had been lost to him after Judge Bracket's death.

You may have whatever music you wish. We'll order from the North.

Misty, I fear you'll think me unduly acquisitive. And the scores will cost a pretty penny. Some of them are hard to come by.

Do you make out the list.

Close in candlelight at the dining table they gleaned names of publishers from Beauty Beast's existing store of music. He said gloomily that many of the selections might be available only in Europe, there would be a long wait for transhipment.

I have been yearning for the opportunity, Misty, to build piano solos out of chosen baroque sonatas, trios, even quartets. Many composers accomplish that, delving into their own work previously scored for other instruments. I am not a composer but—

You are not a composer? Look me in the eye.

He turned his face away.

Beauty Beast, I said, Look me in the *eye*.

Misty, I swear. I've never played a single bar for you which was of my own composition. My own arrangements, my tran-scriptions—ah, that's another thing—

I *thought* that you'd composed. Now I know it definitely.

I'm reluctant to project any of the few things I've attempted. Please do not command me to do so.

Not for company, she said. I shan't. Not yet. Pray when do you play them?

When you're away. Such as, for instance— Monday you were to the Wilkeys. Yesterday you drove into town and dined at the minister's.

(Disconcerting, even to recollect the fact. But Fortunatus Stephens was pastor, so— Mrs. Cadmus Dowson had been among the guests. Her disregard of Sidney Shallop was impolitely evident.)

Beauty Beast said, Faltering things, *gavottes, ballades.* Some I've fiddled with for years. There is one which Judge Bracket—

266

He smiled sadly.

Did it please him?

I composed it in honor of Judge Bracket's sixtieth birthday. He could be very stern, Misty—even brutal and bruising to a hopeful composer. Doubtless that's one reason I'm reluctant to admit to any throes of creative effort. His verdict was, God damn it, you milksop, I've had more fire in my life than *that*.

Ill-tempered unappreciative old wretch!

Misty, quite probably he was correct. Someday, when I can muster courage to play the thing again, you decide.

She sighed. I'd have no basis for rendering opinion. I've never created anything—except dreams, and queer little notions.

And some new varieties of cookies, she added with a laugh. I suppose all who create must be wounded frequently. Tis their lot.

Fruit-colored light wavered and flickered and smoked around and over them.

Bless this night, bless this room.

And, dear God, bless Us.

Beauty Beast said, They were all slaves too.

Who were slaves?

The composers. Patrons were their masters, held every license to make or mar their lives. Mar they did, so many times. And what of critics? Are not the composers slaves to critics as well? Critics determine their fate—not the creators in their own right. Bach was ignored, scorned by that pompous Margrave of Brandenburg. *He* cast six concertos on a shelf, didn't even bother to examine them. An account of the episode was published but recently. Also somewhere I've seen a copy of the letter with which Bach approached the margrave. It was an abject letter, crawling, cringing. It made one crawl and cringe to read it.

She said flatly, I marvel at your erudition.

Misty, what little I possess is the result of grave discipline inflicted, and feverish enthusiasm which followed.

He grieved, But what benefit if a slave possess erudition? He can't use it as a file to cut his fetters! Mozart languished in

servitude, he found himself a captive of the Archbishop Hieronymus. That saintly churchman demonstrated fiendish delight
in whipping an ethereal spirit which he might never prize or
understand. And in our own century— Critics were the masters
and Beethoven was the slave, when it came to his violin concerto. They scouted it with sneers and cat-calls. *Perpetual repetitions,* said the burial service in Vienna. *Vulgar passages.* It
took the genius of Joseph Joachim to rediscover that beauty for
the world. And Beethoven had mouldered in his coffin long
before—

He stood up as suddenly possessed, and struck his fist against
the table. We heard him play it, Misty.

Heard Joachim?

Judge Bracket and I. The first time. When he rescued the D
Major from the grave. More than ten years ago.

Where, Beauty Beast? *Where?*

The Philharmonic Society in London. Joachim was but *thirteen years old.* And, Misty—

Sidney felt cold titillation of her back and neck, excitement
of the mysterious, the supernal.

Might you guess who was conducting?

She could not speak, dumbly she shook her head.

Felix Mendelssohn-Bartholdy.

As if deranged he went pressing across the passage and into
the back parlor (it waited ready with lights for any serenade).
Sidney ran close behind him. Beauty Beast sat down heavily on
the bench, banged up the varnished cover from piano keys. He
struck in resonant chords the D Major *rondo,* its lordliness rang
out briefly with sublimity and challenge. Then he slammed
folded arms across the keyboard and dropped his head upon
them. Dissonance shattered the room and tore through space
beyond.

Sidney hovered in trepidation at that last crash of hammers
against strings, she listened for the combined futile stroke long
after it had ceased to echo.

Tell him now that he shall be free?

In days, even hours?

268

I cannot do so.

Dare not relinquish him, relinquish the power of possession I hold.

What difference between your reluctance and the reluctance of a man named Bracket?

But Bracket was his father. Thus a deed done, far more spiteful—

Once Beauty Beast was taunted with the idea of freedom. Since then his bondage has been more apparent. Thus more tormenting.

But when I bought him, I did not acquire responsibility for the sins of others!

Persuade yourself so, dear Mrs. Shallop. Hasten, before you risk stroking his hair. Which your hand is about to do.

Need him, need him so desperately. Oh, I remember when he spoke his appreciation of my extremity. Therefore by some means I must make him find happiness in acceptance of my ownership.

But this is not yet the time.

To every thing there is a season. I should meditate according to Ecclesiastes. *A time to mourn, and a time to dance. A time to love, and a time to hate.*

A time to love?

Not yet, my Beautiful Beast, not yet.

When he lifted his face (as she'd known he'd soon do) and spoke regret and apology, she said only, Let us now go back to the table and complete our list. May I remind you to be generous to yourself—and to me—in your selection.

Bach, Mozart, Vivaldi, Tartini, Boccherini, Couperin, Albinoni— Twould be a choice in some cases; if one was not available another might be. Sonata in G Major, Suite in A Minor? He sat culling, reviewing, deciding. Aye. And, if it might be permitted, some of the more recent composers—

Misty, this is not generosity on your part. Tis extravagance.

Then an extravagance for myself as well as for you. Should not one be unstinting in the entertainment of one's guests? I'm by way of becoming, instead of a testy recluse, a social celebrity.

Some people, I'm told, talk of little else except the dinners you concoct and the music you offer. Few folks in this vicinity are sophisticated musically. But the sympathetic—there are many such—hang on every measure you award them.

Wishing to blot out vision of his own hysteria, he said roguishly, Then perhaps you can profit in selling me to the highest bidder.

There was no reason to join him in enforced smirking—to speak in trivial fashion of tragedy inflexible. She knew (wisdom born in womanly heart, engendered more by affection than by experience) that Beauty Beast spoke with the pretended light-heartedness of a youth going into battle. Or better— Of the jaunty veteran soldier, many times terrified and bloodied, who profanely terms the bullets to be wasps, the battle to be a ball.

You are entirely too self-centered, ma'am, Mr. Irons said to her that night in the middle of sleep (she supposed it to be the middle; could have been beginning or end; she remembered dreaming nothing else later or earlier).

Am not.

Yes, you be.

On what, she asked frigidly, do you base that distasteful remark?

Mainly on the record. You've never asked me bout *myself*.

But you were always so busy with other matters.

For your sake. Sake of Apoxsee.

She prodded her horse into what might be called a charge (what horse? Grief—not Cinna or— Indeed she was riding that devil Watson, long sold off, who'd wrecked Pettey J.). But Irons floated easily beside her.

Sidney was bound to suggest, Let us dismount and rest.

They lingered on that high place near St.-Germain where you could look down and out, east across the Seine. Please to order some wine for us, ma'am, since I don't speak French, just a little Mexican lingo. Twon't be of any account here.

So they sat, sipping a white Burgundy which to her astonishment held faint flavor of ripe apples. Nathaniel Irons told her, I had no chance at wine when I was a little tad.

Nor I.

My old lady kept preaching at me that I was sickly. She scairt me into taking all sorts of nostrums.

Your old lady?

My mother.

He volunteered that he spent his childhood in the Old North State where his father was a miller. Most men of his immediate ancestry had been either millers or millwrights according to long tradition. A young miller would come to work for an older man who owned a water-mill; and then the young man would marry the owner's daughter. This continued for generations, and seemed a practice in the profession. Irons had two junior sisters, and they went with their father to fish on the dam. All were drowned, father as well as the little girls. It was during a time of spring freshets, but no one knew exactly what had occurred. Perhaps one of the girls fell into the river, and the father dove in, trying to rescue her; and then the other fell— They were gone. Bodies of the children were recovered later, far downstream. Body of the senior Irons was never found.

My mother was named Sissy Belle.

He told that she went into widowhood with wild eye and strident voice, continued so. She made the surviving child, little Nat, a target for hysterical endearment and ugly prophecy. But they did not starve. Sissy Belle managed her mill fairly well. Two old black men whom they owned did the heavy work— lifting, repairs of machinery, dressing of the burrs, dam repairs.

Mr. Irons. What are burrs?

They grind.

Ah.

Nat was always Mother's Boy and Mother's Son. Where's Mother's Son been so long? Don't take you that long to come from school: was you kept in by the master once more? Mother's Boy has got to learn, Mother don't want her boy to be no dunce. Was you made to wear that dunce cap again?

He said with solemnity, I could learn but slowly and literally, because of inferior quality of the instruction, and inferior gifts of the schoolmaster.

Also this education was expensive. At first it cost five cents per day per scholar.

Expensive? Stuff. Very cheap.

Later, in hard times, Master Anderson lowered the price to three cents. The children of more opulent, or perhaps more progressive families, were taught by the minister .and his daughter. But not so myself.

At what did you become proficient?

Greek and logarithms.

À votre santé. Should you care for more wine?

I'm agreeable, ma'am.

Garçon—

Mr. Irons said, Mother was a bitch.

Why do you say that?

He imitated his mother, voluble in high falsetto. You ain't handsome, Mother's Boy. You won't never cut no figure with the ladies. But don't worry, you don't need to get no girl. Mother'll always be here a-waiting.

When he and Sidney were riding once more, he brought his horse close, leaned across and said impressively: I know only that I disliked that woman increasingly—fought shy of her shrieking voice—the voice that went through me like a rusty blade when she yelled.

He fled to the army. Departed by night, never heard screams issuing when Sissy Belle found the note he had left. Years later he came back from Mexican campaigns sporting that rarity: a belly-wounding in which the victim recovered. Surgeons had been stricken mute at the miracle of his survival, and this emphasized heartily to Mr. Irons that he was here only through the grace of God. He returned to Carolina to find his mother dead of an internal complaint (she drank a quart of vinegar daily, claiming that only such acid might allay the pangs within her) and the small estate rotted by mortgages and notes. There was nothing to keep him at home. He even considered rejoining the army, but decided against it. He thought of blazing blue shadows which he and his horse cast on the desert, and said No.

I'm very glad, Mr. Irons, that you didn't go back to the—

Dragoons, ma'am.

Yes, yes, dragoons. Something like—dragons?

A mite.

For then I shouldn't have you here on the place. And I need you. Just as I need Beauty Beast. And he says that he likes to feel needed. Do you, as well?

Oh, yes, yes, he said. Yes, yes.

Pell-mell they rode into the plantation yard, and again Sidney was thrown, but Beauty Beast darted out of nowhere and caught her before she struck the ground. He hugged his mistress tightly though secretly when he set her upon her feet.

She wakened, lay wondering about the dream. Some must have been true, some items. The mother? And the mill?

She decided, Beauty Beast would certainly try to catch me if he stood near.

She entered into a new day, feeling increased love for Beauty Beast, and pity and sympathy for Mr. Irons which she had not held before.

Sidney entertained repeatedly, was entertained. Vehicles rolled on the road to the Big House and disturbed evening owls. Nearer neighbors, some more distant (some were relatives of the Wilkeys) , such as Mansingings, Cowleys, Ludlows, Yorks, Mathesons. They were kindly folk who had not been to Apoxsee since Sidney offered them her first regrets in response to invitations which had followed her period of mourning.

Mourning? What is that? A ceremonial invoked to advertise one's bereavement (which may be no bereavement, may be a boon) . A ritual welcomed by tailors, sempstresses, ministers alike, since in each case their professional services can be offered and usually accepted. She thought again of Calvin Tensley's coffin set up on chairs, of Pettey J. Shallop screaming, *I'll die!* She looked at their memories languidly, turned away, pondered only on amiability of the present and lure of the future.

Many local families, although close in fondness and in shared experience to the elder Shallops, had sickened at Pettey J.'s debaucheries, would no longer see him. Logically or illogically this exclusion was invoked against his third wife. Mrs. Bonaparte Wilkey devoted herself to more than a little missionarying on Sidney's behalf. Once Sidney'd become a widow, invitations went to her in due course, but were generally declined.

In this pleasanter season of 1854 she felt herself no butterfly, nor held desire to be one; but she did find active delight in sharing, giving and (lately) receiving. She discovered old Mr. Mansinging to be attractive in satanic fashion, possessed of a gift of satire. The younger Yorks were a genial pair—bride beaming in the prettiest stage of pregnancy, young husband inordinately pleased whenever he was invited to recite humorous odes which he'd published while still an undergraduate at Oglethorpe. Major Ludlow had been captured by Indians in his youth, and his reminiscences were colorful (if not exactly a novelty to wife and other kin). Mr. Matheson was but recently come from visiting his cousin, a Scottish laird. Mrs. Ryder Cowley made pottery her hobby, had her own kiln, experimented in decorating white ware. Sidney, my dear, cried Jane Matheson warmly. I have a boon to ask of you, and you must surely grant it. When you come to us on Monday next, might you please be so good as to fetch along that talented yellow boy of yourn? I'm having Mr. G. Wash come out and tune our piano, special. You know Mr. Matheson's sister Effie is with us now. She's just so plain lamed up with rheumatic joints that she can't drive out anywhere. But she'd simply *adore* to hear your boy play. I described that magnificent concert of his, over't Apoxsee, and she declared it made her homesick for the British Isles.

Sidney told Beauty Beast of Mrs. Matheson's wish (expressed on an evening at the Ludlows') and saw the argent pleasure in his eyes.

Even a slave, and here among cotton-growers, she thought. How desperately an artist seeks appreciation.

Misty, the lady is too generous with praise.

I intend to honor her request, unless in some fashion it should wound your feelings. If such an appearance is irksome—

I am yours to command, Misty.

274

Of that I'm aware. Sidney could not avoid letting stiffness creep into her tone. Your constant reference to yourself as one in bondage, and having didoes about it— Not that I blame you in the least— I'd do the same thing were our situations reversed. But you are heart and soul a musician. A musician who cooks, shall we say, as one pursuing a charming hobby. I might command the servant to *do* a thing, but I do not choose to offend the musician.

Gravely he spoke. Dear mistress, please to excuse me if I have shown petulance. A pianist should be happy that people choose to hear him perform, under whatever circumstances. In thinking of the lame Scottish lady who's come visiting, I'm reminded that I have an arrangement of the *adagio* from the Scotch Symphony. Also something from the Hebrides Overture.

Excellent. You're bound to play the right thing in the right hour.

On the next Monday, however, a problem of transportation was posed. The better part of that road running between Apoxsee and Gun Grove, the Matheson place, was not in good condition; therefore Sidney had planned on an early start with the carriage.

Nineveh came to her in disconsolation, and tardily.

That Betty horse—

(Never a Betty mare, always a horse.)

She done gone lame in foreleg.

Nigh or off, Nineveh?

Off leg, mistess. Same one she have trouble with before.

When she had the seedytoe?

Yessum. But ain no seedytoe this time. Other time was cause that blame Duke, he hammer em big clips too hard in her hoof. I get him holp me, and we whittle down that crust, and I stuff it with *tow*, long with that medicine you done give me—

I remember the treatment perfectly, Nineveh. And how well her hoof responded. But what is wrong now?

Mistess, I see her, I watch her at rest. All time she hold her one foot right in front of tother. Now, I know that leg gone *lame*.

But, Nineveh, what *is* the difficulty?

Difficulty, mistess, is *splints*. That where you find em: down from knee, inside the *leg*. Now, I *have* seen em, long ago, on *hind* leg, but—

The only way in which such clinical dissertation could be overcome was to accompany Nineveh to the stable. Splints were apparent. Betty whinnied dolefully. *See my agony?*

If we were to work her today in the carriage, Sidney told the coachman, it would become more apparent immediately. Truly serious and aggravated, should it extend into the knee-joint. She's been bruised somehow or other, and will need rest. Pay close heed: we shall follow the treatment recommended by Dr. Yarrow. Hot applications, very hot at first—try the water with your own hand—to take down the inflammation. Then, at night, you're to swaddle her leg in cold-water bandages. Is any left of Dr. Yarrow's liniment?

He produced a large bottle, half-full, and said that already he'd rubbed it on.

Then once more, Nineveh, before bandaging her for the night. You are to repeat the same treatment tomorrow. Hot applications; liniment twice during the day; and again the cold-water wrappings at night.

But, mistess, you planning drive all the way to Gun Grove. You know that Bill horse—he *refuse* work in harness with any other horse in this whole *world*. Cept Betty.

Which poses a problem. Since I am to take Beauty Beast along.

You take you *cook?*

Mrs. Matheson has asked that he play piano for her guests. This is a time when I feel need for a one-horse carryall. Perhaps I should buy another.

(The Apoxsee carryall had been smashed to flinders when Pettey J. drove off the bank of Showcaw Creek on a wager. This happened after a two- or three-day drinking bout. The man who made bold to accompany him in the vehicle, also on wager, might never forget the occurrence. He received a crushed pelvis, and appeared miserable enough whenever he tried to move on crutches even after these several years. More fre-

276

quently he kept a big darkey close, to carry him from his buggy into church. Like many another heedless or downright evil soul reduced to pauperism of body if not of purse, Mr. Stilton McCurf professed to Christianity and asceticism, had them mingled in his mind. Except for the matter of raising voice on the subjects of rum or tobacco in impromptu harangue, he was nearly as much out of circulation these days as Pettey J. himself. The top of the Shallop carryall went out to sea and was washed up on a beach miles away. Sidney suffered heartbreak over the fate of a fine driving mare, innocent victim of this escapade, who had to be destroyed. Pettey J. was protected by a full retinue of Old Nicks. He received only a sprained ankle and lacerated ear, and went haughtily to collect his fifty dollars the very next evening.)

Sidney said, We have no other vehicle on the place which can carry three in comfort. Except for wagon or cart, and I'm not about to journey to the Matheson place in any such vehicle. Beauty Beast shall drive me in the chaise.

You drive as well as ride? She asked of Beauty Beast, after he'd been sent for.

Misty, you should have seen me fulfilling the various offices of coachman, when we were in Provence. Judge Bracket sacked his driver for impertinence, so I was delegated. The judge preferred a light phaeton, not designed for use on those steep hillside lanes. But by God's grace—

Then the chaise can hold no horror for you. I'll have them put Rodney into it. He's reliable, if a bit elderly and slow, but accustomed to being driven solitary. Bill without Betty would make himself obnoxious, and perhaps even run away with that two-wheeler.

Now, what of music? Have you planned our program?

All is in readiness. May I ask, Misty, how should I appear—? As to costume—

Wear the jacket which you were wearing when first I saw you. Sugar berries.

But with indigo. Scorched, and they laughed together.

We should be off by four-thirty at the latest.

Sidney felt her heart leaping and bright, put a hand against her breast as if in tactility she might catch the lilt of its rhythm. Despite concern for poor Betty, and adjuration to Nineveh that he be constant and faithful in nursing the beast— A shimmer of holiday brightened the air. Sidney hurried to direct India at the laying out of her moiré antique gown, in the preparation of her entire toilet. Grief, she cried, girlishly upbraiding the stubby little wench. Did I want an iron so hot, I'd have Duke the blacksmith come do my curls! This iron would fry the hair right off, India. Touch it with wettened finger, you'll soon see.

Sidney thought of Eleanor Wilkey, basking in the ministrations of Linnet, and groaned. India would never have the bird touch, the petal approach. She was greedy for perquisites of improved status without accepting increased responsibility and the sensible discharging of new duties. She was more bent on swishing openly before every black whom she saw in trousers. Beauty Beast looked upon her with repugnance—the mistress had seen him do so—but soon enough India would be put in the family way by one nigger or tother. Then Sidney must indulge in further prodigality by acquiring a new maid.

But she did not wish Linnet back at Apoxsee.

Not for all the world, she sang to herself.

Then again (blandly, selfishly), I wish his attention to be centered on *me*. I am his admired mistress, he is my admired servant. Our interests shall be mutual and undisturbed.

How far to Gun Grove? I wish it were farther.

But there'll be the drive home, later on.

I've never truly *sat* next to him, *tête-à-tête*. Oh, on the piano-bench a time or two (I think our bodies touched slightly). And near him in a chair, as at the dining table when we worked with music. Or those many hours when we've talked, there at the piano. But not together upon a single seat, as in the chaise.

Why, I have the feeling that I'm going to a jolly place, and being *escorted*.

Why, the gentleman will call for me, and—

We'll drive together.

It's very gay. As if we were bound for a picnic.

Return to Willowhurst. Sidney recalled how she'd made a fresh baking of delicious pastry once, a-Tuesday; and Wednesday there'd resounded a chorus of somewhat-less-then-dulcet voices beyond her gate. She went through the yard to find Niece Mamie scrambling and exploring with a dozen other noisy girls. A long-suffering colored couple had charge of the misses. Twas explained amid lurid excitement that they were to enjoy a picnic—a birthday treat for one child, arranged by her parents. They'd stopped at Aunt Sidney's for a drink-a-water. Of course all must be fetched inside and offered currant wine (somewhat diluted) . A huge jar of the fresh cookies was emptied: brown, crisp they were, a raisin baked into the center of each.

Aunt Sidney, this is right *prime!* All us girls want to give you a kerchief salute.

A kerchief salute? And what may that be?

Like this! They howled, gathering round and pulling out their pocket handkerchiefs, waving them wildly in Sidney's face. She screeched in pretended terror, battled them off. The old nurse cried, Miss Emily, Miss Teenie Bet, all you little misses— You ack *lady*like. Now you just ack *lady*like. Come long to the wagon, Jonas been a-calling you I doan know how long. He say we got to get on with the *picnic.*

Sidney helped herd them, they were ranged in rows on planks across the wagon box. They lifted special baskets to show her what they had in them, offered the kerchief salute again as they departed, dear small flower-faces under bonnets. Some began to sing.

Sidney asked herself, Did I say that I should prefer to be young again, prefer to start afresh? In early months when first I came to this cottage? No longer.

I shall never wish again to be *that* young.

What is this medal offered to youth for being young? What is this award, this coronet placed over gleaming hair of an untried child? So now she is to be a duchess, solely because she wears no years under her eyes or in the skin of her neck?

I'd disdain to be fresh-hatched, newly emerged. Rather would I welcome the lines and graying soon to come.

Quick—to the looking-glass and let us see—

But meanwhile, child and children, revel well in your picnic. Munch sandwiches of egg and cress, find happiness in pickles, get grass-stains on your petticoats.

What justification have I (Sidney made further inspection) to continue thinking in picnic terms? The essence of a picnic is eventual arrangement round a picnic cloth—or on the deck, on the shore among baskets. It is formed by a sociability in the sharing of food. When we dine this evening, I shall not be seated next to Beauty Beast, nor opposite him, nor will he be in appearance or even in attendance. He'll be out yonder, kitchenwards, fed grudgingly by shambling rustics who'll peer at him with incredulity and suspicion.

~13~

WHEN I WAS FIVE, I think, and my sister Emma was fourteen (the year before she married) our Uncle Zack came home to Carolina, the only time he came. He was broad, outspoken, bearded, with eyebrows like mustaches. And he had shiny little anchors on his coat lapels. There was some sort of fair down on the riverfront, with barrel-organs playing, gypsies, a bear alleged to dance— A woman who wound a spotted snake around her neck. Perhaps the snake had rings; but it was large and glossy and came, they told us, from some foreign place. Booths were set up where folks could play at darts (they said I was too small, and wouldn't let me throw). But there were wooden balls to toss, so I tried. The balls were heavy, the distance looked quite far, and had me discouraged before I began.

Uncle Zack spent dime upon dime upon us two. He only laughed when Ma called him to account for this, and spoke ill of such extravagance. Pray, what example did he mean to set for us? Well, said Uncle Zack, I've been sailing here and sailing there, and all my tin piling up meantime. Aim to let it tinkle as I distribute it. Let the girls go riding in this here goat-cart, whilst I step over to the grog-tent for a dram or two.

Oh, oh, that goat did *smell*. Emma held her nose when we were riding elegantly behind the goat, with some old nigger leading Mr. Goat upon a halter (though each of us girls was told to hold a rein). The cart was red, and had a small brass rail behind the seat and up above the dash—

Back came Uncle Zack. He talked louder than before, and kept grinning. Every time some friend would call to him, he'd swat the man upon the back until the man went staggering.

Ladies, let's go see. What have they got in *this* tent?

It was hoops—the small round hoops wherein a lady does her fancywork. Embroidery frames indeed, and what a place to see them at this fair! Or carnival, some called it. Whistles blowing all the time, and bells clanging, and people's voices rising up, challenging you to Come and Buy, or Come and Try.

The year before, mother'd given me one of her old hoops—not skirt hoops, but one of those embroidery hoops. I don't know why she gave it to me—perhaps she'd broken the mate, or possibly the mate was lost. Still I had that thing to play with. I'd taught myself an art, in sporting round our lawn. I'd sent my hoop spinning out and flat, whirling as I tossed it. A thousand times I must have spun it so. Catch this flower or that stone, try to catch a baby chick or kitten. Sometimes I could, even when the cats went scooting away from me.

At this fair they had treasures spread upon a table, well behind that counter where the hoops stood piled. There'd be such marvels as a penknife or a ring, or maybe it would be a piece of ore they said was gold, or—they were much more numerous—a peach or posy. Each article was placed upon its slab, a slab the hoop could barely go around. The proprietor would demonstrate: he'd stand alongside the table and drop hoops here and there, and show how they would go completely round the block on which each treasure lay.

Some tell you, Mister Hoops would cry, that these hoops won't go around the blocks! Oh, *no?* Well, ladies, gentlemen, and youngers too: just take a look. Watch me toss these hoops.

The rings would fly, circling and spinning, round and round. Then down they'd come, each snaring one of the best gifts displayed.

Emma tried, and Mother too, and Uncle Zack. They got nowhere. Maybe they won a flower or so; flowers were the most

284

numerous and fruit came second. But still there was a penknife, and the finger-rings. A flask, too—the man said it was filled with Spanish perfume, and he'd hold it up against the light so you could see the perfume. Oh, yes—some sewing shears, and picks for nuts. Smelling-salts, pocket handkerchiefs (he said they came from France). And there were pipes for men, larger knives for boys. Dear, dear, such gifts and trophies.

I kept whining, May I try, Uncle Zack?

And Ma says, Sidney, dear, you're far too young.

Please let me *try!* I started in to pout. So, Lord sakes, they didn't want a tantrum, so they let me try.

I spun my first hoop out, and secured the perfume.

All right, says Mister Hoops. This fine young gal has won her prize. Now step aside, child, step aside. There's others waiting here to try.

Ho-ho, says Uncle Zack. I paid a dime for them three hoops, she's got two left, now let her try again. Let the thing go sailing, Siddy.

I aimed again, tossed. Pocket handkerchief this time. I'd won it fair.

Now, people, people! The man tried wheedling. Give way. There's others. Little gal, you've had your sport—

Uncle Zack leaned across the counter and took that fellow by his shirt. Mate, she's got one left. You understand?

Why, certain, certain! mourned Mister Hoops. I understand! Just toss it out, young lady. Toss ahead!

I let the circlet go. This time I'd seen a locket with a chain, and I wanted those very much. Again I won.

There came sadness later, when I found my golden locket turned to green.

Cozily they drove toward Apoxsee through the umber night.

Misty, much as I have spoken of earlier years, and Judge Bracket— And abroad— This is the first time you've mentioned your own childhood. Twas as if you'd never *had* a childhood. Now you are discovered to have once been a little girl.

Mistress and slave, he mused. Slave and mistress. Yet we've talked.

Ah, Beauty Beast, we have indeed. How strange that we hold such vast area of common interest.

Dinner and the musical hour following had been as congenial as those who contributed. Little Miss Matheson was one of those young-old wisps with wren voice, wren manner, and deep brown circles under her eyes (curved chevrons awarded to those who suffer incessant pain). On starting she told Sidney in her soft West Country accent, Mrs. Shallop, ye should take him abroad wi ye, and make a fortune for the twa.

Also Miss Matheson informed me, Beauty Beast, that there are many others of her family dwelling in the Hebrides and on adjacent mainland.

So she was certain, Misty, to be affected by that figure in B Minor from Fingal's Cave. It was Mendelssohn, not I, who overwhelmed the lady.

Oh, don't talk like a fool!

They jogged in offended silence, pitching over invisible ruts and hummocks, feet of the old horse coming down to scatter mud or flatten clods in uneven cadence. No carriage lamp had ever been arranged upon that chaise, twas a conveyance dedicated to daytime use. A far-seeing Beauty Beast, however, went scouting through rubbish in the blacksmith's shop before departure from Apoxsee. He'd found a piece of wreckage in the shape of a twisted iron pole with a hook at the top; now this stood tightly affixed to the whip-socket. At the top swung a whale-oil lamp taken from the carriage, waving its dull brown beam from Rodney's flank to Rodney's ears, from nearest hedge to nearer ditch.

Presently the driver began, I may talk like a fool, Misty, but—

I'm dreadfully sorry that I was cross, Beauty Beast. I do become annoyed when you deride your own gifts. But let me eat humble pie.

Not unless I bake it for you, Misty.

(Welcome staccato of our harmony. Laughter goes ringing through darkness, telling lonely coverts that here are humans with buoyancy between them.)

Do you pull up for a moment, and I'll look at my watch.

He spoke to Rodney, drew in the reins. Sidney leaned toward the lamp.

We've been gone almost an hour. That means we should be approaching the Dempsey Corner.

Isn't that where the road improves?

Wider from then on, worked more frequently. But go slow at the turning, there are eroded places.

When they'd fallen into the jolting uncertainty of travel once more, Beauty Beast said, I was thinking of my excerpt from the Scotch Symphony. He worked on it a very long time, Misty, starting when he was twenty, and fascinated by Scotland from the first. I remember someone's reading aloud a letter attributed to Mendelssohn after he'd explored that crumbling Palace of Holyrood. Doubtless he felt a fanciful love for Queen Mary. One phrase is still haunting: *Everything around is broken and mouldering, and the bright sky shines through—* Hello, he said as Rodney balked.

Sidney thought of highwaymen. *Do we have any such?* Some peculiar activity ahead, the shape of a vehicle sagged at one side. This was Dempsey Corner, you could see roads which came in to join, confluent with the lane they were on. Dappled horse, tilted buggy or wagon, two men alongside; two women on the rear seat, turning to see who came.

What's ado here?

I'm sure I don't know, Misty. Someone appears to have driven into the ditch.

I recognize the Reverend Mr. Stephens, so do you pull up opposite.

Will Rodney stand?

There's nothing he loves better.

Squat long-armed shape, negro wearing a checkered jacket, stepped toward them. Beauty Beast said, Why, it's Boaz.

Boaz?

Mrs. Dowson's coachman.

(I should have recognized her bonnet, and how those wads of pale ribbon protrude like horns above the brim. Those she should wear: fit growth for Her Satanic Majesty. Oh, her husband's but a lummox, blue eyes too bright, too staring and expressionless; forehead high, wide, shiny; chin dissolving in rolls of flesh, creasing into several chins against his neck. His voice so patently mellifluous, the hallmark of insincerity. And many ladies consider Mr. Cadmus Dowson charming! And Senator Ledge has long forgotten: we did meet at the Fraleys' ball, shortly before Pettey J.'s death, when Dowson was a newcomer. Twas the scandal of the evening as he followed me about. I wanted him not, did nothing to lend encouragement to his pursuit. Heaven knows why the Fraleys invited us; but Mrs. Fraley had been a bosom friend of Pettey J.'s mother, so— My beloved husband, muddled to stupor, sprawled in the McCurf carriage. But twas not because of his improper behavior that I won the undying hatred of Mrs. Dowson, ah no. Twas because her own husband sniffed after me like a big blond dog, making excuse to press my hand, building opportunity to lounge with suggestion of intimacy beside my chair, nodding at every reluctant utterance I made. He disregarded my attempts to converse with others, talked so closely in his whisper that I felt his breath upon my bare neck and back. He murmured those little physical compliments which it is told that Spanish gentlemen utter to perfect strangers, sidling behind a woman when she comes out of a shop, informing her that her ears are dainty seashells, her hair spun by the angels. And because Cadmus Dowson made an ass of himself, I was instantly become Queen Hussy of Mrs. Dowson's realm. Here looms she now, a few yards distant, in company with our local religious. What joy to encounter her when I am gadding in a hooded chaise, solitary at night with Beauty Beast my cook! Near-white. Pray do not overlook that, Mrs. Dowson. *Near-white*.)

Sidney took the reins from Beauty Beast. He vaulted down into the ruts. Bo, you appear to be in difficulty.

Sakes, it's Beauty Beast, and Boaz seized Beauty Beast's sleeve. Reckon I turn too short. We been here while. See—dat dere gully—she run clean out in road. Off wheel, she drop down— He continued with a torrent of explanation while Mr. Stephens picked his way to the side of the chaise.

Sister Shallop, how come you here?

How come you? she asked in turn, contriving a light-heartedness along with the words, and speaking in a voice with strength to reach those women in the opposite vehicle.

We supped at Brother Hutch's. Sister Dowson was kind enough to fetch us along in her buggy. But now we seem in sore straits. I did my best to lift, while the driver drove. But twas beyond my strength.

I'll go see, and she extended her hand. Reluctantly the minister helped her down, crying the peril of mud-holes.

Good evening, ladies, said Sidney. The horns on Mrs. Dowson's bonnet twitched away. Mrs. Stephens returned the greeting in characteristic snarl.

The vehicle was a two-seated Brewster which Cadmus Dowson had freighted by ship from the North. Its right rear wheel hung prisoned in a narrow sluice.

Beauty Beast rose from where he had been huddled with Boaz. I think, Misty, that—with the two of us lifting— And if the minister would be so good as to drive—

He'll be glad to lift and shove along with you. In fact he's been trying, all by himself. Is that not true, Reverend?

Stephens quoted, *Many are the afflications of the righteous: but the Lord delivereth him out of them all.*

You'll make it much more simple for the Lord to do the delivering if the three of you hoist together.

Mrs. Dowson called austerely, Reverend Stephens, I do not drive.

Mrs. Stephens said, Neveh druv a hahss in my life.

Perhaps, then, said Sidney, you ladies will be thoughtful enough to step down out of the carriage? Twill make it easier for those who are attempting to raise the wheel.

It's all mud! yelled the minister's wife.

I know, dear Mrs. Stephens. I've been wading in it.

Sidney addressed herself to the Dowson driver. Boaz, will the horse pull if I take him by the head?

Spot never do dat, mistess. He pull if you *drive* him, not if you tug he head.

Then pray allow me to take the reins. Sidney sought the driver's seat, Mr. Stephens scrambling to help her up. She waited with cold amusement until the other women, rustling in distaste, had climbed down. Then she called to the men at the rear, When you're ready to lift, say *Now*, and I'll start him up. If the wheel doesn't come out, cry *Whoa* before we drag this carriage apart.

Now!

Parson and slaves heaved hard, the obedient horse lunged ahead. Traces pulled taut, the buggy frame moaned in protest, then the wheel was up and out. Boaz cheered. Let us, said Mr. Stephens, sing praises with timbrel and with harp.

Beauty Beast fetched his lamp from the chaise to conduct an examination. Neither he nor Boaz could find any permanent damage. Best to drive slowly, Bo. We'll precede you till we reach the Big Gate at Apoxsee, since we have the light. Thus you'll run no risk of sliding into another hole.

Mr. Stephens had made ceremony of assisting his wife and Mrs. Dowson into the Brewster, and now he escorted Sidney to the chaise and handed her up. Well met, Sister Shallop. Well met indeed.

Lowering his voice. It is one of my regrets that you are not more regularly attendant at Worship. There is to be special afternoon service on Friday, and I pray that you may be present. Two other bishops from presbyteries within the synod will be present. Archibald Atkins Mercer, who serves as moderator when we are in convention, is being honored. He has now forty years in the service of promoting the glory of God. There will be preaching—at least some brief message offered—by each pastor. We look forward to giving Mr. Mercer our right hand, *in token of cordial reception and affectionate regard.*

Thank you, Reverend Stephens, for the reminder. I shall be happy to drive into town on Friday afternoon and greet the Reverend Mr. Mercer.

She thought, For no other reason than to show those two harpies that I'm not reluctant to meet them at such a gathering.

Through dimness he looked up at her and communicated his

stress. She felt warming pity for this self-conscious ecclesiastic, so withdrawn among ritual, form, printed substance of alleged worship, that he was unfit to cope with the slithering animals of vice, large or tiny, which ran amuck throughout his congregation. Sidney recognized that he was aware of his wife's hostility to her; and now, after only a few months in matrimony, had become even more cruelly aware of the enmity which that young woman bore for a great share of the human race.

Assuredly he must be conscious of the fact that neither Mrs. Dowson nor Mrs. Stephens had spoken a word of thanks, either to Sidney or to her pro-tem driver.

Sister, the Fortieth Psalm. *He brought me up also out of an horrible pit, out of the miry clay.*

Beauty Beast came to hang the lantern. Reverend Stephens made some sort of priestly signal with his hand. It is of benefit to us that your talents, Beauty Beast, are not confined solely to cookery and to the piano—

Thank you, sir.

The sad rotund little man waved, turned back to the two-seater.

They started off in the chaise. For a time Boaz kept close in his following, deriving assurance from their passage ahead. Suddenly he fell back as if in response to an order.

Don't wait for them, Beauty Beast. If they choose to go fumbling by themselves, tis their privilege. I hope you did not strain your body in any way, or injure your hands with that lifting?

I've suffered nothing except damage to my shoes and attire. Which can be rectified.

In my case as well.

She put her head back as if to doze. But presently—

I can't help thinking of Mrs. Dowson yonder. Is she the only grandchild of Judge Bracket?

Let me relate, Misty, a fragment of family history. Heaven knows I overheard the details often enough. It goes like this: Judge Bracket was wedded to Samantha Greenthorn in 1808. Their first child was a girl, Leona, named after the judge's father, Leonidas. They had two other children, both boys, who died in infancy; and Mrs. Bracket herself died of complications following the birth of the second boy. The daughter grew to maturity and was wedded to Mr. Ronald Greenthorn, a distant relative of her mother, when she was eighteen or thereabouts. Both of the Greenthorns are gone, having taken the cholera in New Orleans when the disease first appeared there—twas when you were very young, Misty.

He said, But their daughter, named Ronny Lou, is the present Mrs. Cadmus Dowson.

Then you are Mrs. Dowson's uncle, Beauty Beast.

Half-uncle.

He added, I fear that the fact of the relationship is unknown to Mrs. Dowson, and would be staunchly denied. For she it was who inherited *me*. And sold me off— To you, Misty.

I know, she said sleepily. To me.

Later. You were something I caught with my hoop.

But I may turn to brass.

Sidney confided, I had a dream wherein Mr. Irons chided me for never having asked him about *himself*. You mentioned tonight that I've never told you about *myself*—

Misty, I am supposed to offer anything which I can offer. Is that not the legitimate demand put upon a slave? I had nothing else to award except whatever skills I possessed. You wished to know how they came about. Therefore— I told.

You figured in my dream as well.

I figured?

At the conclusion. I rode into the yard too rapidly, and was thrown. But you were standing near and caught me.

I'd have tried to do that, Misty. Were I there.

I know.

This time Sidney dozed happily until they turned in at the Apoxsee gate. Then she became alive, awake in a twinkling.

Beauty Beast, do you pull over. Here, beneath these low-hanging branches where the moss drips down. Douse the carriage lamp.

Misty, I don't understand.

I should like, if possible, to listen to the conversation of *mine enemies*. As Reverend Stephens might say.

Presently they heard the Brewster buggy approaching. It passed, with Mrs. Stephens' nasal voice stringing out over sound of wheels and hoofs.

—Flittin round the countryside by night with that yellow fellow—

As they went up the driveway Sidney asked, You heard?

Yes, Misty. Twould seem that they have little tolerance for my ability as coachman, even though we rescued them from a bottomless pit.

She murmured, Suddenly I'm very tired. To have communed with the Infinite, as represented by your playing tonight— I can still hear that echo from the overture. And then to be reminded of the pettiness, the indecent little hates we humans hold in our hearts. Mrs. Dowson holds hers against me, so does Mrs. Stephens. For what reason I cannot well imagine in the latter case, except that I felt an instinctive dislike for the woman when she first came.

And I, too, she told him in low intense voice as they reached the front gallery. I'm as petty as they. Just now I've skulked—made you skulk, under those trees—eager to hear whatever trivial condemnation they uttered. God knows I should be above that. But I'm not.

Of course not. You're Misty. A very human Misty. It helps me, to hear you confess to weakness.

And to go to a house of worship, she said, as I'm going, come Friday. Not for sincere purpose of honoring any visiting clergy; but merely to see whether I'm spoken to, and how I shall feel in return.

I'll do it, she said.

And swore for the first time in his presence. Damn it, I'll *do* it.

Friday afternoon saw Nineveh robed in black frock-coat (faded to olive-green across the shoulders) and with an ancient beaver hat jammed above his ears. Betty stepped out bravely, no longer favoring her right foreleg. Pleasure in being behind the team again. Sun glared and hid, hid and glared, in some manner an insolent sun affronting with its brass. Hard clouds were chewed by winds which seemed blowing fast aloft, yet never touching fields below. Nineveh had fetched a light carriage-robe and put it across Sidney's knees. Coolish now, considerably cooler by evening.

In town they halted under waxy magnolias in front of the vine-grown church. Services were not yet commenced, and the Presbyterian community spread in chatting groups along graveled paths. Sidney found sisterly affinity represented by Ronny Lou Dowson and her accolyte, Mrs. Stephens, who conversed with two other women a rod or two from the steps. This was as close as Sidney would ever again approach to the church's interior.

For a certain Mrs. Williston looked upon her with cordiality, smiled, beckoned. Why, Mrs. Shallop, I've not seen you in *such* a while. I should like to make you acquainted with my cousin, Mrs. Kayle. In that moment the other two women turned away, Mrs. Stephens pretending to seek out something important beyond, and Mrs. Dowson performing a gesture of contempt as old as costumes worn by women. She was tall, dark-haired, with a handsome sullen face hidden by width and depth of her bonnet. (Ha, straw. So it's summer still? Hurrah for those horns.) Ronny Lou Dowson's hand stole down to her skirts and pulled them tight against herself, away from Sidney. Mrs. Williston and Mrs. Kayle stared agape.

So now I'm done with admission into this communion. Just as well.

Sidney bowed to Mrs. Williston, smiled gently upon the cousin, said, Pray excuse me. She moved forward and pushed deliberately between Mrs. Dowson and Mrs. Stephens. Am I to be churched, she asked with clarity, because I came upon you at night and rendered assistance? My *dear* Mrs. Dowson, are you not aware that Beauty Beast, my cook, is your half-uncle?

She turned, nodded in politeness at a few friends, went down to where vehicles were ranged. Nineveh, she called, I've decided not to attend the services after all. Bring the carriage round.

~14~

RETURNED to Apoxsee, and while they were still at some
distance down the drive, Sidney became aware of that
which she would not tolerate among her people: disturbance.

Nineveh cried out in disgust, Niggers fussing—

An altercation was taking place somewhere behind the Big
House.

Stir the team.

The carriage went bounding. Sidney's velvet reticule lay
beside her on the seat. Directed by no reason—not understanding and yet actuated to a purpose—she snatched up the reticule,
twitched tiny knobs apart, pushed her hand inside. They tilted
round past chinaberry trees and Nineveh swung his horses out
of the track. This was necessary: the rear drive was blocked by
an assemblage of field hands who scattered momentarily, wailing, falling over children when the team plunged. The horn
had sounded some time before, and hands were well in from the
fields. They'd been weighed, they should have been eating
at their own quarters, must have lost their wits in congregating
so close to the Big House.

Here appeared Mr. Irons, pale and tense, coming from the
office with strides.

Adam the gardener sat upon the horse-block, mountainous
shoulders hunched, head hung sullen. He breathed heavily and
his narrowing eyes studied the trampled ground. Beauty Beast

stood perhaps three yards distant, challenging Adam, confronting him but saying not a word. Sidney turned toward the house. India crouched fearfully on flagstones outside the rear door. She'd fled that far and then her limbs betrayed her.

Knew this would happen, Sidney scolded in her mind. Knew it all along.

She called out, Mr. Irons.

Ma'am? Mumble of the throng fell lower.

Mr. Irons, what is happening here?

Whatever twas, it just happened. I didn't see.

Please to clear these people out of the yard.

Yes, *ma'am*. Come now, git!—he snapped at the slaves. Git, all of you. To your quarters!

They broke back a little, moving wide, giving ground with reluctance, some looking at him almost piteously as to say, Please, we want to watch. Irons snapped his fingers and made more motions of pushing them away. A few of the eldest did move, and turned off toward the quarters, and several women caught up their children and followed. As for men and boys, most of those remained, yielding immediately in front of the overseer, but oozing back whenever he turned in another direction.

So it's Adam again, said Irons.

Didn't you-all hear Mr. Irons? Sidney yelled with her throat hurting her. He told you to *go*. Obey immediately!

They murmured, some more broke away, some few. Most of the hands merely spread apart and surrendered ground once more. Sidney told Nineveh to hold steady, and he creased a wheel against the side of the carriage to give stability. Sidney shook out her skirts and, gripping the reticule, balanced her slipper on the iron step, then sprang to the ground. Her right hand was still sheathed in the velvet.

Bound to come, Sidney repeated to herself. Awareness was giving voice as it were a separate essence. Saying, I was here all along. Inevitable. Fear me and hate me as you choose, but I am here. Will persist.

She addressed Beauty Beast, and his eyes flicked toward her

and then away. He barely turned his head. Misty, I must stand here.

Have you been having trouble with Adam?

I daren't move. He might come at her again.

Come at her?

India. He tried to drag her into the weeds.

On the flags, the little maid jumped with sob and scrambling. She flung open the door with its loose mosquito-bar billowing, and rushed into the house. Sidney could see that her gown had been ripped down the front.

They were arrayed as ornate Spaniards of the bull-ring, on tapestry in embroidered past. Sidney here, Beauty Beast there, Adam crouched vindictive, Mr. Irons at the side. The blacks themselves, field hands and all, made the ring. The bull: Adam.

Beauty Beast said quietly, I got him to loose his hold on her, Misty, but then he flung me off. He's just too mighty.

Mr. Irons prepared for battle. Do you go into the house, Mrs. Shallop. I'll take care of this. It's my task.

A last smash of sunshine was discharged quickly behind windy trees, and on an instant pines and oaks and moss were dancing dark against it, with rays shooting up in Biblical composition, fanlike. And presence of night all around, even before night fell.

He's in liquor, said Irons.

Through what stupidity did that occur?

Reckon he stole it, Mrs. Shallop. I had nigh onto a full bottle of rum yonder, well hid, using it sparingly as I do. Suddenly the bottle was gone. I went for it, after I'd et my meal, like I always do, and twas gone. Reckoned I'd mislaid it. But he must have crept in a-thieving.

Sidney told Adam, If you've stolen liquor you'll be whipped. Thrashed soundly.

Ain't no man, said Adam, going thrash me again. The assertion was a rumble from out his chest and throat and wide sloppy mouth. No one could have told exactly what he was saying when he said it; you had to evaluate the meaning an instant later, then it struck you.

For the first time Adam lifted his head. When he blew out his breath and faced Sidney she could smell the rum, it was a permeation mingled with his own grease.

Ain't no one *ever* thrash me again. No driver, no overseer, no mistess, nobody.

Adam, we've enough of this. I'm going to sell you. You'll go to the swamps. To *rice.*

Hates yellow-hide, said the gardener, and he lifted his jet fist as it were a weight attached to the end of his arm. Then he loosened his fist, and the finger pointed toward Beauty Beast.

He get in my way.

Again. I hates yellow-*man*-hide. Likes yellow-*girl*-hide good enough.

Mr. Irons ordered out Honga and Maddy, told them to fetch a rope. Adam was to be tied. The two drivers went toward the toolhouse, but slowly oh slowly, and looking back as they moved. They stopped in their tracks when on a sudden Adam stood up and kicked a bare heel at the horse-block behind him. Women squealed.

You could see now: Adam had kept a sickle concealed beneath his body as he sat. He'd held it flat there. With the sickle he made a cutting motion toward Beauty Beast.

Aim slay him.

For the last time in this life, or perhaps in any life: Yellow-man-hide. I hates—

Stop where you are, Adam, said Sidney Shallop. Her voice thin, nasal. Open velvet reticule fell away from her right hand.

Slice him, Adam repeated. He lifted up the sharp curved sickle and staggered in implacable force toward Beauty Beast. The negroes spilled away and howled behind him. Sidney shot Adam through the heart.

I, Fenton Ledge, as foreman of this inquest, have diligently inquired and true presentment made, on behalf of the State, how and in what manner Adam (Shallop), here lying dead, came to his death, and of other such matters relating to the same as were lawfully required of me.

As also was lawful, the Coroner issued due process for witnesses, commanding them to come forward to be examined, and to declare their knowledge concerning the matter in question; and the said Coroner did administer to every witness an oath or affirmation, in form following: *You solemnly swear (or affirm) that the evidence which you shall give this inquest, on behalf of the State, touching the death of Adam (Shallop), shall be the truth, the whole truth, and nothing but the truth.*

This inquest recognizes, under the Code, that a slave is a human being, though in a servile condition. It recognizes his right to live, until an overwhelming necessity shall deprive him of life. It holds that his true condition, in this State, is one of subjection and bondage. But at the same time it accords him certain rights which may not be taken from him except in conformity with the law of the land.

This inquest finds that the deceased came to his death by the hand of his owner, one Sidney Veck Tensley Shallop (Wid.); and that this death occurred as the result of a bullet wound, said bullet being fired from a .28 caliber revolving pistol owned and wielded by Sidney V. T. Shallop.

The Penal Code, in its subdivisions, enumerates the cases in which homicide, commited upon a slave, is justifiable.

1st. When a slave is in a state of insurrection.

2nd. When a slave forcibly resists any lawful order of his master, overseer, or other person having legal charge over him, in such manner as to give reasonable fear that the action of said slave may result in great bodily harm to others, or even in loss of life by others.

3rd. When a slave uses weapons calculated to produce death, in any case other than those in which he may lawfully resist with arms.

In consideration of the sworn testimony of all witnesses examined, it is the opinion of this inquest that the slaying of Adam (Shallop), here lying dead, should be pronounced a justifiable homicide; and this finding shall be delivered to the Superior Court of this County at its next session.

So say we all.
Fenton Ledge, Foreman
R. Cowley
Willis Hutch
Elijah Iverson
J. R. Mansinging
Bonaparte Wilkey
Gordon G. York

Inflexible truth claimed her.

There abide Those Who Have Killed. Loose from the rest, disunited permanently.

At incredible distance, oceans and continents removed, are other inhabitants: the vast innocent throng named Those Who Have Not. They constitute the bulk of the living. Wicked or beneficent, they walk unbranded: children, mild-faced mothers, aunties, gaffers, uncanonized saints, sedentary fathers wrapped in their work of the world. Pure or impure, they still seem filmy, tender-skinned, unmauled. Many have done great wrongs, and many of those may be bothered in their consciences by recollection of what they've done, although others will go unvexed. But whatever offices of life they did fill or now fill or seek or will seek, they seem devoid of tarnish.

At a single bound you've left their ranks and villages—crossed this space—versts, deserts, polar regions. Ho!—you're away, and the wall is up. You consort with some of the most despicable natures ever evolved, and some of the most heroic. For each one of you, in this new category where you find yourself, has been a trigger-finger on God's hand or the devil's.

Not one of you can give, but all have taken. And each would say, if examined and able to speak with articulation, There was no choice. It had to be done.

It happened unexpectedly on the edge of a sharp split sliver of Time. Or you were trained for it as warriors are trained. Or you plotted cannily; or you were so disturbed that you could not remember when you thought or what you thought, or exactly how you conducted yourself during that irrevocable moment. There loomed only the dank emptiness of your drunken state or the spitting spark of rage. You were retreating, trying not to do it; or perhaps you went preying with bayonet in hand. You did it in self-defense or in defense of another human; or you did it because your Nation was at war, and in war there must come campaigns when each of those engaged will try to slay as many of the others as he can.

You were an executioner, you did it under and for the Law; yea, you were paid.

Extenuation?

Not so. Move over here with us, coz.

There blows a different odor in the air you breathe, and you must sigh and accept, and say, It will be so. Later, much later (are you fortunate) you'll become so accustomed to the scent that you'll never be able to isolate it more.

Sidney told Fenton Ledge, If only I would not still hear that deep voice of his talking to the things he planted. Vegetables, shrubbery, things he put into the ground. I've put him into the ground. Can I talk to him? No. Say nothing.

Child, you showed courage. Must continue to show it.

She appealed pettishly, twisting her hands, snarling her mouth, setting her jaw and rocking her head stiffly from side to side as nerves tightened. That's merely saying, Be brave, Mrs. Shallop, be brave! Is that all the help you can offer?

She began to cry again.

Patient voice told her, That's all the help, my dear. No one can do more than I, no one can give you a benefit. That must come within your own heart.

Later he got up in heaviness and went searching for a book, found it eventually. Blind man, he said. Poor John.

Ledge began ruffling pages. Finally he was reading.

> Infinite wrath and infinite despair?
> Which way I fly is hell; myself am hell.

Tis what the most brilliant sawbones nowadays call a traumatic experience. That's their name for it. You've been struck from outside, as it were, and the blow spread blood beneath your skin. Discoloration—black-and-blue and yellow-and-pink. It shows when you're badly bruised.

Oh, damn Mr. Irons! For leaving rum around, so Adam could get at it—

The evidence might suggest, dear Sidney, that if it hadn't happened on this occasion it would have happened on another. Testimony showed that he was dangerous, had been dangerous before.

Then he said (regretting instantly after the words passed his lips) — If only you'd sold him, first time it happened.

Coarse sound of grief and revulsion. Sidney pushed her face down into her hands.

(Burst away from any genial pastorale. You have chopped with your axe, poured your poison, tossed your grenade—stabbed, shot, set off your bombard, strangled. On this side, gardens may grow the same but they will be colored differently, as if you looked at them through tinted veils. A mourning dove gurgles with new intonation, no longer to be only a meek gray-brown bird with enticing speckles about him. His fluting will hold significance never noted before.)

I know, said Fenton Ledge. I've killed.

His hand on her head. She felt that her hair was flying dis-ordered, twould be ragged like that, blowing in strings till the end of time.

When? She sobbed the question.

Let's see. First time was when I was very young. An affray with North Africans. There was a raid in port, and I had been stationed with a pistol—in fact a brace of pistols. This critter climbed up over the bulwarks. He had a knife, some sort of dagger, I could see it glimmer. Put my pistol to his head and fired. The lantern kept shining down, and I saw his face. Never'll forget how surprised he looked before he toppled and I heard the splash.

But that— Was war. At sea.

I was on guard, he told her, as you were on guard. It hap-pened suddenly, there was a threat, some innocent person would be slain. So you killed. I killed in almost identical fashion.

Dear Sidney, he said, taking her hand and bringing it up to kiss. You must say to yourself, Twas a circumstance put upon me, and I could not resist, could not deny the need. No escape, twas essential. A part of my own life that had to be lived.

Keep saying that, teaching it to yourself.

(Grass has a different green. Hoofs strike the ground, instigating an echo foreign to be heard. The very wind whispers in occult language, a dog trotting down the road has a pace never discerned before. You Who Have Killed are a race apart. Your mourning dove makes a personal mourning because he is lamenting for the one or ones you slew.)

~15~

THROUGH various weathers the mistress of Apoxsee
sought to find reason and purpose in observing God's
manifestations, His orb, His first frost, spicy stars. In racing air
He seemed especially evident, but He ran on, gave her no
answers. Nevertheless she welcomed wind. *Per* example (that
brought brief notion of Fenton Ledge, she sent him his own
brand of tenderness) there came one ominous afternoon
when autumn roared extravagantly about winter long before
winter actually descended. Within an hour after gusts twisted
out of the northwest a favorite ancient oak had gone down.
India gave report, relayed from Mr. Irons: privies upset at the
quarters, shakes torn from various roofs. A double row of
stunted cabbage palms marched along both sides of the driveway, they staggered aside where the driveway bent, turned their
columns where it turned. Hurricanes and weaker storms had
lashed them often but not one had ever been uprooted. They
waggled unhappily, tossed jagged unkempt heads, rocking,
seeming to say, No, oh no. Swooping in over her shoulder and
across a corner of the gallery, Sidney saw clouds made of thin
gun-metal, evil light above and behind them. They ran low,
broken, once in a while the sun drilled through. Sun seemed
not a part of this scene: an unbidden observer quickly frightened away. Wind coursed harder, colder, keener, you thought
of having people build up fires. No, oh no, said the palms, posturing, complaining.

Birds and rats living in them? They must be hanging by their toes.

Sun again, distilled on green-brown lawn, sun always a stranger in afternoons like this, not belonging or really caring to belong. Go away, sun. You're false. Sun slides into its steely sluice and is vanished for good. A rat is projected from her nest in one of the nearest palms, she lands uncertainly, travels in heaviness on short feet and legs, crossing the yard in little dashes, going she knows not where.

Sidney sought for comparison, some pattern, a parable among winds, something she could touch and make applicable. She found nothing. She was sequestered. In time the gusts diminished and left her in apathy.

God is dumb. Cannot speak. Or chooses not to.

Nervously the woman brightened and thought of going to far places and doing strange things, shaking off Apoxsee and its riddles and repetitions of Nature, shaking it away from her, claiming land and house and people no more, being emancipated therefrom.

On a better day than that, India carried up Sidney's breakfast, and said, Beauty Beast wan talk to mistess.

Bid him come.

India went stamping down the stair (her shoes were still a novelty, she enjoyed making clatter) and Sidney flew to her dressing table the moment the capped head was out of sight. By the time Beauty Beast appeared she was returned to chair and tray.

I thank you for these excellent croquettes, and the more-than-excellent sauce.

He stood soberly, not smiling, only bowing in thanks. Tis gratifying to realize, Misty, that the season for turkey is come again.

India returned to the bedroom, choosing this moment for tasks dealing with chamber-pot and *bidet* behind their respective screens. Hastily Sidney packed the maid off to more appropriate duties below.

You wished to speak with me, Beauty Beast.

Yes, Misty.

Then—?

I am— Worried about you. Deeply concerned. Strangely enough, it was dealing with the turkey which set me to thinking—

Her throat grown bone-dry on a sudden. Why are you worried?

Because of the great change which has come over you. Since the—tragedy.

Tis but natural, I suppose.

I know, Misty, that notes have come from your friends. I've carried in two of them myself. Have you not received invitations?

She nodded silently, watching him with wide amber gaze.

But you go nowhere.

Tis but natural, also, that I am reluctant to go forth to—to—

To laugh, Misty?

Difficult.

He spoke at some length, compassion in his tone made her close her eyes to be more completely medicined by this unguent. Misty, there is something I might tell you which would make you see yourself and Apoxsee—indeed the entire situation —in a new light. There was an experience of my own past which, if related in detail, might change your attitude. For the happier, Misty. But I should need to speak to you for several hours at least— there's far too much to relate and explain in a single evening in the back parlor. With my playing as—

An excuse? she whispered.

Excuse for our being together.

You are so understanding, Beauty Beast.

Everything which I can offer should be yours. By authority and by—

She smiled wearily. And by the dictates of humanity? Or something similar?

Yes, Misty. Here at the Big House we'd be subject to interruption.

Then have you a suggestion?

He tapped his foot on the floor, looked down, watched the rapping foot as if it were a separate entity, finally stilled it and lifted his glance to meet hers.

Would you be reluctant to go off in the chaise again, with me driving Rodney?

Not at all. Where could we go?

To the shore. There's seldom anybody about, except perhaps niggers fishing. Crabbing, oystering—

She told him, nearly in eagerness, And on our own shore there'd be none of those, for I'd send no one on such excursion.

But— Nineveh? What would he—?

None of his concern. I *am* the mistress.

He bowed again in silence.

Should I decide to go forth in our freight wagon, with Clemmy or Molly holding the ribbons, would it not be a case of *avoir droit?*

Of course, Misty.

Sidney's eyes went to the window. *Why, the day is fair. I had not realized. And no blowing. Gulf will wear those polished virid plates across its shallows.*

Seemingly so long before: that cheerful suggestion of a picnic.

Today, Beauty Beast?

À votre gré, madame.

Then send word about Rodney and the chaise. And do you put up a bite to be taken along. For the two of us, she said firmly. And some of your ginger beer. There's no drinking water to be had yonder, no spring.

By ten o'clock they reached the Gulf. Long before that he had begun his account of a journey into the iniquitous.

Senator Plesser's two plantations were located on a good-sized island off the coast of Georgia, one devoted to rice culture, the other to long-staple cotton. Just why Judge Bracket needed to confer with the senator, and in seeming emergency session, Beauty Beast could never be certain. It had to do with a subject tiresome to the boy's ears: the independent treasury system.

Judge Bracket and Beauty Beast took ship from Baltimore to Savannah, and proceeded by a small steamer to the sandy straggling town of Darien. There they were met by their host, accompanied by his overseer from the rice plantation, one Mr. Gallant, who'd come along with the master to do some errands.

(Beauty Beast said, The rice place was called Emilion, and the long-staple cotton place, Avenida. Both could have been called Avernus and no harm done.)

They journeyed for miles on a series of twisted waterways, writhing between dikes built to hem the rice fields. Looking far toward the landward you could see only vast wilderness weed beds of the coastal region. They seemed as a generous crop which people had planted and then deliberately abandoned. Even in winter, as now, flocks of birds rose from the reeds, fell again like smoke blown down, rose and fell darkly, saying that they were neglected and bereft, haunting in a manner to remind the observer that Man would never offer fidelity.

Sometimes a little schooner made the trip from and returning to Emilion, but not with winds as they were this day. Instead there was employed a long shallow-draught barge with eight rowers and a helmsman. A mast sprouted but the sail was furled. Beauty Beast wrapped his arms about this mast, against roll and plunging of the boat, and gazed out at wet deserts of weeds stretching far to west and north, and then back at the bleak rice beds they approached. He saw timberland, banks of cypresses massed upon the southeast horizon, seeming to palpitate in raw wind, seeming to harbor wolves. The barge or scow or baby *dhow* went through a cut whittled out of mud and roots by the shovels of men. The way was shaped long before, when Oglethorpe took his troops to the region.

There came a lying-to, a holding against force of current. Yells sounded, people leaned over the gunwale, poking at something. Judge Bracket and Senator Plesser went to look, and Beauty Beast followed after. A balloon afloat, or something swollen: small purplish object, round and bouncing. Slaves tried to reach it with oars and it bobbed loose and bounded back; then a pole caught and whirled the thing closer to the hull, and they could peer over, and see what it was. Body of a negro baby, swollen hugely, fat face pushed back by swelling. How the little mouth pouted hard and round, and how the eyes squeezed shut. The hand who'd seen it first yapped in amusement, and said he'd thought it was a dead fish.

Mr. Gallant, asked Senator Plesser of his overseer, did you hear of any loss of a child by drowning, on either place?

Gallant insisted that he had not, nor on any other plantation in the region. He might have heard, had such a thing befallen. That body'd been in the water for days, you could tell by the way it stunk.

If you wish my opinion on the subject. I'll tell you that some wench somewhere bore her child in secret, and then drowned it to get rid of it. Didn't want to lug it to her task, and bother nursing, and such.

Avid fish nibbled and struck, darting close to the body. You could see them thick, even in yellow precipitate of the opaque water.

May I suggest sir, that we just shove the thing off. In the end it'll reach salt water and the tide'll take it out. After all, we don't think it's *our'n*. Have no reason to believe so. Twould be a right smelly bit of cargo to take aboard, and we've nothing to put it in. Just be a nuisance to bury, once we got ashore.

Plesser nodded, so oars thrust out and poked the body into currents where it went voyaging. Gulls observed, and wanted it or the busy fish which nipped. They came down, struck with yells, soared again, came back and dived. Tooth or beak, which might puncture the bulb first, and destroy its buoyancy? It did seem so lonely under sweeping gusts which cut across the channels. Away it went, falsely skylarking—out to sea, it should be hoped. Beauty Beast felt tears in his eyes for a moment; he thought this a sad abandonment to leave this plump voyager behind. Covertly he whispered a Goodbye, but by that time all they could see were gulls.

The steamer had come tardily to Darien, and there had been contrary tides, and then the other delay. It was very late when they reached the pier at Emilion, with sun gone under gray metallic clouds, wind increasingly bitter. Before they came up to the dock a great trooping and crowding could be seen. Black people had finished with their day's work and were gripped by excitement of both master's and overseer's departure on this same day, and their return in dusk. Not only that: they'd brought visitors from the outside world. (It made no difference to them whether Judge Bracket was a Justice of the Supreme Court or no, or whether there existed a Supreme Court, or any Justices, or any justice.) Certainly this massa was one of great importance, but what of the well-clad yellow youth behind him? Massa Boy, they yelled in general understanding, and that was Beauty Beast's name throughout his stay in the accursed area.

He'd thought of damned souls before—considered them according to the way they were presented in Biblical lore or, say, by Dante. But he had not imagined what it would be like to be pressed by them, close-packed in proximity. They were more ragged than any rag-pickers who ever crawled the streets of Washington—their scraps of sagging garments so crusted with filth, so stained by soil or in many cases by effluence from their own bodies, that they seemed reduced to a uniform fringe of rags, a common smelling pigment.

Beauty Beast's first fear was that these scarecrows attempted to make off with Judge Bracket's luggage. They had their paws on sacred carpet-bags, the leather portmanteau. True, he realized vaguely that they might mean no harm—they were only touching and feeling substances strange to them, something to wonder at, something different from rice-straw, hulls, sticks, compressed earth and grimed walls of huts which made their lives. But they were dirtying the baggage, and almost automatically Beauty Beast struck with the wrapped umbrella; neither had they seen anything like this, or perhaps not recently. So they whooped about it, and tried to touch the umbrella (he thought they were trying to wrest it from him, and resisted vigorously) until a driver came whipping, *snap, lash, snap*. Then they broke back, tumbling and squalling. Some house servants appeared— They were nigh onto being as filthy as the field hands, but their clothing hung together more wholly— They gathered up the visitors' bags, as well as crates and packages which the senator and Mr. Gallant had fetched from a shipment waiting in Darien.

Judge Bracket held a habit of making intimate or musing comments from time to time, addressed solely to Beauty Beast (probably this was true because Beauty Beast was most often with the judge). In this instance Judge Bracket turned from his host and from the other white man, looked down at Beauty Beast, smiled, and said quietly, So help me God. I never saw anything like this before. Not in all my born days. How now, Beauty Beast? Would you trade Shearwater for this? Then he laughed aloud, shrugged, and moved impressively to join Senator Plesser. Even these ragamuffins respected and feared him, they gave space for his walking, did not reach to stroke his clothing (except cautiously when his back was turned, and then to touch only coat-tails).

Women and most of the children might have been gotten up for a masque: heads bound in cloth turbans tightly wound, so saturated that they seemed pasted round their heads. Notion of uniform or some sort of professional headgear came upon you again.

Much lameness and hurt, you heard coughing and wheezing on all sides, spitting, heavy breathing. Elder men and women looked as if they'd been squeezed by gigantic remorseless hands, the fat and force of living pressed out of them. They gaped, mouths open, strings of matter hanging sometimes from eyes or noses, not wiped away. Knobs of their shoulders stuck out like limbs of trees dead in a place where the ground had become permanently inundated: exaggerated elbows, legs seeming to have been pulled from the pelvic sockets and turned to one side or the other. Gnarled they were, but not in good seasoned gnarling. Rather than pity you felt an awful desire to have them removed, wiped out. *Blot them from me. I don't wish to see them, don't wish to know that they are here. Or anywhere.*

They continued giving voice, a herd of animals who could not resist baying about the strong scent that came to them. So they milled along, all the way to the Big House, such as it was.

It grew in a chunk against night approaching from forests to the east, built of squared logs and planking, with plaster forced between. There came a fleeting thought that here lay charm, as in pictures of half-timbered houses in Old England; then the entire idea of charm was demolished, you knew that these walls held only starkness. The area within would have no more attraction than trodden ground outside, where no shrubbery waved, no flowers prettied, no vines draped.

Abominable place, Beauty Beast heard Senator Plesser saying to the judge. You can well understand, sir, why I come here as infrequently as possible.

(You could build a better house, couldn't you? The nettled Beauty Beast imagined himself in response.)

He heard Judge Bracket saying equably, Bound to be rude country, here on these coastal islands. A crude shelter is more appropriate than would be a place high-ceiled and with fine verandahs. Especially since there are no womenfolk in the *ménage*.

Three rooms. A draughty dining-living room in the middle, with its shallow stone fireplace spitting and smoking along one wall, and rough tables and benches scattered. It might have been the public room of medieval tavern customed only by rankest outlaws. Large private chambers stood at either end of the house. One of these, at the south, was occupied by the host; Mr. Gallant used it for his own quarters when the owner was absent. Judge Bracket would be housed in the north bedroom. Cut into each outer corner of the chamber was a kind of closet. When viewed from the exterior these stood out like turrets on blockhouses of Colonial times. Beauty Beast investigated, whilst unpacking the judge's bags. He found that one of these closets was a place for storage, and the other a privy containing a wooden seat with a receptacle placed underneath—a weighty tublike specimen of the cooper's art. It had not been removed for cleaning recently. But folks used it: house servants, he thought grimly. He lugged the smelly thing out and demanded that some housemaid should empty and scrub it immediately. These darkies spoke in accents which a stranger could barely

317

understand in many cases, and in some cases not at all. The girl whom Beauty Beast addressed seemed addle-tongued. *Ah-na, she po keen dah.* The girl kept repeating it, looking at him with large eyes and a little laughter. Eventually he made out that she was telling him, Anna was supposed to clean *that*. Since there appeared to be no Anna about, he lugged the thing down to the dock himself, still boiling at implied insult to Judge Bracket. He found a morsel of rope, tied it to the bail, dropped the big bucket into the water, dumped and doused, brought it back, found a stick, stirred, scraped. He got it cleaned after a fashion. Throughout this sortie he was accompanied by a throng of hands, mostly male and mostly youthful, who watched raptly through the darkness and jabbered about what he was doing, and gave thin shrieks at seeing this younger—whom they considered an elegant gentleman, but inexplicably colored— engaged in menial pursuit.

Beauty Beast carried the receptacle as far as the house door, opposite a log kitchen where negresses swarmed. Then the bail was wrenched from his hand by a towering black woman who had the effrontery to reprimand him stridently. He made out that she believed he was shaming her. So he was. He wondered if she might not be Anna, and asked: Anna, who was supposed to clean, et cetera? For reply she yelled invective and came at him flailing. Beauty Beast snatched Judge Bracket's umbrella which had been left hanging carelessly on a peg outside the door (twas a wonder it hadn't been stolen already). When the big woman struck, and as he dodged, he whirled to give her a good poke in the stomach. She doubled up, cursing, and the other servants were convulsed with laughter. Splendid household, he thought. I'll get on nicely here! He caught up the handle on the privy bucket and carried it to reinstallation in the corner closet of Judge Bracket's room. He doubted that Anna would trouble him again, or try to attack physically. Indeed she did not. He'd pushed her with the umbrella tip more brutally than he realized.

(She went around coughing and moaning, bending over now and then to hold her middle and to rebuke him with rolling eyes. She postured through his dreams. He was overcome with remorse and wished somehow to make amends, but had no notion where to begin. Later, when they left this plantation of Emilion for good and all, Beauty Beast was still distressed by his wounding of the woman. Though it seemed that she had recovered: she walked briskly, chatted or snarled in conversation with the rest. When he was called to follow Judge Bracket aboard for departure, Beauty Beast took a quarter-dollar piece from his small hoard and appeared suddenly in the group at the kitchen door. Anna, this is for you. He pressed it into her hand, scurried away. In enormous delight he looked back from the boat and saw her walking to join the crowd on the pier and to stand waving.)

In Washington, Judge Bracket strode one night to interrupt Beauty Beast at the piano, as he did often when a whim struck him.

I've ordered Arnold to pack me for departure early Thursday. Herewith I instruct you to get your own duds together for a brief voyage. That suave sly-boots does well enough in a mansion in the Nation's Capital, but he'd be in sad plight on a wilderness plantation—which I take it, is what we'll find. I must confer with Senator Plesser at once, Beauty Beast. He's down for his semi-annual visit to properties he owns off the Georgia coast. Gossip has it that accommodations are of the most barbaric sort, with the noble Plesser too stingy to make better. Ah, well. Parsimony in personal attitude may breed parsimony in statecraft—

Nor should I fancy Arnold's company on any sort of voyage. He complains that the very sight of ocean waves turns him seasick; therefore who'd lay out my drawers, who'd brush my gaiters? Tis a pity for you to lose time at the pianoforte, but no help for it: you must return to valeting for the nonce. Thursday morning, d'ye hear?

He stalked away, leaving Beauty Beast in glee at contemplating a God-given midwinter vacation from drudgery at Master Drummond's.

(Little did I know, Misty, what was in store.)

Plesser had spent his childhood in Darien and, as sole heir, inherited the two plantations from his uncle. He'd been schooled at the North. There he settled into practice of law, whence he went to Congress when still quite young: first to the House, then to the Senate. As a Northern statesman he'd gained power, and this was the reason Judge Bracket sought him out. During the journey south, the judge made amusing observations, mostly to himself; but sometimes directing them to Beauty Beast (who paid scant heed. He was having too good a time in dashing about the deck to capture the few flying-fish which flopped aboard, and then in carrying them to the galley to be cooked for breakfast) . Mr. Justice Bracket spoke of how at least a few dedicated souls must remain alert and able, if any of Old Hickory's ideals were to survive the hocus-pocus of current administration. Relics of his words did hang through the years in Beauty Beast's memory, but never as a vital substance—they were mere ornaments on the wall of Time, rusting as years went by.

Nevertheless, on this first night at Emilion, Beauty Beast was so alarmed and disgusted at what he'd already seen, that he made every excuse to cling close to host and guest while they dined. He held no abiding curiosity about their conversation; but realized, even in early teens, that a man of Plesser's stripe offered horrid fascination. It would be well to learn as much about him as possible.

In Washington the senator's turn-out was the subject of raillery: antique carriage with creaking wheels, moth-eaten horse, pop-eyed driver. His sweethearts were tired-looking women—widows mostly—who came from good backgrounds. Usually they were women older than himself, and would cost him nothing, would be glad to accept whatever pallid masculine favors Senator Plesser might choose to offer. The house which he took, not far from Judge Bracket's, was too small for a busy politician's purpose. Spotted cushions, worn carpets, cracked soup-bowls, wine glasses which looked as if they'd been gnawed on the edges. His straggling servants were the cheapest which money might secure. Plesser himself was a pale-faced pudgy man with soft white hands of which he was intolerably vain. He carried a little French knife with folding files and shears attached, and he was always working at his nails in public, especially when he sat in committee sessions. Then he would polish his nails with a yellow silk handkerchief which gave forth an odor of oily perfume. He managed just the same to wrap those flabby hands around so many reins of political prestige that his ill-favored house was a busy place. Men of promise and distinction could be found there—tongues in their cheeks perhaps, but still they could be found. When Senator Perry Plesser entertained, jokes went rattling around town. Even Beauty Beast heard many. One anecdote had it that a man was accused by his wife of being drunk. Impossible, he said loftily. I'm not drunk, and I'll prove it. How so, my dear sir? I, he told her, was entertained this very evening at Senator Plesser's. No one could possibly become intoxicated on the amounts he serves. The wife apologized. I find you innocent, dear husband. Pray forgive the charge.

Or the story of a shellfish-monger who was told when he came into his shop, Senator Plesser's housekeeper was by, and bids you send up oysters and lobsters for twelve. Shall I then take the cart and deliver a keg of oysters, plus twelve of the lobsters—or twenty-four?

Did you say Senator Plesser, boy? Then you shan't need the cart. Take up a pint of oysters and one lobster.

Scrawniness and bleak aspect they were then prepared for, but not for downright savagery and hardship of the place as they found it. Most articles of furniture in the house had been made by negroes at Emilion—those who were called carpenters, but had only the axe-man's skill about them. The very chairs were rough unplaned wood, they'd had splinters rubbed out of them through usage. Benches were of the same sort found in negro shacks—a slice of log split off, with legs stuck into the curved portion beneath. There loomed a few stained chests-of-drawers which it turned out had been fetched long before from the uncle's house at Darien. Every table, large or small, rocked on the uneven floor when touched or moved; there lay chips scattered to push under the legs and try to build stability. Smell of wood-smoke palled the place, smoke hung solid against light; nor did it offer a pleasant odor, it was too mingled with aroma of unwashed darkies, grease and grime of their cookery. Whenever a door was left open, even for minutes, poultry made for the interior. Ducks came quacking, even a goose or two. They were chased out, but not before their pasty droppings had lumped on the floor.

In the main the overseer, Mr. Gallant, was responsible for such conditions. He was a round-shouldered, long-armed, long-legged man with a hurt pocked face. One eye had been gouged in a fight and stared awry (this scared the colored mightily). Mr. Gallant gave up the south bedroom in the house only when Senator Plesser came, and Plesser was not there more than a few weeks out of the entire year: hence Gallant now regarded himself as dispossessed, and was surly about it. He'd moved into his office which stood not far from the kitchen. Gallant seemed to hold what amounted to pride in the filthy situation abounding. Actually he pointed out an open ditch nearby, where servants went to squat and relieve themselves, and where their sewage drained reluctantly through a hollow log placed under the dike. My own idea, he said pridefully. Before this was dug, you use to step in turds all the while.

For the evening meal Senator Plesser arranged himself and Judge Bracket at a table some distance removed from the fireplace. Fresh sparks flew to scorch the floor in tiny craters. On a rough hearthstone the bulk of flying embers accumulated, but many spat beyond. Stray tufts and spirals of smoke rose from the planks; some burnt deeply, dangerously. Servants who'd stuffed that fireplace should have known the sparking proclivity of cedarwood. Either they did not know or did not care. From beneath floor puncheons emanated slithering sounds, moans, grunting, an occasional squeal: hogs or dogs, seeking their own allotment of flea-ridden comfort. Sometimes both species seemed to be present, their incense rising through cracks.

Beauty Beast blessed himself that he'd had the foresight to pack a jar of flea-powder put up by the judge's favorite chemist, twould come in handy. But oil would help; already his mind was busy with plans for a wholesale clean-up of that room and an oiling of the planks, once the gentlemen were out of the house next day. If oil could be had. He'd seen a big stationary engine puffing its smoke at a distance from the house: something to do with rice, perhaps there would be oil on hand. Beauty Beast knew that darkies heeded a voice of authority, once they understood that the authority was actually delegated (with penalty for non-compliance attached). This whole experience might prove to be a series of challenges to his ingenuity, and he mounted with spirit to the charge.

Judge Bracket made no secret of reposing confidence in Beauty Beast. My dear senator, he ventured amiably when the first weird figures had come grunting and spilling with preliminaries to supper. May I suggest that you allow my personal boy to take charge of the meal? He's trained in all essentials.

To use slang borrowed from other scholars at Master Drummond's, this was pie in Beauty Beast's pantry. He waited only until Senator Plesser condescended to the necessary orders, then sprang eagerly. He cleared another unsteady table for a service buffet, he warned the shambling leering women to set their platters on it. There was no wine; host and guest were provided with some variety of blackstrap rum; they downed this with water, and Judge Bracket rumbled in his throat at every swallow. The fish course was an unsavory pilau made from rice, crayfish, peppers, with ragged wafers of shell ornamenting the mass. Cornbread accompanied throughout the meal, thin as a plank and, Beauty Beast discovered, fully as easy to masticate. Worst of all was a platter of lamb: huge cubes of greasy stuff with bones penetrant in every direction, lumps of fat and wads of tissue tangling. It would be found that there was no butcher. Not a soul among the kitchen staff knew how to cut up meat.

Except perhaps possum.

Or wildcat meat, thought Beauty Beast. They'd probably cook that too, and never know the difference.

Who carved the lamb, Mercy? he asked of a snuffling lip-licking creature who admitted to that name.

Kahve? Wha you mean *kahve?*

Who cut up the lamb?

Bob kuh im. He carpenter.

During journeys to the cook-shack Beauty Beast learned that the staff dined concurrently with the master, or in many cases before, and on the same fare. Some had already finished, and were amusing themselves by tossing chunks of lamb or charred cornbread to a throng of field hands compelled to squat outside the household circle. There were enough and to spare of the latter: young mothers crouched, suckling babies; children wrestling and fighting over possession of scraps; hollow-ribbed dogs slinking.

With eyes grown more or less accustomed to persistent smoke, and with initial responsibilities of his task mainly discharged, Beauty Beast had opportunity to halt and gaze at an existing phenomenon. A mural, he thought. Frescos? Statuary? (Of late the judge had set before him a lengthy treatise on Greek sculpture as revealed at ancient temple sites, and bade him study it well. He was prepared for the idea of human bodies, robed or unrobed, marshalled motionless against a wall.) Between visits to the dining table, he made a cautious circuit of the house exterior. Fastened to east and west walls of the central chamber were a collection of fringed figures held, tight as gravity might have held them, by the impulse of curiosity. Solid wooden shutters were drawn down and hooked over each window; but a sufficiency of cracks could be identified by fire-glow within. These apertures were now stoppered by eyes of watchers outside. Also poorly-mixed plaster between logs had yielded to usage and the elements. In profusion these areas served as peep-holes. Smaller fry swarmed up like rats, toe-holding and hand-holding to higher portions of the outside walls. Crone, slattern, hobbler, doomed hoyden, a dread starved audience paid undiverted heed to the drama within. It was a play with but two actors. Master and guest sat at meat—the supercilious little-glimpsed master who was almost as much a stranger as that

324

guest whose tone and bearing gave testimony to imperial status. The gaunt auditors built no conversation amongst themselves. They did not wish to be driven off; they knew that they would be sent scooting if they disturbed, they might even be whipped. Within experience of each tattered individual there must have been a sense of blows raining unexpectedly in a punishment—to their notion—unmerited. Beauty Beast recalled a chronic lazy-bones at Shearwater whose eternal complaint was, Didn't do nuffin, but get beat jus same.

His lean athletic imagination ran and chased. He fancied that he heard the primal thinking of these people, heard it translated into words he could understand—common plantation nigger talk, not the jargon employed here. Actually the only communication or audible response was an occasional growl, a snorting through the nose, quick gulp or intake of breath, a soft *Wooo* of incredulity when perchance they observed Judge Bracket opening his snuff-box.

Young Massa, he not so big as Big Old Massa.

Big Old Massa, New Massa Come, he got big big watch-chain.

He watch-chain gold.

Oh, oh, oh!

Big Old Massa Come, he got diamond hang from he watch-chain.

Oh, oh.

Em Massas, dey not eat much meat.

Reckon our Young Massa, he not like meat.

No, no, doan want eat no way.

Big Old Massa Come, *he* not like dat meat.

You give *me* dat meat. Ho, ho!

You give me dat meat, I eat whole big pile.

Eat big cup full.

No, boy, I eat more den dat. I eat whole *piggen* full.

Hi. I eat whole bucket full.

I eat big *barrel* dat meat, you give me chance.

You ask em niggers in kitchen, dey maybe give you little bit.

Oh, oh! Big Old Massa New Come, he take out he *watch*.

Now dey boff drink.

What you reckon dey drink?

Reckon dey drink spirits.

Why dey say white folks drink *spirits?* You drink spirits, dey *hant* you.

You reckon maybe spirits hant white folks *too?*

Were it a question of haunting, The Watchers managed. They remained with Beauty Beast, rigid but breathing in silent emblazonment. They hung in his mind, loomed when he'd shut his eyes against any light remaining; he saw them lumped in faint color, as if he'd looked at objects in too intense a sun, until these were those rows, gray dabs hovering against muted blood-color, dark blood-colored dabs against green, insistent, following a form of vision long after the eyes were closed.

During the cold broken night which followed, he found himself starting up as in response to his own voice which had demanded, What do they want? What do they *want?* In later understanding he realized that they wanted everything because they had nothing. There was nothing for them, nothing adhering to or possessed by them except the breath of life, and even that was terminated in misery.

Another time when he awakened, they were still there. On this occasion he was asking, But what can I give them? I can give them nothing. For I, too, am a slave. Then he dreamed that he was weeping lustily for them. Replete with sobbing, he tried to spread lamentation over them like layers of blanket. He did not have enough, could not reach far enough, most of these victims would remain out in the cold.

Shearwater boasted the usual rows of cabins (especially neat; they were not far from Judge Bracket's scrutiny or from his olfactory discernment; they stood scrubbed). At many other plantations Beauty Beast had seen much the same. Up in Maryland some two years previously he'd accompanied the judge to a brick house shaped like a square U; and one of those rear wings was actually occupied by the colored. Sufficient partitions had been inserted to build a dormitory for household staff and their children. But this partook of the unusual: it came about because an agèd grandmother lay an invalid, and it was essential that nurse, cook and handmaidens of various sorts be in the house at all hours.

Beauty Beast had supposed that when the evening's work was done these Emilion hawks and harridans would go shuffling off to their cabins. The fact was that they had no cabins. No provision was made for their housing. If they could not subsist in the open or in the kitchen itself, then they need not subsist.

Through past experience on entering into a new situation where he was accepted as the body-servant of a distinguished visitor, Beauty Beast had been put into the hands of some dusky major-domo by mere gesture from housekeeper, butler, or even the mistress. He had been told, You bring you things, boy. Obediently he brought them, although on a few notable occasions his bag had been carried eagerly by some youngster who hoped to be awarded a scrap of silver, and was. Always Judge Bracket kept Beauty Beast appropriately turned out. He wanted no beggarly-looking hobbledehoy attending him.

The youth was guided to a clean bed in an outside cabin; sometimes he might be installed barracks-fashion with other male servitors. Once he'd been invited to share the bed of a fluttery valet whose main topic of conversation was the elegant new wardrobe recently acquired by the mistress in Paris, and who later behaved in a manner which Beauty Beast thought novel but offensive. The valet earned a kick in the teeth from a stout little bare foot, in result. The visitor spent the rest of that night (twas in a sizeable mansion) on a sofa in the billiard room.

He had been quartered in basements, attics, on a cot in a cooper's shop; and he considered any such diggings to be satisfactory. Here at Emilion no one had told him where to stow himself or his possessions. All were oblivious, uncaring. His ordinary traveling equipment consisted of a sturdy knapsack. It had been gifted by a former Swedish soldier, the servant of neighbors in Washington, who hung about trying to court one of the bronze kitchen-maids at Judge Bracket's. *Korpral* Olaf demonstrated wonderful pockets and pouches which were properties of the knapsack; the boy toted the thing proudly.

On entering this reprehensible establishment, he'd shoved his knapsack under a table near the door leading to Judge Bracket's bedchamber, that it might not be thieved away from him too easily. He'd folded his greatcoat atop. It was one complete with cape across the shoulders, and cut out of genuine Scottish plaid: a pride and love of a coat, with ornamental frogs down the front. He wondered now if he'd be compelled to sleep in it, and just where he'd lie and wrap himself. While the two gentlemen sat opposite the fire, sipping what proved to be the last of their coffee and liquor (Senator Plesser did not smoke, but provided the judge with an old churchwarden pipe and some particularly unpleasant tobacco—probably both were the property of Mr. Gallant) — Beauty Beast went into the bedchamber for night-time preparations. He arranged pillows and bolster; there were only rags of curtains round the bed, but he pulled them this way and that in order to give as much protection against weaving draughts as could be managed. Temperature of bedclothing? Icy. The bed had been made up clumsily a long time before, and the nearby river's dampness claimed it. Beauty Beast went in search of a warming-pan. He could find none, nor could he find any person who'd ever heard of such implement. He made clumsy substitute with a large ash-covered stone which lay near the living room fireplace. Unobtrusively he heated the stone there, wrapped it in scraps of flannel which he found crowded into an old chest drawer, and lugged the heavy thing to make its great dent in feather-beds. Feather-beds? His hands went exploring and evaluating. No, indeed: these thin mattresses were filled with some other material. There was a gaping seam, he spilled some of the stuff out. Spanish moss indeed, reduced almost to a powder. (Each time after that when he stood politely in the presence of Senator Plesser, he felt increased and abiding contempt.)

No fire in that bedchamber, nor provision for one. Beauty Beast reasoned that he could not well go out and warm Judge

Bracket's nightgown and cap in the living room where the gentlemen sat. He smuggled them to the kitchen-shack, warmed them there. Whole log-piles of scrofulous children had lain asleep on the floor earlier but now adults reposed as well. There ensued an awareness which prompted scorn at first, then pity hardening into rage. These people owned neither mattress nor pillow nor any proper covering which they might call their own or think of as belonging to them, or even feel cozily familiar with.

The old cook, Mercy, was hunched in a corner nearest the fireplace, spooning up a substance called pudding, but which had been rejected by the diners in the house.

Where do you sleep, Mercy?

She looked around, bloodshot eyes rolled and roamed. Sometimes I sleeps over *there,* was what she said, in essence. Sometimes I sleeps over *there.* And pointing vaguely each time. Tonight I guess I sleeps right *here.* She shoved her empty bowl, it rolled into the smouldering embers. Mercy spread herself in a position as foetal as her strange shape would allow. Before Beauty Beast left the shack she was actually groaning in sleep.

Host and guest were vanished for the night, retreated into their own chambers. Mr. Justice Bracket sat on the edge of the bed, unwinding his stock, and Beauty Beast knelt to pull off his boots.

The judge quoted derisively, *The boast of heraldry, the pomp of pow'r—* D'ye hear me, hey? Finish it out.

Or all that beauty, all that wealth e'er gave—

This then you've committed, as I bade you. Good indeed!— and you should have won better for yourself than this pigsty. But I shall try to make it up to you in the future, Beauty Beast, with lodgings in one doge's palace or another. That shall be *th' inevitable hour.*

Sir, I fetched flea-powder—

What say?

The insect powder, put up by Mr. Walpole.

Then dust me, boy, dust me.

Beauty Beast dusted. The judge stood in socks and drawers,

329

and held out his arms for Beauty Beast to draw on the night-gown.

Now then, my noble Moor, can you give me the dates for Thomas Gray, whom we've quoted?

He was born, sir, in 1716, and died in1771.

Year after the Boston Massacre.

Yes, sir. That occurred on the 5th of March, 1770.

Ah. And who was the ringleader of the citizens who pelted the Redcoats, Beauty Beast? Who—was—the leader?

Some say that it was one Crispus Attucks, sir, who was shot down. Others declare Attucks to have been an innocent by-stander.

But what was the *color* of Crispus Attucks?

He was a mulatto. Unless he was of Indian blood. I like to think, sir, that he was a nigger. *And* the ringleader.

You're spry, said Judge Bracket. Still, at best it's but parrot-ing. Fact learnt, fact lodged, fact let forth, recited. Essential at times, extremely effective on many occasions. Yet in no way indicative of cerebric activity. Your ordinary uninspired stu-dent has his accumulation of facts. He spews them forth when demanded, and we'll all be bound tis a convenient faculty; but never be deluded into the notion that it is Thought. Are you entertaining Thought, Beauty Beast? My own notion is that it's too chilly for bedside prayers.

Judge Bracket rolled into bed. The boy helped him to adjust pillows and bolster behind him (the judge scrolled his face at encountering their rancidity) . Habitually he slept half-propped as a much older man might have done.

I asked you. Have you been thinking?

I have, sir.

What are the form and substance of your meditations?

Beauty Beast frowned, hesitating before he replied. There's not much form to them, sir. But the substance— I've been thinking about these people, here on the place.

This rabble of savages polluting the very air? Pray expunge them from consideration. Take herons, partridges, mud-hens, minnows, mandrakes, mountebanks— Speculate on those in-stead. They're finer forms of life.

Bracket's feet encountered comfort of the warm wrapped stone and regions surrounding it. Bushy eyebrows went up in surprise, he gave a complacent nod.

These critters. They're demons, and a disgrace.

Beauty Beast asked boldly, Then who's made them so, sir? Their master, or masters? The overseer, sir?

Tis their natural bent. Entire tribes and villages exist like this in Darkest Africa. I've heard from seafaring people who've gone there: their own chiefs and kings disgrace them, debase them, let them decay so.

The unhappy Beauty Beast cried, But we've nothing like that at Shearwater! I've never seen the like, never believed that it could be!

Then it's meet that you should accompany me here and have a look at the seamy side. Observe how wind at this end of the house comes through and ripples the draperies! Ah, well, perhaps tis a benefit; otherwise we might succumb to presence of the hogs down below. Pray fetch my Bible, Beauty Beast. I'll read you a chapter before I slumber.

Here, sir. Right beside you.

Shadows jigged in the room, the candle flame leaned and smoked to south, to east again. Judge Bracket motioned for Beauty Beast to take up the Bible.

Light is better beyond the bed. Draw up that stool, boy, and read.

What shall I read, sir?

Proverbs.

Hesitation again. Then, Make your own choice. Can you see to read by that abominable flame?

I can, sir. Straining close.

When the righteous are in authority, the people rejoice: but when the wicked beareth rule, the people mourn. . . .

If a ruler hearken to lies, all his servants are wicked. . . .

Where there is no vision, the people perish. . . .

Judge Bracket said drowsily, Tis the Twenty-ninth Chapter you're reading from, or I'm a dolt. But I seem to remember something else: *He that delicately bringeth up his servant from a child shall have him become his son at the length.*

There was a long silence, shared actively, knowingly between them.

(Twas often so, Misty.)

Have they offered you a place to bed yourself? Nay? I suspected as much. Then do you take your greatcoat, and my cloak as well, and bed down on the floor out yonder. Those grate-stones hold the heat. Even stench from beneath can be forgotten if you're warm enough.

Sleepily. Both the Old Andy and I slept with hogs, or worse. Long ago.

Not only did recurrent spectacle of The Watchers persist before Beauty Beast's eyes (behind his eyelids) throughout a spectral night. Also he heard Judge Bracket's quotation from Gray as mockery and accusation. The man Plesser was pompous enough in power. In Washington he flaunted his mischief in failing to abide by practiced rules of hospitality, embracing a niggardliness almost to the point of dementia. Here at Emilion he could reasonably be said to occupy ancestral soil as he slept, and Beauty Beast was unable to understand how the senator's dreams might remain unsullied. In an outlandish setting he demonstrated pomposity to its final and cruelest degree, by ignoring every ugliness conveyed to him by his senses, and in managing complete withdrawal from responsibility. He was an aloof and feeble Pilate washing his hands. As for heraldry: the boy wondered whether the tribe of Plessers boasted a coat-of-arms. Back home, in Washington, there were books relating to heraldry in the library. There the boy'd examined during rainy holidays or—rarely—when he was in enforced idleness, ailing with sore nose or throat. Mostly sleepless on his first night in these dreary wilds, he sought to beguile himself by designing a shield appropriate to Senator Plesser. Mysterious terms could not be applied, they were jumbled—tinctures, pales, gyrons and the rest— He was at a loss to employ them. He did fancy the shield as being quartered, with a glaring skull in the first quarter, whip in the second, bottle of poison in the third (symbolic of food served), and a white worm in the fourth. (The worm was Senator Plesser.) Also he should devise a crest. Something to do with a dollar sign. Dollar sign with two crossed bones?

What of lives in which there could never be found *all that beauty, all that wealth e'er gave?* All? Not a shred, not a figment. Nor even most hackneyed comfort, direst necessity. He thought of his native Shearwater from toilers' standpoint, chattels' standpoint. He gulped aloud, his near-empty stomach felt inclined to reject and eject the few morsels he'd managed to put into it.

From afar delicious odors returned: sizzling pork, mush, roasting ears, mustard greens, okra, a yam dusted with white ashes, drawn from the fire with a hooked stick, cracked open, good smell and steam bursting; and hot drippings to dress it with. Fried chicken—

Hands at Shearwater might keep poultry for their own use, just so a few simple rules were observed. Feed was not supplied from plantation stores, wild feed might be used. Such stuff as grew in the woods, and whatever table scraps were left from the hands' own rations. Hogs were reared under the same conditions but hogs must be kept penned. And any darkies' chickens which strayed through the fenced yard of the Big House stood their chance of being kidnapped into the master's flock maintained by old Jeems. Black people were adjured to self-betterment through edict and example. Ah, when he, Beauty Beast, skipped in the shirt-tail brigade, how many times had they stuffed themselves with a bounty of forest grapes! And when the boys were grown a bit taller and might on occasion scamper to the sandy shore— Well, he remembered the pickle-weed—picklevine, some called it—and how they'd pull up long strands of the stuff with oily fat pointed leaves, and carry armloads home, munching as they went. The leaves were stuffed with goodness, flavor of butter and salt, they'd pop when you bit them. Back to the quarters, and bursting in at a cabin where he lived with Aunt Suke and Uncle Jag who'd reared him from babyhood.

Crying, Look what I got.

Why, dat's saphire you done fotch me, cheered Aunt Suke in appreciation.

(Actual name of the plant was samphire, he discovered later.)

I makes you wash dat real clean, get sand off. Den we plucks de leaves—doan never keep de bad ones—and we puts dat saphire down wid vinegar an pepper an a speck of cane juice. We has bes pickle in no time tall.

When she'd made her pickle it never lasted long. Uncle Jag and Beauty Beast loved it, they'd spit pieces of pone and slide the green stuff inside, munch with glee.

Such joy was simplicity itself, all the more joyful for being simple. But both wealth and beauty were inherent in such recollection.

Aye, there was work, back-breaking work. Aye, drudgery. Aye, weariness. This was slavery. Oh, Lord, said Uncle Jag, dragging himself from his corn-shuck mattress. Dere go dat bell. He rose groaning with a rheumatism which plagued him before his natural time. Oh, Lord, dat bell, dat bell. Black man born pick cotton, white man born ride hoss.

Still there were riches in every season. Come autumn, on a fitting Saturday night with no bell to clang disturbing on the next morning, Uncle Jag would lead out a hound called Old Clip. Off they'd go to the woodland, maybe tree a coon. Uncle Jag would prod the critter down, and Clip'd grab and hold, the club'd pound, there'd be roast coon Sunday. Wow, wow, that scent of meat again, and yams going with it.

Weather colder, snow flurries trailing and tracing, though on fair days there'd be cotton picking right into the middle of winter.

A four-day festival, four whole days and nights.

Christmas giff!

Often ladies and gentlemen came to the Big House. The more were there, the louder and more frequent the petitions.

Christmas giff! Christmas giff!

Beauty Beast's one sound pocket was weighted with big

334

pennies, a glinting dime, three half-dimes. Judge Bracket gave pocket-knives to every boy, a string of beads to every girl. The overseer received a colt, his wife a new lamp, the drivers had silver watches—at least they looked like silver. Aunt Suke and Uncle Jag displayed with pride their dollars, Aunt Suke had an apron and a new tea-kettle, Uncle Jag got three bandanna handkerchiefs, each of a different color, and a clay pipe.

Christmas giff!

The echo awakened Beauty Beast, he reëntered this baleful abode. Pigsty smell, wind through cracks more determined, fire but a few scraps of orange-colored fluff. He hated to leave his hard bed. Twas warmth: greatcoat and cape wound together had kept him in comfort, but a righteous chore should be performed. The fireplace must remain hot, Judge Bracket would appreciate decent temperature in which to breakfast. No wood in the chimney corner, all had been burnt up. Forage for more. Immediately beside the cook-shack: yes, he'd seen a pile there, disorderly jumble, not stacked. So he forced himself out into the night. There he saw them sleeping, The Watchers. Every exterior bench or raised portion of planking—a kind of loading platform, for instance—had its huddled inhabitants. They gave vent to faint animal coughs and grunts as they lay. Covering? Beauty Beast bent to feel. Long moss again, nothing else. (Tree moss, they'd call it; or, as he learned, *tee mouse*.) God's thin gift to tired people when they were cold, and so beaten down by brutish demand and neglect that they might not even recognize the colossal wickedness of which they were a part.

With first light Beauty Beast became possessed of brilliant ambition: to secure a good breakfast for Judge Bracket. In so doing he'd have to secure a good breakfast for Senator Plesser as well, and nothing could have been less to his desire. But there existed certainty that the judge would look kindly on the provider of the feast, if a feast came about, and say, Do you save these remainders for yourself.

In nearby waters fish must abound. Beauty Beast loved to

fish, and went sometimes with schoolmates (when he could escape the incessant demands of pianoforte or other studies) to the creek which bordered Georgetown northwest of the H Street house. At his native plantation he had fished ever since he could remember, and counted himself as skillful. When informed that they would be visiting wildernesses, he'd made haste to pack a spindle wound with fishline, box of hooks and weights, a few chunks of cork.

Neither guest nor master was as yet astir, not even after Beauty Beast finished building up the fire. Some negroes still roosted on the woodpile, and groaned when he disturbed them in pulling out fuel. Two or three cursed and struck, but feebly. He rallied them for this, said that his master had ordered him to fetch wood.

He wound himself in a wool tippet and went prowling. Some fifty rods south of the house a stream entered the river, and the boy took himself in that direction. There were straggling palms, he hoped to find green tree frogs as at Shearwater. But winds of night, fallen to nothing in this hour, had sent most of the frogs to some other cover. By dint of repeated search he observed one specimen, chilled and seemingly lifeless. His hand shot out, swept it off the back of the frond, and he impaled the creature on a hook, where it refused to wriggle, dangling its legs hopelessly. There was a broad stump on the bank, conveniently close to a pool backed in from eddies; there he suspended his lure. Nothing happened except a bobbing and weaving, faint tremor of the line. When he drew up the frog, he found that it had been nibbled by something apparently too small to swallow the bait. This gave him the notion of dispatching the frog, cutting it into bits, and trying a much smaller hook. Promptly the cork went under, and Beauty Beast swung out a miniature black catfish. Bullheads, he thought. They'd be prime! A host of the slippery creatures wallowed at depth in the pool. With twigs and whipcord he constructed a stringer, and added to his hoard every minute or so. He warmed to sport so ardently that it was necessary to remove first his tippet, then his jacket. Bullhead after bullhead slid down the stringer. He'd wrap it around a root of the stump, let the fish dangle, rebait the hook, drop it into the pool, there'd be another. He wished that Franklin and Maurice could see him. Franklin was the son of a congressman, Maurice the son of a French diplomat, and both fellow-scholars at Mr. Drummond's, and rivals on those fishing expeditions to Rock Creek. But Beauty Beast longed for an audience, here and now, that he might enjoy words of envy and commendation.

There did come an old woman wrapped in scraps of dirty sailcloth. She hobbled close, peered, gave a caw like a crow each time another bullhead was secured. She reached up to tug at the boy's pantaloons as he stood on the stump. *Mah oh man ee oos tap fih.* He asked what she was saying, truly, in as polite fashion as he could muster; but she only spoke the same words. *Mah oh man ee oos tap fih.* She pointed a short distance down the creek to its juncture with the main river. Then, muttering because he couldn't understand her, she turned and walked a lame pitiful path toward the cook-shack.

It dawned on him that she had been saying, My old man, he used to trap fish. Probably she'd been pointing out the very place where the traps were set. He looked again. Something else there at the moment: another observer had approached silently in a boat. It was a quaint craft, shaped something like a squat canoe, but there were rowlocks and the occupant had oars. He clung against the bank, watching the fisherman.

The person in the boat was a boy or young man of peculiar coloration. His skin was neither jet-black nor brown, but black as if viewed through a gauze screen—grayish hue, ash-colored. Also there loomed peculiarity in the form or expression of his face, but distance was too great to discern in detail. Odder than his face was an item of garb. Hood, cape, cloak? Something over his head and falling down around the shoulders, and seeming to be made from fur in patchwork fashion.

Where this stranger had come from might not be reckoned. Certainly he was not one of those at the landing-pier the previous night, nor had he been dawdling near the kitchen. Still desiring applause, Beauty Beast bent down again to lift the cord on which bullheads were arrayed and squirming. He held it high as he could, for the other's delectation, and he saw a dusky arm rise and a hand wave in salute. Oars went into operation, the odd little craft swung round the bend, headed downstream. From his vantage point Beauty Beast could observe the pier, but the wayfarer did not come ashore, he splashed past straggling quarters and on in direction of the threshing area.

Count them: twenty-seven bullheads, though several were exceedingly small. The aggregate could provide an ample breakfast for two—with, he prayed, sufficient left over for himself. He rolled the line upon its stick and carried his catch to the Big House through a crowd of women, children, bent old men, and their hubbub of wonderment. Idiots. Any of them could have done the same thing, even elder children. All they'd need were hooks and line and— Hold. Where'd they get fishhooks? Not from that slimy Mr. Gallant, twas certain.

He dropped bullheads on the hearthstone, went to tap at Judge Bracket's door. Light as he touched, the crooked door sagged open and revealed Judge Bracket splashing himself at the crazy washstand. There was neither mat nor bath-rug, and water spread over the puncheons.

The judge glowered. You deserted me, you yellow—

Master, I've been catching your breakfast.

Catching my—?

Fresh fish, sir. I've an ample supply, and if you'll but give the word I'll cook them myself. Aunt Suke taught me to fry fish—

(This was in the year before the fatal duel, and Judge Bracket's retirement from the bench, and from the world; and before his insistence that Beauty Beast take up culinary pursuits.)

It seemed that the provender was so unworthy last night, sir, that your host might honor you with better fare, if I made it available—

You're bleeding.

Just one hand. Those sharp daggers on the little fish. Bullheads, master.

Bullheads!—repeated the judge, brows arching up. What did you with my fustian pantaloons?

In that corner place—the press, or closet. But let me wash my hands, and I'll fetch them—

No, no. You're to suck your wounds!

I did, sir.

Then suck them again!—Judge Bracket roared. And get along to your preparation of fish, and management of those black lice in the kitchen. I'll garb myself. I prefer that you remain devoted to the creation of something better than that pukish fare—

He thought of Plesser, and lowered his voice.

—Which was deeded to us at the evening meal. No tricks to my toilet today, boy. It's to be rough garb, the senator and I are bound for some shooting. He declares that there should be doves in plenty, so we may be able to continue our conference among birds and powder and shot. Ah, this lodge is a rarity! He says there are only two horses on the plantation fit to carry us to the hunting grounds. Which are, I take it, some miles distant, well beyond the rice. Nor are there any bird-dogs, only these sickly hounds. They employ children instead.

And shoot over the *children?* asked Beauty Beast in horror.

So he says.

But children can't scent out—

Assuredly they cannot. They fling stones into coverts or something of that sort. At least, in so doing, birds will rise well ahead of you, and you'll have a chance at them. They won't be twirling out from under your own feet, dashing away through stubble, giving you no target. But get to your cookery, my precious blackamoor, get to your *cookery*. Have your bullheads been cleaned?

No, sir. I but just—

Then clean them!—and Beauty Beast fled to the chore.

Preparing the satiny little fish was a simple matter ordinarily. There were no scales, you had only to slice off the fins, slit body cavities, scrape out entrails, rinse, roll in cornmeal, and they were reading for frying. Skin was a mere film, tender and sweet —the very bones could be crunched happily. Judge Bracket was one who munched his bullheads down to their skulls. But the

339

young cook was hard put to find a pan in the first place. One had to be scrubbed out, and this with the usual crowd staring, smelling, jostling around him. To his disgust, when he attempted to dump accumulated guts, the dishpan was snatched away and people tussled over the remainders. Some carried off their portions to be cooked; but others selected choice tid-bits and munched them raw. That stuff's not fit to eat, Beauty Beast yelled at them. Response came promptly, almost with serenity. *Wha fo doan eat, goo fo blah fo.* Out of such reiterated jargon he culled the fact that entrails of fish were not eaten by white folks, but were good for black folks.

He knew that he should have pitied them, driven to such desperation by a crying need for flesh to supplement the eternal mess of rice or meal rationed to field hands (these who loafed round the kitchen-shack were codgers and dried-up female husks, except for offspring of house servants) but instead his grim desire was to herd the whole lot into the river and let them perish. Did they not possess one spark of resource or ingenuity? Fish swarmed hereabouts, bird life as well. They needed only to sit and take it, but such ambition was beyond them. Fish-traps? His decrepit acquaintance of that morning had told him that her husband used to trap fish—

Ignore these cringing mummies, forget their stench if possible.

He cooked his catch and served it up to an appreciative pair. Even Senator Plesser expunged the slight sneer in which his face seemed perpetually cast, and managed a nod of approval. Beauty Beast made bold to request the pantry keys and, in utter astonishment, received them. Since the gentlemen would be in the field all day, the youth wished to prepare a snack for them to take along. With glee he visited the storage chamber and found that ham, cheese and sea-biscuits had been included in a shipment brought from Darien the evening before. Hangers-on tried to follow him into the log room built adjacent to the kitchen; he barred the door against them. Mice raced, roaches slithered, but for all their presence he packed an adequate lunch in an old saddlebag. Then he ran to see the hunters on their way, and to eat his own breakfast after they'd gone. He chased off the tattered maids who came creeping to giggle at this young yellow stranger, sitting now in his master's place at White Folks' Table. In the end there were three left-over bullheads which he awarded to old Mercy in the kitchen.

He sought the rice-threshing engine later, and met up with a truculent operator who would spare him no oil. The engineer growled that ordinarily he did not even have a sufficiency for proper care of his equipment. Far out beyond, rice fields shone within their embankments, raggèd and stubbled squares seeming in no way fertilized by the bodies of those who'd been worked to ruination there. Folks in the fields were up to their knees in water and mud all day long—he knew of that, he'd heard tell. Beauty Beast started back to the Big House. He'd given up all idea of a campaign against fleas in the living room, twas futile. Then clanging of a hammer drew him toward the blacksmith's shanty.

He stopped, gazed, went forward slowly. Seated on a barrel outside the smithy door, swinging bare legs in the sun, was that same oddly-accoutered youth whom he'd seen watching him from the small boat in an earlier hour.

The boy slid off the barrel, grinning in friendly fashion. My name M'Gu. Come from Aneeda. Who you?

My name's Beauty Beast. My master is Judge Bracket. He's down from Washington to visit Senator Plesser.

You so dress up! exclaimed M'Gu.

City clothes are all I've got, save for an old pair of— But if we're to talk about clothes, what is that you're wearing?

M'Gu removed his cape-bonnet and passed it over with all the pride in the world. The garment was of fur, and he'd made it himself.

Beauty Beast was delighted to find one apparent native with comprehensible speech, though his manner of talking was bizarre. M'Gu omitted many short words, especially articles and prepositions; he often employed a singular instead of a required plural; he even trimmed out syllables in the middle of words.

Nevertheless Beauty Beast held his diction to be that of a Clay or a Bracket, compared to the gibberish which prevailed here. This was a desert island figuratively as well as in literal fact. Twas good to have someone to talk to.

M'Gu was half a head taller than he, and also above him in years. The boy did not know his exact age, but thought himself to be fifteen or sixteen. I can count, he said. Can you count? I count all way to hundred by ones. One time have old mistress, she teach me count to hundred by fives. This way: five, ten, fifteen, twenty—

Beauty Beast interrupted, saying that he too could count, and asked if M'Gu could read.

Oh yes, I read, read very well. Old mistress teach me, though it gainst law. She *say* gainst law, I never know. You read?

I can read anything, said Beauty Beast with charming modesty.

The taller boy flung out his long arms in a wide gesture and flapped his hands. Oh, good, good. Maybe you teach me more? Maybe you read much, you read more'n I read. How come?

How come what, M'Gu?

How come you read so much?

Because I was taught, and studied hard.

Good, good!

Kinks of peppercorn wool were tight against his head. His brow slanted, his scarred nose seemed squashed in the middle, nostrils spread. His lips were twice as thick as most negroes'. The lower jaw seemed hard as stone and protruded noticeably.

(Misty, he had an air— I don't know what to say. Almost of jolly contempt, as if he were some sort of royalty. Your driver Honga is the only person I've ever seen who reminded me of him.)

M'Gu said that he and his mother and father had belonged to one Mrs. Skeen who lived at Darien. She was an eccentric widow, in sore financial straits when her life ended. The negroes could not be inherited by her children, they were sold off to help pay debts.

Bad day for us. Oh, very bad day. We get sold this place. First we here, then Aneeda.

(That was what he and most of the others called Avenida. Emilion was Meeon.)

Bad days both places, said M'Gu. But Aneeda not so bad as Meeon, because Meeon rice, and we cotton up there. Just same, my daddy work death, my mammy work death. I all alone when small. You know what? My father African. Yes, yes! My mother, she ordinary nigger. But my daddy real live African, when he *was* live. You know how did he get here? Got smugged, smugged in. Because trade all stop so my daddy got to be smugged.

Beauty Beast held M'Gu's cape and stroked it, held it to the light, marvelled anew. Twas put together from scores of small patches of bristly fur—dark brown, pale brown, every shade of brown, edging into gray, or gray along the sides of each piece.

Yes, boy, M'Gu told him. Rice rats. Kill them all myself. How I kill them? Easy. But take long time get enough make this. They thick, oh very thick. Sometimes they many more than other times. I keep old cat one year, two years. She go out, catch rice rats, oh many, many. She fotch home for kittens, sometimes three, four, five, six, same night. And I take them away from her, but I give insides to kittens anyway.

His laughter rose.

Hunt rats myself? Yes, yes. Long stick, big sharp nail on end. Wait where they make path, all along edge of bank, stick them real quick. Oh, sometimes they cry, not like to be stuck. But I stick them just same!

He'd tanned the hides—not too ably, there was still an unpleasant smell to the cloak. But he wore it with satisfaction, it kept off winter.

Feel like I wild African too. Like my daddy.

Across the low bridge of M'Gu's nose, down one cheek and into his chin, ran a pinkish scar. Say it was whitish-pink— When blood flushed beneath the skin in excitement, the disfigurement shone more vividly.

Get this scar, he explained to his new friend, from Mistuh Turbey.

Who's Mr. Turbey?

Overseer at Aneeda. Oh, big man, very bad man. Very— He hunted for the word and found it. Very *fierce* man. He give me

343

this maybe I only ten years old. He whipping my mammy, and she cry bout it. I get pitchfork, try stick Mistuh Turbey with fork. But oh no, fork too big, I too little, don't stick him much. Would be nice kill him, but oh no, I too little. He give me just one crack he whip. All he need, do this to me. One crack.

(Misty, when he said *crack,* you thought you heard the sound of the blow.)

He say learn me lesson. Maybe so, maybe so. I still afraid Mistuh Turbey. So I run off once, run off twice, three times I run off. So— See?

He held his hands close before Beauty Beast, that mutilation might be observed. On both right and left hands the first joint of the little finger had been hacked off, there were knobs of scar tissue.

First time run off, cotch me in Darien. Fotch me back Aneeda; I get whip, whip, but so much go faint, never feel whip till come to, and Mistuh Turbey have drivers throw bucket water on me. He say, That learn you run off. Next time run off, get all way Savannah because hide on steamboat, nobody know I there. But men cotch me—runaway nigger boy, Savannah, put me in jail. Fotch back Aneeda again.

Boy, say Mistuh Turbey, cut off you tail one inch at time! But you ain't *got* no tail, so put you hand down on this block. He make somebody hold it there. Take out he great big knife and give one chop. Left hand. Next time run off, some niggers they see me go, they run tell. Get cotch nearby, second night after run away.

They bring me back. Come, boy, say Mistuh Turbey. You want next joint off same finger, or first joint off *this* finger?

Oh, I say, don't cut off no more, Mistuh Turbey. Never run off no more. That truth.

Which hand, boy? he say. He grab right hand, hold down on block— No more I got joint *right* little finger. So I run off no more, not for some time.

Some day— He muted the words. I maybe run off. But never know how do.

He stupefied his listener by again bursting into hearty laughter. Come long, I show you boat.

344

He'd journeyed from Avenida in the capacity of errand boy. M'Gu said that he did this frequently. In the tiny pirogue, or whatever the vessel might be called, he could travel more rapidly than ordinary oarsmen. He was thin but seemed manufactured of pliant steel, he had incredible strength in those gaunt arms. He hallooed once more and cried, Current never bother me. I go like bubble!

The blacksmith at Avenida was sick with a pneumonic complaint, and urgent repair jobs accumulated in result, on various machinery. None of the broken pieces was especially large or weighty, but all required forging. These parts were put into a canvas bag, and M'Gu hustled them down-river to have the work done at Emilion. He'd set out the previous afternoon, and Beauty Beast thought of how the wind must have blown against him. But I go fast, M'Gu said, cause downstream all way. Then I get to place, know where I am: big dead tree, got nice hollow. Old bear den, I know that place, sleep there twice when run off. So I pull in, pull boat up on land, crawl in log, chase out old snake— Don't know what kind, too dark see. Then I go to bed with moss, and I so very very glad. Sleep long time, then go out, light enough see boat, put boat in water, so I come. See you cotch little little fish. I call kitten-fish, cause they small *cat*fish, and again he howled.

Beauty Beast dropped into M'Gu's boat and attempted to manage it. Steady as he might balance himself on the single thwart, wisely though he tried to pull the short oars, this task was beyond him, he floundered in circles. M'Gu stood on the pier, teasing.

City boy never know how. Wild boy know how!

As interesting as the home-made canoe were M'Gu's weapons contained therein: a bow, and a skin quiver holding different types of arrows. Also a great knife in a sheath of gator hide.

Make that myself, said M'Gu proudly. Though Cato, blacksmith, he good friend, he holp. Make of old sword, busted sword I find, all rusty. One time soldier have, I think. Or maybe pirate, and his eyes danced at the idea.

When returned to the forge M'Gu consulted with the smith. The parts would not be ready until midafternoon.

Not till sun start down sky. We got long while yet. You been to sick-house? Many things see there.

Stench struck them like a board slapped across their faces as they walked inside. Patients lay upon the floor or huddled against log walls, some motionless, some squirming. All men this room, said M'Gu. Women in other room, but old Pommy she nurse both. Pommy was the crippled creature who'd approached Beauty Beast that morning and told him that her old man used to trap fish. At nursing duty she hobbled sorely, bearing food or medicine as the case might be. Kettles of various sizes were crowded together over a dying fire; the cat-and-clay chimney did not draw well, smoke thickened. Pools of vomit spread on the uneven dirt floor, Beauty Beast stumbled when he stepped upon a dead rat.

Nighttime many live rats come. These people, they all fraid me, and M'Gu snapped his fingers toward poor Pommy who groaned and cowered back. These people not walk much, lost many toes. I show you.

Without By-Your-Leave he bent to lift the leg of one old man who failed to utter a sound, only watched with oozing eyes. See, he got this wrap in tree moss cause toes coming off. So they were: three toes on that foot rotted away, bones showing where the flesh had sloughed. M'Gu said that one man had an entire foot gone, and where was he? One foot, and toes gone from other foot? He asked Pommy. Fearfully she told him that the man had died since he, M'Gu, last visited the place.

This come from stand too long in rice, feet in water, mud. Some kind of sick only nigger get. No white folks get. So some die. Much better off when die, he concluded philosophically. He led on to the door of the women's room. Beauty Beast followed, but stopped in shock and turned back. He would squeal himself awake afterward, dreaming on what he'd seen. One girl was an epileptic, foaming and writhing. Two other females were ill of some condition relating to their menses. Side by side, backs propped against the wall, they lay with legs

346

extended, tattered garments pulled up. Moss was their only bandage. Nor was it effective as such. There returned to Beauty Beast that charring hurt with which he'd first read "Of the Visitation of the Sick" in Judge Bracket's Directory for Worship.

> He shall instruct the sick out of the
> Scriptures, that diseases arise not out
> of the ground, nor do they come by chance;
> but that they are directed and sent by
> a wise and holy God, either for correction
> of sin, for the trial of grace, for
> improvement in religion, or for other
> important ends.

You sick? he heard M'Gu inquiring from some far planet. You sick, we go. Outside the lazaretto Beauty Beast leaned against a post and continued to be sick. M'Gu told him cheerfully, Aneeda sick-house not bad as this one. Nothing so bad at Aneeda as Meeon, cept Mistuh Turbey. Oh yes, Mistuh Turbey worse. You come long now, forget bad things. I show how kill turkeys.

Turkeys?

Wild, said M'Gu. Old Chidsey know how.

Who is Chidsey?

M'Gu puffed out his chest and said that he was Chidsey. Mrs. Skeen in Darien had named the darkey baby after a favorite setter, a superannuated pet about the place. Chidsey die same day I get born, so she name me so. But my daddy, he mad. Say nobody, not even mistress, name his child for dog. He call me M'Gu; mean something in African, never know what. And everybody call me M'Gu. Finally even old mistress, she give, she write it on roll. Though sometimes she call me Chidsey, sometimes M'Gu. Call myself Chidsey sometimes, all for fun. I like fun. You like fun?

Yes, said Beauty Beast, feeling better. I like fun.

In high dry woods well up the river and at some distance inland from the opposite bank, they made ambush behind a fallen oak draped in moss. M'Gu did his gobbling on a little pipe fashioned from turkey-bone. He'd rushed into the forest noisily, and the visitor was hard put to keep up with him at plunging through the brush. Noisy way to begin hunting, Beauty Beast thought. He recalled lying in wait for hours at a time, when with Jeems or Uncle Jag. But in this region the birds were of a different habit, they assembled in large flocks.

Better to have dog. Dog scare them quick, they go every way. And what I do? I call them back. He instructed Beauty Beast to lie without speech or motion. He'd just frightened off a large flock of birds from that very site, and they were bound to return. It seemed to take forever. Beauty Beast, weary from a disturbed night, fell sound asleep, awakening only when turkeys arrived. A huge gobbler came first, M'Gu shot it dead with a blunt arrow, first shot. He missed his second bird, it rushed off in alarm. But a third came soon, and this was secured.

M'Gu swung the dead birds in his mutilated hands. These I give you for Mastuh Plesser. Then maybe he never think M'Gu so bad.

Does Senator Plesser think you're bad?

Oh, very very bad. He know how I run off, I hear Mistuh Turbey tell him.

They traveled back downstream, crowded in the dugout with their prey, and heard Cato beating on an iron bar swung from a chain outside the smithy door. This was the agreed signal to inform M'Gu that repairs had been completed, and he might start back to Avenida with the mended equipment.

Not stop to eat fore I go. Take longer reach old tree for spending night, because upstream. Take longer, even though I *say* current never bother me. He made a grimace. You hungry, Beauty Beast?

Not I, replied the youth, still plagued by thought of the sick-house. What will you eat, M'Gu?

Turkey. He indicated a package wrapped in rags of a picking-bag. Already cook. I eat maybe half turkey coming down, half turkey going back. But Mistuh Turbey going be mad.

Why?

They think it not take long, fix these things. He think maybe I come back late tonight, early tomorrow morning sure. But now— Maybe tomorrow noon.

He shrugged.

Beauty Beast felt unwelcome coldness forming within him. What will he do, M'Gu, if he thinks you've been deliberately late?

I never know. Maybe whip. Maybe—

His voice crawled low and smooth.

He cut off any more my finger, and I kill him sure.

Beauty Beast swallowed. How would you kill him?

M'Gu shipped an oar, reached into his home-stitched quiver, and took out an arrow with a barbed head. He twirled it, put it back.

There had been the usual rabble of old folks and children at the pier, but when they made out who was approaching they scattered like chicks. Fraid me, said M'Gu, once he was on the dock. Everybody at Meeon, cept Cato, fraid M'Gu. He dropped the one turkey he was carrying (Beauty Beast had the other) and jumped into the air, flapping his hands, shrilling out a kind of cock-crow. The fugitive blacks ran even faster. *Fato fing inta feng,* said the wild boy. Africa words, my daddy teach me. Mean, Black man no good. You member, Beauty Beast. *Fato fing inta feng.*

(I remembered, Misty.)

After M'Gu had gone back up-river, Beauty Beast found to his satisfaction that Mercy knew how to pick and draw turkeys; she set several children to the picking immediately. Beauty Beast had never cooked a turkey himself, but he'd watched Aunt Suke often, and was determined to make an attempt. Once the big birds were plucked, singed, plumped and drawn, he built up the kitchen fire to his liking and fastened a turkey on the spit. He hid the other under a bucket in the locked pantry.

The hunters rode in shortly afterward, tired and sullen. Judge Bracket breathed maledictions once he was alone with

Beauty Beast. Seven doves, he kept repeating. Seven, for a day's riding and shooting! Furthermore I made no headway with that insufferable— Best not to speak of it. Best not to recognize what I've endured in behalf of a principle. Well, well—tis but another few days at best. Or at *worst*. But if I am indeed to influence mine stubborn host, I must accompany him to the other plantation up-river tomorrow. So we go voyaging again.

Master—

What say?

I still have the pantry keys. Perhaps the senator forgot that he gave them to me. And when I was looking up victuals—

Yes?

I discovered a bottle of peach brandy. Twas behind some other articles on a shelf. Unopened, sir, but marked distinctly. It must be very old brandy—

Then— The judge started to bellow, cast his eyes toward the door, finally spoke in a conspirator's whisper. Fetch it. Fetch it here at once. And under your coat, boy, under your coat.

From time to time Beauty Beast ran to lard his turkey, nourish the fire, explore for other viands to be served in accompaniment. He contrived a stuffing of rice and onions, packed it into the body cavity, hoped for the best. When at last they were served, the hungry men greeted his efforts with enthusiasm— Judge Bracket in particular, peach blossoms on his breath. Beauty Beast wondered what the senator thought when he scented the brandy. They drank more of the blackstrap rum, grew almost convivial.

Quite diffidently, Beauty Beast informed Senator Plesser that the turkey was obtained by M'Gu during his visit.

Ah, that limb of Satan.

Who might he be? asked Judge Bracket between mouthfuls.

Plesser explained that M'Gu was not worth a quarter-hand when it came to picking cotton, but kept the white folks at Avenida in game and fish. There were, he said, a number of whites on the place—not only Turbey and his wife, but also two brothers-in-law with their families, the men serving as assistant overseers.

Scarcely worth their salt, said the senator. But Turbey pockets a tolerable wage, along with bonuses which he demands for good crops above an agreed figure. His sisters' husbands receive only their keep. Since the boy M'Gu hunts and fishes for them, they cost me next to nothing.

He wiped his mouth with that same stained silk handkerchief. We've considered selling off the boy M'Gu, and tried to, since he's forever attempting to run away; but no one in the region wishes to buy. Tis rumored that he's actually killed a nigger or two. Generally speaking, Turbey manages to keep him in line.

Aye, thought Beauty Beast. By hacking off his little finger-joints.

Our replacement figure is on—approximately—a seven-year basis.

Judge Bracket put down his fork and looked at Plesser stonily. I do not understand your reference, sir.

Slave replacement. It averages out to a complete turnover in seven to seven-and-one-half years.

Bracket's brows came together. Am I to assume, sir, that your black people on these plantations must be replaced by other hands each seven years? Do you not think it possible—

The judge's voice was trembling.

—That you might reduce that appalling figure, were you to provide adequate food, quarters, clothing, medical attention?

Plesser smiled, he motioned for Beauty Beast to remove his plate. Then he produced the gold knife with which to clean his nails.

We make out comfortably as it is. Both Gallant and Turbey recommend this system, and the results prove their point. Pampered niggers simply won't function. We fare well enough with no coddling.

(Misty, we never did reach Avenida. There were delays, and we had a late start. M'Gu was dead. We were so informed by Mr. Turbey and some niggers whom we met en route, perhaps an hour below Avenida. What happened was this: M'Gu

351

arrived late, as he'd feared he might, though at the time Mr. Turbey was gone to a distant field. The eldest of the brothers-in-law, one Mr. Shanton, accused M'Gu of malingering, and ordered that he be given thirty lashes. On the legs, he said, and that'll teach him not to run again. After the flogging M'Gu waited in some bushes for Shanton to go to his quarters—just as he'd lain in wait for the turkeys. But this time he held one of those barbed hunting arrows against the string. Shanton came, M'Gu shot him halfway through the chest. We rowed back down the river in our barge, traveling by torch and starlight, with Shanton delirious in the stern. We left the boat at Emilion, but the wounded man was carried to Darien. He was still alive when we sailed from Darien two days later; although Judge Bracket never inquired of Senator Plesser what the outcome had been. He'd grown to despise Plesser too much for that, would have no further confabulation with him. As a result he never won Plesser's support on treasury legislation, though it passed without Plesser's help later on. But of M'Gu. After he'd put his arrow into the man, he headed for the swamps. His legs tricked him, he'd been too cruelly beaten to begin with. He bogged down, was caught and dragged back to the plantation. There Mr. Turbey had him tied—swinging off the ground, held by the wrists—and M'Gu was flogged again. This time over his entire bare body as he twisted: buttocks, back, face, chest, belly. Turbey grinned when he told of it. My idee, he said, was to whup him senseless. But I do guess we just laid it on a mite too long. So we toted him back mongst the cypress, to a hole where there's some big gators, and heaved him in. Reckon the gators'll bury him, way they do. Judge Bracket blasphemed to high Heaven, declared that if such a thing'd occurred within his own bailiwick he would personally have put a hole through the overseer. Senator Plesser said, Please to remember that the boy gave us a great deal of trouble in the past. Tis well settled.)

That was slavery, Misty, as practiced on those two plantations. Life for the darkey at Apoxsee, at Shearwater, at Yaupon, is a tea-party in comparison.

I ask you one thing, Beauty Beast. Should I find peace—or even stimulation—in witnessing that I have not been an accomplished fiend?

Misty, tis only this: I've revealed a horror which has remained since the first tasting. You are far more generous in management of your human properties than those in the outside world—the industrial masters who'd have their fate in hand, were those same blacks no longer properties, did they stand free. Free as laborers in mills at the North—

And I'm more concerned with their welfare than was Senator Plesser? And I'm not brutal as the monster Turbey?

Misty. I meant in no way to—

But still I've been executioner. That can never be rubbed out.

He cried in anger, Then let me tell you the truth, e'er we reach the Big House. With this long recounting I attempted to purge myself of worms. Nor was I successful. They're still active in my innards. I can feel them squirming, they're live and busy.

There must be some panacea, she said softly, for both of us.

Face hard-set, he looked into hostile space, did not reply. Though by the next day he was all gentility again.

~16~

O N THIS NIGHT Beauty Beast's playing became a river of
pale glass (though warm cordial currents turned beneath
the surface. Their humanity emanated, enfolded you, you
glided smoothly without waves. No rapids to provoke). Sidney
found herself borne here and there, could not remain seated.
She drifted, light canoe on the stream, going to door or window, or sometimes finding herself at door or window without
knowing she'd walked. Through pellucid air, air already
touched by frost—but not knowing it in this hour—air suspended motionless between warm weather and blasts to come.

Air saying, I am intimate with the moon.

When the musician's hands went away from the keys she said
aloud without turning, A pity that music calls for candles.

He seemed to consider this. Misty, candlelight is not essential.

But— The score? Your music?

If the selection is well familiar, and the pianist can play by
ear— What of the blind who play? There are many such.

Come, see this moonlight.

She felt and heard him moving near, halting before he was
close enough to brush her gown. She continued to hold gaze
upon the grace, the nearly motionless draperies of moss outside,
showing whitish, silver, black, according to slender position.

My dear mistress, you would seem to be out there.

Why say that?

Because you're Misty.

But it's not misty, truly. Look—all those regions of shadow and lightness, with lightness growing wider every minute. As the moon rises and swings southerly.

But it's misty, way over yonder. You'd be there somewhere.

I should chide you. Do you mean to infer that I'm gone again in haze? In fog?

Perhaps in frost. You're Misty.

It shall be tonight?

The first. We've waited long enough.

Tonight?

Her whisper reached to him. Let us dispense with candles. Then you'll play.

He obeyed, stepped away, she heard quiet assured motion, heard tinkle of the snuffers. Layer by layer, yellow light vanished behind her. Darkness in the room, all glory beyond.

Instantly on hearing fresh and stately melody Sidney entertained illusion of a prayer-wheel. Prayers engraved thereon, they went round and round. Mozart, she cried in identifying the loveliness. And further, Do you suppose that nasty old archbishop had a prayer-wheel? Twould be a heathen object, never in accord with his accustomed ritual. But he was so cruel to Mozart—

Beauty Beast's noble fingers pressed out a message. Here are love, expectancy, later a resignation. Take them apart, dissect them as you will. Certain delicate appurtenances hang round these comely things like loose lace, but we are twitching laces aside, revealing only tenderness strung beneath and behind. We must never try to penetrate the complete mystery, because we would be only robbing ourselves.

Beyond the window, variations ascended into pines and oaks, came down again to step in ornate measure on the grass.

Not greensward, she thought. Not now. Variations walking on silversward.

She turned away, was drawn through shadows to the piano, waited near. She saw Beauty Beast lift his head when notes ceased running and rolling, when the fairy thought was gone behind draperies again.

You liked that, Misty?

God.

Then I'm proud.

Why haven't you played it before?

He chuckled, he was a little boy who unexpectedly had done something which pleased him very much. Actually tis one of two sets of variations for piano and violin which Mozart composed.

He meditated briefly. I *think* there were two. That may be incorrect. At any rate, I worked the thing into a piano solo partaking of both instruments. As you heard, the piano is stressed. But—grief—why shouldn't a performer like Mozart stress the piano? He said that he took a simple French air—perhaps a folk song, I'm not sure—with a title something like, *At the Edge of the Fountain.* Some critics have been inclined to sneer at it—too *galant,* they say. An eternal puzzle to me. Why should a celestial presentation or rendition be required of every composer, or even of every performer, once he sits down to the task? Is there no room in this world for a *partita* as well as a symphony?

She said, It may be that sometimes a *partita* or a slight variation can reach deeper, affect more profoundly, than a symphony. Aren't there moments when we need not the brilliant sunset? Or artillery of the thunderstorm? We can be content with holding one leaf. One spider-lily.

After silence. Misty, yours is a beautiful voice. I do wish that you sang.

I cannot sing.

Neither can I.

Ah, yes. I've overheard you lilting away with a *chanson.* Or nigger songs—

Folk balladry, he said. When I'm in good spirits, I do like to *make a joyful noise unto God.* But it's never singing. Any more than a child's reaching up and thumbing at piano keys is playing.

She said, I squawk. Sounds so dreadful that I never allow anyone to hear me even attempt—

He broke in upon her words as he had done more frequently

of late (when they'd been sharing, when many restraints were gone). Because, he said, if you sang, we'd have mirth. I'd find such pleasure in accompanying you.

Accompanying me?

In music, in songs only?

Ho!

It shall be tonight.

But once more—

Beauty Beast, you must play it again.

It? Those variations in G Minor?

The *Fountain*. We shall pretend that we are there. Or somewhere. With Mozart.

He went into the work afresh with Sidney motionless nearby. She fashioned another room in which they were together, she wondered whether it might be in Salzburg or in Vienna. Friends were gathered, along with the young Wolfgang of course. (Vicious Archbishop Hieronymus? No admittance to him!) Sidney approved of her own dress—saw it as of apple-green Lyons brocade, *décolleté,* she felt a fastidious puckering at the bodice, was glad to be a woman and to be inside that gown. Beauty Beast presented an *andante con espressione.* Twas odd: he did not wear powder, he'd let his shining hair grow long and tied it with a ribbon, with the queue down below his collar. Other gentlemen had their hair queued and powdered, some of the elders clung to periwigs. Other ladies? She saw them but dimly. The small figure of Mozart leaned squatly out of his chair in a position to watch Beauty Beast's playing as well as to listen, he nodded in approval. Sidney thought, What do we here, so far from home? King's Mountain is well in the past, the Americans have whipped Tarleton, people say that Cornwallis is driven against the sea in Virginia. But here we bide in Austria, listening. Ah, the answer!—there is that universality about all good great music which transcends space and time.

Mozart must have stitched out this beauty nearly seventy-five years ago. Will it be as polished, as translucent, seventy-five years hence? Aye, a hundred years, two hundred, on and on into Time.

Excellent living thing.

Shakespeare walks in at the door today and sits rapt among us in the audience. We are in no way surprised to see him.

Once more the reiteration had passed into silence.

Beauty Beast, please do not relight the candles.

As you prefer, *madame*.

Why should you call me *madame?* You haven't—for so long—

He laughed through prettiness of reflected pallor from outside. I don't know, Misty. Twas as if I imagined myself back abroad once more, whilst I sat playing.

I did as well. Except in a different time. Imagined ourselves actually *with* Mozart. He was watching you play. Sanctioning you.

Thank you, Misty.

She said with distinctness, I am now going to my room. Beauty Beast, do you but wait a few minutes—not more than ten or fifteen at the most, say. Then you are to come up the stairs, to my room.

Mistress! I—

Silence following this first utterance, before he spoke again. By then Sidney was at the door, rustling toward the gallery. He hurried after her, that he might not have to lift his voice. On the front gallery she turned to face him.

Misty, *pardon*. Did I understand you correctly? That I should come to— Your chamber?

In a little while. There's something which I wish to give you.

Again silence. Slowly he bowed, assenting.

When he approached she lay in readiness: on the bed, undressed, with but a sheet across her body. Beneath that sheet she sensed the sleek embrace of her nightgown—one which Pettey J. had insisted that she have sewn when they were last in Paris. She'd never worn it since he died. Twas a garment appropriate to costly women of a certain persuasion, women whom he'd known before marrying Sidney. (When he was potent still. They must have affected such night-garb and so he desired her

to copy after.) Reviling his whole memory, she'd sought to
burn the garment. Often she thought to slip it into a fire when
no one stood to observe. But the thing itself was not evil, it was
such rare beauty, rare silky prettiness, poppies growing against
black. So adroitly made. She'd unfolded it from its retirement
on occasion of late, played with enticing folds. Thought, Perhaps I shall. No I shan't.

But twas intended for rapture, and the nightgown never
found rapture any more than I.

If unqualified love but once touches this gown, any taint of
evil is driven from its tissue forever.

Beauty Beast reached the open doorway, and drummed falter-
ingly with his knuckles.

Yes, she said.

Misty, you— You said that I was to—

That you were to come to me here.

He took a cautious step beyond the doorway. Stopped.

Misty, excuse me. You said that you had something which you
wished to offer me?

I wish to offer you myself.

She heard the long intake of breath, and lay pulsing in
natural expectancy, knowing how she desired him and how he
must desire her.

Yes, dear heart. Myself.

He came springing toward the bed. She'd thought, *In eagerness.* Instead he came foaming with hatred.

You wretched woman, I'm your *slave.*

Then— Mine to command?

Devil with your commands! You're white.

Dreaming, I'm dreaming. This cannot be actuality. Wake me
up. Oh, please, please to release me from nightmare imagining.

Someone, she moaned in her soul. Beauty Beast— *Anyone.*
Wake me up!

God damn you, Misty. Why did you have to be *white?*

Vile whites. They could never leave well enough alone, had
to go prying and poking over the world. Only a few Orientals

resisted them. But, time, time— Give the whites time, they'd have the bars down which held them from the Orient.

Indians? Here in America? Either they'd been slaughtered or else pushed off their lands. Were being pushed, each decade, further and further to the west. They resisted still, on the Great Plains? Give the whites time.

Misty, they dragged Osceola's people out of their underbrush, put them on ships, lugged them away. I hold a recollection of other folks herded to the shore and carried off. African blacks, and their blood is in me. *In me.* Can never come out, never be bleached. But no one who does not own black blood will ever—

You had slaves.

Oh, we niggers managed our own brand of slavery, in many ways worse than what you *buckree* have practiced. But it was black holding black, black capturing or killing black, d'ye see?

(Tone of Judge Bracket sounding from his tomb, using antiquities of speech, saying *Hearken.*)

Twas on our own continent, among our own kind. Nigger gainst nigger, nigger selling nigger, nigger buying nigger. As for the ones taken in war—

Mungo Park tells of it. Gad, how you treat your slaves!

Ah, you've read, Misty, but you don't feel black liquid bubbling inside you. Thick as tar. You don't feel weight and stew, activity of the black blood. When you possess that, the whole diabolical pattern is repeated within your body and mind. Blood *tells* you. It gabbles and moans—the way these niggers here on the place gabbled and moaned when you-all were laying away the girl who was drowned. *Poor little child in clean water. Missed so much.* What was her name? Tickle? We have queer names, do we not? Beauty Beast. There's one for you.

Droll, to have the colored come around and say it of your own child—droll, if you were Judge Bracket. To say, He a little beast, in their comical darkey manner. Then you laugh too, and think, This *is* a delight. So ludicrous, yet so natural, so very primitive.

Prim-i-tive. Hammer hitting me in the middle of my skull.

Three strokes, blacksmith's hammer. Your blacksmith Duke's hammer coming down, the way it pounds on one of those red shoes when he's shoeing your precious Cinna, or Bill, or Betty.

Prim-i-tive. Welcome the word.

Misty, it strikes home.

Every slave should have his own father for a master. There are so many advantages entailing. Ah, you couldn't even be aware! All sorts of coddling, development of one's wondrous talents. Who but his master's slave and his father's son, shall we say, could ever be a student at the very keyboard of Frédéric Chopin? I've never told you that, but I was. Eight times in all. Chopin was nervous and— I loathed his fidgety disposition, his imperious attitude, all the snobberies attending him. Then in a very happy moment he went away from Paris, and thus broke off relations with us several students, whose families were paying fortunes for the privilege. But no other slave was represented. Of that I'm sure. No other master was paying a ransom in francs to Chopin for his slave's lessons.

Ah, the benefits accrued. I must count them up.

All the while he'd been ranting softly, with that vicious firmness of the low fluid voice— (If my voice is metal, she thought, then the voice of Beauty Beast is dark ice. Or dark water in icy chill, still flowing, not yet solidified? But you'd die if you were to fall, fall *into* that voice) —

All the while he'd been ranting, paint of moonlight expanded across the room, pieces of paleness advancing gradually. They were milk-colored burglar ghosts who'd crawled to be stealing something, wishing to remain unheard and undetected; therefore they moved gingerly, minutest fraction of an inch at a time, white feet and legs going ahead, progressing.

Now a portion of this chair is revealed, and a garment tossed there. Now that patch of shine has walked to reveal the Chippendale splat. So it goes, they creep, planes and puffs of moonlight stalking.

While his voice continues.

For a good solid black, take Adam. Whom you shot to death.

Sidney's anguish choked her before she could speak. You yellow wretch, I killed for you! Killed to save your life! How dare you sit here—

I'm kneeling. Beside your bed. Bed you want me in.

Ah, she wailed, I do, I *do*.

Please to God, mistress. Let me rave, there's honesty in my ravings.

She could feel stickiness, oil of tears over her face. Tears were a paste to smother, she'd drown in them. Bitter and burning in the nose, her very eyes would liquefy and run down cheeks and make the face blind and hideous.

Take Adam, Misty. Who did not have the benefit of white blood. In consequence he was not borne across the water to visit European highways and byways. Never did he attend Mr. Drummond's school, nor was he enabled to thrum upon a golden harpsichord. Never fetched a bottle for Andrew Jackson's sake, never delivered a letter at the White House. Consider the prerogatives I've enjoyed because of white parentage! But for that, I might have soaked myself in rum—and now, like Adam, be lying up there on the ridge, in a grave remote from others, and turned into a spook to frighten all hands.

They say—

He lowered his voice cautiously, and freighted it with tribal significance. He descended into dialect which made Sidney clamp her jaws to keep from yelling.

Say dey see him on dat chopping-block, middle of de night.

Teeth were still grown together, but she managed to talk through them. Stop it. *Stop* it—

What'll you do if I *don't* stop it? Have me whipped? Order Maddy to lay on the first twenty-five strokes, Honga the next twenty-five? Then continue until— Or should you prefer to shoot me quickly with your revolving pistol?

She whispered, Give a nigger an inch—

Oh, I know I've taken my mile. Let me go all the way. It's not for long. Hear me, Misty.

(Again the explosion of a remembered father and honored Mr. Justice. *D'ye hear? Hearken!*)

Won't be for long—

Not for long?

Because I know. There were *gitanes.*

Gypsies—

Your French vocabulary must be more extensive than you admit, dear mistress. Gypsies, *certainement.* We were in the chateau of a widowed countess not far from Carennac. Judge Bracket had become acquainted with our hostess in Paris, and she sought to marry him. He was still a vigorous man at the time. Perhaps it runs in the family? Twill make no difference in my case. Because—

He spoke thinly, and leaned to grip the sheets above her in closeness nigh to intimacy. Not richest intimacy, but still he was near, probably with face distorted by exaggerated fury of his outburst. He was bound to indulge in the posturing and leering to accompany any desperation so revealed.

Misty, did you ever observe my life-line? Life-line of my palm? When a chiromancer scrutinizes your hand, one of the things he seeks— Gypsies *know.* I recall their word for it, but not in French. They call fortune-telling *dukkerin.*

She spoke from the next county. I wouldn't know, Beauty Beast. Wouldn't know.

There was an object laid down in the road below our gate. I mind seeing it there, stepping over it in some alarm. Twas made of yarn or cord, binding twigs in a peculiar shape. Armand the gardener crossed himself and asked to be defended from evil. So that little *patrin,* whatever twas— Oh, we niggers have them too. Sometimes ancient words come oozing out from black mouth and black brain. They speak of *saphies,* some say *grigri.* You hear other words—

Conjur words—

Surely. So we knew that gypsies were about. Next time I came by, there was a gypsy woman crouched on the turf—waiting, beckoning—putting out her hand and making motions. And I supposed she wished to pick my pocket as well; but I didn't have much money about me. We agreed what I should give her when she'd told my fortune. This was the first time I can remember having it done. Except of course— A couple of old women at Shearwater sought to indulge such tastes. They put up philtres and potions and similar rot. Niggers! Full of it. Full of rot. Stink of their jungle exuding.

Sidney groaned. If you'd cease these antics! What are you attempting? To emancipate yourself? Are you taking this childish way to achieve a manumission? Freedom from my clutch? Naw, I shan't, she said.

She repeated it, voice rising riled. *Naw, I shan't free you. Or* sell you.

Misty. Please— Not to be so loud—

You fear the house servants? They hear me speaking to myself, days and nights. I've no one else to talk to, want no one else. Except—

She fell into a peevish fit of coughing.

Beauty Beast put his head down on the bed as he were placing it on a block. *Where be you, Headsman?* Moonlight spilled closer and made shine and sheen out of his pomaded hair. Sidney questioned in her mind, same question again. Joel? Has he come back? Is Joel returned *in him?* Then knowing that Joel had not, that Beauty Beast replaced Joel in entirety, took up Joel's space, sent out Joel's heat.

He mumbled, They've all told the same thing. Must be true. The life-line of my hand. It's naught, it's truncated, goes nowhere. Why haven't I died before this? They shake their heads and give the tidings: I'll never make old bones.

He rose up amid cream and shadows, lifted his left hand, held it before her eyes. No. You can't see it, not in this light, no matter how bright the— But it's there. Little life-line, thick and strong. But oh, so short, Misty. Short.

Beauty Beast, I thought you were too wise, too able, and sophisticated— Far too wise to cringe at the babble of gypsies.

We niggers *feed* on superstition. Fatten on it. Thus I feel that every prophecy is true, and know my days are numbered. Nor do I mind. Misty, I'll die, but I don't care.

(Again. *Hearken. D'ye hear?*)

Don't care.

Voice sank down, his head was on the bed once more, face resting, moonshine on hair.

Moonlight? Moonshine? Poetic word. Tis all the same.

Jesus, God, she said. God, Jesus. What a fool you are.

He began in reverie, *Whosoever shall say to his brother, Raca—*

Don't go quoting Scriptures to *me,* you wretched nigger, you. I've read em, studied em, absorbed em all my life. Know em far better than you do.

He told her, The judge used to read the Bible to us every day, when we were at the place down here, or home in Washington. And a special service on Sundays. He was forever to the— To the pulpit born? He identified himself with the speaker; and when it was Our Lord, with one of His sermons, I fancy that Judge Bracket thought that he was nigh on to *being* Our Lord. *He shall be in danger of hell fire.* He identified himself closely with nobility. He could not bear to mention nobility without acting the part, looking the part, and considering doubtless that he was a practicing nobleman.

She cried, You've no right to hold me responsible for what he said or prayed. Or believed. Or performed!

Misty—

What?

I'll speak in manner of the vanished Adam.

If you value your life, don't mention that name to me again.

Value it, Misty? What makes you think I do? I've told you: I don't *care.* Then you called me a fool, and then— Damn you, white woman, if I valued my life, would I put up with your strumpetry? Your seeking the manner in which to coax me into your chamber? If I valued my life, I'd be no more kneeling here beside your bed—almost *on* your bed. Or in it. With you, as you desire.

Beauty Beast. Do you wish me to have you killed?

Kill me yourself! You've killed before. You say you killed for me. Ah, I suppose that was in your mind. He was drunk, I might have been able to dodge away from that sickle. But then of course he might have turned on you whilst— It all happened so very quickly.

368

Do you not think—that it— Happened quickly? With *me?*

The poor lubber had no sense in his head when he'd been drinking.

Did that make it any less perilous to be nigh him?

Misty, my mind is torn apart as it never was before! It's been teethed and teethed and teethed again, like cotton going through the gin. My mind's been plucked apart until it only knows one thing. That's why I'll speak with the words of Adam.

Have me killed, then! he almost shouted. When he sat up it was as if the gloom fell apart and let day blaze, reveal all, display his suffering gold face.

I uttered that name again. You forbade me on peril of my life.

Very well, Beauty Beast. Speaking with the voice of Adam, then— What say you?

(*Hear me?*)

Villainous mimic. You mime!

Because he spoke in frog tone, toad tone, resounding growl of the dead.

I hates yellow-man-hide.

You're a yellow nigger yourself.

Hates yellow-skin. But I've *got it.*

There recurred immediately her saturnalia of Africa, complete with apes and Terrors and crocodiles, darkies' musk, jackals yapping at night. Currently it was as if men came from a hunt. They had been dealing with elephants, also were proud at having chunks of lion fat with which to be rubbed (braveness going into them). She heard their approach long before she saw them, but so did Beauty Beast. He lifted his head, his more sensitive musician's ears catching remote disturbance before Sidney became alerted.

Hunters approached from iniquitous if moon-laced closets of night. From infected jungle, and they had scored, were carrying meat, hallooing about it. They'd be bearing light-wood, flaring and dripping at length of their arms, so that they might not be deceived by the moon itself, and wander into baleful quags. Yankees spoke of pine-knots, and up in Carolina were many who spoke of pine-knots too. But here they called it light-wood: fat rosined splints which burned like fabled Chinese fireworks a-sputter. Flame painted each polished black face to pink on the bones, made pink on low slanting foreheads, reddened taller ridges of the cheeks, ornamented the ears. (Light-wood? Dozens of angry old fires had raced, eradicating palmetto scrub or crowning through tops of trees, over all that woodland; and left the usual wreckage of trunks which never sent out green needles again. Sap within was crystallized, could explode almost with the ease of gunpowder.) Cool season. No frogs talking, few insects caring to make their voices heard, but there were owls speaking at night. The big ones grabbed gulls from bars along the beach, and carried them inland and tore them to shreds while perched, and gloated in rolling horn sounds as they swallowed. But generally the forest softened at this time of year, except for whicker of coons, sometimes a bobcat's yowling. There roved bears and panthers on islands in the deeper swamps, but they did not come to Apoxsee longer.

Apoxsee? Seminole word. What right to be spoken, when we're considering *Afrique noir?* Call the place by drum-sounding names, call the place Ibo, Dahomey, Susu, Ibibio, Gaboon. Shall I ask Beauty Beast, What think you of these? Which do you select as the new name for Apoxsee? Why, why, what, what—you recoil? Is not the nigger coming out in you?

They've been hunting possums, he said in a kind of envy.

Yes. I saw them traipsing off, with dogs and clubs—the usual coon and possum hunters. Mr. Irons was bound to go along, liking such adventure. I think it makes him feel that he's with the dragoons again. Both drivers relish it, and some of the hands. Boys like Flash and Eddie, though they prefer to fish.

> Yeeeee,
> Possum ain dead.
> Ain dead tall.
> Jus pren be dead.

You could not yet see them against tremble and sputter of torches, they were far down the drive. Yet Sidney recognized her massive panorama of warring dancers and dancing warriors. Chalky slime dried on ribs, spears brandished, metal clanking, hair tied into wads, badges made of bones.

Conjur hair, conjur grease.

Delusion recurrent, twas not the homely fact at hand. Twas not the fat little rats of possums carried with tails tied over sticks. And anticipation of yams to be roasted along with them—

Hush. This is Africa. You're considering—

Considering only blackness. No yellow-man-hide.

(*Hear me?*)

Beauty Beast said in scorn, But listen to them. Damnable lingo which they cry. And yet— Musing. I cried it when I was half-a-hand. Old Jeems and I: we'd hunt the varmints down because they'd been taking chickens. And I hated the chickens. But—

His wretched plaint. I hate so *much*. Oh, I hate so *much*.

Idiot, she said. I offer you love which you sorely need. Yet you keep hating.

She shut her eyes, and Furies fresh from Congo and Niger and such coarse regions were springing as if to pound her to death, brutalize her in other ways—perhaps let their snag-toothed women and monkeys of children come clawing her face. Sidney heard advance, massive and irrefutable. Mobs and battalions of them, prancing with endless clangor and endless rolling of eyes, jangle of little bells they'd bought from traders.

(Oho. *How* did they buy bells from traders? By capturing other blacks and selling them. In this way they got rude guns as well, got red cloth and the doodads they wanted.)

We didn't begin it, she said soft against oncoming noise.

Misty?

We did not originate negro slavery.

Oh, no, I reckon we nigs initiated the pretty business. But you palefaces had to come bumbling. Couldn't leave poor lil ole black folks lone. No, no, no. Yah-yah-yah.

Incredible.

What's incredible?

That you can be so utterly witless. There never was a lunatic

371

like you. You could have anything and everything. You're brilliant. You have— You can give—

Keep deviling me, Misty, and I may kill *you*.

With automatic contempt. Yes. And be hanged for it.

But under impact of his words a fear solidified, fear like a tree, trunk and branches fastened inside her body, twigs extending into fingers and toes. Tree of dismay, remorseless. Such apprehension had never befallen before, not even in sore hours when, a whimpering child, she'd been raped and blemished by Calvin Tensley. Nor when she came to be excruciated by Pettey J. Fleetingly Sidney renewed the latter scorn and hatred, recalled her twisting away from his words: Divorce, you say? I'll never give you a divorce. How'd you get one? Sit in open court, and tell what I do to you? Not likely, Mrs., not likely!

Dismal truth in what he said, she observed its validity.

But why shrink in atavism at thought of the outlander, the other race, the brute? Do I yield to hysteria? He should slap me smartly in the face.

Pray no didoes, Mrs. Shallop. You've coped with worse, can cope with this.

She said, You'd never murder me, Beauty Beast. I offer you my devotion. You recognize frankness. Tis in your nature. As you've told me, as you've demonstrated.

He said hoarsely, I wouldn't accept a scrap of your love. Not a driblet. Misty, believe me. It's not only that I wouldn't or won't. It's that I *cannot*.

Fear was no longer existent. It watered down into pity for herself, pity for them both.

Why can't you?

Because you're white.

She sat up writhing, and again aware of clamor made by hunters as they traveled and as young negroes' voices hooted satisfaction in the catch they'd made. A faint reflection of lightwood began to waver on the opposite wall.

Don't speak as an imbecile. So I'm white, am I? You're nigh onto being white yourself. You scream your blackamoor's gabble, it's become a fetish with you, one of the *saphies* you've mentioned. Why, we'll not continue here, you dear stupid creature. I'll sell Apoxsee, we'll be gone. Anywhere we might choose to go.

(Quickly she heard herself relating to herself in personal reminiscence not intended for Beauty Beast or anyone else: Once before I built the same chimera. But it was not the same, not a question of color. Question of—)

Flesh swatting flesh. She saw him tall in splotched light, striking with his fist, swinging it against the palm of his other hand. Remember a night when he soared from the piano bench and knocked candelabra and—

Judge Bracket did it to me, Misty. Grained it into me. I tell you, he *grained*.

She gasped. Something else? Like that oath?

The black and the white of it.

Beauty Beast ignored the hunters, his voice cut sharply.

Or white and brown of it. Or white and yellow. Once we were abroad, and I'd grown older, and began to wish for women— He let me know in divers ways. He branded me with my yellowness, even though crying that it was a fault of his. He carved his guilt upon me.

Never cross the line, Beauty Beast! There's misery for those who do, and for children who follow after. You should know it now, perhaps, but you'll know it far more bitterly later on.

Hear me, you yellow bastard? Never lie with a white woman.

He told me, The half-breed's a miserable critter through all history, the quarter-breed is worse. Ah, day'll come when you'll damn me to a hundred hells for begetting you, for rogering your mother. She was such a beauty, boy, a beauty! But the two strains can never mingle harmoniously. You'll always be at war with yourself, and with all else. Mulattoes: ho, an untrustworthy lot in the main. I don't care a fig for your talents. You'll still be tormented in your soul, and thus an enigma to all. Who wants to be a walking enigma? Do you desire to father one, hey?

By the eternal God, you mustn't. Because that single drop of black, that iota—wee black pearl, frail as a bubble blown from

373

its syringe by the physician— It muddies the entire crystal pool, the dye spreads. A tiny amount of dye, but it's there, and you're a nigger.

Never forget that. Nigger in your tongue and in your soul and in your fingernails. You may look like some sort of tawny god, but the darkey's present, and you cannot run away from him. Neither can your children.

Sidney asked, not in mockery, Did he contrive some other vow for you to take?

Beauty Beast growled as if through foam clustering on his lips. Vow? The judge put his beliefs into my consciousness like tiles set in cement. You'd have to riddle the whole structure to get them out. You may not have understood before— I thought you were thick in the cranium, Misty, thought you mulish— But I'll make you understand, and never mince words a-doing it.

He prowled restlessly for a while, bedside to door, back again. Then he told Sidney, I came into what should have been the bliss and power of physical manhood, and already I was harmed to the death, and didn't even guess. I've spoken of the countess whom we visited in the Dordogne. She had a daughter, a voluptuous young woman, free with her charms. One night we were whispering, long after dinner, and it was agreed that we should meet in a far corner of the garden after everyone else retired. We did meet. She lay ardent, skirts drawn up, her body ready for mine.

An hour earlier I'd thought to perform great feats with her. But when faced with the act, I was limp as a leaf.

Sidney heard herself chuckling warmly, harboring tenderness, wishing to make him understand that she did. Oh, poor thing, poor fellow! To labor under such belief. Why, you were a *child* still. A virgin. Common for them to be disturbed, reduced to weakness, there's a dread of the bodies' meeting—

Beauty Beast sneered down at her, consumed with such ferocity that he might have been spitting in her face.

Virgin, you say? I'd been with women a score of times, young as I was. In Paris, Marseilles, in— But *black* women, niggers of whatever color. Some niggers even lighter than I, but their race

374

showed. Oh, I'd been tempted by white servants a time or two, but they weren't to my taste. Then this young demoiselle, with her tricks— I groveled away from her.

I am impotent with whites. A cruel way to find the truth, but I learned it—

Shut your mouth! he gasped when she strove to interrupt, to beat him back into a state of humility and penance. I tried again—other women, other whites—and it was the same. Judge Bracket had plied his arts too long and too well. He'd taken his scalpel, keen as any surgeon's, and opened up my scrotum and cut out my seeds. *Where white women were concerned.*

She whispered, I hear Mr. Irons and the rest, closer in the drive. They've left off with their noise, fearing to disturb me. Be silent, and think. I shall give you something to think about. Beauty Beast, I swore that I would never free you; but what if I were to go back upon those words? What if I give you your freedom? Will you come away with me, of your own free will?

She huddled in bed, saying no more. But desiring to hiss at him, Beauty Beast, you must.

> *Then was Jesus led up of the spirit into the wilderness*
> *to be tempted of the devil. . . .*
> *Again, the devil taketh him up into an exceeding*
> *high mountain, and sheweth him all the kingdoms*
> *of the world, and the glory of them;*
> *And saith unto him, All these things will I give thee,*
> *if thou wilt fall down and worship me.*

Bible's in my mind, Misty.

Bible?

Matthew. Tis one of the early chapters, wherein the devil says to Jesus—

Sidney stormed out of bed and rushed upon him. He fell back toward the chamber door, fending off her charge with one long arm.

Damn your yellow soul. Comparing yourself to Jesus, and me to the devil!

Misty, you're the devil, come a-tempting. Devil can take any guise. It's Judge Bracket's soul which you should be cursing now, not mine. He did it to me.

In awful clemency. But I took revenge.

She halted amid shadows, hearing rapping of the angry heart within her ribs, whistling of the angry breath she sought to control. Revenge? What do you mean?

I killed him, Misty.

You're talking twaddle, and I'll not be impressed by it. I remember listening to Dr. Nugent who was called to attend him. It was a stroke of palsy.

Yes, Misty, and he lay unable to speak or lift a finger before he died. But how did that stroke come about? That's what they don't know. I caused it, I brought it on.

She believed him, and asked quietly, How?

We'd had that brief time, back at Shearwater, and nothing more said about the promise to—

About the manumission?

Yes. Oh, I wandered round, tried to keep my spirits up. It was then that I dyed the old jacket which he'd given me. I still felt great affection for him. But I wanted to be out and gone. Wanted most of all to be free, as he'd said I'd be.

After those years abroad, plantation life was not for me. There was no area where I might fit in. I had a few friends still, or new ones, among house servants or the old women. But most of the men hated me, or were at best suspicious. Fact of my paternity had become a legend among the hands. I thought that if my father would free me at last, I might return to Europe. I could make my living—of that I was confident—in the concert field. So I went to Judge Bracket one evening, and begged again. He said something about the time not being ripe. That was when I blew to bits. I was heedless in my speech. Said something I should never have said. Reminded him that he'd promised to execute the manumission, once we were back in the States. And had he been *lying?*

From far curve of driveway north of the Big House rose a cluster of sounds: hoof-fall of the Irons horse and some mules, padding of barefoot youths, mutter and squeak of distant conversation. But no multitude of insects giving out their throb, because already frosts had struck.

Misty, the sight is always there, I'll never forget it. Judge Bracket got up out of that chair behind his desk and said— Said something about, You—you yellow— A threat, an accusation? I don't know. His face was purple as a beauty-berry; and then his eyes seemed to go back in his head, and both hands flew against his head. He was tottering forward over the desk. I ran and caught him and carried him to a sofa. You could hear his breathing all the way down the hall. Not long afterward he lay dead. There had been nothing the doctors could do.

I brought it on, Misty. As if it were contrived.

He said, I suffer long, recognizing the burden of sin I carry. Therefore I give little heed because the life-line is so short.

Beauty Beast, dear heart.

I'll give you your freedom.

At once, tomorrow! Soon as the legalities can be attended to—

In some way among fragments of moonlight and shade he eluded her. Sidney reached, trying to touch and grasp him, but still he was evading. She struggled forward, knocking her knee against a chair, striking elbow on a table. Ah, no— Where? Then she recognized him beyond the door, tall in moonlight. Those shirts she'd made him wear, of flower-sprigged-Joel-babyhood cloth. His face was a blur, formless as he looked down at her and whispered. Misty, I do hold love for you. A mirth and gratitude, often, when we are together. But if I had my freedom I'd go a thousand miles. Ten thousand. Often I think of running off as it is.

(*D'ye understand? Hearken.*)

Far from you. I could never be your consort.

She jabbered, Pray to eat those words, my dear *cook*. I'm white. I have station, have a life to keep. I've laid myself down before you, as surely as the daughter of that Frenchwoman did. Do you dare to hazard that I'll let you loose, knowing what you know? What I've said and done, what I've offered? You might be wallowing with some other Linnet—

Misty. You knew, then? Somehow you *knew*. That's why you sold her. I could never—

Wallowing with nigger wenches of your own stripe or other stripes, and telling them what you know about *me?*

His big feet went crashing across the gallery.

Heard the brain within her skull yelling, Let me out.

Sidney whirled to an expanded distance, away through walls and ceiling and roof to some lone place outside. There she was left quickly mute, and looking down and seeing herself rooted in that gallery door, and listening to her own shriek. It began very low in throat, but somehow in mouth as well. A whine which grew stronger and stronger; and then all the air which she had drawn into her lungs got behind the sound and pushed it high and knifing. Small night beasts yonder, not yet captured by hunters— They must have stopped incredulous to hear the sound.

She screamed not only in rage and thwarting, in despair at the retreat of Beauty Beast. She cried also against miseries which had marked her from childhood (I wanted only to be joyful, to wind myself in a Willowhurst swing, to bake gingerbread men). She informed the cool listening night of her loathing for Calvin, her revulsion from Pettey J. who'd tormented. Over all was the loss of Joel; and then the growing love for her slave. And now he— *Now he—*

Had no happiness, can never have.

Can but feel agony.

Is no release to come?

I'm burning, my skin's a torture, who has a salve?

No one. Keep burning.

Always? Please— Always?

Let the scream go on until it freezes and you see it hanging there.

Polished shaft of that screech seemed as a bright hard rail or tube down which Beauty Beast went hurtling. In immediate response beyond the north end of the house, came up a hubbub of exclamation, men and boys speaking amazement. Saying Ho and Hey and Listen Dat; making also ejaculations without words, the whole surmounted by the overseer's distinct cry, That's the mistress! Someone's got into the Big House! Without being there to see the man, you could imagine how instantly he thrust a foot into the hooded stirrup and swung up across his sorrel horse. A specter or (in dangerous flesh) an enemy was present. No one needed to be told more. Maddy and Honga would be whipping their mules into gallop, with Irons leading, and the pack of barefoot darkies spilling behind.

Beauty Beast had begun thundering down the stairway, but before he was halfway to the bottom he heard that rush in the driveway. Clearly Sidney saw him slap one hand on the banister and vault across, dropping down, ripping through dry-leaved vines into bushes. Roof of the gallery held the moon away as Beauty Beast thrashed anonymously, getting himself loose and then darting across the short breadth of lawn. There he could see to run. Something distorted in his pace: he'd twisted knee or ankle when he made the jump and landed among stones penning the shrubbery. Still he seemed eight feet tall in his flashing costume, gleaming head all silver, arms bent as he swam the air. He looked over his shoulder once, to see the riot of critters and people clattering in pursuit. That was enough: he must leave the driveway.

Irons sang out, There he goes. Under them trees!

Hoofs muted as they struck on turf instead of hard road. For a moment you could see the uneven leaps Beauty Beast made, from area of shade to area of brightness, and disappearing again. Bent and hobbling worse in his gait, and then bouncing to shelter of another tree. Sorrel horse danced after him, guided surely, surely. Also there sprang a lean stringy shape which would be Honga. He'd left his mule and was racing on foot, and lifted high the club with which he'd pounded trees where possums clung.

Sidney discovered herself partway down the stair, she must be standing at the point from which Beauty Beast had vaulted. She

379

gave a plantation yell (no such scream as uttered before) and then brought all force she could bring into her voice, shrilling, *Stop! Stop!*

Who would stop, and why? A fugitive loose, knowing well why he must be a fugitive; the others going in grit and vengeance to take him.

Stop! Stop!

Faintly the sound of contact, blows struck. A single syllable from Beauty Beast stung across the glades. Did he intend to beg for mercy, or was he saying, Ah, as if intending to reveal a secret? The solitary cry cut short, hammered flat by a K-sound; so the note he sang was *Ahhk*. It stood in Sidney's hearing long after it was uttered and there were only thuds to be heard. Still the *Ahhk* assailed her.

Later she observed distinctly Chopin's Prelude in E-Flat Major tinkling from the back parlor. She walked the lower front gallery, going toward front steps. She wore robe and slippers but no cap. She held no recollection of ascending to her room for robe and slippers, but here they were.

Here they are, she said.

Mr. Irons led his horse up the driveway.

Why on earth is he not aware of unleashed music? How can fleeting phrases fail to touch him?

Run and play in sun and water. But escape so much.

Light-heartedly. She spoke when Nathaniel Irons reached the lower step. Can you not hear it?

Ma'am? Irons made a motion as if to pull off his hat; then the hand went lamely away from his head because he had no brim to grasp, his hat was yonder under trees.

Ma'am. Lucky we heard you yell. We got him. Ma'am, are you—hurt?

Oh no. Smiled wisely through moonlight, though he could not see her smiling, her face was shadowed from where he stood.

But a ghost come to greet him.

You're sure you're— All right?

She echoed brightly, All right.

Did you get a chance to—to see who twas? Sorry to tell you: twas the cook. That yellow fellow. Beauty Beast.

Hates yellow-man-hide.

She selected words carefully, picking them up, looking them over, hesitating for portions of each second before choosing. She thought the words were on a shelf, more or less like bricks in a row, as if masons were laying brick. Then she became a mason, and reached out and took one brick (it was a word that she took). She spoke the word, spoke others.

Did—you—catch—him?

Sorry, Mrs. Shallop, but you've done lost a piece of property. I'm scairt to tell you. He's dead.

Not with all that Chopin bursting from the back parlor! Well, bursting's not exactly what we should say, because the notes are sprinkled, running together radiantly like *little girl running in sun.* That sort of thing.

He went this way, that, mongst the trees. I was riding hard after him, and then— I guess twas Honga or Maddy, come in on foot from the other side. He jumped back, and went right under the forelegs of my horse. Was stomped, kind of. Then Maddy give him a lick or two with his club, then the others come in. Guess maybe they beat him too hard, Mrs. Shallop. But— Awful thing, hearing you scream, and then seeing him attempt to flee away. We were— I mean, I was badgered to death at the whole business. Sure you're unhurt?

Unhurt. Repeat it doggedly.

Thank the Lord that he didn't get *to* you.

I believe—I—screamed.

Sure enough you did.

Irons looked back down the driveway, and at a distance (I never knew they were so far away when it happened!) there walked a muddle of figures, figures carrying something.

There'll have to be another inquest, said the overseer.

She echoed it after him, although disdaining the first syllable. Said, Nother inquest.

What I think I'd better do, if it's agreeable, and you're not afraid— I hear the maids squawking around, out in back.

They're roused now, and they'll be with you. Hadn't I better get into town, right hasty, and wake up Senator Ledge, and fetch him out here? Or ought I to go for Mr. Wilkey first? You say, ma'am.

Sidney held up her hand in gesture of warning. Listen, it's stopped.

What's stopped, Mrs. Shallop?

Music.

I didn't hear no music.

She said with pleasure, There it goes again. Hear it now? But so different. No E-Flat Major any more. Rather I think it's what he was playing the very first day. Telemann, transcribed. Maybe some peasants dancing.

It persists. As if he were playing still.

Sidney turned around and started up the stairway. Once she believed that the balustrade had dissolved under her hand and that she was melting into stairs. She heard herself lecturing, Control yourself. She brightened and tightened, managed almost to run the next few steps. Down on the lower gallery the overseer was asking in bewilderment, Ma'am, are you *all right?*

From the head of the stair she called to Mr. Irons, I think it best that you go for Senator Ledge first. It'll take so much time. Then, if we're to put it on the market—

His hopeless words, in nasal puzzlement and desperation. Put what on the market, Mrs. Shallop?

Apoxsee.

She went in and lay across the bed. There was a scent of Beauty Beast's pomade, and Sidney kept wriggling her nose, not sure what the perfume might be. Nigger grease?

Clear she heard the last cry he gave.

Ahhk.

But it dissolved presently, ugly sound left her, and there were only some new loose sweet piano notes rising through woodwork from the back parlor.

Fuengirola, Spain, 1953
Sarasota, Florida, 1967